8/15

R

GRANT OF IMMUNITY

GRANT OF IMMUNITY

Garret Holms

ISBN: 1503114783
ISBN 13: 9781503114784

FOR SONNY

BOOK ONE
Los Angeles, 1976

1

Danny Hart

Sunday night, July 4, 1976

It was just before midnight when fifteen-year-old Danny Hart heard Snake tap on his bedroom window. Snake motioned for him to come outside. Danny was wide-awake and ready to go—he'd slept in jeans and a T-shirt, and even had on his canvas-tops. He scrambled out of bed, shoved open the window, and climbed out into the hot, humid July air.

A full moon illuminated the yard, but Snake stayed within the shadow of a fruitless mulberry tree. Even so, his six-foot-two muscular profile was unmistakable.

"You got the money?" Snake's breath smelled of beer and the sweet scent of pot. He stepped into the moonlight and held out his huge, calloused hand. A mosquito buzzed; Snake glanced down at the insect on his forearm and crushed it, splattering and smearing its engorged blood.

Danny nodded, looked into Snake's cold eyes, and then had to look down. Snake's stare always intimidated him, since that first day they'd met at the pet shop where

Danny worked after school. Danny reached into his pocket and pulled out six crumpled ten-dollar bills. It had taken him eight months of cleaning cages at the shop to save that money, but it was worth it. Snake was taking him to the reservoir tonight—giving him a chance to "grow up and be a man"—to hang out, drink beer, and smoke dope with Snake and his girlfriend, Sarah. Danny just had to "do as he was told, keep his mouth shut," and pay for his share of the beer and the dope.

Sarah wasn't waiting outside her apartment building when they drove up. Snake parked the GTO in front. She'd moved since the last time Danny babysat her kids, and he noticed it was one of those rundown places, maybe even public housing. Trash littered the gutters. Two rough-looking guys sat on an old couch someone had dragged outside. They were smoking and drinking beers.

"Shit," Snake said. "Bitch is always late."

Danny saw the door open. His breath quickened at the sight of her. She was taller than him, and so pretty with her long, red hair, swept up on one side, and blue, blue eyes. She hurried up to the car and motioned for Danny to get out. As he did, he noticed immediately that she was not wearing a bra.

She smiled. "Sorry to take so long, but Sean had a nightmare, so I had to read to him till he dozed off." She looked at Danny. "Both he and Erin are fast asleep, so you shouldn't have any problems."

"Danny-boy's not babysitting tonight. He's coming with us," Snake said.

Sarah frowned, hesitated. "I don't know—"

"Get in the car," Snake snapped. His voice had a hard edge to it that Danny recognized. This was a command to be obeyed. "We'll only be gone a couple of hours—just to the reservoir to chill out. They won't wake up. I told the kid he could get loaded with us tonight, as a reward for babysitting last time, and you're not going to make a liar out of me."

Sarah paused, shrugged, and then slid in. When Danny moved next to her, she was wedged between him and Snake, and Danny could feel the heat of her thigh next to his. He inhaled her clean, shampoo smell.

"Okay," she said. "But *no more* than two hours."

Snake grunted, floored the gas pedal, put the stick shift into first gear, and popped the clutch. The tires screeched as they grabbed pavement and launched the GTO forward. To get to the reservoir, Snake drove to the top of Lake Hollywood Drive. There, he forced open a gate and drove over the gravel access road. They parked ten feet from the water's edge. Snake opened the trunk and took two six-packs of Brew 102 out of a Styrofoam, ice-filled cooler. They walked down a narrow landing over the water and climbed up onto the flat roof of a roundhouse at the end of the pier. Each took a beer.

Snake lit a joint and passed it around.

The three of them sat, looking out at the moonlit water. Gradually, Danny began to relax and to feel a buzz coming on. He heard the chirp of crickets, felt an insect bite, became aware of the hard surface of the roof he was sitting on. He took a sip of beer, savored its crisp, bittersweet tang, and contemplated the lake. He noticed the sounds of traffic from the highway below, inhaled the pungent

5

aroma of pot. He threw a rock, listened to the sound of the splash, and studied the expanding circles it created, finding himself fixated on the liquid motion of the waves. For the first time since his parents died, Danny felt like he belonged, like he was okay, not someone to make fun of. He decided Snake was his best friend—his only friend.

Sarah Collins was old—twenty-two—two years older than Snake. She was Snake's girlfriend, even though she had two kids. She unfastened the combs holding up her red hair, and it fell over her shoulders and down her back. She was barefoot and wore jeans and a loose-fitting pull-over blouse. Danny felt a deep stirring inside as he noticed the movement of her loose breasts whenever she shifted position.

The moon vanished behind a cloud. The only light came from the burning cherry tip of the joint, illuminating their faces as they inhaled. Snake put his arm around Sarah and started kissing her. Sarah kissed Snake back—a long, lingering kiss. It was very dark, but Danny thought he saw Snake put his hand on Sarah's breast. Danny's heartbeat quickened. He was glad it was dark, so no one could see the bulge in his pants.

Snake unbuckled Sarah's belt and started to unzip her jeans. Danny felt a thrill so intense that he worried he might come in his pants.

But Sarah pushed Snake's hand away. "Don't," she whispered. "Not in front of the boy."

"It's okay," Snake replied. "He likes it."

"I don't," Sarah said sharply.

She climbed down from the roof and rushed to the car, shaking her head and fastening her belt as she walked.

Snake tensed and his eyes darkened. "Don't you fuckin' walk away from me," he shouted after her.

Sarah turned, and then a little more slowly continued toward the car.

Danny remembered the last time he had seen Snake's rage—that night when Snake had cut Danny's arm and then locked him in the shed with the boa constrictors. Just because he'd refused to help Snake get food for them. By the time Snake let him out, Danny was nearly out of his mind with panic. Thinking about it scared the shit out of him.

Snake's face contorted. A vein on his neck began to throb. He jumped off the roof and caught up to Sarah as she reached the car.

"Please," Sarah pleaded. She started to cry.

Despite the sweltering heat, Danny shivered. He decided to get the hell out of there. Sixty bucks or not, he was terrified. He maneuvered down from the roof and tried to sneak away. He knew of another path that led toward the highway, where he could hitch a ride home at Barham Boulevard.

"Where're you going, Chief?" Snake called after him. "The fun is just starting."

"I'd better get back," Danny said, turning. "My grandmother is probably missing me right now."

"Let's all go," Sarah said. "It's late and I need to get back to my kids."

"Shut the fuck up," Snake said to Sarah, then called back to Danny. "I thought you said the old lady wouldn't even know you left the house."

"Sometimes she wakes up in the middle of the night."

"That ain't what you told me. Get your ass over here, Chief."

There it was again, that angry edge to Snake's voice. Danny hesitated an instant, and then hurried to where Sarah and Snake were standing.

Snake said to Sarah, "We're gonna put on a little show for the kid. Take off your clothes."

She didn't move.

"I said take ... off ... your ... clothes."

But Sarah stood still, glaring at Snake.

Finally Snake said, "Okay. Then I'll take them off for you."

He put his hand at the neck of Sarah's blouse and yanked, tearing it down the center. Sarah jumped back with a startled look on her face. Danny's heart raced uncomfortably when he saw her ragged top dangling, her breasts showing.

Then she lunged at Snake. "You son of a bitch. You cocksucker. That blouse cost forty bucks!"

She tried to scratch him with her fingernails, tried to hit him with her fist, but Snake caught her wrists, and bent them back, forcing her to her knees. She screamed. Snake let go of her, but before she could get up, Snake drew back and punched the side of her head with his fist. The force of the blow knocked her flat on her back. She lay there, dazed.

Danny felt the blow as if he'd been struck. He couldn't believe—couldn't accept—what he'd just seen. Snake unsnapped the leather holder on his belt and took out his hunting knife. He went behind Sarah and dropped down on one knee. Pulling her up so she was sitting, he put one arm around her neck and held the tip of the knife at the side of her neck. The knife drew a drop of blood as Snake spoke directly into her ear. "Fucking cunt. You're gonna pay. You'll do everything I say or you're dead. Understand?"

"No!" Danny said.

Snake took the knife from Sarah's neck and pointed it toward Danny. "You want some of this, Chief? Keep your fucking mouth shut and do what you're told. Like her."

Sarah, still dazed, still crying, was nodding. "Please don't hurt us. I'll do anything you say. Please."

"Okay," Snake said. He put the knife back in its leather holder. "Strip. Get naked."

This can't be happening, Danny thought.

Sarah began to undress, taking off her torn blouse. At that moment, the moon vanished behind a cloud, and it was dark again. Danny couldn't see anything other than movement. It seemed that Sarah was still on the ground. She took off her jeans and her panties. She started to shiver, although it was hot and muggy.

Snake unzipped his fly.

"Now, suck my dick," he said.

Sarah got to her knees, reached into Snake's pants, put it in her mouth, and began. "That's it. Good," Snake said. Danny could see Sarah's head moving back and forth.

Again Danny tried to sneak away. "You can't leave!" Snake called. "It's your turn next!"

Danny froze. *His turn?* "No," he said. "I don't want—"

"You're part of this, Chief," Snake said. "Either she sucks your cock, or you suck mine. And then I put you back in the shed with the boas. Only this time, I cut your balls off, first."

Danny considered running for it. After all, Snake couldn't manage Sarah and run after him. He could run as fast as possible back to the highway and hitch a ride home. But he knew Snake would find him later and hurt him the way he was hurting Sarah.

So he stayed. Even though he knew this whole thing was wrong. Even though he knew he should do something to stop Snake. But he didn't know what.

Snake's body tensed. He grunted, shuddering.

Then he looked at Danny. "Your turn, Chief. Come here!"

Danny walked over to Sarah. Snake stepped back and pushed the boy to her. "Take out your dick and put it in her mouth."

No, Danny thought.

He leaned over to Sarah and whispered in her ear, hoping that Snake couldn't hear. "It's okay. We'll pretend. It's dark. He won't know."

Danny unzipped his pants, but didn't take out his penis. Sarah put her face against Danny's crotch, and pretended to suck.

Just then, the moon reappeared.

Snake came near to them, peering closely. "What is this shit? You're not doing anything. We need some light. Come with me."

Snake grabbed Sarah by the arm, forcing her to stand. He pulled her toward the GTO. The boy followed but stopped a few feet before the car. Still holding Sarah's arm, Snake forced her to walk with him around the car. At the driver's side, Snake opened the door, reached in, and turned on the headlights. Then he took Sarah to the front of the car and forced her to her knees again. Bright light illuminated her naked body.

He spoke to Danny, "Come here and take out that dick, Chief."

This time Danny did as he was ordered.

Sarah was once again on her knees in front of him. She put his flaccid penis in her mouth and started sucking. Danny could see her face and naked body clearly. Could feel the warmth of her mouth. Sarah's eyes were closed and tears were streaming down her cheeks. Danny started crying, too.

He closed his eyes. But still he felt her mouth on him and heard her sucking sounds. Sarah kept on sucking, but the boy could not, would not have an erection. In desperation, he told Snake he was done.

"Did you get your rocks off?" Snake asked.

"Yes," he said, lying.

Sarah stopped, pulled her head back and away from Danny's penis and looked up. There was gratitude in her eyes.

As Danny put himself back into his pants and zipped himself up, Snake reached down, took Sarah's arm, and pulled her to her feet. "Get in the car," he ordered her.

"What about my clothes?" she asked.

"Don't worry about them. Just get in the back."

"I'm not getting in the car without my clothes. Let me get dressed first."

Snake dropped her arm and took out his knife. Sarah stepped back, turned to run, but Snake caught her arm and swung the knife at her. Sarah slapped Snake's wrist.

The knife fell.

Sarah managed to scoop up the knife and tossed it at Danny. "Run!" she screamed. "Run!"

Danny picked up the knife and ran. Behind him, he could hear Sarah screaming.

Then, suddenly, she stopped. And Danny stopped. He waited, listened. No sounds. *Maybe Sarah got away. Maybe everything is okay.* He started walking again, toward the highway. Then he paused. *Maybe Sarah's not okay*, he thought. *Maybe she's hurt. Maybe she needs help.*

He had to find out. He turned and went back.

He still had Snake's knife in his hand.

2

William Fitzgerald

Tuesday morning, July 6, 1976

Although his boss, Lieutenant Becker, had warned him, LAPD Detective William Fitzgerald was taken aback by the reception area at MacLaren Hall, L.A. County's foster home for abused, neglected, and abandoned children.

The reception room was sparse, the only permanent fixture being a giant concrete trash receptacle adjacent to the entrance he had walked through. The black-tiled linoleum floor was scuffed and littered with wadded-up candy wrappers and take-a-number numbers.

People—mostly women, some with crying babies—sat on folding chairs and waited for their number to be called by a receptionist behind a Plexiglas-fronted cubicle. A dusty display case along the back wall housed faded photographs and trophies. The room had an unpleasant musty odor, tinged with perspiration and punctuated by the smell of dirty diapers.

Fitzgerald approached the receptionist, showed his badge and ID, and told her he was there to interview Sean

Collins. The receptionist told him to wait, that Sean's caseworker would be out shortly.

After a few minutes, a woman came out through a doorway beside the receptionist's window. She appeared to be in her mid-thirties, with brown eyes and brown shoulder-length hair in a layered cut. She introduced herself to Fitzgerald as Flo Murphy. She smiled and Fitzgerald, who hadn't realized how tense he was, relaxed.

"I'm afraid I'm a little out of my element here," Fitzgerald said. "Is there a place where we can talk?"

"Follow me."

She turned and led Fitzgerald back through the same doorway and into a long hall, about fifteen feet wide. The walls were white, with unframed drawings posted all along. They were obviously drawn by kids: Each had a name and age written beneath. Some were by four- and five-year-old children. Against one wall stood a row of hospital-style beds, all neatly made with gray wool blankets and turned-down sheets.

Kids were running everywhere. *Utter chaos*, Fitzgerald thought. *How do they keep track of all of them?*

"Do you have any news about Sean and Erin's mother?" Flo asked, as they walked.

"I'm afraid I do." The images of Sarah Collins's body would be fixed in his mind forever. Her eyes not quite closed, pupils visible, unseeing. A naked female corpse, lying in blood-soaked mud and weeds, her mouth open, legs unnaturally spread, one knee up, the other out. Fifty-plus stab wounds—an ugly, unliving thing.

"Her body was found late Monday morning by hikers who were exploring the hills surrounding the Lake Hollywood Reservoir," Fitzgerald said.

"I was worried about that," Flo whispered. "Her poor kids."

Flo led Fitzgerald to a partitioned cubical with two desks. She sat at one and motioned Fitzgerald to a chair beside her desk.

"What about Sarah's kids?" Fitzgerald asked as he sat down.

Flo grabbed a spiral notebook from a drawer and read from it. "The boy is five years old—name is Sean. Erin, his sister, is only two." She looked up. "Do you know who killed her?"

Fitzgerald shook his head. "No. Only that two were involved—not much else to go on. We interviewed neighbors, searched for family, friends, ex-husbands, boyfriends, etc. Checked telephone records. So far, we've come up with nothing. That's the real reason I need to talk to the children." He looked directly at her. "What can you tell me about them?"

"They are both exceptionally bright children. From what I understand, when Sean awoke around four a.m. on Monday and realized that he and his sister were alone in the apartment, he dialed zero and spoke to a Bell System operator. She called the police. Officers went to the home, found no caregiver, and turned the kids over to Child Protective Services, who placed them here."

"We've searched the home," Fitzgerald said. "Found utility bills and photographs, but no luck at finding the whereabouts of relatives. Apparently, the victim was a single mother. Moved here recently from Iowa. Both her parents are deceased. She was on food stamps and aid to dependent children—no job, no other source of income."

The two sat in silence for a moment, then Fitzgerald said, "I have to question the kids."

Flo frowned. "Impossible. Sean's not doing well. His sister is worse, won't stop crying, keeps screaming for her mom. The news about their mother has to come from someone who can hold and soothe them. Someone who loves them." Her expression hardened. "They can't be interrogated, Detective."

"That is not an option. Those kids represent the only source of information we have left. It's likely they've seen or heard something that may lead us to suspects. There was no evidence of foul play at the residence. As far as we can tell, their mom left of her own accord."

Flo didn't reply.

"I'd like nothing better then to leave this place," Fitzgerald added. "I don't even know how to talk to kids, let alone tell them their mother is dead. Can't you please help me tell the children? They at least know you. Perhaps we could explain the situation to them together?"

The two stared at each other. Fitzgerald had said all he could. If she refused, he'd have to go over her head, which would only make everything worse. But he knew enough about people to keep his mouth shut until she replied.

He watched as Flo considered. Finally, she said, "All right. I'll do what I can. I'll take you to Sean and Erin. They're in the TV room. Come with me."

They went into a large dayroom with a black-and-white television playing cartoons. It was on a roll-around stand at the front of the room. Some of the children were sitting on a couch directly in front of the TV. Others were lying on mattresses scattered on the floor. The TV reception wasn't very good. Flo walked over and spoke to one of the kids, who said something Fitzgerald couldn't hear, and then pointed in the direction of a small boy squatting against the wall. Beside him, in a playpen, a red-headed toddler played with alphabet blocks. *That had to be Erin,* Fitzgerald thought. *Same red hair and blue eyes as her mother. So sad.*

As Flo approached, Fitzgerald joined her.

She whispered to Fitzgerald, "That's Sean. Erin's in the playpen. Obviously, you can't question her—not that you'd be able to get much from a two-year-old."

"Of course," Fitzgerald said. They walked over to the boy.

Sean was staring straight ahead, but not watching TV.

He looks so small and fragile, Fitzgerald thought. The boy was wearing blue corduroy pants with an elastic waist, a long-sleeved T-shirt with little cartoon characters on it, and Winnie the Pooh tennis shoes. His face was dirty, his brown hair uncombed.

Sean looked up as the adults approached. He didn't smile, but his gray eyes showed recognition as he looked at Flo.

"Hello, Sean," Flo said. "Why aren't you watching television?"

"I'm not supposed to watch TV during the day. My mom says it's not good for me." He brightened. "Is she here yet?"

Flo hesitated. "Sean, this is Detective Fitzgerald. He's a policeman who's come to see you."

Sean frowned. Fitzgerald held out his hand. "Hello, Sean. You can call me Fitz. I need to talk to you for a few minutes."

"You don't look like a policeman," Sean said, still frowning.

"Well, I am. Look. Here's my badge."

Fitzgerald took out his ID and showed the badge to Sean. Sean touched it and moved his index finger over the badge. "Not all policemen wear uniforms," Fitzgerald continued, "but I used to."

"Why did you stop?"

"I'll tell you all about that. But first, we need to talk about something else." Then to Flo: "Is there a place where we can talk to Sean alone?"

She shook her head. "We're very crowded. I'm afraid there's no place where there aren't half a dozen kids."

"What about outside?"

She looked thoughtful. "Well, I suppose it would be all right. Follow me."

She went to a door that led outside to a fenced playground. Fitzgerald and Sean followed. There was a bench against an outside wall. Sprinklers were watering and there was the smell of fresh-cut, wet grass.

"We can talk here. There won't be any children out until lunch, at eleven-thirty."

As they sat down, Sean asked, "When are we going home?"

Fitzgerald took a moment to answer. Sean was looking at him, his eyes shining. "I'm afraid you won't be going home today, Sean—you'll have to stay here just a little longer."

"But what about my mom? Can't she take care of us?" Before Fitzgerald could answer, Sean spoke quickly. "Is she sick? Sometimes Mom gets sick. But she still takes care of us. She stays in bed, and I help her by getting stuff she needs."

"She's not sick, Sean."

"Then why can't she take us home now?"

Fitzgerald wasn't sure how to tell the boy. He thought of saying something like "your mom has gone away," but he could see that Sean was too smart for that.

Fitzgerald decided on a direct approach. "Your mom can't come to get you, Sean, because she died. Do you know what that means?"

Sean didn't answer for a moment, and Fitzgerald thought the boy hadn't heard him. Finally Sean said, "We had a goldfish that died. I buried him in our backyard."

The boy looked thoughtful. Then he said, "Can I go home now? Is my mom there? Will you take me home?"

"Honey," Flo said, "your mom can't be at home. When someone dies and their spirit goes to heaven, they can't come back. Even though we love them and they love us."

Sean said nothing, just kept looking straight ahead. Flo put her arms around him and hugged. They sat there in silence, until Flo reached into her pocket and took out a Snickers bar. "Would you like some candy, Sean?"

Sean said nothing.

"Aren't you hungry, honey?" Flo said.

Sean shook his head.

Flo said to Fitzgerald, "I'm afraid you'll have to come back tomorrow. That's all you're going to get from him, for now."

Fitzgerald nodded.

Flo stood up and took Sean's hand. "It's time to go back inside, Sean," she said.

"I wish I could take you home, Sean," Fitzgerald said. "I know it's not much fun here. I'll try to visit you again tomorrow."

The three of them walked back to the reception area, where Flo let go of Sean's hand and Fitzgerald shook it. "It was nice meeting you, Sean," he said.

The boy allowed his hand to be shaken, but said nothing in response. He was crying.

Fitzgerald couldn't help it. He knelt down and hugged Sean, feeling the boy's soft, wet cheek against his face.

3

Danny

Monday morning, July 5, 1976

S unlight woke Danny. Bright, unfiltered sun shone into his room, and he opened his eyes. His first thought was that last night had been a dream. No, not a dream ... a horrible nightmare.

Danny looked at the clock. Eleven-thirty. The morning was so beautiful. He could hear birds singing outside. Through his open bedroom window, he could see the backyard. It was lush and green, with his grandmother's roses in full bloom. He felt a warm, flower-scented breeze on his face. *Was it only last night that Snake was in his backyard, knocking on his window? For that matter, could last night have really happened?*

As the grogginess of sleep left, he knew that last night *had* happened. He felt sick to his stomach. Tears came to his eyes. He felt unspeakable, staggering grief. He put a pillow over his head and forced himself back to sleep.

Some time later, the hallway phone outside Danny's bedroom rang and woke him again. At first he ignored it, thinking his grandmother would answer. But it continued to ring.

Looking out the window, he saw his grandmother on her knees, wearing canvas gloves, pulling weeds from freshly turned earth.

Danny got up and answered the phone.

"Hey, Chief," Snake's voice said.

Danny considered slamming the phone down, hanging up. But he didn't. "What do you want?"

"You left last night just when things got really good. It wasn't very polite of you, especially when I needed you to help me clean up."

"I have to go," Danny said.

"Did you ever get a blowjob like that before, Chief?"

Danny didn't reply.

"The reason I'm calling is to tell you that I got to go away for a while. But I'll be staying in touch. And in case you think that you might want to tell anyone about our little adventure last night, I wanted you to know what'll happen. She sucked your dick. Your fingerprints are all over that knife. If you happen to say anything to anyone, anyone at all, the police are going to get that knife."

"But your fingerprints are there, too, aren't they?"

"Of course they are. After all, it was my knife that you stole." Snake paused. "You'll find all about these details, if I have to give the cops the knife. Even if I'm away, I'll always know what you're doing. And if I ever think that you might be about to say something to someone, that knife will wind up with the police. Remember that, Chief."

Snake hung up.

Danny put down the phone. He tried, but he couldn't block out the image of Sarah Collins, naked, on her knees before him, sucking. Or block out the sounds of her screaming.

4

Danny

Thursday morning, July 8, 1976

Danny had been in bed for three days. Had refused to leave his room. Had told his grandmother he was sick. And the boy was sick. And numb. Nothing seemed real to him anymore. It was a summer-session school day, but he couldn't get out of bed.

The clock radio alarm had gone off over an hour ago, but he'd just turned over and gone back to sleep. He didn't care whether or not he was late for school. He didn't care whether he ever went to school again.

"You have to get up," his grandmother said, poking her head into his room.

At first, his grandmother had been understanding, had accepted his story of illness. Today, however, she was insistent.

"What's wrong with you?" she asked. "I thought you liked school."

It was true. He did like school. He enjoyed learning and talking with teachers, and his grades had shown it.

Before this week, he had not missed even one day during the last five school years.

But none of that mattered now. Not compared to the death of Sarah Collins. He hated himself for what he had done. He couldn't believe he would never see Sarah again. Couldn't get the memory of Sarah, pleading with Snake, out of his mind. Couldn't stop hearing the sound of her terrified voice, begging to live. Couldn't stop thinking about what might have been.

Somehow, he got out of bed, got ready, and went to school. But the dark thoughts stayed with him, reliving that night, detail after detail after detail. He worried he might be going crazy.

He was sure the police would eventually find out and come after him. In his third period English class, his teacher told him that he had to report to the principal's office. On the way, through the empty hallways, he imagined walking into the room to find police officers waiting to take him away. But it turned out that the principal just wanted to personally notify and congratulate him that he had won a scholarship for which he had applied.

By the end of the day, Danny decided to go to the police.

He walked eight blocks from his house to the police station, feeling relieved that the ordeal was about to end. He went over and over in his mind what he would say, and how he would explain his behavior. He didn't need to tell them what Snake had done to him. The thought of that made his face burn. It didn't matter about his fingerprints.

Whatever happened would be better than living with the guilt that tortured him.

He walked into the police station. An elderly couple was arguing with the uniformed officer at the reception desk. Danny waited patiently, but the dispute became more heated, until the couple turned abruptly and left.

Danny hesitated. What if the cop arrested him? Danny pictured himself in a jail cell while the police called his grandmother. What would she say? How could he explain what he let Sarah do to him, or why he didn't throw away the knife? What if they did find out how Snake used him?

The officer looked at him coldly. "May I help you?"

He stared at the policeman, but couldn't speak. Danny realized he didn't even know Snake's real name.

"May I help you?" the officer repeated.

"Uh. No. No thanks," he said. He turned and walked out.

As the days went by, Danny discovered that he could distract himself by studying. Whenever he began to remember about that night, he would study. Math. English. Science. Anything at all to keep his mind occupied. His grades soared, and teachers hinted he might achieve valedictorian. But that meant nothing to him—he didn't deserve awards. What he deserved was death ... but he wasn't man enough to kill himself.

He had a thought. Maybe. Just maybe he could redeem himself for what he had done. Dedicate his life to finding a way. The thought eased his pain.

Almost.

Except for the dreams.

BOOK TWO

NIneteen Years Later

5

Judge Daniel Hart

Monday, June 12, 1995, 1:30 p.m.

Female defendants charged with prostitution were always arraigned in the afternoon. Each time Judge Daniel Hart viewed this procession of handcuffed and chained women, he couldn't help thinking how much these creatures were like trapped animals. Trapped in a system they despised, based upon rules they didn't understand. Women in a cage.

Today, like every day, he was surprised by the number of young women charged with prostitution. He'd seen too many of these cases. They were strikingly similar. Women not just accused of prostitution, but of streetwalking. Strolling down Sepulveda Boulevard, standing at intersections, provocatively catching the eye of single male motorists. Now, clad in orange jumpsuits and without makeup, they stood, feet shackled, eyes down. It always moved him. *They look like high school kids*, he thought. *How incredibly sad.*

At thirty-five, Hart was one of the youngest judges on the superior court bench. An ex-trial lawyer and ex-prosecutor, he'd been lucky. On the exterior, he was impressive. Thick brown hair, a symmetrical face with a strong jaw, and a kind demeanor. His intelligence was clear to anyone who appeared before him. But despite this outside appearance, he was filled with personal doubts. The most difficult part of being a judge was overcoming his own self-contempt.

That was why he worked hard and drove himself even harder, hoping that he could prove to himself that he was worthy, in spite of it all.

The governor had appointed him judge two years ago, but to this day, he was still handling high-volume arraignments, pleas, and case assignments in Division 103 of the Van Nuys Unified Superior Court. This included virtually every case that arose in the San Fernando Valley. Other judges in his position—especially those like him, up for reelection next year—would have stayed away from courts like this and looked toward high-status, high-penalty felony trials: murders, robberies, rapes.

But Hart felt he wasn't ready for felony trials. Perhaps he never would be. He first wanted to prove to himself that he could handle high-volume pressure, show to himself that no matter what, he could give each person individual attention. But it took a heavy toll. By the end of each day, he was exhausted as a result of the deep concentration and reflection required. He knew it must never show, but decision-making was difficult. Especially with these young women he saw every afternoon.

The defendants were lined up in the same order as the files stacked on Hart's bench. From his point of view, the bench was nothing more than a big desk, but since it was elevated and had a wooden front, it had an impressive appearance to the public. Hart picked up the first file and called the case of the first defendant.

She was about five-foot-three, with dark hair and clear, smooth skin. *How out of place she looks—she should be at home, watching television or doing homework while her mom cooks dinner.*

"My client would like an indicated sentence," the public defender said.

This was the accepted way of asking what the sentence would be if his client were to plead guilty. Hart looked toward the prosecutor, Doris Reynolds, who was sitting at the counsel table in front of him. Reynolds was forty with brown eyes and shoulder-length, carefully brushed blonde hair. She made sure that everyone knew she was the representative of the State, and that she had a key role in the system. Hart remembered her from the days when he was a DA. She had a thing for cops—had been married several times, always to a police officer, usually to someone who'd been a star witness in one of her cases. Today, as usual, she wore heavy makeup and clothing that emphasized her legs and her figure.

"Ms. Reynolds," Hart said, "what's the People's position on this case?"

"It's a standard second offense, Judge." Doris had the defendant's rap sheet. "I notice a petty theft, and an eleven-five-fifty. She's just another hype. She needs to be locked up."

Like all judges and lawyers in the criminal system, Hart used the criminal code sections as shorthand to describe the crime with which individual defendants were charged. The eleven-five-fifty was a Health and Safety Code Section conviction for being under the influence of heroin. Hart knew that this, too, was typical of many streetwalkers.

"Then if she pleads guilty, her sentence will be forty-five days plus an AIDS test," Hart said. "She'll take it," the public defender said.

The defense attorney came forward and handed the clerk a written and signed waiver of constitutional rights form. His client had already signed the form; he'd obviously told her in advance what the sentence would probably be.

After taking her guilty plea, Hart recessed the court and went into his chambers while the prosecutors and defense attorneys met to discuss plea bargains. His intercom line on the telephone buzzed. It was his clerk, Louise Moreno.

"Judge, we need you to take the bench again, and I need to talk to you."

"Why?" Hart asked.

"There are television cameras."

"Okay, come back here and tell me about it." Hart put down the phone and waited for Louise. If there was a big case in his courtroom, Hart wanted to know about it before he entered the courtroom. He needed a chance to think about the possible issues first. Especially given the upcoming election.

Under California election law, if no one opposed him, his name would not appear on the ballot and he would automatically be elected. On the other hand, if someone ran against him, he would have to wage a costly campaign—easily over a hundred thousand dollars—even if no serious opponent ran against him. Hart was glad that he was almost invisible in this assignment. If he could just keep it that way, no one would think of running against him.

Louise came into his chambers with the case file and some documents paper-clipped to the folder. Hart was grateful to have a clerk as organized and knowledgeable as Louise. Her previous judge retired after thirty years on the bench, and she'd been with him the last twenty. She knew the system inside and out. Slim and fit, with smooth skin and salt-and-pepper hair, she didn't look nearly old enough to have so much experience.

Hart looked at the documents first. They were requests from the press to bring cameras and microphones into the courtroom. He didn't like that. Cameras meant posturing by the lawyers and his having to be on guard at all times. But the public did have a right to know, so his policy was to allow cameras in, unless there was a good reason not to.

He looked through the file and read the criminal complaint. He didn't recognize the name of the defendant, Gina Black. It was a vehicular manslaughter case, but that was all he could discern. Because the law required a judge to learn about a case by taking evidence during a hearing, court files contained no police or other reports. If a defendant pled guilty, or if there was a plea bargain, a judge would order a probation report, which would summarize everything about the case and include an entire background history on the defendant. After reading that report, the judge could decide whether to accept the plea bargain, and also determine what the appropriate sentence should be.

He looked up at Louise. "What's the deal on this case?"

"The defendant is represented by Amanda Jordan."

Hart smiled. If the lawyer was Amanda Jordan that explained a lot. She was one of the most prestigious defense attorneys in the country. Five years ago, she represented Patricia Huntington, accused of murdering her husband, Senator Arthur Huntington. The acquittal received national attention. In Hart's early days as a deputy district attorney, Jordan was a public defender, and they were often on opposite sides in court. She was one of the most thorough and professional lawyers he'd ever been up against. In fact, he'd never beaten her in court.

Louise handed Hart a document. "The lawyers have filed a stipulation that you may read the pre-plea probation report."

Hart read the report, which indicated that the defendant, a female surgeon, had been driving at a high rate of speed down Kanan Dume Road to get back to the hospital for an emergency surgery. She took a curve too fast, crossed over the double yellow line, and hit another car head-on, forcing it off the road, into a ravine. The defendant was okay, and had not been drinking, but both people in the other car were killed. The victims were the pregnant wife and six-year-old son of an LAPD lieutenant.

Now Hart understood. It would be a difficult and emotional case. What happened to this Gina Black could happen to anyone. But the law was clear: If a death happened as a result of a violation of a statute, even an infraction such as crossing over a double yellow line, it was manslaughter. Driving too fast on a mountain road could constitute gross negligence. That could mean state prison.

It was a no-win situation for the sentencing judge, no matter what the sentence. The cops would be all over this, demanding the harshest penalty and unforgiving if they didn't get their way. On the other hand, Dr. Black was a surgeon rushing to save a life. If that was true, didn't she deserve some consideration?

"Give me another minute or two, and I'll come out," Hart said.

Louise left, and Hart studied the file carefully, checking if he'd missed anything. Confident that he was as prepared as possible, he signed the order allowing cameras, buzzed his clerk twice to indicate he was taking the bench, put on his robe, and walked into the courtroom.

Louise hadn't exaggerated. Every seat was taken. A large number of cops in uniform sat in the spectator section behind the prosecutor. The audience had been buzzing with conversation, but that ceased immediately when Hart entered.

A single television camera at the side of the spectator area pointed toward the counsel table where the defendant, Dr. Gina Black, sat. She was elegant looking, with dark hair pulled back, accentuating her blue eyes. Mid-thirties. Pearl earrings. Wearing a black suit, a white silk blouse, and no other jewelry. Next to her was her lawyer, Amanda Jordan, equally elegant. Brown hair, shoulder length. Dark, expressive eyes, high cheekbones. Dressed in an expensive-looking gray suit with a burgundy blouse, she wore a gold Cartier watch. The two looked more like women you might see at a Beverly Hills cocktail party.

Hart picked up the file on the bench and called the case. "People versus Gina Black, Case number VF22794."

Lawyer and client stood.

"Doctor Black is present, Your Honor, with counsel Amanda Jordan. Good morning, Your Honor." Jordan was well known for her polite, friendly, and sincere manner of speaking. When referring to her client, she used her client's name and title, rather than the negative description "defendant." This placed emphasis on the fact that she represented a person and a physician, not some object.

"Deputy DA Doris Reynolds for the People, Judge."

"Good afternoon," Hart said. "This matter is here for arraignment. Ms. Jordan, does your client waive the reading of her constitutional rights and plead not guilty?"

"No, Your Honor." She handed the clerk a waiver of constitutional rights. "My client wants to plead guilty—an open plea. Has the court had a chance to read the probation report, Your Honor?"

"Yes, I have."

Hart was surprised to find out it was to be an open plea. Usually the prosecutor and defense agreed upon a sentence, and the court decided whether or not to approve it. An open plea meant that the defendant was placing her future completely in Hart's hands. He did not like that prospect. Hart said, "Would Counsel approach at sidebar?"

Jordan and Reynolds walked to Hart's left, where there were two small steps leading up to the bench. Hart stepped down and met them. The three could talk quietly at this spot and not be heard by anyone else in the courtroom.

Hart looked at Jordan. "Is there some understanding between the two of you?"

The DA interrupted before Jordan could reply. "There most certainly is not," she said. "And this is outrageous. I told Ms. Jordan that there would be no deal. This is a state prison case."

"You're out of your mind." Jordan responded. "Doctor Black is a respected and highly successful physician. The only reason this accident happened was that she cared more for her patients than for her personal safety."

"She cares for nothing other than money. Don't you realize that her grossly negligent conduct not only killed two people but also destroyed the life of everyone in the victims' family? The victim was pregnant, for Christ's sake." Doris Reynolds's face was red.

Hart admired Jordan. He liked the way she stood up for a client and refused to be bullied by the prosecution. Nevertheless, a judge maintained control by being even-handed and fair, so he must treat them equally and not assign fault to any side. "Quiet, both of you," Hart said. "I'll have no bickering. And Ms. Reynolds, please keep your voice down. Is no plea bargain possible?"

"Not on your life, Judge," she said. "And this comes directly from my head deputy. There are no deals in this case. It has to go to trial, and she has to go to prison. The victims were the wife and six-year old son of an LAPD lieutenant. Every cop in town knows about this case and expects justice."

"That's why this must be an open plea, Your Honor," Jordan said. "I've watched the way you handle cases, and I think that you have compassion, fairness, and common sense. I'm not certain the same is true for the other judges in this building."

That's the butter-me-up-to-get-your-way approach, Hart thought. *Even Amanda Jordan is not above it. It would be interesting to see if Jordan will still have that point of view if I sentence her client to prison.*

"And that's exactly why she doesn't want to go to trial, Judge," Reynolds said. "She knows that her client would be convicted, and she knows that any trial judge in this building would do what was right and sentence this defendant to prison. Judge, the People will not stand for anything less!"

"I didn't call you to sidebar to hear you argue with one another," Hart said. "I wanted to get some background on each of your positions, and you've filled me in. Thank you."

He turned, walked back up, and sat down at the bench. Both lawyers returned to their respective positions at the counsel table.

During their sidebar conference, the clerk had put the written plea and waiver of rights form on the bench. Hart looked at it. Yes, it was an open plea, all right. The defendant had initialed each constitutional right waiver and had signed the bottom. Jordan had signed a statement that she had advised her client about the possible defenses to the case, the maximum sentence, and other consequences, and that she concurred in the plea.

Hart spoke at last. "The waiver forms appear appropriate. Ms. Reynolds, do you want to ask any questions of the defendant before her plea is entered?"

"No, Judge. But the People oppose the plea and ask that the court reject it. This case must go to trial."

Generally, and especially with a crowded courtroom, there's a low buzz of spectator conversation. With Reynolds's statement, the courtroom went absolutely quiet.

That comment was extraordinary. Reynolds knew that if a defendant wanted to plead guilty to all charges, there was nothing the People could do to prevent it. She had to be saying this for cops and the television cameras, which were suddenly trained on Hart. "Ms. Reynolds, as you know, the defendant has the absolute right to plead guilty if she wishes. Do you have any legal basis for asking the court to reject the plea?"

"Yes, Judge. The People want a continuance. We'd like to decide if more charges are appropriate in this case. We demand that the court give us a two-week continuance and not accept the plea today."

Jordan stood. "Your Honor, there are no other possible charges in this case. My client opposes any continuances and requests that her plea be entered and that she be sentenced today."

Hart pondered for a moment, then said, "Ms. Reynolds, your motion to continue is denied. Doctor Black will be allowed to enter her plea of guilty today. The sentencing hearing will be in sixty days. However, the members of the victim's family do have a right to be present at the sentencing hearing. Please notify them."

"Your Honor," Jordan said, "may I ask that the sentencing be in ninety days? I'm going to be in a federal trial in Washington, D.C., and will need extra time to prepare and bring together the people who want to speak on Doctor Black's behalf."

"All right," Hart said. "Sentencing will be set for September eight in this division." *And I'll need the extra time to decide what the sentence should be,* Hart thought. *There go my hopes of remaining invisible before the election. One side or the other is going to be outraged, no matter what I do. I can't give the defendant a light sentence just because she's a physician. There's a dead child and a dead pregnant mother. But this woman certainly isn't a criminal and didn't intend to hurt anyone. The public expects judges to make the right choice. But what if making that choice costs me my job?*

6

Jake Babbage

11:00 p.m.

LAPD Sergeant Jake Babbage—once, a long time ago, known as Snake—had been surveilling Erin Collins for eleven months, although she had no inkling of it. For years he'd been trying to duplicate the intense thrill he'd experienced that night when he'd drained the life from Sarah Collins. He'd almost succeeded during his tour of duty as a U.S. Marine—he'd enlisted right after his night with Sarah. There, he had volunteered for a covert assignment to Operation Condor in Chile: Working with DINA (the Chilean secret police), he'd interrogated female subversives and communists.

From military police to civilian police was a natural progression for Babbage, one where he could apply what he'd learned in the Corps.

He called them projects—finding, stalking, molesting, and ultimately snuffing his prey. Just like in the military, he was doing a service—eliminating a pestilence: in this case, women who sold their bodies—while at the same time satisfying his own sexual hunger.

Babbage uncovered Erin while foraging for new projects. He routinely monitored local prostitution arrests. When he saw her name, age, and booking photo, he knew immediately that she was Sarah's daughter, but ruled her out as a project. It was too risky—he was a professional, after all. But his mind kept returning to her image and her uncanny resemblance to her mother. So much so that he couldn't get her out of his mind.

Finally he gave in.

Had to.

For weeks now he had studied everything he could find about her. Projects always took time, but not the enormous commitment of this one. He was stepping into dangerous territory where any mistake could cost him everything.

Erin Collins was worth it.

She was a bartender at the Traffic Stop, on First and Los Angeles Street, a place where many off-duty cops went to have a drink and grab a meal. Although he normally avoided the place, Babbage made it a point to stop in at random times, while off duty.

Like her mother, she had red hair, blue eyes, and beautiful tits. Thin, but not too thin. She worked late afternoons until closing at 2 a.m., when she usually let one of the guys walk her to her car before driving home.

Now, sitting at the Traffic Stop's bar, Babbage noticed she was sipping from a glass she kept under the counter. Sipped a drink between the jokes, the laughing, the flirting, the puffs on her cigarette. The top two buttons of her blouse were undone, and he saw that both her neck and the swell of her tits had an alcohol flush. He was convinced that by 2:30 a.m., when she got behind the wheel of her car to make her way home, she'd be well over a .20 blood alcohol level.

Two weeks earlier, he had run her plate through the computer in his patrol car, even though he had to be careful using the fucking computer nowadays because the dickhead lieutenant kept track of everything. Just as he'd thought, she had a couple of outstanding traffic warrants out of Van Nuys, including an open one for a DUI last year. At Parker Center, Babbage pulled the police report for the last (and open) DUI case. He couldn't justify running her rap sheet, but he could find out most of what he needed to know just by looking at the report. It showed she'd been stopped, and tested .26 blood alcohol level; .08 was enough to get a conviction. You had to be a heavy drinker to score a .26. Light drinkers, especially women, would usually pass out before swallowing enough booze to get that high.

Babbage then went to the traffic court on Hill Street and pulled the case file. As he knew it would be, her rap sheet was in the file. He found out that Erin would be in deep shit if she were arrested again. She had two prior DUI convictions. And the 647(b) arrest for prostitution (but no conviction) that had first brought her to his attention. She was a fucking whore, just like her mother. The present open case was for a third DUI, where she'd jumped bail and, as a result, had an active bench warrant for her arrest.

Now, sitting in the bar and watching, everything had fallen into place. She was facing a mandatory 120 days on her outstanding warrant. A fourth DUI would be charged as a felony and, with her record, would probably mean eighteen months in state prison. He looked at his watch, drained the bottle of Heineken he'd been nursing all evening, left the change in front of him for a tip, and exited. It was a clear summer night, the air outside hot and dry. Babbage took a deep breath to clear his lungs of the sweat, smoke, and sawdust.

Three hours later, at 2:30 a.m., Babbage was parked in his patrol vehicle on the street in front of Parker Center, just across from the Traffic Stop. His lights were out. Because so many other black-and-whites were parked on this street, he knew his wouldn't be noticed.

Since Babbage was a sergeant, he had no partner. As he sat there, he monitored the video terminal in his patrol vehicle, reading the cop-to-cop communications for the people he supervised. His incompetent lieutenant gave him free rein. So as long as there were no fuck-ups, Babbage could do as he pleased while on duty. In the small of his back, in a leather sheath, was his Marine combat knife with a tempered steel blade, buffalo-horn handle, and solid brass fittings.

There she was.

Two obviously drunk assholes walked her out to her car, a white, 1990 Honda Accord. She stood there chatting with them for a while. Babbage grew impatient, but he controlled himself. *It'll just make it better*, he thought.

Finally, she got into her car and drove away, heading north on Los Angeles Street toward the Hollywood Freeway on-ramp. The two assholes watched her disappear, and then got into their own cars and left. Babbage waited for a few moments so he wouldn't attract attention, then made a U-turn and drove off after Erin.

When he was midway between First and Temple, he switched on his headlights and accelerated. He saw Erin's Accord up ahead, moving slowly. She was driving straight as an arrow, giving no objective indication that she was DUI. Normally, before stopping any suspect, an officer would have to have some justification for the detention, and then, according to LAPD policy, would be required to immediately notify dispatch. But Babbage didn't bother and neither did he give a shit whether or not he had probable cause to pull her over. He knew the bitch was drunk. That was good enough.

She turned right, just after Aliso Street, and entered the Santa Ana Freeway, going east. Babbage guessed that she intended to merge into the left lane, heading down the San Bernardino Freeway, toward her home in Monterey Park. He followed, knowing that she couldn't tell by looking in her mirror that a patrol car was behind her. Besides, as drunk as she was, there was no way she would take her eyes off her straight-ahead path to look in the rearview mirror.

While they were still on the transition road to the San Bernardino Freeway, Babbage switched on his overheads. As he would have predicted, she did nothing. He gave her a three-second blast with his siren. That got her attention. He got on his vehicle public address system. "Pull off at the Mission Street off-ramp." Mission Street was a perfect place for the stop. Almost no one got off the freeway at Mission at this time of the night.

She did as he commanded, moving slowly off the freeway, turning onto Mission Street. She proceeded about twenty-five yards further, and then stopped curbside. Babbage followed her, parking behind. He left his engine running, his overheads flashing, his headlights on bright, his spotlight shining directly through her back window, illuminating the inside of her car. Before opening his door, he removed his name badge.

Babbage exited his patrol vehicle and, using his service three-battery Maglite, scanned the surroundings. To his right, a vacant lot strewn with debris; across the street, a boarded-up gas station covered with graffiti and surrounded by cracked, stained concrete. There was a faint stench of garbage. As he walked toward the driver's side, Erin rolled down her window. He shone his flashlight directly into her face.

She was shit-faced all right: stinking of gin, blue eyes glazed over, hair out of place.

"May I see your driver's license, please?" Babbage said, his neutral tone giving no indication of his intense state of excitement.

"Was I doing anything wrong, Officer?" Her speech was a little slurred, but she had a smile on her face. "I'm Erin. Maybe you've seen me at the Traffic Stop? I work the bar." She handed him her driver's license.

She thinks she can flirt her way out of this, Babbage thought. *Good*. Things were going exactly as he had hoped. "Would you step out of the car, ma'am." It was not a question.

Hesitating briefly, Erin opened her door and got out, stumbling. *She's at least point two-five*, Babbage thought.

"Perhaps you know Steve Curtis?" she said, her voice a little more urgent. "I think he works patrol out of Rampart. Is that where you work?"

"Could you step over here, ma'am?" Babbage, all business, directed her to the curb. "I'm going to have you do a set of simple field sobriety tests, ma'am. For this first test, I'm going to ask you to stand straight, put your head back, and your arms out like this." Babbage then demonstrated how she should put both her arms out, palms up. "I'd like you to close your eyes, keep your head back, and touch your nose like this." Babbage touched the tip of his nose with his right index finger. "First use your right hand, then your left, each time touching your nose just as I have demonstrated."

She leaned her head back and stretched out her arms. Before she could attempt to touch her nose, she lost her balance and stumbled. She recovered and tried again, but each time she leaned her head back, she became disorientated.

"I can't do it," she admitted finally.

Babbage just looked at her. "Okay, we'll try this. I want you to imagine a straight line on the street in front of you. I want you to walk forward, putting one foot in front of the other as you walk, always keeping your feet on the straight line." As before, Babbage demonstrated.

Erin again tried to do as she was shown, but each time was unable to put her foot in a straight line.

"All right," Babbage said. "I'd like you to count backwards from one hundred by twos, like this: one hundred, ninety-eight, ninety-six, etc. Do you understand?"

"Yes." She began. "One hundred. Ninety-eight. Ninety ..."—she paused and thought—"Ninety-six. Ninety-five. No, I mean ninety-six. Wait. Did I say that before? Ninety-five. Ninety-three. No. Ninety-five. No. Can I start over again?" Her speech was thick and slurred.

"No, ma'am. That won't be necessary." She failed the tests so miserably he knew he had her. "I'm taking you to the station, ma'am. You have a choice of three alcohol tests: blood, breath, or urine."

"Am I under arrest?" she asked. He could tell she was scared. "Because if you'd check around about me, you'll see I'm practically one of the guys. You wouldn't arrest another cop, would you?"

"We'll take that up at the station, ma'am."

"No! Wait!" Her voice had taken on a tone of deep urgency. "Please! This is my first DUI. Can't you give me a break?"

"Sorry."

"Look," she continued, "if you can cut me some slack, I know you won't be sorry."

"What do you mean?" he asked.

"Well," she said. She paused, then: "I'd be glad to give you a drink on the house any time or even a free meal at the Traffic Stop."

"Ma'am, I ran your driving record, and this is not your first offense. You have three prior DUIs. You're not only a liar, but now you're trying to bribe me."

"A bribe?" she said. "Jesus Christ, I just offered you a drink. That's not exactly a bribe."

"Besides," he said, "I'd be in deep trouble if I gave you a break. After all, with your record, this would be a felony arrest."

"You wouldn't be in trouble!" There was desperation in her voice now. "How would anyone know? I'd never tell! And I'd be so appreciative!"

Tears made mascara lines down her face. Babbage said nothing for nearly a full minute. Out of the corner of his eye, he became aware of a movement in the darkness of the vacant lot. But it was just a rat, scurrying out across the pavement and into a distant gutter. He looked back at Erin and said, "Just how appreciative would you be? You're asking me to put my job on the line."

"What do you want?" she said.

He pointed to his now obvious hard-on. "Take care of this for me. Now. Right here."

She started to speak, then hesitated. "And ... and if I refuse?"

"Then I take you down to the station, and all bets are off."

"I don't think so," she said. "What do you think would happen to you if I told anyone that you asked me for a hand job?"

Babbage was stunned that this fucking bitch was actually threatening him. He took a deep breath. His voice was almost a whisper. "You're on my turf now and don't forget it. You just failed all the FSTs, your BA is probably three times the legal limit, and you tried to bribe me. Who the fuck do you think they'd believe? Some drunk? Or me, the arresting officer and a sergeant? When I'm through with you, you'll be doing hard time at the joint, being eaten by bull dykes."

He had an incredible urge to hit her. He imagined, could almost feel his fist making contact with her face. His hands twitched with impatience, but he controlled himself, anticipating the terror he'd see in her eyes. And the ultimate thrill—the moment those eyes went glassy, then blank.

So, he waited.

He saw a wet patch appear at her crotch, and smelled the stench of urine.

Finally: "Okay," she said. She was crying. "I'll ... I'll do it. I mean ... I'll give you a hand job ... but ... nothing more."

"Oh no, Erin," he said. "No hand job. You're going to suck my dick. And you're going to suck me until I come. Or else, no deal."

At first she didn't move. Tears streaming down her face, she couldn't take a breath without sobbing. She was defeated, and he could see she knew it. "Okay," she said.

He stood with his back to the Accord and unbuckled his pants. The bitch went to her knees and began. Babbage put his right hand behind her neck and reached back with his left hand for the handle of his knife. Soon. Her head moved back. Forth. Back. Soon ... soon. His fingers curled around the knife.

Release. He climaxed.

The radio of his patrol car squawked. "Two-L-Fourteen. Code Three. Ten-ninety-nine. Officer in trouble."

Shit. He'd have to finish later. "You can go," he said to Erin. Hastily, he zipped up and hurried to his vehicle. As he drove away he kept an eye on her in his rearview mirror. Still on her knees, she hadn't moved.

Except that her head was in her hands.

7

Fitzgerald

Friday, June 16, 6:30 p.m.

Detective William Fitzgerald Jr. sat at his desk on the third floor of Parker Center and compared two autopsy reports: one, a recent unsolved murder he'd been working on; the other, an open Lancaster Sheriff's case. He studied the included photos, shook his head, and sighed. He'd been an LAPD cop for twenty-five years, assigned to Robbery-Homicide for the last twenty. He'd earned every gray hair on his head.

He still hadn't received the results of the various DNA requests he'd made during the last six months. He punched in the phone number for Rich Grabowski, the Crime Lab DNA coordinator, and asked what was going on.

"Backlog." Grabowski replied. "We're about six months behind on trial stuff. Your cold-case comparisons are at the bottom of the heap—maybe a year. Couldn't get to your prostitute murders either. Don't feel bad, no one's doing any better."

"You've got to move my stuff ahead. I got trials coming up."

"You and everyone else. Want better service? Send it to a private lab." He laughed. "Won't break my heart."

"At five thousand a pop, that'll happen," Fitz said. "Thanks"—he slammed down the phone—"for nothing." He'd have to get Becker to light a fire under this guy.

Fitz returned to his reports, but then realized that someone was standing at the doorway of his office enclosure. Without looking up, he knew it was Hardy. The thick smell of Old Spice cologne always announced him, and lingered after he left. "What do you need, Lieutenant?" Fitz said, still looking at his reports.

"Got a minute?" Hardy said. Then without waiting for an answer, sat in the steel chair next to Fitz's desk. The lieutenant was a short, muscular man who spent every spare minute pumping iron.

"Not really," Fitz replied.

Hardy eyed the documents on Fitz's desk and frowned. "What are you doing with a Sheriff's case?"

"Both victims were young female prostitutes." Fitz said. "Both stabbed numerous times. And—very unusual—both had bruises to their wrists, and lacked defensive wounds to both the hands and arms.

"Okay," Hardy said in an exasperated tone. "And this proves what?"

Isn't it obvious, you pompous moron? "That there's a possibility the same perp did both. That's why I've ordered our crime lab to do a DNA comparison from the two victims."

Hardy scowled and shook his head. "Based on three common factors? Bullshit. Let the sheriff worry about their cases and pay for their own comparisons. If they're not willing to pay, why should we? You're wasting the city's money. For some fucking Lancaster Sheriff's case not assigned to you." Hardy brushed a piece of lint off his tailored suit jacket. "Cancel the request."

Fitz felt a flash of rage deep inside. "The hell I will. And what if it is the same offender? What do I tell the next victim's family? That my lieutenant thought it wasn't worth it to save another life?"

Hardy leaned back in his chair and folded his arms across his chest, flexing his biceps and glaring. "That makes five DNA comparisons you've ordered in the last six months." The lieutenant's tiny eyes flashed. "Thousands of bucks and you haven't solved shit. What the fuck is going on with you?"

Fitz glared back at Hardy. "Those were authorized by the captain. There's a serial killer out there—possibly the same perp as in the Collins murder."

"What the fuck are you talking about? The Collins victim wasn't a prostitute."

"But the rest of the signature is identical, Lieutenant. We just need a little luck."

"Luck? Jesus, Fitzgerald." Hardy sighed, and squeezed his eyes shut then opened them. "That's the reason I'm here." Hardy poked his finger in the air at Fitz. "Captain Becker and I agree on this. As of now, Collins is transferred to the Cold Case Unit. Send the murder book, with all its photos and autopsy and crime reports—everything—to the unit ASAP. Understood?" Hardy got up to leave.

Fitzgerald jumped up, furious. "You talked to Becker about my case without checking with me?"

"Damn straight I did. Someone needs to pound sense into you. You haven't solved the case after nineteen years. I don't see the point in continuing. Any of my other detectives would have archived that case years ago—or at least turned it over to a cold-case specialist. Obviously a fresh point of view is needed."

"We'll see about that," Fitz said.

Hardy's face reddened. "I've had enough of your insubordination, Fitzgerald. You think because you and the captain were partners years ago, you're entitled to special treatment? Well, here's a flash: The next screw-up, the next wisecrack, and I'm writing you up. Remember that."

"Yes," Fitzgerald said, then added, "sir."

Hardy turned and left.

Fitz watched him walk away, then scooped up his files and headed to Captain Becker's office.

The door was open, but Fitz stood in the doorway and waited for the captain to acknowledge him. Behind his desk, Becker was studying a computer screen. Without turning his head, he said, "Sit down, Fitz. I'll be with you in a moment." Fitz sat in one of the seats in front of Becker's desk. Becker typed something on his keyboard, and then turned toward him.

Fitz put the prostitute autopsy and crime reports on Becker's desk and brought the captain up to date on the two murders. "I need the comparisons. Hardy ordered me to cancel the request."

"He's your lieutenant, Fitz."

"The man has his head up his ass. I'd bet my badge the same perpetrator killed both women."

"Did you check the FBI's Combined DNA Index System?"

"Yeah. No match on CODIS. Same with the state DOJ. I'm checking other open prostitute cases—maybe we'll get lucky."

The captain ran his hand through what was left of his hair, but said nothing in reply. His lined face seemed deep in thought. He inhaled sharply. "I've been asked to head up the Internal Affairs Division. It's a lateral move, but it could lead to something more."

Fitz was surprised, but tried not to show it. "Congratulations."

"Fitz," Becker said, "I'd like you to come with me to IAD."

Fitzgerald shifted in his chair and looked away, out the window of Becker's office. From where he sat, Fitz could see both the Criminal Courts Building and the old Hall of Justice, damaged and shut down after last year's Northridge earthquake and now permanently closed. He'd heard they were planning to tear it down. *Too bad,* he thought. *So much history in that old building, but its time to retire had come. Maybe the same was true for him.*

"What do you say?" Becker asked.

"May I speak freely, Captain?"

"Of course," Becker said, then added, "Christ, after all those years you watched my back, you don't even need to ask."

Fitz took a breath before speaking. He needed to say this the right way. "Investigating cops is not my style,

Captain. For me, being a cop is tough enough. I don't think I'd be any good snooping—sorry—prying into the way some cop does his job. Besides, I've always planned to stay in Robbery-Homicide until I retire."

"That's a long time. You're still a young man."

"Anything else, Captain?"

"I could have you reassigned without your consent."

"You're the captain," Fitz replied.

Becker picked up the autopsy reports, started to look through them, then put them down. He looked at Fitz. "Damn it, Fitz. I need you. You're the best detective-three in the division. I knew you'd be when I brought you in as a D1 all those years ago."

Fitzgerald looked at Becker. "I need you to rescind Hardy's order. DNA comparison between the two cases is essential. They occurred less than four months apart and have the identical signatures. If it's the same DNA profile, we're dealing with a serial killer."

"I can't set aside Hardy's order. Sorry," Becker said dryly.

"And something else, Captain. Both cases have the same signature as the Sarah Collins case."

"At least think about it, Fitz. As a favor to me for all the years we've worked together."

Becker was damn persistent, but Fitz had no intention of reconsidering. He respected the man. Truth be told, Becker was the best captain in the department to work for. Fitz realized he had to give the captain something, if only the courtesy of seriously considering the offer. "What about my cases?" Fitz asked.

"You'd have to give them up—other than those already cleared and filed, requiring your testimony and the like."

"I'd have to keep the Collins case," Fitz said. "She left two kids. I owe it to them."

"Can't do that," Becker said. "It belongs in the Cold Case Unit, and that's where I'm sending it, whether you join IA or not." Becker's expression softened. "Come with me, Fitz. There's a lieutenant's spot opening up next year when O'Grady retires. You'd be perfect for it."

"Since you're leaving, Captain, why not let your replacement make the cold-case decision?"

Becker stiffened. "I'm not going to put this on someone else. Besides, Hardy's in favor of it, and I'm not going to overrule him. If you change your mind about IA, I'll need your answer by Monday morning. Understood?"

"Yes, sir."

Fitz left Becker's office, went back to his desk, and took a sip of his cold coffee. It was stale and bitter, but he swallowed it anyway. Fitzgerald took a breath and stared out of his office enclosure into the office bullpen, at the two rows of gray steel desks lined up like so many gravestones in a military cemetery. Where had the years gone?

Fitz pondered Becker's invitation to join IA. *No. Impossible.*

Sitting at his desk, he looked at the two small photos he kept under the plastic of his desk blotter: a fading sepia ID shot of his father, the late Police Captain William Fitzgerald Sr. in full uniform, and a color picture of his wife, Elizabeth, who died of breast cancer ten years ago. He removed her photo and gently brushed a speck from its surface with his thumb. It was his favorite picture, a close-up shot he'd taken when her dark eyes were deep in thought.

Like his father, Fitz had been a cop all of his adult life, assigned for the most part to the Robbery-Homicide Division. What would the old man have said if Fitz actually moved to IA?

And how could he tell Sean and Erin Collins that he was going to turn over the case of their mother's murder to unknown hands?

The ringing of the phone on his desk interrupted Fitzgerald's thoughts. It usually meant business, since he had very few non-cop friends.

He picked up the phone. "Robbery-homicide, Fitzgerald."

"Fitz?"

The detective smiled, recognizing the voice. "Hello, Sean. What's up?"

Fitzgerald had known Sean Collins since he was a little boy, since right after his mom's murder. He could still picture five-year-old Sean and his two-year-old sister as they looked when he arrived at the foster home that morning nineteen years ago. Fitz had remained close with Sean and Erin, and had watched them grow up. He'd encouraged Sean to go to law school and written letters of recommendation. He'd even assisted Sean in finding a family in Westwood, near UCLA, that would trade housework and babysitting chores for room and board. Fitz could not have been prouder when Sean became a lawyer, although he'd wished that Sean had become a prosecutor instead of accepting a job with the public defender's office.

"It's Erin," Sean said. She was assaulted last Monday night. Says it was by a cop."

8

Erin Collins

Tuesday, June 20

Erin was terrified of Babbage and the thought of going to court, no matter what Sean said. He'd assured her everything would be okay, and that Babbage, the bastard cop who had abused her, would go to prison where he belonged. Told her it was her duty to prevent another woman from being victimized. But inside, she couldn't shake the feeling that she would regret reporting the incident.

The last few days had gone smoothly, and Erin was beginning to think everything might be all right, after all. She had no idea how to find the man who had abused her, but she'd remembered his sergeant stripes. It turned out there weren't that many patrol sergeants at Rampart Division, and she'd picked him out from a photo lineup.

Now they wanted her to call Babbage while they recorded every word he said. Get a confession, and the man would have no choice but to plead guilty. It meant going to the Criminal Court's Building in downtown L.A., to the seventeenth-floor District Attorney's Office. No problem, Sean had said. He'd drive.

And he had. But now, waiting for the elevator with Sean and Fitz in the crowded lobby, Erin felt panic rising inside her, paralyzing her. Despite Fitz and Sean's assurances that she was a victim and that Eric Lundy, an experienced deputy district attorney, would treat her with courtesy and respect, Erin couldn't make herself believe it.

They squeezed into an elevator packed with shabby-looking people on their way to court. The first fifteen floors were courtrooms, and the elevator stopped at every floor.

"This is a bad idea," she whispered to Sean. "Let's go home."

Sean squeezed her hand. "You can do it," he replied.

By the time they reached the seventeenth floor, they were alone in the elevator, but the sweet smell of cologne tinged with sweat remained. Erin's throat tightened, and she thought she might vomit.

Fitz showed his badge to the guard, and they were buzzed into what looked like a doctor's waiting room.

"This is where cops come to present police reports and file their cases," Fitz said. They sat down. "Detectives wait here until they're called into one of the filing prosecutor's offices," Fitz added. "Lundy is a prosecutor in the Special Investigation's Division, SID—that's the section that prosecutes cops."

After about ten minutes, Lundy appeared. He looked to be mid-forties. His round face was topped with thick brown hair. He had a high-blood-pressure flush, was close-shaven with no sideburns, and wore a short-sleeved, white shirt with a plaid bow tie. "Detective Fitzgerald, nice to see you again," he said. Then to Erin: "Ms. Collins, I'll be handling your case." He looked at Sean. "I presume this is your brother, Mr. Collins?"

She nodded.

"We'll talk more in my office," Lundy said. He ushered them down a hallway to a medium-sized office with light-gray walls and dark-gray vinyl-tile floor. He motioned them to hardwood chairs and sat down behind his desk.

Erin glanced at the rear wall, at the awards, plaques, and diplomas. On the credenza behind Lundy were framed photos—a young girl in a soccer uniform, the same girl older and at Disneyland, and as a young woman, smiling in cap and gown.

Lundy explained that a DA investigator was going to place a recorded call to the suspect she'd identified, a police sergeant named Jake Babbage. He picked up his telephone, told the investigator to begin the call, and then handed Erin the telephone handset.

Erin listened to the phone ring. "Babbage here," the voice she'd recognize anywhere answered.

"Officer Babbage?" Erin said. She tried to sound friendly, but her mouth was so dry she had to swallow before speaking.

"Can I help you?"

"It's Erin." She hoped her voice didn't shake.

"Who?"

"From the Traffic Stop," She said.

At first Babbage did not reply and Erin feared he'd just hang up. But then he spoke. "What do you want?"

Now was the critical part. The words she had carefully rehearsed with Sean and Fitz. "I need to see you," she said. "Tonight. After work."

"You know I can't take personal calls," Babbage said evenly. "As a supervisor, I've got to set an example for my officers."

Erin tried to sound seductive. "It'll be worth your while." But her voice cracked. *Shit, shit, shit.*

"Didn't you hear what I just told you?" Babbage snapped. "No personal calls. I've got to hang up now."

"Wait," she blurted. "Don't you want to see me? Don't you want more of what you got Monday night?"

"What are you talking about? Is this some kind of shakedown? If so, you've picked the wrong guy to mess with!"

"You bastard!" she shouted. "You threatened to arrest me unless I ... unless I gave you a ... blowjob. Don't try to deny it."

Babbage shouted back. "I don't know what your game is, but I'm going to find out, and when I do, there'll be some justice done. You can count on it." The phone went dead with a loud click.

"Now what?" Erin said, hanging up.

Lundy took the handset back, listened, and nodded, confirming that everything had been recorded as planned.

"We still file the case," Lundy said, putting down his earphone. "It's not going to be a problem. Thankfully we have the DNA on your blouse, so it won't just be your word against his. It would have been good if you'd come in immediately afterwards; we could also have prepared a sexual assault kit and might have gotten hair or semen samples."

"I know," Erin said. "That's the first thing Sean said when I called him, but by then I'd taken my shower. I was going to trash my blouse—no way I'd ever wear it again without remembering what happened to me. Luckily I talked to Sean first."

Sean handed Fitzgerald a plastic bag. "The blouse is inside," Sean said. "I hope the lab finds something. If only—"

"What's done is done," Lundy interrupted. "We're okay with the corroboration we've developed. Your six-pack photo lineup identification; the fact that he's a sergeant, on duty and unaccounted for during the incident; and, very important, his knowing your first name and acknowledging that he'd talked to you. With all that, it's an automatic conviction. In fact, I'll be surprised if he doesn't plead guilty to get a lighter sentence rather than face a trial he's sure to lose."

"I hope so," Sean said. He picked up the six-pack Erin had looked at. "Which photo?"

"Number three," Fitz said.

Sean frowned and studied the photo. "There's something vaguely familiar about him. Something about the eyes."

9

Babbage

Thursday, June 22

Yesterday morning his lieutenant had broken the news to Babbage. Internal Affairs had notified the captain that criminal charges had been filed against Babbage, based on the Erin Collins's complaint. Babbage had to turn in his badge and weapon and was being suspended with pay pending his trial on the matter. Internal Affairs would not be interviewing him or scheduling any Board of Rights hearing until the criminal charges were resolved.

From the lieutenant's office, Babbage went straight to Henderson, the union rep, who told Babbage that the union would hire a lawyer to represent him at all proceedings. An hour later, Henderson called Babbage. The lawyer was a hotshot named Anthony Giovanni, and Babbage better be early to his 10:30 appointment—the lawyer's time was valuable, and the union didn't want to pay for lawyer-time spent waiting.

Babbage arrived at 10 a.m.

The office was impressive. *These fucking assholes really know how to spend the union's money,* Babbage thought, looking around at polished hardwood floors, fancy Persian rugs, and oil paintings, and hearing piped-in classical music. *But what kind of lawyer would work in a place like this—with flowery smells, leafy plants, and soft lighting?* He almost turned around and walked out.

But he couldn't.

At 10:45, a secretary escorted Babbage to the lawyer's office. Anthony Giovanni stood behind a huge desk and held out his pudgy hand. Giovanni was squat, flabby, and balding. He had a U-shaped fringe of dark brown hair, cut short. He was wearing a tight-fitting, buttoned, camel-hair sports jacket and blue wool pants, wrinkled at the crotch.

Babbage was not impressed. He shook Giovanni's cold hand and sat down in a soft chair in front of the desk.

"Would you like a cup of coffee?" Giovanni asked.

"No thanks."

Giovanni took out a legal-sized manila folder and studied it carefully. Finally, he looked straight at Babbage. "Let me give you some background on how we're going to proceed. You don't mind if I call you Jake, do you?"

"Whatever you like."

"To begin with, at this time, I'm not going to ask you any questions about the allegations, and I don't want you to volunteer any information about these charges. Instead, I'm going to wait until I've read all the reports and done all the investigation of the case against you, and then I'll question you in detail." Giovanni tapped his fingertips together.

"When I question you," Giovanni continued, "it is absolutely critical that you be completely open and honest with me. I tell you this because you need to know that

I will not allow you to get on the witness stand and say anything that I know to b e a lie." Giovanni paused to let this information sink in. "Any questions so far?"

So far, this out-of-shape asshole sounds more like the prosecution than the defense. But Henderson said the guy was okay. Babbage would wait a little longer and see.

"If you're not interested in my side of the story, what are we going to do today?"

"Today, we're just going to discuss the case in general. I've read the reports and called the DA. I'm going to give you my appraisal of the case and suggest a strategy. Fair enough?"

"Go on," Babbage said.

"All right. Here's what's happened so far. This woman, Erin Collins, alleges that you stopped her and threatened to arrest her for DUI and an outstanding warrant, unless she gave you a blowjob. She claims that because she was afraid and thought she had no choice, she complied with your demand, and you let her go. She's filed a complaint against you with Internal Affairs, filed a police report, and cooperated with the investigators by telephoning to get incriminating statements from you."

"She didn't get shit," Babbage said.

"I told you not to volunteer any information," Giovanni said. "Goddammit, Babbage, there's a reason for everything I do. Don't shoot yourself in the foot by ignoring me. Please keep quiet until I'm done."

Anger flared inside Babbage, and his hands clenched into fists. Nobody talked to him like that. These fucking defense lawyers all thought they knew everything, and that everyone else was as stupid as their gang-banging clients. Giovanni would find out soon enough that he was dealing with someone who knew which way the wind blew. Too bad he didn't meet this shithead lawyer on the street. That's where people found out what happens when you mouth off to Jake Babbage. But back to the present—he needed the fucker for the time being.

"Here's the bottom line, Jake. You're charged with oral sex under color of authority. In this state, that carries the same penalty as rape—three, six, or eight years with no probation possible."

Babbage leaned forward, focusing his eyes on the lawyer.

"In order to beat this, you've got to either prove it didn't happen, or admit it happened and prove consent. I can't advise you about your case until I know what they've got. If they've got evidence that establishes this woman gave you a blowjob—such as DNA from semen swabbed from her mouth—then I'll investigate the consent issue. Only after I know all these facts, and after I bring you up to date on what I know, will I question you. Now do you understand why I need for you to keep your mouth shut?"

Babbage was beginning to understand. Maybe this lawyer was not so dumb, after all. Giovanni would make sure that Babbage knew everything the other side had, make sure that Babbage knew what the best defense would be, and then and only then, would he question Babbage. Giovanni didn't really care if Babbage lied, didn't really care whether or not Babbage was guilty. The lawyer just wanted to cover his own ass and keep Babbage from saying anything before knowing what needed to be said for an acquittal.

"Okay," Babbage said. "So now I know the rules. What happens next?"

"I've called the DA's Office and spoken to the deputy who's filing the case. Because you're a cop, they've agreed to release you on your written promise to appear, and not require you to put up bail money, provided you surrender today at one-thirty p.m. and get booked and fingerprinted. The arraignment is a week from Monday, on July third, in Division 30 in the Criminal Court's Building."

10

Fitzgerald

Thursday, August 24

Fitz thought about the last few weeks. He marveled that they'd actually made it to trial. It had been a continual struggle with Erin, but Sean had been a godsend. Erin kept changing her mind about whether or not she could go through this all. Fitz and Sean kept reassuring her that she had to persevere. After all, Sean told her, even if she didn't care about herself, how about other women that Babbage would surely victimize?

As part of his preparation for trial, Deputy District Attorney Lundy had not run Erin's rap sheet. When Fitz objected, Lundy explained that he wasn't concerned about Erin's arrest record because California's victim anti-blame law protects sexual assault victims and does not allow the accused to go into arrests and sexual background of their victims. The open DUI warrant—called a bench warrant, because a judge issues it from the bench when a defendant jumps bail and doesn't appear in court when scheduled—was a different matter and had to be resolved immediately. Fitz and Lundy met with Erin's public defender, and the three of them went to the issuing judge. The warrant was recalled, and a date and time was scheduled after the Babbage trial for Erin to surrender in Van Nuys.

Fitz asked Lundy when he was going to go over testimony with Erin.

"I don't do that," Lundy said. "That way the testimony is spontaneous, more impressive to the jury."

Fitz shook his head. "No, you need to go over what Erin is going to be asked. Give her tips on possible cross-examination. She's very nervous and that will make her feel more in charge."

"Absolutely not," Lundy said. "Besides, there's nothing to worry about—the case is a slam dunk."

As the trial approached, Lundy continued being confident. But as late as yesterday morning, before court, Erin called Fitz to say that she couldn't do it—couldn't testify. Fitz called Sean and the two of them went to her apartment to support and reassure her. What she was doing was difficult, but important, they told her. If she could stand up for herself now, she could end being a victim. And she'd be saving other women who would be victimized if Babbage weren't stopped. When Fitz and Sean left, Erin seemed more determined, and even ventured a smile.

Fitzgerald watched as the jury filed into the courtroom and took their places in the jury box. The trial was moving along quickly. Jury selection had taken only two days. Opening statements had been heard that morning and early afternoon. Erin would be the only witness, and Fitz was concerned. He'd asked around about Babbage's lawyer, Giovanni. Word was that Giovanni was a clever son of a bitch. He specialized in defending cops and was very effective.

Giovanni had waived the preliminary hearing six weeks ago, and Fitz was troubled about that as well. Giovanni had something up his sleeve, and Fitz worried that the eight-woman, four-man jury might not understand why Erin was so terrified of arrest that she could be intimidated into giving a cop a blowjob.

Erin had asked Sean not to observe the trial. She was going to be nervous enough recounting the sexual details of what happened that night in front of complete strangers. Having her brother present as well would be too much for her. Sean understood.

Fitz gave Erin a reassuring nod when the judge entered the room.

"Call your first witness," Judge Catherine Morley, a middle-aged black woman with salt-and-pepper gray hair, said.

"The People call Erin Collins, Your Honor," DA Eric Lundy said. Fitz had asked Lundy earlier about Morley, and the news was mixed. "If Babbage is convicted," he said, "you can be sure that Morley will max him out. But she'll force us to prove our case. If we don't, it's all over."

Now, in the austere fluorescent light of the courtroom, Fitz watched as Erin made her way to the witness box. Her dark hair was pulled back in a bun, and she wore a conservative, but attractive, charcoal-black pants suit with a light-blue cotton blouse. How could the jury not like her?

But her complexion was pasty, and she had that nervous look he'd so often seen in victims who testified. Victims who were powerless during the crime and now power-less in court. At risk again of being manipulated—this time by lawyers. Before sitting in the witness box, Erin turned toward the court clerk and raised a shaking right hand.

The clerk asked, "In the cause now pending, do you swear to tell the truth, the whole truth, and nothing but the truth, so help you God?"

"I do," Erin said.

"Please be seated. State and spell your full name for the record."

Erin obeyed.

Lundy began his direct examination from his chair. "Ms. Collins, I'd like you to remember back to June thirteen of this year, around two-thirty a.m. Do you remember the events of that evening?"

She leaned forward, looked at Lundy. "Yes, I do."

"Please tell the jury what happened." In a flat voice, Erin described how she'd been stopped by Babbage and how he'd administered field sobriety tests to her.

"And then what happened?"

Erin paused and took a breath before answering. "He told me"—another breath—"that if I would ... if I'd give him a blow ... er, I mean ... if I'd orally copulate him, he'd let me go."

"And did you orally copulate him?"

"Objection, Your Honor," Anthony Giovanni interrupted. His voice was loud, irritated. "The prosecutor's leading the witness."

"Sustained," Judge Morley said.

"What happened next, after he told you that?" Lundy asked.

Erin straightened in her chair, cleared her throat. She folded her arms in front of her as if shielding herself from Giovanni's anger, from Babbage's stare and said, "I was afraid. I didn't know what else to do. So, I ... I performed oral sex on him."

Fitz silently sighed with relief. She'd said what she'd been dreading to say. They had gone over this again and again, looking for ways that Erin could say what happened in a way that wouldn't embarrass her in front of a room full of strangers. She couldn't bring herself to say "blowjob," but "oral copulation" seemed too clinical, too foreign. But Fitz knew her real ordeal had not yet begun.

"And then what happened?" Lundy asked.

"He left, and I drove home."

Erin described how she had discovered semen on her blouse, how she'd almost trashed it, then recovered it and turned it over to the prosecutor.

Lundy said, "Your Honor, we have a stipulation to enter into the record."

"Proceed," the judge said.

"May the following be stipulated? That the semen on Ms. Collins's blouse was analyzed July third of this year, by the Scientific Investigation Division of the Los Angeles Police Department, that it was compared to blood taken from the defendant, Jake Babbage, that the result of this comparison revealed the semen to be the defendant's."

Fitz turned to look at Babbage, who sat perfectly still, looking straight ahead, expressionless. From the slight redness around the neck, Fitz could tell the bastard was furious. Fitz was grateful that SID had been able to retrieve DNA markers that confirmed the blouse stains came from Babbage.

"So stipulated," Giovanni said.

"The court accepts the stipulation," Judge Morley said, evenly. She turned to the jury. "Ladies and gentlemen," she said, "you are instructed that a stipulation is an agreement between parties concerning any fact or facts in the case. You are to treat such a stipulation as a fact that has been conclusively proven."

Fitz noticed that all the jurors had been leaning forward during Erin's direct testimony. After the reading of the stipulation, several scribbled in their notebooks. Lundy sat down. "I have no further questions for Ms. Collins at this time."

So far, so good, Fitz thought.

"Mr. Giovanni," Judge Morley said, "you may cross-examine."

Giovanni stood. Babbage glared at Erin. "Thank you, Your Honor," Giovanni said. Then he frowned at Erin. "Let's get this straight," he began. "You're saying that you orally copulated my client because you were ... you were afraid?" He said the word "afraid" as if it were unbearably preposterous.

"That's right," Erin said, her arms folded in front of her. She shifted in her chair.

Giovanni's eyes narrowed. "Were you afraid that Sergeant Babbage would harm you?"

"No. Not really."

"So you didn't feel that you were in any physical danger?"

She shook her head. "No."

"Was it being arrested that caused you to be afraid?"

"Yes. I was afraid of being arrested."

Giovanni parted his lips in a thin smile. "I thought so." His tone became accommodating, even sympathetic. "But you'd been drinking, hadn't you?"

"What do you mean?" Erin glanced at Fitz.

Although he was careful to keep his face impassive, Fitz was cringing inside. Lundy was a fool not to have gone over Erin's testimony with her.

Giovanni said, "Please look at me while I'm asking you questions. Detective Fitzgerald can't help you answer. Do you want me to repeat my question?"

She nodded, "Please."

"You'd had too much to drink that evening, hadn't you?"

"Well, I did drink some. But I don't think that I was drunk, no."

Giovanni picked up his yellow pad, and appeared to be looking at notes. He nodded to himself. "Are you saying that you were not driving under the influence of alcohol that evening when you were stopped?"

Erin paused, and then said, "I may have had a little too much to drink. I'm not sure."

"So you were afraid of being arrested because you'd broken the law, correct?"

"It's not like you make it sound—"

Giovanni interrupted. "Objection, Your Honor. The answer is non-responsive. Motion to strike."

"Sustained." Judge Morley looked at the jury. "Members of the jury, you are to treat the answer as if you'd never heard it."

Erin turned to the judge. "May I have a drink of water, Your Honor?"

The bailiff brought a paper cup with water to her. She took a sip and cleared her throat.

Giovanni continued his questioning. He folded his arms in front of him. "Please listen carefully, Ms. Collins. I want you to think back to that moment just after you took the field sobriety tests. To the moment when you realized that you were being arrested. What exactly did Sergeant Babbage say or do that caused you to believe you were being arrested?"

Fitz noticed that Babbage's eyes were locked on Erin—with the intensity of a cat staring at a wounded bird.

Erin closed her eyes briefly, and then opened them. "He said that he was taking me to the station, and that I had a choice of three tests: blood, breath, or urine."

"So you knew that if you had too much to drink, these tests would prove it, didn't you?"

Erin sipped her water. "Yes."

"You also knew that if you passed these tests, you would not be arrested and would be released, didn't you?"

"I didn't think about it exactly that way, no."

Giovanni picked up a document from a folder on the table in front of him. Still looking at the document, he asked, "But you knew how the process worked, didn't you?"

She frowned. "What do you mean?"

Giovanni looked up, turned to the jury for a moment, and then looked back at Erin. "Ms. Collins, I'm a little con-fused." His tone was sarcastic. "A few moments ago, you said that you orally copulated Sergeant Babbage because you were ... afraid of being arrested, correct?"

"Yes."

"But if you weren't breaking any law, then you wouldn't have been arrested, would you?"

"He was going to arrest me anyway. He said so."

"Are you saying that he said he was going to arrest you, even though you'd broken no laws?"

"Yes. I mean, no. He said that I'd failed the FSTs, and that he was going to take me to the station."

"But if you broke no laws, wouldn't that mean, at worst, you'd just be released?"

"It doesn't work that way," Erin said softly.

Giovanni shook his head slowly and said, "You've been through the arrest process before. You know what happens, don't you?"

"Objection, Your Honor." Lundy stood. "Counsel knows this is irrelevant, prejudicial, and assumes facts not in evidence."

"Your Honor," Giovanni shot back, "it goes to her state of mind. The witness has said she was afraid. I'm entitled to inquire."

The judge overruled the objection and said to Erin, "You may answer the question."

Giovanni looked at Erin. "You do know what happens at the police station, don't you?"

"I do," Erin said in a defeated voice.

"And that's because you've been arrested for driving under the influence before, haven't you?"

"Yes."

Fitz could see stress, and even fear, in her eyes.

Giovanni picked up the document he'd been looking at, glanced at it, then dropped it.

"Twice before," he said. "Isn't that correct?"

"Yes." Erin's voice was so soft now that Fitz could barely hear.

"And that's really why you were terrified, wasn't it? You weren't afraid of Sergeant Babbage. You were afraid you'd go to jail." Giovanni didn't wait for an answer. "You'd do anything to stay out of jail. So you bribed your way out of the arrest by orally copulating Sergeant Babbage, and now you want him arrested for agreeing to let you go, don't you?"

"No!" Erin shouted. "He made me do it. He made me! He said I'd go to prison."

"Objection!" Giovanni cried. "Nonresponsive. Motion to strike. The witness is trying to justify her sexual bribe."

Lundy was on his feet. "The People object, Your Honor. Counsel is testifying. May we have a sidebar conference?"

"Quiet—both of you!" Judge Morley said. "I'll have no speaking objections—argument must be done at sidebar, not in front of the jury. It's been a long day. Court is adjourned until tomorrow morning at nine a.m." Judge Morley stood up and left the bench.

The jury slowly filed out of the room. Erin remained seated, staring into space, all color drained from her face.

11

Babbage

Giovanni was waiting in the reception lobby of his office, reading through a file, when Babbage entered. The lawyer had taken off his suit jacket. His tie was loose at the collar, and his wrinkled shirt barely covered his gut.

Giovanni walked toward Babbage and held out his hand, grinning. "Jake, right on time as always. Well, what did you think? From my point of view, it couldn't have gone any better."

Babbage ignored Giovanni's extended hand. "From my point of view, you couldn't have fucked up any worse."

Giovanni dropped his hand and gave Babbage a long appraising look before speaking. "Let's go to my office and talk," he said quietly.

They walked out of the reception room. Neither spoke until they were inside Giovanni's office. "I don't understand you, Jake. Erin Collins all but admitted she sucked you off in order to bribe you."

"That's my point. You're supposed to defend me, not make me look like a crooked cop." He had the urge to smash his fist into Giovanni's mouth. *Not yet,* Babbage thought. *Not yet.*

Giovanni shook his head angrily. "You obviously don't get it. I saved your ass today. Now, if you take the witness stand, your word will count for something. The jury will be sympathetic. You were seduced. That's the reality of what happened. You're human; you had a moment of weakness. The jury will believe you because it makes sense to do that, and because Erin Collins all but admitted her motive. So instead of going to prison, you face, at worst, getting fired and, at best, getting a few days' suspension."

Babbage couldn't believe how stupid Giovanni was. "There's no way I get out of this with anything less than termination. You claim to know how to defend cops. If you did, you'd know that any Board of Rights panel is going to recommend firing anybody who accepted a bribe!" Babbage paused. "Because that's not even what happened."

Giovanni's expression hardened. "I told you not to tell me anything about the facts of the case until I ask."

"When the fuck are you going to ask? We've started the damned trial. How the fuck can you defend me if you don't know my side?"

Giovanni was quiet for a time. "I tried to explain to you that I wanted to know all the facts before I asked you any questions. In this case, that meant after I'd heard all the testimony from everyone else. I planned to interview you the night before you testify. Now you've blurted something out, and I have to follow up. But remember, I told you that there's no way I put you on the witness stand if I think you're lying."

"So?"

"All right then. Let's hear your side of the story."

"It's simple," Babbage said. "I met her at the Traffic Stop. I could tell she wanted it, so I asked her to meet me after work. One thing led to another, and that's how it happened."

"Really?" Giovanni said. "Why did you stop at the Mission Street off-ramp? Why didn't you take her to your place? Were you in uniform or out?"

Giovanni paused and looked at Babbage, then continued. "If you were out of uniform, that would mean that you went back to Parker Center before leaving to meet her. Did you talk to anyone about it? Can you prove any of the things you're telling me?"

"Are you calling me a liar?"

"You tell me," Giovanni said. "Why else would she accuse you of forcing her to her knees?"

"Because her skinny ass should be in jail right now. She has an outstanding DUI warrant—a bench warrant. Why is she not in jail? The only answer is that she's made a deal with the DA. The fucking bitch would sell her soul to stay out of jail. She's a whore!"

"Wait a minute," Giovanni said. "You never told me she has an open DUI warrant. As a police officer, you must know that under the anti-blame law, the defense can't get a rap sheet on a sexual assault victim."

"You never gave me the chance, remember?" Babbage squeezed his right hand into a fist. "I looked her up at the station. She's got a bench warrant out of Van Nuys for failing to appear for her arraignment."

Giovanni mused, "That means any cop, including the court's deputy sheriff bailiff, would have to arrest her on the warrant. Unless ..."

"Unless a judge recalled the warrant," Babbage finished. "And no judge would do that unless a DA asked for it. That's what I've been trying to tell you. The bitch made some kind of deal with the prosecutor."

Giovanni said nothing for a moment.

"That's it," he said. "That's how we'll get her. That's the way we win this case without any Internal Affairs Board of Rights hearing. If I play it right, you won't even have to testify." He drummed his fingers on the desk. "Why'd you call her a whore? Do you have evidence that she's sleeping around with cops?"

"I got something better. The bitch was arrested for P.C. 647(b), prostitution. Two years ago."

"Was she convicted?" Giovanni asked.

"I don't think so."

"Can you get me the report for that arrest? It could be the clincher for everything."

Babbage shrugged. "I'll call one of my guys." Babbage added, "Now do you get why I wanted to tell you my side, hotshot?"

He picked up the phone on Giovanni's desk and called Rampart Police Station. After a quick conversation, he looked up at Giovanni. "He can get it to us in fifteen minutes."

12

Fitzgerald

Friday, August 25

Fitzgerald studied the jury as they filed into the court-room, and then looked to Judge Morley as she sat down at the bench.

"Ms. Collins," the judge said, "please take your seat in the witness box. You are still under oath. Mr. Giovanni, you may continue asking your questions as soon as the witness is seated."

Erin walked to the witness box and sat down. *On the surface, she seems to be holding up,* Fitz thought. But he worried that her complexion seemed a bit pasty, and she looked tired. *Poor kid is nervous and wary.*

Giovanni had been sitting at the counsel table. He stood up and walked toward the jury, and then paused in the space between the counsel table and the jury box. He had a reflective look on his face. "Ms. Collins, have you been promised anything by the prosecution in order to testify today?"

Erin looked at Giovanni, then at Lundy, then at Fitzgerald. "What do you mean?"

"It's a simple question, Ms. Collins. I want to know what the prosecution is doing for you in exchange for your testimony?"

"Nothing."

"Then," Giovanni continued, "you're testifying today simply because you feel it's your civic duty? Nothing else?"

Erin's face flushed, and she straightened in her chair. "I'm testifying because I'm a victim. The defendant forced me to perform oral sex on him, that's why."

"I see," Giovanni said. He wrote on his legal pad. "May I have a moment, Your Honor?"

Giovanni went back to his chair at the counsel table, leafed through a folder, and pulled out a document. He examined it for a moment. Still holding the document in his hands, still looking at it, he spoke without looking up. "Do you know what a bench warrant is, Ms. Collins?"

Shit, Fitzgerald thought. He looked to Lundy, who stood.

"Objection. Irrelevant," Lundy said.

"Overruled," Judge Morley said. "You may answer the question, Ms. Collins."

"I'm not sure," Erin replied.

"Would it refresh your recollection to know that a bench warrant is something the court issues when a defendant fails to come to court after being released on bail?" Giovanni asked.

Erin hesitated.

"Your Honor," Lundy said, "may we approach at sidebar?"

"No, you may not," said the judge. "Ms. Collins, please answer the question."

Fitz was concerned. His jaw clenched. Once again, Lundy had dropped the ball. This should have been discussed with the judge without the jury present. Now all eyes were on Erin.

She looked at Giovanni, but Babbage—who was sitting in the seat beside his lawyer—glared at her. Erin turned away, and looked straight ahead again. Fitz could see she looked flustered. "Could you repeat the question?"

Giovanni did.

"Yes. I do remember what a bench warrant is," Erin said.

"I was certain you would remember, Ms. Collins," Giovanni said. "Because that's precisely what happened to you in your second driving under the influence case, correct?

Erin looked at Lundy. "Yes."

"A judge issued a bench warrant for you, because you failed to appear at your arraignment. Correct?"

"Yes," Erin said, quietly.

"And you knew, didn't you, that once a judge issues a bench warrant, any bailiff, sheriff, or police officer would have to arrest you and bring you to the court where the bench warrant was issued?"

Erin nodded.

"You have to answer out loud, Ms. Collins," Judge Morley said. "For the court reporter."

"Yes," Erin said.

Fitz wanted to rush up to her, tell her everything would be okay, tell her not to worry. But he was worried. Very worried.

Giovanni walked to the bailiff who stood at the side of the courtroom. "I notice, Ms. Collins," Giovanni said, looking at the bailiff, "that there is a bailiff in this court-room. In fact, there is also a police officer, Detective Fitzgerald, here in the courtroom." He nodded in Fitzgerald's direction.

Fitzgerald looked back at Giovanni, fought hard to keep his expression passive. *The son of a bitch is getting to her.*

Giovanni went back to the counsel table, and then looked directly at Erin. "Have you ever discussed your bench warrant with Mr. Lundy?"

Lundy was immediately on his feet. "Objection, Your Honor. We again request a sidebar conference."

"Objection overruled. Your sidebar request is also denied." Judge Morley looked at Erin. "Ms. Collins, you may answer the question."

"I have discussed it with him," Erin said. "Yes."

Seconds passed. Giovanni took a deep breath and exhaled before speaking. "So, the prosecutor knew about your bench warrant, and he did not have you taken into custody, correct?"

"Yes."

"Was Detective Fitzgerald present during your discussion?"

"Yes."

"So, both the prosecutor and the investigating officer knew there was an outstanding bench warrant against you, and they did nothing about it. Correct?"

"No. That's not correct. They went to the judge who issued the warrant. They said—"

Giovanni interrupted. "They said that if you testified against Sergeant Babbage, that you'd stay out of jail, didn't they?"

"They said that would be up to the judge."

"But the warrant was recalled, was it not?"

"Yes, it was."

"In other words, based upon the efforts of the deputy district attorney and the investigating officer in this case, the warrant was recalled. Correct?"

"Yes."

"And this was done in exchange for your testimony in this case, wasn't it?"

"As far as I know."

"What this means is that, in effect, you've succeeded in getting from the prosecution what you tried to get from Sergeant Babbage. Is that a fair interpretation—"

Lundy jumped up. "Objection! Argumentative, assumes facts not in evidence, and Counsel is testifying."

"The objection is sustained as argumentative," Judge Morley said.

Giovanni peered at his notes briefly, nodded to himself, and then looked up at Erin. "Ms. Collins, you've testified that you participated in oral sex with my client, Sergeant Babbage, because you were afraid. Correct?"

"That's correct."

"Who mentioned it first? The oral sex, I mean?"

"The defendant told me that if I wanted to avoid jail, I would have to give him a blowjob."

"Really?" Giovanni replied. "Didn't you say yesterday that Sergeant Babbage told you he was going to take you to the station and that you had a choice of three tests—blood, breath, or urine? You did testify to that, did you not?"

"Yes. That's what happened."

"So, Sergeant Babbage said nothing about sexual favors before telling you that? Is that what you're saying?"

"Yes. He first told me I was going to the station."

"What did you say in response to that?"

"I asked if we could talk about it."

"So, at that point your intent was to talk Sergeant Babbage out of the arrest?"

"I was hoping he wouldn't arrest me. Yes."

Giovanni started looking through his folder again. "May I have another moment, Your Honor?"

"You may," Judge Morley said. She peered down at Giovanni, an annoyed look on her face. "If you have an exhibit, you must mark it and hand a copy to the prosecution," she said.

Giovanni pulled out a document. "Not just yet, Your Honor."

Fitzgerald could see Giovanni had a police report. Fitz didn't like one bit what was happening. Lundy had assured him that Erin would be protected by the victim anti-blame law. Why wasn't Lundy asking to approach the bench at sidebar?

Giovanni appeared to read the document to himself. After a moment, he looked up. "Ms. Collins, Sergeant Babbage isn't the first police officer you offered to orally copulate, is he?"

Lundy interjected, "Object to the word 'offer' as assuming facts not in evidence, Your Honor."

Before Judge Morley could rule, Giovanni spoke. "I'll withdraw the question, Your Honor. Ms. Collins, Sergeant Babbage is not the first police officer that you ever discussed oral sex with, was he?"

"Object," Fitzgerald whispered to Lundy. "Now."

Lundy rose. "Objection—"

But Erin answered before Lundy could finish.

"I don't know what you're talking about," she said.

"May we approach at sidebar to discuss my objection?" Lundy said.

Before Judge Morley could respond, Giovanni added, "Oh, I don't mean that evening with Sergeant Babbage, Ms. Collins. Perhaps it would help you to remember a time in the bar at the Marina Hotel?"

Why isn't the judge ruling on the objection? Fitz thought.

Erin flushed. Giovanni continued. "You do remember such a time, do you not?"

Erin glared at Giovanni. For a moment, it seemed like she might run from the witness box. *I should have warned her,* Fitzgerald thought. *Anything would have been better than to let Giovanni surprise her like this.* Fitz was angry with Giovanni, angry with himself, and outraged at Babbage. *That bastard just might win this thing,* he thought. Again, he leaned close and whispered in Lundy's ear. "You've got to do something. At the very least, try to get a recess so Erin can catch her breath and recover from this."

Lundy stood. "Your Honor, a moment ago, I asked to approach at sidebar. May I?"

Giovanni interrupted. "May we get an answer to my question first, Your Honor?"

"Your request to approach is denied," Judge Morley said to Lundy. "Ms. Collins, please answer the question."

Tears were trickling down Erin's face. She said to Giovanni, "What happened at the Marina Hotel has nothing to do with today. You're taking everything I say and turning it against me. It didn't occur like you say."

"Didn't it, Ms. Collins?" Giovanni said. "Didn't it occur exactly the way I described it?"

"No," Erin said.

"Yes, it did. You told Detective Donald Rufus at the Marina Hotel bar that you'd give him a blowjob if he'd give you one hundred dollars, didn't you?"

Erin tried to wipe the tears away with her hand. She said nothing.

Giovanni looked at the judge. "Would the court instruct the witness to please answer, Your Honor?"

Lundy stood once again. "Your Honor, Ms. Collins needs a recess. Could the court take ten minutes?"

Judge Morley looked at the clock over the jury box. "It's almost noontime. We'll take our luncheon recess." She rose from the bench. The jury filed out of the courtroom.

But Erin didn't move. She remained in the witness box, her head in her hands, weeping.

13

Fitzgerald

After the judge left the bench and the jurors filed out, Fitzgerald rushed to Erin. Her look of stunned anguish broke his heart. She was the closest thing Fitz had to a daughter, and he'd been unable to protect her. He stood beside the witness box, feeling helpless, not knowing what to say or do.

Lundy approached. His face was grim. "Let's go to my office."

"How could the judge let him do this to me?" she asked. "You said everything would be okay. I didn't want to come to court, didn't want to do any of this."

"We have to leave," Fitzgerald said. "We can't talk here." He led her out of the courtroom, and they returned to Lundy's office.

While Lundy telephoned a sandwich order, Fitzgerald sat down with Erin in the two chairs in front of the lawyer's desk. "Don't give up," he said.

Erin looked down and said nothing.

Fitzgerald was still reeling from what happened to Erin. Giovanni was a ruthless bastard—a typical defense attorney. Fitz had expected as much. But Lundy had made it clear that the anti-blame law protected Erin.

Lundy hung up the phone. His eyes flashed anger, and he looked at Fitz. "You're the investigating officer—you know we don't run rap sheets on victims. Why didn't you tell me about this Marina Hotel thing?"

"Because you made it clear to me that Giovanni couldn't go into Erin's background. That the anti-blame law protected sexual assault victims."

"It does," Lundy replied. "The judge is clearly wrong."

"So what can we do about it?" Fitz demanded.

"Nothing. The jury has been exposed to the information, and even if Judge Morley admonished them to ignore it, they've already heard it."

Fitz was devastated. "So what do we do now?" he asked.

"It doesn't matter. I just can't go on," Erin said. "What's the use?"

"You've got to try," Fitz said. "You've come this far—don't let Babbage get away with this."

"Fitzgerald is right," Lundy said. "Hey, there's highs and lows in any trial. What counts is how the jury sees things after hearing *all* the evidence."

Erin didn't reply, and they sat in silence for a time.

"Please, Erin," Fitzgerald said.

"Okay," she said, finally.

Fitzgerald exhaled. He hadn't realized he was holding his breath. Waiting and worrying.

"All right," Lundy said, smiling. "Let's get to work. Tell me what happened that night."

Erin took a deep breath. "It was two years ago. I've almost been able to put it out of my mind—until now. I was lonely and depressed, and thought a drink would cheer me up. I wanted to be around people who'd like me and make me laugh. A place where I could have fun and forget my problems. I'd been to the Marina Hotel once before, and I really liked it. It had an outside bar, a view of the ocean, and lots of people. I decided to go there."

Fitzgerald interrupted. "It's a popular hotel since it's near the airport and near the ocean," he said to Lundy. "A lot of successful businesspeople stay there. The bar does a booming business; it's always crowded. They have a big prostitution problem—that's why the vice cops practically live at that place. They make lots of arrests."

Erin nodded. "I know now how stupid I was to be so trusting."

"Go on," Lundy said.

"I got there around eight p.m. As I said, the hotel has an outside bar by the water. I sat on an empty stool at the end of the bar. I ordered a martini, straight up, and felt a buzz immediately."

Erin sighed. "Somebody asked if anyone was sitting next to me. I turned to look. He was tall, six-one or six-two, dark-brown hair, wearing a beige cotton T-shirt and faded jeans. He looked to be in his mid-twenties. Honest face. Handsome. With a carefully trimmed beard."

"Yeah," Fitzgerald said. "Most people don't expect a cop to have facial hair. Vice cops grow beards just for that reason."

"He definitely did not look like a cop," Erin continued. "He sat down. We talked for about an hour. He said his name was Don or John or something—I don't remember exactly. That he was a salesman, attending a conference at the hotel, was from San Jose and knew no one in the area. We continued to talk. He had a great sense of humor, and was a good listener. And he seemed really interested in me. He took my hand and didn't let go."

"He had to know by then you weren't a hooker," Lundy commented. "No hooker would spend an hour talking to a potential john. Time is money. And no hooker would ever hold hands. I'm beginning to understand why they never filed on you. What happened next?"

"He asked me if I wanted to go to his room for a night-cap. My head was swimming, and I was attracted to him. I found myself following him to the elevator, heading for his room.

"In the room, I had another drink. He asked me if I needed any money. I said no—insulted that he'd even offered it. I got up to leave. He took my hand. He said he was on an expense account and had plenty of money. He pulled a wad of bills from his pocket. 'No, really,' I said, 'I wouldn't be comfortable taking money.' But he said it was okay and put a hundred dollar bill in my purse.

"But then I began to think that I really did need money—especially the fifty dollars for my next month's rent, so I hesitated. Then he put his arms around me and kissed me. 'Can we do it?' he whispered in my ear. I nodded. 'Yes,' I said. Then abruptly, he pushed me away and stepped back. He flashed his badge. Somehow I was arrested for prostitution. He was really an undercover vice cop."

"Classic entrapment," Lundy said. "And it's clear to me he knew you had no criminal intent. When did you find out that you weren't going to be charged?"

"My brother called a local bondsman who bailed me out a little while later. At the jail, they gave me a piece of paper telling me to report for arraignment in the Van Nuys courthouse in two weeks. I went to the Public Defender's Office, and they agreed to represent me. When we went to court, my lawyer told me the charges had been dropped. I was so relieved. But I didn't know it would come back and haunt me."

"We need that police report," Lundy said. He looked at Fitzgerald and said to him, "Can you get it by Monday morning?"

"I think so." Fitzgerald said.

"Good," Lundy said. "You get the report. When Erin testifies after lunch, I'll help her explain to the jury what really happened that night. I'll arrange for this cop, Don what's-his-name to be available Monday as our next witness. If things go the way I expect, we'll be okay."

Fitz wasn't so sure. Call it cop's intuition, but he had a bad feeling that he just couldn't shake.

14

Fitzgerald

J udge Morley started the afternoon court session promptly. The jury filed into the courtroom.

Fitzgerald looked at their faces. The jurors looked straight ahead. No one smiled. It was hard for him to read what they were thinking. Generally, when it was a prosecution jury, they smiled at the investigating officer, so their blank stare couldn't be good. On the other hand, what happened to Erin was serious stuff. Maybe that accounted for it.

"We are returning to the People versus Jake Babbage case," Judge Morley said. "Ms. Collins, please take your seat in the witness box. You are still under oath. Mr. Giovanni, you may continue your cross-examination."

Giovanni stood. "Your Honor, we have no further questions of the witness at this time."

Fitz considered this. Giovanni must have decided he'd accomplished everything he needed. *Maybe he had,* Fitz thought. *Well, now it's our turn. Let's see what Lundy can do.*

Judge Morley looked at Lundy. "Redirect examination?"

Standing without notes, Lundy began. "Ms. Collins, there was no answer to the last question posed by Mr. Giovanni, so I will re-ask it. Did you ever tell an undercover vice cop that you would perform oral sex for one hundred dollars?"

Erin shook her head. "Never."

"Did you perform oral sex on the officer?"

"Never."

"Were charges ever filed against you in connection with that case?"

"No. The case was thrown out of court."

"Objection, Your Honor," Giovanni said. "It calls for a legal conclusion on the part of the witness."

"Sustained."

Lundy asked Erin, "Did a jury ever hear your case?"

"No."

"Did you ever appear in front of a judge in connection with these events?"

"No. No charges were ever filed against me."

"Ms. Collins," Lundy continued, "do you remember the events that surrounded that arrest?"

"I remember them very clearly."

"Tell us what happened."

"Objection," Giovanni said. "Calls for a narrative answer."

"Sustained."

Lundy began again. "Tell us how you met the vice officer that evening."

"I was sitting at a bar at the Marina Hotel when he approached me."

"Who spoke first?"

"He did. He seemed interested in me. He looked into my eyes and said romantic things and took my hand."

Fitzgerald glanced at Babbage, who seemed amused and unconcerned. Giovanni leaned forward. *Probably waiting to pounce when he hears an objectionable question,* thought Fitzgerald. The jury seemed interested. Everyone was taking notes. *Maybe things will turn out okay, after all.*

Lundy continued, "At some time that evening did you go to a room with him?"

"Yes."

"How long after he first approached you did that happen?"

"About an hour."

"And what did you do during that period of time?"

"We talked, laughed, and held hands."

"Who suggested that you go to his room?"

"He did."

"Was money mentioned at anytime before you left for his room?"

"No. He just said we could go there and talk."

"When was money first mentioned?"

"When we were in his room, after he kissed me."

"Who mentioned money first?"

"He did. He offered to give me one hundred dollars, and I said no. He kept trying to put the money in my purse. Finally, I got tired of saying no and didn't remove it, and that's when he arrested me."

"Let me get this straight," Lundy said. "An undercover vice officer picked you up in the bar, spent an hour holding hands and talking to you, asked you to his room, forced you to take money, then arrested you for prostitution. Correct?"

Giovanni stood abruptly. "Objection! The prosecutor is leading the witness. In addition, the question is compound."

"Overruled."

"Ms. Collins," Lundy continued. "Did you offer to commit an act of prostitution for Officer Donald Rufus

"No. He seduced me, put money in my purse, and arrested me."

"Objection!" shouted Giovanni.

"Overruled," said the judge.

"I have no further questions, Your Honor." Lundy sat down.

Fitzgerald looked at the jurors. The bald man in the front row was asleep.

15

Fitzgerald

itzgerald, Erin, and Lundy met in Lundy's office. Fitzgerald had a manila envelope in his hand.

"Did you get the report?" Lundy asked.

Fitzgerald tossed the envelope on Lundy's desk. "I picked it up at the records division at seven this morning. I've already shown it to Erin." Fitz knew what Lundy's reaction would be, but Fitz hoped that Erin would be okay when she heard it.

Lundy opened the envelope, took out a document, and began to read it. "It's pretty sparse."

"That's standard for these sorts of reports," Fitzgerald said.

Lundy read out loud:

> Reporting officer (RO) observed lone female suspect sitting with her back to the bar at Marina Hotel bar, a known location where prostitutes frequent. Hotel

management cooperated with vice operation and provided a room in the hotel.
RO observed suspect looking at male
patrons and smiling. RO approached suspect. After brief conversation, RO asked
suspect if she was working. This is street
vernacular for working as a prostitute.
Suspect asked RO if RO was a cop. RO
denied being a cop and asked suspect
to go to RO's room, which was provided
by the hotel. Suspect complied. In room,
suspect demanded RO show his penis
to her to 'prove that he was not a cop.'
RO refused but put a marked one hundred dollar bill, which RO obtained from
department funds set aside for this operation, in suspect's purse. Suspect asked
RO if he would like head. That is street
vernacular for oral copulation. At this
time, RO arrested suspect for a violation
of P.C. 647(b), prostitution.

"It's all a damned lie," Erin said. "I never asked him if he
was a cop. I never asked to see his penis."

"I understand why they didn't file it," Lundy said. "He
put the money in your purse before you asked for money.
That totally violates our filing guidelines. But if I put him
on the stand, and he says what he said in the report, it
looks terrible. Plus, it's Erin's word against the police officer's. Then we're right where Giovanni wants us. A prostitution trial of Erin instead of concentrating on Babbage's

crime." He paused. "That settles it. We can't put this damn cop on the stand."

She gave him a startled glance. "But you said you would!" Erin insisted. "You said Babbage was as good as convicted."

"I was wrong," Lundy said. "I'm sorry."

Erin looked to Fitz, silently pleading.

"I have to agree," Fitzgerald said. "It would be a disaster to put him on. I'm sorry, Erin."

She sat still and stared straight ahead at nothing.

16

Fitzgerald

Tuesday, August 29, 9:30 a.m.

Fitzgerald was a realist. The crime was reprehensible. Babbage's semen had been found on Erin's blouse. That one fact should have convinced the jury that Babbage had no right to walk about freely. But this was Los Angeles. Throughout his career, time and time again, juries did stupid things. No juror who heard the evidence in this trial ought to do anything other than convict, but Fitz was gravely worried. Because, time and time again, he'd been astounded by criminal jury verdicts that freed the guilty. Freed them in the face of overwhelming DNA evidence, fingerprint evidence, even video evidence that proved the crime beyond a shadow of a doubt. The list of these outrageous miscarriage-of-justice verdicts was endless, and the public knew the names of the accused defendants by heart.

Deputy DA Lundy was a nice guy and a professional trial attorney, but Fitzgerald could see that Giovanni had outmaneuvered him throughout the trial, resting without Babbage even testifying and without presenting any additional evidence. During defense argument, every juror's eyes were on Babbage's lawyer as he spoke.

At first Giovanni talked softly, but toward the conclusion of his closing, his voice became strong with anger. The People had failed to prove their case, he said. Babbage was only human, and he'd been seduced by a prostitute. A woman who sold sex and who attempted to use it as a bribe, attempting to corrupt a man dedicated to law enforcement. Fitzgerald noticed that even the dark-haired woman juror—who earlier appeared sympathetic to Erin, leaned forward and took careful notes.

"Giovanni just made a major tactical error," Lundy whispered smugly to Fitzgerald. "The jury won't fall for that." Fitzgerald didn't respond. He was getting sick to his stomach and his head ached.

Lundy's rebuttal was direct and to the point. Babbage had misused his power as a police officer to violate an innocent victim. The prosecutor argued that Giovanni had attempted to obscure Babbage's outrageous abuse by attacking Erin. It was a smoke screen. The jury must see through it and send a message to Babbage that he would be held accountable for his acts.

But Fitzgerald worried throughout the rebuttal argument. He studied the jurors' faces. They didn't look at Lundy as he talked, didn't take notes.

The judge instructed the jury and, finally, the matter was in their hands.

They went to Eric Lundy's office to await the verdict.

Lundy was confident, he told them. But he didn't look confident, Fitz thought.

Erin sat in the chair at Lundy's desk and quietly stared out the window at the condemned Hall of Justice, across the street from the Criminal Court's Building.

Despite everything, Fitz relaxed a little. Maybe it would be okay. In any event, he'd done all he could, and so had Erin. Regardless of the result, she could be proud, he told her. She'd shown Babbage that win or lose, there was a cost to victimizing her.

She didn't reply.

Two hours later the clerk informed Lundy's secretary that the jury had a verdict. Fitzgerald had always believed that quick jury verdicts usually meant that the jury had voted guilty. He certainly hoped that's what it meant today.

Back in the courtroom, Fitzgerald noticed Babbage watching him as the jury filed in. Babbage continued to look at him as each juror sat down.

"Remain seated. The court is now in session," the bailiff said.

Judge Morley looked to the jury. "Which of you is the foreperson?"

A young African-American man in the back row raised his hand. "I am, Your Honor."

"Has the jury reached a verdict?"

"We have, Your Honor."

"Please hand the verdict to the bailiff."

The foreperson handed a closed manila folder to the bailiff, who took it to the judge. Judge Morley examined the verdict form carefully.

Fitzgerald was weary. He was tired of seeing innocent victims like Erin blamed and attacked as if they'd caused the crime, tired of seeing victims treated as if they deserved whatever they got.

Judge Morley handed the verdict form to the clerk. "The clerk will read the verdict."

The clerk started to read. "The People of the State of California versus Jake Babbage ..."

Fitzgerald held his breath.

"We, the jury in the above entitled case, find the defendant to be ... not guilty."

Babbage grinned at Fitzgerald

BOOK THREE

17

Erin

Friday, September 8, 8:15 a.m.

For today's court appearance, Sean had come along with Erin for moral support. She was surrendering on the bench warrant, which had been recalled, and was to be arraigned in Division 103 at 8:30 a.m. Her public defender, Beth Daniels, had told her that the judge, Daniel Hart, was a fair guy. Sean knew and worked with Beth and had nothing but good things to say about her. Erin agreed. Beth did nothing to fix herself up, wore no makeup, didn't color her hair despite some premature grey strands of hair, and, as a consequence, looked older than her twenty-nine years

But she had a warmth and inner beauty that Erin admired. She gave Erin her cell phone number and told her to call if she had any questions at all. For today's hearing, Beth was optimistic that Erin might qualify for the thirty-month alcohol rehabilitation program. If she did, she could avoid the mandatory 120-day jail sentence and the equally mandatory revocation of her driving privileges. But if she didn't complete the program, or if she consumed even one drink, she'd go to jail for sure.

Erin made her way up the steps to the Van Nuys courthouse. She was very nervous, almost as nervous as she'd been for the Babbage trial.

She was terrified of Babbage. He was sure to be twice as dangerous now that he'd been acquitted. Fitz had told her that Babbage wouldn't dare try anything, but Fitz didn't know Babbage the way she did. Now that he'd gotten away with what he'd done to her, he must think that he was invincible. When the jury came back with its verdict of acquittal, Babbage, after grinning at Fitz, had turned to look at Erin and smiled. *That son of a bitch,* she thought.

Maybe it was her imagination, but ever since the trial, she saw police cars everywhere she went—in the parking lot at the market, across the street from her gym, even at the car wash. She didn't know what she would have done if it weren't for Fitz. He'd given her his home phone and cell/pager numbers. He'd promised to keep an eye on her, to see that she was okay, and he had. He called her every evening, and drove by her apartment during the days when she slept in late. He had even taken her out for breakfast twice.

Fitz had promised to be at the hearing, and Erin was glad to see him waiting in the hallway as soon as she and Sean got off the elevator.

The three of them entered the courtroom, which was already crowded and noisy. In the rear were two rows of uniformed cops. Beth, her public defender, had told her it was going to be a busy day in court, with lots of cops there for a high-publicity case. Erin averted her eyes from them.

She was to check in with the bailiff, and Beth said that she would be there by the time the court called Erin's case.

———

Jake Babbage watched as Erin and Fitzgerald walked past him, spoke to the bailiff, and then moved to the first row of the spectator section. Babbage had arrived early, and because he and the other cops were in full uniform, the bailiff had allowed them to enter the courtroom before it was open to the public. The officers were all there for Dr. Gina Black's vehicular manslaughter sentencing. When Babbage arrived, he was astounded to see that the judge was named Hart.

Daniel Hart.

Babbage had been following Hart's career for years, knew he'd become a Los Angeles County judge, but hadn't had the opportunity to find out where Hart was assigned. For Hart to be the one who decided Erin's fate was an unbelievable stroke of luck. And Babbage knew exactly how to make use of Hart. There was no telling just how valuable this was going to be.

As Fitzgerald and Erin sat down, Babbage smiled. After the acquittal, Fitzgerald had tried to get a Board of Rights hearing initiated, but since Erin had been totally discredited, Anthony Giovanni was able to convince the captain that Babbage had been through enough. After all, he was a respected sergeant with a spotless record. A tough cop like Babbage occasionally received groundless complaints, and the department ought to stand behind its best cops.

Bottom line, it was a relief to be back at work. It felt good to be in uniform and to be armed. Now he could finish up with Erin without worry. As long as he was careful, there was no reason why he couldn't take care of her. Especially if the judge controlling her fate was Daniel Hart. All Babbage had to do was ensure that Judge Hart handled all future proceedings involving Erin Collins. And, if things went the way he expected, that fucking Fitzgerald would soon be out of the picture, too.

Erin and Fitzgerald showed no sign that they'd noticed him sitting among the other uniformed cops. But they had to have seen him. *Good*, he thought. *Let them squirm.*

Remaining in the spectator section, Fitz watched as Erin and Beth made their way forward to stand in front of the judge. He realized he was nervous again. Erin had been through so much—she really needed a break—but was it realistic to hope she could avoid jail? He didn't think so. He spotted Babbage in the middle of a bunch of cops here for the Gina Black case. The asshole probably *came* to gloat. Well, fuck him.

"The court calls the case of People versus Collins," Judge Hart announced.

"The defendant is present with Counsel, Deputy Public Defender Beth Daniels, Your Honor. My client would like to request a thirty-month alcohol program, Your Honor. If the court would allow that, she's prepared to plead no contest today."

The prosecutor, a fortyish woman with longish carefully brushed yellow hair stood up. Even from the back,

Fitz recognized the woman as Doris Reynolds. He cringed. She was well known by local cops.

"Ms. Daniels knows," Reynolds said, "that the People oppose, and the court doesn't allow the thirty-month program." She turned to speak directly to Beth. "Your client belongs in jail."

Beth stared angrily at Reynolds, and then looked at the judge. "Your Honor, Ms. Collins has been through a lot as a result of her drinking. She tells me that she's been sober for over a month, and that if the court would give her a chance, she'll prove worthy of it. And Detective William Fitzgerald is here to speak on her behalf. May he address the court?"

"What for?" Reynolds broke in. "Every judge in this building has a policy of no thirty-month program."

Hart didn't appear ruffled in the least. "If you have legal grounds to oppose a sentence that involves the thirty-month program, present it. Otherwise, please sit down."

Reynolds shook her head and remained standing.

"Please come forward, Detective Fitzgerald," Hart said.

Fitz walked to the counsel table and stood next to Daniels. "Your Honor, I know Ms. Collins and can vouch for her. I was the investigating officer on a case where she was the complaining witness. As a result, I spent much time with her and observed her carefully. She tells me that she's been sober and that she's been attending AA meetings. During the time of this case, I have not seen her take a drink or smelled alcohol on her breath. I believe that she's an excellent candidate for the thirty-month program."

"Ms. Collins," Hart asked, "if I put you in this program, are you confident that you'll stay in it? Be aware that you would have to agree to attend a rehabilitation program, along with your Alcoholics Anonymous meetings, and also maintain absolute abstinence from drinking. Most people find they are unable to do this. If they are unable, they go directly to jail. You would also have to pay for this very expensive program yourself. Do you understand all this?"

Erin looked directly at the judge. There was determination in her voice. "Ms. Daniels told me about the costs and how difficult the program is, Your Honor," Erin said. "Money is very tight for me." She turned and looked toward Fitz, then looked back at Judge Hart. "As a result of the court case I was involved in, I had to quit my job, and I don't want to return to it. But I have a little bit saved, and I can also borrow some from my brother. I *will* finish the program, and I am going to remain sober. I'm determined to overcome my addiction."

Judge Hart looked down at a folder on his bench. For a moment, the court seemed very quiet. Finally, he looked up. "Very well, Ms. Collins," he said. "I'll allow you to attend the program."

Fitz breathed a sigh of relief. The judge continued. "In order to be in the program, you must formally plead guilty and agree to pay for and complete the alcohol program. Also, I'm going to require, as a term of your probation, that you attend an AA meeting at least three times per week, without exception, for your entire five-year probationary period. Do you understand and accept those conditions?"

Erin nodded. "I do, Your Honor. Thank you. Thank you so much."

"You're welcome, Ms. Collins," Hart said. "Good luck to you."

Fitz couldn't help himself. He knew it was unprofessional, knew he should wait until the recess or until they were out of the room, but he grinned at Beth and Erin and gave them a thumbs-up. Erin beamed.

Judge Hart called another case while Beth assisted Erin in completing the constitutional rights form. After her plea was taken, Hart officially placed her on probation for a period of five years, on the conditions stated. She could not drive unless going to or from the alcohol program or to or from her place of employment. In addition, she would have to be properly licensed and insured at all times.

When the three of them left the courtroom, Fitz was elated—almost as if he'd been the one who'd avoided jail—even though he was aware that Babbage's eyes followed them as they walked out.

———

Before leaving the courthouse, Erin stopped in the restroom and ran into Doris Reynolds. Erin had no intention of acknowledging her, but the prosecutor walked up to her, hand extended. "Congratulations on your probationary sentence," Reynolds said.

Erin's eyes widened. What was going on? "I don't think I'm supposed to talk to you," Erin said.

"You're not, but it's okay," Reynolds said, smiling. She made a motion with her hand. "In here, everyone's equal." She became serious. "I hope you make it."

"I'm sorry," Erin said, "but you're confusing me. Weren't you demanding out there that I go to jail? What gives?"

"That's my job," Reynolds said. "And if you screw up, I *will* put you in jail. But that doesn't mean that I have any personal animosity toward you. I really do hope you make it."

Reynolds turned and left without another word.

18

Babbage

B abbage parked in the beach lot adjacent to the Wharf Restaurant. Off duty and in civilian clothes, he'd driven his personal vehicle, a red Toyota pickup. It had been a month since the trial, and things had gone well. Giovanni had averted Babbage's Board of Rights hearing, arguing that the DNA on the blouse was the product of consensual, off-duty sex and that Erin Collins was a liar who was not to be trusted—the jury verdict proved it. But it had been too much of a close call.

It was time for him, once and for all, to complete his project: Erin. And at the same time, ensure that the asshole Fitzgerald would not interfere. Because Fitzgerald had taken a special interest in Erin—obviously because he was fucking her.

It was a crisp, cloudless night. Babbage got out of his truck, inhaled the saltwater smell of the marina, and walked through the gate leading to the dock entrance of the restaurant. He walked past the hostess station, turned left, and went into the bar. He sat on one of the empty stools toward the end of the counter. An over-the-bar television was playing a closed-captioned news program with the sound turned off.

A bartender washed glasses. Babbage studied him. The guy appeared to be in his late twenties, clean-shaven, with a short haircut. Babbage noticed he was wearing a wedding ring.

The bartender looked up. "What can I get you, buddy?" he asked.

"Do you have Bud on tap?" Babbage asked.

"You got it," came the reply. The bartender filled an iced mug and placed it in front of Babbage, who watched the silent television for several minutes, until he drained his glass and signaled for a refill.

"By the way, what's your name?" Babbage asked.

"Jimmy," the bartender replied. He filled another iced mug, scooped up Babbage's empty mug and put it in a sink behind the counter.

"Jimmy. Jimmy," Babbage repeated. "Aren't you Jimmy Flanagan? Seems like I remember a Jimmy Flanagan that worked the bar here."

"No. My last name's Riley. I don't remember anybody named Flanagan, and I've been here three years. You must be mistaken."

"I could have sworn the guy was named Flanagan," Babbage said. "I think he worked the day shift. What's the name of that guy?"

"Not a guy. Two women. I work from six to closing, except on Monday. My day off."

"Maybe it was the owner?"

"No, his name is Alex."

"I guess I was mistaken about the last name," Babbage said, shaking his head. "I think the guy I knew was married to a someone named Martha. What's your wife's name?"

The bartender paused, and for a moment, Babbage thought he'd gone too far and might have to find another way to get the name. But then the bartender answered. "Barbara."

"I'm batting zero tonight. I must be thinking about another place." Babbage continued drinking in silence for a time, watching the TV. Meanwhile, the bartender went to the other end of the bar and took an order from a couple who were holding hands. Babbage drained his mug, stood up, and pulled out his wallet. The bartender returned with a check.

Babbage took a ten out of his wallet and placed it on the counter. "Thanks, Jimmy. See you around sometime."

Just one more thing, Babbage thought, as he got back into his truck. *The stop has to be in the Valley—under the jurisdiction of Judge Daniel Hart. Just in case.*

19

Erin

Thursday, October 5, 4:30 p.m.

Erin was on edge and restless. She needed a drink badly. With the stress of a new job, it had been a long exhausting week. She was working as a waitress at the Wharf, an upscale restaurant at the harbor in Marina Del Rey. Because they had an adjoining bar, and it was the only work she could get, the judge had made an exception to her probation condition that she not be in any establishment where alcohol was served—but had cautioned her to stay away from the lounge. The judge emphasized that any consumption of alcohol would be a probation violation, resulting in jail time.

She so wanted to show her new boss, Alex, that he was right to give her a chance as a waitress, but it had not been easy. To be closer to work, she had moved from her apartment in Monterey Park to West Hollywood. It was still a trek to the Marina, but this was as close as she could afford to live, even with a roommate.

Since there was no court-ordered alcohol program tonight, she decided she had to find a way to relax and go to bed early. Maybe a hot soak in the tub would do it. Afterward, in pajamas, she'd eat, watch a little television, and then turn in.

Erin was running water into the bathtub when the phone rang.

"Erin? Erin Collins?" said the woman on the other end.

Erin did not recognize her voice. "Speaking."

"Thank God. I'm so glad I was able to reach you. My name is Barbara Riley, Jimmy's wife. Jimmy needs a big favor from you."

"What is it, Barbara?" Jimmy the bartender had always been nice to Erin. This was her opportunity to be nice back. And to show Alex that she was a team player.

"Can you fill in for Jimmy tonight from six to midnight? He's got some kind of stomach flu. He says you used to tend bar."

Erin took a deep breath and held it for an instant. She wanted to help Jimmy, but if she tended bar, she'd be violating a term of her probation—to not to be in a bar ... certainly not to be in any room where primarily alcohol is served.

"I'm not sure I can do it," Erin said.

"We've already called two other people," Barbara said. "We wouldn't ask if it weren't really important." There was desperation in her voice. "Jimmy will have to go in sick. Isn't there any way you could help out just this once?"

Erin considered. Was she being overly cautious? Or just plain dumb?

"Alex told me to call you. Said it will be a personal favor to him."

That cinched it. She'd do it. No one would ever know she did it this once. And besides, if anyone asked, this was a legitimate emergency. The court couldn't be that inflexible. "Okay," she said, "I'd be glad to help out. But this one time only."

"You're a sweetheart," Barbara said, then added, "Oh, another thing—I'm so sorry to impose—but could you come by and get Jimmy's keys? You'll need them to lock up at two a.m. I know it's a little out of the way we live in Sherman Oaks, but I'll drive out and meet you at the Ventura Boulevard off-ramp. There's a Hughes Markets parking lot right as you come off the freeway. You won't be able to miss me. I'll be in a white BMW convertible, top down. You'll be able to turn around and get right on the freeway, heading back."

"I think I know where that is."

"Great. It should take you about thirty minutes to get there. Thanks again. Bye."

Erin looked at the clock. It was 4:55 p.m. She'd have to hurry to meet Barbara and get to work on time. She dressed, brushed her hair, put on makeup, and started to walk out the door. It occurred to her that maybe she should call Jimmy to see if he had any special things she needed to know for tonight. She looked at her watch: 5:10 p.m. She had to get moving. She had her cell phone—she'd call from the car. It was okay to drive to work, but it would still be on a different schedule than she had given her probation officer. If she were stopped and her DMV record were checked, she wasn't sure what a cop might do ... She'd just have to hope that didn't happen.

Once in the car, Erin drove very carefully, making certain that she obeyed all laws. No racing through yellow lights, no speeding—just sensible, defensive driving. She watched everything around her, checking the rearview mirror every few seconds, particularly watchful for cops. Once, she thought she saw a black-and-white behind her, but when she stopped for a red light and looked around, she decided it must have been her imagination.

She got on the San Diego Freeway, heading north. Rush hour traffic was heavy. She glanced at her watch. Almost 5:40. It was going to be close.

She took out her cell phone and dialed the restaurant to get Jimmy's home number. The line was busy. No surprise when people were phoning in for reservations.

At Wilshire Boulevard there was a traffic jam, and it took her nearly twenty minutes to get through the two miles of stop-and-go traffic. Finally, she was through it and the freeway was moving again.

She was about a mile from the Getty Center Drive off-ramp, when she saw the flashing red lights of the police car in her rearview mirror. *Shit*, she thought, her heart pounding. She decided to call Fitz. It was dinnertime, and he might be eating, but this was an emergency. She dialed his number, turned on her blinker, and slowed down, pulling over to acknowledge the red lights behind her.

Fitz answered on the first ring. "Fitz? It's Erin. I'm just being pulled over by a black-and-white. What should I do?"

"Why are you driving?" he asked. There was surprise in his voice. "You know you can't be out tonight."

"I'm on my way to work. The regular bartender is sick, and I'm filling in for him, on my way to get his keys. The point is I'm about to be stopped. I'm near the Getty Center off-ramp of the San Diego Freeway, and a black-and-white is right behind me with its lights flashing."

"Get off at Getty Center and park. Don't hang up the phone. Tell the officer I'm on the line, and that I'll speak to him." Erin followed Fitz's instructions. As she stopped, the police car pulled in behind her and also stopped. Its high-beam lights were on, and its spotlight illuminated her from behind. The light blinded her, so she could not see who was getting out of the patrol car. She kept her cell phone in her hand, while she rolled down her window.

The officer stepped out, and she recognized Jake Babbage at once.

"It's him," Erin shrieked into the phone. "Babbage." She had the sudden urge to drive off—to run away.

"Should I leave?"

"No," Fitz said. "That'd be the worst thing you could do. Just follow my instructions. I'll be listening to everything. If necessary, I'll call Captain Becker and radio to get someone to your location ASAP. In the meantime, hang in there."

20

Babbage

With his headlights on high beam, his spotlights on and directed straight into Erin's car, Babbage could observe the overall interior as he walked toward the passenger side of Erin's vehicle. He'd use his flashlight to illuminate and examine the inside of the car. Although he was certain she was alone, years of experience had taught him that things were not always as they seemed. It would be just like that bitch to have someone or something that he needed to be careful of. He was at his best: his world, his turf, his project. He motioned for Erin to roll down the passenger-side window.

She complied.

Standing at the open window, he used the flashlight beam to scan. He needed to see her hands first, then everything in the front seat and on the floorboard. He saw immediately that Erin held a cell phone in her right hand. What the fuck was she doing?

"Put the object you have in your hand on the passenger seat, ma'am. Then put your hands on the steering wheel where I can see them." Babbage had decided that until he was certain they were alone and unmonitored, he would play it straight. For all he knew, the bitch was wired or had a voice recorder with her.

Erin did as he commanded. Her hand shaking, she placed the cell phone on the seat next to her. She put her hands on the steering wheel. Her knuckles were white—*she's clutching it like a life raft*, Babbage thought with satisfaction. It felt good to be in charge. He continued to scan the interior of the vehicle. The rest of the vehicle was clean and neat, with a purse on the passenger-side floor and a folded sweater-jacket on the back seat.

When satisfied that all was safe, he spoke again. "Please exit the vehicle, ma'am. At the passenger side, please."

"Sergeant Babbage, is this really necessary?" she asked. Her voice wavered, but she continued. "You can be sure I'm not giving you a blowjob this time. And don't think you caught me driving outside of my restriction. I'm on my way to work."

Babbage felt his face flush. *Fucking cunt*, he thought. She actually thought she could outsmart him. But she was having an effect on him. He wished he could tell her his plans for her—that would wipe that arrogant look off her face. Just the thought of what he had devised for her sent a jolt of pleasure to his groin.

"Who were you talking to on the phone?" he asked.

"Detective Fitzgerald. He's still on the line, listening. He wants to talk to you."

"Is that so?" Babbage said. He smiled to himself. *Fitzgerald must have fucked her*, the way he followed her around. Well, he made a big mistake this time.

"Give me the phone," Babbage snapped as he grabbed it. "Who's on this line?"

"Babbage? Fitzgerald here. We have to talk."

"About what?"

"About Erin. She has every right to drive. Her restriction allows her to go to and from work, and that's exactly what she's doing."

Babbage snorted. "You'll have to do better than that, Fitzgerald. You know as well as I do—that's the line that everyone uses when they're caught driving. I've got her work schedule, and tonight she's off. And her work is in the opposite direction. Unless she's driving to her program or work, she's in violation of probation, no matter what phony story you and she concoct."

"I don't give a damn what you think. The woman is driving within her restriction, and if you don't let her go immediately, I'm going to call Captain Becker."

"Okay," Babbage finally said, an exasperated tone in his voice. "I'll check out her story. I'll permit her to call the restaurant on this phone. If the manager verifies it, I'll let her go. Otherwise, I'm taking her in."

"Suit yourself. But you'd better let her go in the next five minutes. No one's ever going to buy the coincidence that you just happened to stop her."

"You can think whatever the fuck you want," Babbage said. "She's a drunk and a whore, and she belongs in jail. I'm going to put her there. And just to show you that I'm operating by the book, I'll call you back and inform you of the results. If she's driving legally, I'll let her go. If not, then she's going to pay the price."

Babbage flipped the phone closed and looked at her. "According to Fitzgerald, you claim you're going to work, even though you're heading in the opposite direction. Is that right?"

Erin nodded. "That's right. I'm meeting someone to get keys, and then I'm going directly to work. If you'll give me a chance, I'll prove it to you."

Babbage said, "What's your work number?"

She gave him the number. Babbage opened the phone and dialed. "It's ringing," he said. "What's your supervisor's name?"

"Alex. Alex Brennan."

Erin's stress eased, and she felt a little better. Fitz had come through for her and Babbage was grudgingly giving her a chance. He'd have to let her go now. Things were going to be okay.

"Hello," Babbage said into the phone. "This is the Los Angeles Police Department calling. Official business. May I speak with Alex Brennan?" A moment passed. "Mr. Brennan, this is Sergeant Babbage of the LAPD. Do you have an employee by the name of Erin Collins? Can you tell me if she is scheduled to work tonight? She's not?" Babbage smiled. "Thank you, Mr. Brennan—"

Stunned, Erin grabbed the phone from Babbage. "Alex, this is Erin. I'm filling in for Jimmy tonight. His wife called me and told me he was sick and couldn't make it."

"Jimmy came in ten minutes ago," Brennan replied.

Erin felt a sharp pain in her stomach. *Please, God*, Erin thought, *let this be a mistake*. "Could I speak to him, please?" she said.

"Hold on a minute."

She waited.

"Erin?" It was Jimmy's voice. "What's up?"

"Jimmy. I got a call from Barbara about forty-five minutes ago telling me you were sick and asking if I'd fill in for you tonight."

Jimmy said, "That's impossible. Barbara's visiting her mom in Seattle this week. Someone must be playing a joke on you."

Mechanically, Erin hung up the phone.

Erin felt like she was drowning. That shark Babbage had to have planned this whole thing. She realized now that Babbage had allowed her to grab the phone away. He knew all along. She had to call Fitzgerald back before Babbage took the phone again. Frantically, she punched in the number, hoping she hadn't misdialed. She looked up at Babbage, expecting him to yank the phone from her hands, but he just watched her.

The phone rang. Finally she heard Fitz's voice. "Fitz, I was set up. They didn't know anything about me working tonight. What am I going to do?"

"Where's Babbage now?" Fitz's voice was calm.

"Right here next to me. I'm still in the car."

"Hand the phone to him," Fitzgerald said. "If I don't get a chance to talk to you after this, try not to panic. I'll find out where you are, and as soon as I hang up, I'll drive out to meet you."

Erin handed the phone to Babbage. "He wants to speak to you."

Babbage took the phone, continuing to watch Erin. She glared back at him. Tears of anger and helplessness rolled down her cheeks.

21

Fitzgerald

Fitzgerald's mind was racing. Of course Babbage had set Erin up. And if that maggot was capable of going to this length, he was capable of anything. He had to be stopped, but how? Fitzgerald's first thought was to call Captain Becker. But without proof, he knew that Becker would never intervene. And without intervention, Babbage would arrest Erin and she'd be completely at his mercy.

Somehow, some way, Fitzgerald could never let that happen. He'd start with reason. If that didn't work, goddammit, he'd call Becker and, by Christ, make him intervene.

"Babbage?"

"I'm listening," Babbage replied, evenly.

"I know how you feel about Erin, and maybe you have a right to be pissed. But surely you must see how bad this could look for you. She makes a complaint against you, and you just happen to arrest her. I don't want to get Captain Becker involved in this, but I will. Tell you what. Give her a break. I'd be glad to come and pick her up. I'll even arrange for a tow of her car. She really believed she

was going to work. I told her that under those circumstances, it would be okay to drive, and I stand behind my
word."

"You'd drive all the way out here to pick her up and
arrange a tow?" Babbage paused, and then said, "You
really have it bad for this woman. What, are you fucking
her?"

Fitzgerald's hand tightened on the phone. *Control*,
he thought. He forced himself to be calm again. "I'm not
fucking her, whether or not you believe that. But it's in
your best interest to give her a break. How about it? I'd
owe you one."

"You bet your ass you'd owe me one." Silence, briefly.
Then, "Okay. We're on Getty Center Drive, just south of
the off-ramp to the 405. I'll have her cuffed and sitting
in the back of the patrol car. I wait forty-five minutes,
exactly. If you're not here by then, I'm taking her to the
station and booking her."

"I'll be there. Don't leave."

Fitzgerald rushed out the door, apprehensive but hoping that maybe everything would be okay.

Half an hour later, Fitzgerald arrived. Babbage was
out of the car, his hand-held radio in his left hand as he
directed a tow truck to the front of Erin's car. The truck
was backing up, positioning itself for the tow. Babbage's
car was behind Erin's. Fitzgerald parked his car behind
the patrol car and got out. He could see Erin in the back
seat of the police car. Her head was bowed. Fitzgerald
started toward her, to tell her that things were going to be
okay, but Babbage must have seen him arrive and walked
over quickly.

"Well, well, Fitzgerald," he said. "True to your word, you're here in just ..."—Babbage looked at his watch—"... thirty-two minutes. You must have dropped everything. And you're telling me you're not sleeping with this woman?"

"I see you've got the tow truck all squared away," Fitzgerald said. "You can release Erin to me. I'll see that she gets home okay."

"Just a minute. Let's get something straight. I stopped Erin Collins when I caught her driving illegally. You claim it was all right, and that I should release her to you. But she lied to me — her boss said she wasn't scheduled to work. What the hell do I put in my report on this thing?"

"Does dispatch know you made the stop?" Fitzgerald asked.

"Of course. You don't think I'd pull a suspect over without checking in with dispatch first, do you?" Babbage's tone was sarcastic.

Fitzgerald grimaced, furious at his dilemma. No doubt Babbage was planning something. Reporting in to dispatch would mean that there would be a record that he stopped Erin. There would have to be an incident report, and Babbage would have to explain why he let Erin go.

He made a quick decision. "Put in your incident report that she was legitimately going to work to fill in for a sick colleague."

"And just what are you going to do for me to justify my lying in my report? It better be good."

"I'm sure you'll think of something."

Babbage grinned. "You stupid son of a bitch." Then he put his hand-held radio up to his mouth and spoke. "Did you get that, Lieutenant?"

"It's all on tape, Babbage," a voice said from the radio. "Tell Fitzgerald to report to Captain Becker tomorrow morning at oh-eight-hundred. Book the female and see me at oh-three-thirty hours. I'll take responsibility for approving the crime report."

"Thanks, Lieutenant. I'll be there at oh-three-thirty. Babbage out." Babbage walked to his patrol vehicle and placed the hand-held in the front seat. He turned to Fitzgerald, still grinning. "You dumb bastard. I pulled the same fucking trick on you that you tried to pull on me. You heard the lieutenant. Be in Captain Becker's office tomorrow morning at oh-eight-hundred."

Babbage got into his vehicle and drove off slowly, waiting for an opportunity to merge with freeway traffic. Fitzgerald stood there, watching the patrol vehicle leave with Erin in the back, handcuffed. She turned, desperation in her eyes—then she was gone. Fitzgerald watched the tow truck drive off with Erin's car.

22

Fitzgerald

Fitzgerald jumped back into his car and took off after Babbage, not letting the bastard get out of his sight. He hoped that Babbage was too smart to try anything after reporting in, but Fitzgerald wasn't going to take any chances. He caught up and then slowed to keep pace. Babbage must have seen him, but it didn't matter. Fitzgerald had to make sure Babbage drove straight to the jail and followed proper procedure. If Babbage didn't like Fitzgerald behind him, too fucking bad. What could he do? Call the FBI? Complain to his lieutenant?

They reached the Parker Center jail in downtown L.A. Fitzgerald parked in the employee lot and walked back to where Babbage had parked. Babbage had Erin handcuffed, her hands behind her, and out of the back of the patrol vehicle. He was escorting her to booking. Fitzgerald followed.

Babbage turned. "Just what the fuck do you think you're doing?"

Fitzgerald didn't reply, just gave Babbage a hard look, and then spoke to Erin. "I'm here. It'll be okay."

Babbage glared at him. "Back off, Fitzgerald. You're in enough trouble. Don't compound it by interfering with my arrest or attempting to communicate with the prisoner."

Erin turned, her face contorted with hatred, and spoke to Babbage. "You bastard. You set me up. Who was she? What did you give her to get her to call me? Or was she another one of your victims?"

"Shut up." Babbage pushed Erin forward so hard that she stumbled, but regained her footing.

"This stinks, Babbage," Fitzgerald said, "and you know it."

Babbage shoved Erin through the rear entrance door.

It was all Fitz could do to keep from punching Babbage in the face. Never had he come so close to losing it, but he knew that he had to control himself for Erin's sake. It gave Fitz some satisfaction to see Babbage so pissed. His face was red, and a vein on the side of his neck throbbed.

The three walked down a short hallway leading to a large, open booking area. Uniformed cops sat at metal desks entering booking information and taking arrestees' fingerprints.

As they passed the watch commander's office, a sergeant came out and approached them. Fitzgerald recognized the sergeant as Jerry Smith, one of the two watch commanders. Smith had been assigned to the Parker Center jail for the last fifteen years. Barrel-chested, with close-cropped white hair and dark-blue eyes, he wore a perpetual frown that intimidated the younger cops. But those who regularly worked with him found out he had a wry smile and a dry sense of

humor. Smith knew every detective in the Robbery-
Homicide Division.

"I've got a female to book," Babbage said, pushing Erin
forward.

"Okay, Sergeant," Smith replied. He motioned toward
the bench at the wall. "Sit her there, and I'll have a female
officer process her."

Smith looked at Fitzgerald and smiled. "Hey, Fitz.
What brings you here?"

"He's friends with this female," Babbage said. "He's
already interfered in the arrest process. He's not to communicate with her, by order of Lieutenant Hardy."

Smith frowned, looked at Fitzgerald, and started to
say something, but Fitzgerald shook his head. Smith's
eyes flashed understanding, and he didn't speak.

Presently, a uniformed Hispanic woman appeared.
Her dark hair was pulled back in a bun. She was of medium
height, stocky, but looked to be in excellent physical condition. She smiled at Fitzgerald and said, "You have a
female to book, Fitz? Kind of late for you detectives, isn't
it?"

"I'm the arresting officer," Babbage snapped.

The policewoman gave Babbage an icy stare. "Aren't
you a patrol supervisor, Sergeant? What are you doing
making an arrest?"

"Just do your job and process the female," Babbage said.

"Go to hell, Babbage," the policewoman said. "You
may be hot shit in your unit, but in here, we know all
about you." She looked at Erin. "Come with me, ma'am."
She took Erin away to be searched and processed.

Babbage said to Smith, "I've got to see the lieutenant briefly, so I'll be back later to sign the paperwork. Remember, Fitzgerald is not to talk to the female. I'll ask the lieutenant to call you and fill you in on the details."

Babbage left.

Smith looked at Fitzgerald. "What's with him, Fitz? What the hell's going on?"

"I'm in trouble, Smitty," Fitzgerald said.

"What do you mean?"

"I can't give you all the details, but I tried to convince Babbage to release the female. This is a bullshit arrest. He says I told him to lie on his report."

"No one who knows you would believe that, Fitz."

"This is the woman who accused him of forced oral sex under color of authority. I was the investigating officer on that case."

"Jesus," Smitty said. "We've all been talking about it. What happened? The fucker should have been fired. I couldn't believe the guy got reinstated."

"He had a good lawyer," Fitzgerald said, and then took a deep breath. "I expect that Lieutenant Hardy will confirm you're not to let me talk to her."

"Do you really need to?"

"I'd like to, but I don't want to get you in trouble."

"I appreciate it," Smitty said. "I have an idea. Go home. After she's booked, I'll let her telephone you there. She's got a right to call whoever she wants, so I won't be violating any orders."

"You're a pal, Smitty."

The phone rang and Smitty picked it up.

"Smith here."

He listened. "Yes, sir. I will, sir. I understand, sir." Smitty looked at Fitz, nodded, then hung up. "Get out of here, Fitz."

Fitzgerald drove back to his apartment, poured himself a tall Scotch, and waited by the phone. He was exhausted. The clock over the TV said 11:15 p.m.

The ringing of the telephone on the table next to his chair woke him. His glass had fallen on the floor and spilled. He picked up the phone.

"What am I going to do?" Erin was crying, and there was panic in her voice.

He shook off his sleepiness. "We know he set you up. We're going to find out just how he did it and shove it down his throat."

"But how?"

He had no idea. "One thing at a time, all right? Do you know what your bail is?"

"Twenty-five thousand dollars. I don't have that kind of money."

"You don't need it in cash. You can use my place as collateral for a bond. I'll call someone I know and arrange it for you."

"But don't I need to pay something for the bond in cash?" Erin asked.

"Just ten percent. Don't worry. I have some money put away. I'll take care of the bond premium. Just pay me back when you can."

"I will. I promise," Erin said.

"Once you're out on bond, you can postpone the hearing on your violation of probation for at least a couple of months. That'll give us time to uncover the details of how he tricked you and to hold him accountable."

Fitzgerald didn't mention his other thought—that if he didn't bail her out, and a judge sentenced her to jail, then this would be the beginning of a long jail stay, with no chance to arrange her affairs or help with her defense.

Erin said, "I don't know when I'll be able to repay you."

"Don't worry about it. I have nothing more important to spend my money on."

"Oh, Fitz. What would I do without you?"

"You'd be just fine. After I hang up, I'll call the bondsman. You'll be out in a couple of hours. I've got to be back at the station at eight this morning. I'll check on you, and then I'll call Sean. We'll meet this evening and discuss a strategy."

"Thank you, Fitz."

Fitzgerald immediately called Thatcher Bail Bonds. He looked at the clock. It was close to 5 a.m. There was no way he could get any sleep. He took a shower, made a cup of coffee and some toast, and headed back to Parker Center.

23

Fitzgerald

Friday, October 6

At precisely 8 a.m., Fitzgerald walked into Captain Becker's office. Becker was sitting behind his desk, studying paperwork. "Sit down, Fitz," he said.

Fitz sat down on the edge of a wooden chair, his back straight, his hands gripping the sides of the seat.

Becker continued to look at the work on his desk for several moments, and then looked up. There was disappointment in his eyes. Fitzgerald shifted in the chair.

"What the fuck were you thinking last night?" Becker said.

"Captain," Fitz said, "there's more to this than Babbage's report shows."

"I listened to Lieutenant Hardy's voice recording of your conversation with Babbage." Becker shook his head. "Jesus Christ, Fitz, what possible reason could you have for asking him to lie on his police report? You know better than to try to get a patrol sergeant to release a suspect who committed a crime in the officer's presence."

"There's a reason, Captain."

"If you think you can justify this behavior, by all means go ahead."

Fitzgerald took a breath. "The suspect we're talking about is Erin Collins. She's the woman who accused Babbage of forcing her to give him a blowjob after being stopped for a DUI."

Becker leaned forward, raised an eyebrow, and nodded. "I know. Go on."

"It's a setup, Captain. She hadn't been drinking, hadn't committed any traffic violations, and wasn't driving suspiciously. And she had a valid restricted license, which permitted her to drive to and from work and to and from her DUI program."

Becker interrupted. "But according to the report, she wasn't going to work or to a program."

"That's the bullshit, Captain. The woman really did get a call to come to work. From someone—probably Babbage's girlfriend."

"So she says," Becker interjected. "That's a pretty serious allegation. And why would Babbage do that—why would he set up a lie that could easily get him fired? It makes no sense."

"I don't know why, but I can guess," Fitzgerald said. "Probably revenge. Or, what worries me is he's one sick sociopath."

Becker said nothing, just shook his head.

"Look at it logically, Captain. Babbage says she was not driving to work. But how the fuck did he know that? And this happens a month after Babbage's trial where the very same woman accused him of misconduct?"

Becker leaned back in his chair, looking thoughtful. "Let's assume for the moment what you suggest is true. Babbage stopped this female, and he did it without probable cause. But it's not unusual for a good cop to follow up on suspects he's had contact with before, or to detain that suspect randomly. In fact, it's rather common, isn't it? You don't need probable cause. After all, he knew she was on probation."

"I know," Fitzgerald admitted. "But this wasn't a random arrest. She was never detained when she was driving legally, like during the day. She got a phony call to lure her out. That son of a bitch set her up. At the very least, he's been watching her apartment. He stalked her and stopped her in a location where anybody would be unlikely to see what he was up to. The fucker planned the whole thing."

Becker considered and then spoke. "Assuming that's true and he's rotten, why did you attempt to get Babbage to lie on his report?"

"Actually, I didn't ask him to lie. What I said, I believed was the truth. Because I thought Erin was in danger, and I did not think she lied, I had to protect her. When I asked him to cut her some slack, he promised to let her go if I'd drive out to the location and meet him. At the time, I still thought he'd be able to release her without having to write an incident report."

"Can you prove that?" Becker asked.

Fitzgerald shook his head. "There weren't any witnesses. It was all done over the phone."

"Over the phone?"

Fitzgerald told Becker about the bogus work-request call Erin had received earlier. Fitzgerald described how Erin had called him from her cell phone, how he'd instructed her to leave it on, and how he stayed on the line, listening to what was said during the traffic stop. Finally, he described how Babbage had agreed to release Erin if Fitzgerald would come to the arrest location within forty-five minutes.

"That's another suspicious thing," Fitzgerald added. "If Babbage wasn't doing anything wrong, why would he even talk to me over the phone? Wouldn't he just make the arrest and refuse to talk to anyone that a suspect might want him to talk to?"

Becker shook his head. "He covered his ass, you showed yours."

Becker picked up a document from his desk. Fitzgerald saw it was a preliminary investigation report. "There's no mention of any cell phone conversation in the report."

"But there *was* a conversation, Captain ..." Fitzgerald frowned. "Wait. Babbage told me he radioed in the stop prior to pulling over Erin. Her cell phone bill would have to indicate the time and length of the call as well as my phone number. That would prove that Babbage and I talked before I arrived at the arrest location, and *before* Babbage recorded his conversation with me."

Becker looked doubtful. "That doesn't justify trying to get him to lie on his report."

"A moment ago you asked me what I was so paranoid about. I think I have good reason to believe that had I not been on the other end of the phone last night, Babbage was planning to hurt Erin Collins."

Becker shook his head.

"Captain," Fitzgerald said, "as I said before, Babbage is a fucking sociopath. Four months ago, he stopped Erin at some deserted freeway off-ramp. The Scientific Investigation Division determined that his semen was on her blouse. It doesn't make a shit of difference whatever else happened that night. Babbage had oral sex with a female detainee while he was in uniform and on duty. And that means that he doesn't deserve to wear the uniform, no matter what he says."

"I agree with you," Becker said. "And I still don't know what his lawyer said that convinced the Board of Rights people to forego a hearing and reinstate him. But it happened, and you and I have to live with it. And right now we're talking about your actions, not his. You can complain all you want, but the fact remains that you asked him to lie on a report. The bottom line is, you don't have a shred of proof that he did anything last night other than what any good cop would have done."

Becker pulled out his bottom file drawer.

"I might just have that proof," Fitzgerald said.

Becker stopped what he was doing and looked up at Fitzgerald.

"I'm willing to bet my badge," Fitzgerald said, "that Erin Collins's cell phone records will show that the call she made to me last night ended before Babbage radioed in that he was detaining her."

"And what would that prove?" Becker asked.

"That Babbage lied when he told me during our recorded conversation that he notified dispatch *before* he pulled Erin over."

Becker raised an eyebrow. "You're saying he made a night traffic stop without calling in? Without a license plate check and without anything to support probable cause?"

"Exactly," Fitzgerald said.

Becker said, "When can you get those phone records?"

"I'll get on it immediately. If I'm right, Babbage wouldn't have called in the stop because he didn't plan to arrest Erin at all. And that's the reason I asked him to lie. Because I'd do whatever was necessary to stop him from harming her."

Becker looked over Babbage's report again, and then made some notes on the legal pad on his desk. Finally, he went back to the file drawer in his desk and took out a multi-part form.

Fitzgerald recognized it immediately. It was a suspension notice.

Becker signed the notice, looked at Fitzgerald, and handed it to him. "I have no choice. I'm suspending you, pending your Board of Rights hearing. With pay, of course, but effective immediately. You'd better work on getting those phone records ASAP. For the sake of the department, I hope you're wrong. But you're a good cop and a good friend, and when this is all over, I hope you're vindicated."

After turning in his badge, ID, and weapon, Fitz went to see Smitty and verified that Erin bailed out the previous night. Smitty told him that Erin's arraignment on the probation violation was set for Friday, October 27.

Fitz returned home and phoned Sean.

Despite reeling from his suspension, Fitz felt a flash of pride on hearing Sean's voice. Had it really been nineteen

years since he'd first interviewed that lost little boy at
MacLaren Hall?

"Hi, Fitz." Sean said. "Sorry you had to wait. I was in
a meeting with my boss. Looks like I'll be trying my first
case next week. A petty theft case. My client was charged
with shoplifting cosmetics at a drugstore. She teaches second grade. If she gets convicted, it's the end of her career."

"Sounds like a challenge."

"It's a lot of pressure. She's innocent. She absentmind-
edly put a lipstick in her purse and left without paying for
it."

Fitz had heard that line before, and he smiled to himself. Sean was still an idealist. Good for him. "Well, if you
work on this case like you work on everything else, the
woman is as good as acquitted."

"I appreciate your confidence. What's up?"

"I need your help."

"*My* help? This has to be a first. You know I'll do whatever you need me to do. Just ask."

Fitz swallowed. "I've been suspended."

"Holy shit. For what?"

"It's complicated."

Sean pressed for details and Fitz told him about the
events that led to his suspension, ending with the conversation that morning with Captain Becker. It felt good to
get it all out to someone he trusted.

Sean had said little during the narration. "Well," Fitz
said finally, "was I stupid last night, or what?"

"I don't see how you could have played it any differently. If you're right and Babbage didn't radio in until after
your conversation with him, he was up to something. And

any cop who'd use his power once to coerce sex from a woman is capable of anything." Sean paused. "But if he radioed in prior to the stop, you're in real trouble."

"My analysis exactly," Fitz said. "So, my number one priority is to find out about that phone call and the exact time of the stop."

"I can help you find out the time of the stop," Sean said. "Erin can get her own phone record online."

"Erin's arraignment on the probation violation is in three weeks. Friday, October twenty-seventh, in Division 103."

"Division 103—that would be Judge Hart," Sean said.

Fitz smiled. Sean had a natural, instinctive understanding of the law. Fitz had sat through many hearings in his years as a cop, and he'd learned that the most important quality a lawyer could have was to believe in a client's case and possess a willingness to do whatever was necessary and ethical to get justice. Without that quality, the most experienced and knowledgeable lawyer wasn't worth a damn.

"I'll talk to my boss and see what he thinks, too. In the meantime, I'll research the law and find out exactly what's involved. I'll let you know." He paused. "Can we meet tonight and talk more about this?"

"My place at seven o'clock? I'll order a pizza."

"I'll be there," Sean said.

24

Babbage

Monday, October 23, 8:00 a.m.

Babbage sat outside Lieutenant Hardy's office, waiting impatiently. Hardy had ordered Babbage to be present at a 7:45 a.m. meeting to go over the evidence and testimony needed for Fitzgerald's upcoming Board of Rights hearing. Fucking Hardy was like all the asshole lieutenants in the department, Babbage thought. He'd gotten his job using politics rather than ability. But Babbage needed Hardy, so he put up with his jerk-off crap.

Hardy motioned him to come into the office. Babbage sat down in a chair in front of Hardy's desk. The desk was piled high with papers and manila file folders.

"I've been here since six a.m.," Hardy said. "Too much paperwork to clear up, especially with Fitzgerald suspended. That fucker created so much work for me all last year, and since his suspension, the shit has gotten much worse." Hardy shook his head. "It pisses me off that until now, nobody had taken my complaints about Fitzgerald seriously."

"Fitzgerald had everyone convinced his shit didn't stink," Babbage said.

"Now that everyone knows Fitzgerald is a fuck-up, I've got to scrutinize everything he's done. That means looking at all his cases—I know I'll find more crap and more evidence for the Board."

Babbage didn't like the idea of anyone going through Fitzgerald's files, but he kept his mouth shut.

Hardy pointed to a stack of six banker's boxes containing Fitzgerald's case notes. "The fucker ordered lab reports on cases that weren't even his, if you can believe that. Look at this one."

He handed Babbage an analyze-evidence request for a Lancaster Sheriff's case. Babbage was suddenly on high alert. He studied the request, careful to keep his expression blank.

"Look at that," Hardy said. "Goddammit. It was dated and signed two months ago, *after* I and the captain specifically ordered Fitzgerald to cancel all requests."

Hardy picked up the phone and punched in a number. "I'm calling Grabowski, the head of the crime lab. I'll put this on speakerphone—I want you to witness what he says. Everyone around here tries to protect Fitzgerald, so I need you to back me up in case someone tries to piss backwards on me."

"Grabowski?" he barked into the phone. "This is Lieutenant Hardy of Robbery-Homicide."

"Yeah, Hardy. What do you want?" Grabowski said.

"I'm following up on an analyze-evidence request submitted to you two months ago by Detective Fitzgerald."

"Hold on, I'll get the file."

Babbage could hear the sound of paper shuffling.

"I've got it." Then Grabowski added, "Oh, yeah, I recall. Fitz had his ass in a ringer over how long it was taking to get DNA profiles. Weird. The guy bugged me every day for weeks asking when the results would be in, and then when they finally came in, I never heard from him."

"He's been suspended for misconduct—he'll probably be fired," Hardy said.

"No shit," Grabowski replied. "It must be a mistake. What's he supposed to have done?"

"You know better than to ask," Hardy said. "It's an official investigation."

"You always have to have a rod up your ass, Hardy? Chill out."

The lieutenant ignored the comment. "Didn't Fitzgerald tell you I'd ordered him to cancel the request?"

"Cancel? Not that I know of. Whether or not he did, the profiles are here. What should I do with 'em?"

Hardy considered. "Keep them. As well as any other DNA profile comparisons Fitzgerald submitted. I'll get back to you when his files are reassigned.

25

Hart

Friday, October 27, 8:30 a.m.

Upon entering chambers, Hart saw his clerk, Louise Moreno, sitting in one of the chairs in front of his desk. Hart sat down at his desk. "What's up, Louise?"

"I just found out something," Louise said softly. She was always careful with confidential information. Hart generally left his chambers door open, and someone could walk in or be outside in the hallway. "Doris Reynolds is planning to run against you in next year's election."

Hart thought about that for a moment before responding. He would likely need to hire a consultant, line up a committee, and try to raise money. It went on and on. *That also explains why Ms. Reynolds has been so aggressive in court,* he thought. *She's trying to appear like an ideal, get-tough prosecutor in front of the "soft on crime" judge.*

After Louise left, Hart remained seated at his desk and looked around chambers. Law books on floor-to-ceiling white-oak shelves to his left. On his right wall were framed line drawings of courtroom scenes by Terrance Flanigan, an artist he admired. This was where many judges displayed their certificates, diplomas, and various commendations, but Hart saw no purpose in doing so. Behind him was a huge window facing north that made it unnecessary to turn on the interior fluorescents except on the cloudiest of days. He stared at the wall calendar hanging on the back of his closed door. The primary election was next June, a little over eight months away, and each day until then was going to be hell. And now there would be the pressure of having his opponent, Doris Reynolds, appear day after day in his courtroom. There was a knock on the door.

It was Louise again. She walked in, holding today's calendar in her hand. "Another busy day, Your Honor."

Louise always called him "Your Honor," even though he had asked her time and time again to call him Daniel. But she'd been around too long, and her respect for the bench was a habit she couldn't shake.

"We're ready for you to take the bench," Louise said. "But there's an LAPD Sergeant Babbage who wants to see you first to get a search warrant signed."

Hart had to prepare for his upcoming hearing. It was going to be a busy day. "Tell him to come back this afternoon."

"He says it's critical—urgent." Louise said. "He has to get it signed now."

"Okay. Send him in."

Moments later, the door opened, and in walked the sergeant. There was something vaguely familiar about the man. Babbage wore a half-grin on his face, which smacked of insolence. He'd have to set the man straight as to the proper demeanor in a judge's chambers.

"Sergeant, raise your right hand to be sworn for your search warrant affidavit."

Babbage didn't reply, just sat down in one of the desk chairs. His grin widened. "You don't remember me, do you?"

Hart noticed that the officer didn't end his statement with "Your Honor," which he would normally expect from a police officer. "Should I?"

"Yeah," the officer said. "But that's understandable. The last time you saw me, I was a lot younger. In civilian clothes."

Hart frowned. "I'm sorry," he said. "I don't ever remember seeing you before."

"Sure you do," the officer said. "Think back about nineteen years. Incidentally, *Chief*, have you had your dick sucked lately?"

Hart stared at the man. It was him, all right. *Snake.*

Instantly, Hart was transported back, to that night, to the murder of Sarah Collins. Once again he was fifteen. Powerless, humiliated, scared. Face burning, he wanted to run, to hide, to go anywhere. Away from Snake. Away from reality.

But he had to get hold of himself. To force himself to think rationally. To analyze the situation and determine what he should do.

He couldn't believe that Snake was now a cop. Over the years he'd wondered, worried. He'd hoped that Snake had just disappeared, died even. But here he was, confronting Hart.

But *why*? Why would he show up now?

"I was told you wanted to see me to sign a search warrant," Hart said slowly. "If that's not the reason, exactly what is it you want?"

"Just to say hello, *Judge*." He was still grinning.

"Well, you've said it. Now say good-bye."

"Not so fast," Snake said.

Hart studied the man and said nothing. That night nineteen years ago had changed Hart's life. Snake had taken a fifteen-year-old boy and made him an accomplice to rape and murder. The boy had trusted Snake on the way up to the reservoir that night, and despite what then occurred at the car, the boy had stupidly believed that Snake wouldn't actually kill Sarah—until Sarah Collins's final moments. Hart had replayed the awful night again and again in his memory.

"This afternoon there will be a probation violation hearing in your court," Snake said. "I'll be testifying as the arresting police officer. The woman probationer, Erin Collins, will claim I set her up. She'll talk about a time I stopped her for a DUI. There was DNA evidence as part of that stop. You will order that the DNA evidence and results be brought to court and admitted. Then you make certain that evidence is destroyed, or, if it's easier, lost—"

Hart interrupted. "What the hell are you talking about?" Hart felt the blood rushing to his face. Pounding. Hot. His jaw twitched. "You miserable son of a bitch," he said. "How *dare* you come in here and tell *me* how I should rule on a case?"

Snake smiled. "I still have the knife," he said calmly, "with your fingerprints on it. The knife used to kill Sarah Collins."

Hart froze.

"By the way, the woman probationer is Sarah Collins's daughter."

Something inside of Hart snapped.

He could not put up with this one instant longer. If it meant giving up his career, so be it. If it meant giving up his freedom, or even his life, so be it.

He looked directly at Snake. "You disgusting maggot," he said. Then he reached for the button underneath his desk.

Within five seconds, two armed deputies were in Hart's chambers; within ten, six more arrived.

"Arrest this man," Hart ordered. "I find him in contempt and order him remanded to the custody of the sheriff immediately. He just attempted to extort the court."

The deputies gaped, astonished that an in-uniform LAPD sergeant was ordered arrested. But they obeyed and quickly disarmed Babbage, handcuffed him, and led him out of chambers.

Babbage glared, but said nothing as he was escorted out.

Hart picked up the intercom line. "Louise, I've just found Officer Babbage in contempt and ordered him jailed. I'll prepare a written order for the remand, finding him in contempt and sentencing him to five days in custody. Call the LAPD liaison and the head deputy DA, and ask them to come here tomorrow morning at eight a.m. I'm also disqualifying myself from the Erin Collins matter. Send it out to another judge and cancel my calendar for the rest of the day."

Hart then got an outside line. He dialed the number for attorney Amanda Jordan. A secretary answered. "This is Judge Daniel Hart. I need to speak to Ms. Jordan."

"Ms. Jordan is out of the office, Judge," the secretary responded, courteously. "She's in a court hearing."

"Do you expect her back soon?"

"She said she'd be back later this morning."

"Fine," Hart said. "I'll be there in half an hour."

"But I just told you that Ms. Jordan isn't here, Judge."

"I know. This is urgent. I'll wait until she gets back."

Hart prepared his judgment and order of contempt, and took it to Louise. Then he put on his jacket and headed for Amanda Jordan's law office.

26

Babbage

O n one side wall of every courtroom in the Van Nuys courthouse is a heavy steel door, with a prominent, large, and unusual lock in place of a doorknob. The key for this lock is six inches long and too big to put in any person's pocket. Behind the door was the lockup area—two to ten jail cells, depending upon whether or not the adjacent courtroom was a mass court. A mass court heard cases for hundreds of people but held no trials. It was primarily for arraignments, where cases were processed until they were ready for trial, and for probation and sentence hearings. Daniel Hart's court, Division 103, was a mass court, so there were ten jail cells in lockup and a bailiff-jailer who was responsible for in-custody defendants and others who had been remanded by the court for any reason.

Babbage was in the latter group. He was so outraged he could barely function.

The bailiffs had disarmed him, handcuffed him, and were now escorting him through the door to the Division

103 lockup area. They couldn't believe that Hart would remand an LAPD officer. "Jesus Christ, Babbage. What the fuck did you say to the judge to cause him to go berserk?" a bailiff with sergeant stripes asked. His name badge read Powell.

"Beats the shit out of me," Babbage replied. "We were talking, and all of a sudden, he goes off the deep end. Look, Powell, would you do me a favor and get me to a phone? I've got to call my lieutenant. I'd also like to call the union lawyer. I want to get the fuck out of custody before you have to ship me to county jail."

"No sweat. Make as many calls as you like. If I have to send you to county, I'll be up to my ass in paperwork."

The other deputies left and Babbage accompanied Powell to a small desk just outside the hallway leading to the lockup. Powell took off Babbage's handcuffs, handed him the phone, and stood next to him. Babbage phoned Anthony Giovanni's office.

Giovanni didn't seem surprised that Judge Hart had just remanded him and that he was calling from lockup. "Spare me the details, Babbage," the lawyer warned. "And keep your mouth shut if anyone asks."

"I'm not a fool," Babbage replied. "But I need you to get down here and get me out."

"I'll try to get there sometime before noon."

"That's two fucking hours from now. Get yourself down here before they ship me to county jail on the noon bus."

"That's the best I can do. See if you can convince the bailiff to wait until this evening to ship you to county. I've got another appearance this morning. When I come, I'll

bring a bondsman, in case I can't get you an own-recogni-
zance release. What amount did Hart set for bail?"

"He didn't set an amount," Babbage answered.

"Good. That was his mistake, and we'll take advantage
of it. Sit tight until I get there. And don't call your lieutenant or anyone else. I'll take care of notifying everyone if it
becomes necessary." Giovanni hung up.

Babbage looked at Powell. "My lawyer says he can't
be here until noon, but he says he'll get me out when he
arrives. Can you hold off shipping me out to county until
the five o'clock bus?"

Powell hesitated, and then said, "I can do it. But your
lawyer better get you the fuck out of here when he comes.
I don't want to stay late filling out paperwork just because
I did you a favor."

Powell took Babbage to a single cell at the end of the
lockup. "This is the one we use for females," Powell said.
"We'll put you in here, so you won't get hassled by the
other defendants."

The women's cells, smaller and fewer because fewer
females committed crimes, were eight feet by ten feet,
with bare, stainless-steel benches along the ten-foot walls.
The eight-foot-wide sliding door was a row of jail bars. On
the eight-foot back wall was a stainless-steel toilet with
no seat. A nearby stainless-steel dispenser allowed one
sheet of toilet paper at a time to be removed.

Babbage walked into the cell. Watched Powell lock
him in and leave. The stench of urine was overpowering.

He sat on one of the steel benches and thought about
his situation. Hart had surprised him, and Babbage was
not easily surprised. His position might appear hopeless

to most people. But not to him. He'd been in difficult positions before, but instead of worrying about what might have been, he looked at it as just another problem to be solved.

The problem was he had underestimated Hart. He wouldn't make that mistake again.

But Hart had underestimated him, and in Hart's case, that wouldn't mean a morning in the cooler. That mistake would cost. Big-time.

27

Sean Collins

Sean Collins awoke early on the morning of Erin's probation violation hearing. He was excited and anxious at the same time. He viewed Erin's hearing as his chance to do something for Erin, as well as Fitz, the closest thing to a father figure he'd ever had.

Sean's supervisor had come up with the ideal training solution that would permit Sean to help with Erin's probation violation hearing. Sean would simply associate with Beth Daniels, Erin's public defender. Sean could do all the investigation and research, and might even conduct part of the hearing—with Beth at his side. If Sean got into trouble, Beth would be there to help.

Fitz was happy with the arrangement. The four of them had met last night to discuss the mechanics of the hearing, and what would be expected of Erin and Fitz.

"You really don't need me, Sean," Beth said.

Sean wasn't so sure. That's why he was glad she'd be there. He'd become good friends with Beth—admired her courtroom presence. She knew how to stand up for her client's rights without giving offense to the court or her opposing counsel. At twenty-nine, she was almost five years older than Sean. She had a natural beauty, he thought. Brown hair, blue eyes—wore almost no makeup, but always looked great.

"Possibly you can get Judge Hart to reinstate probation without a hearing," she said. "If that fails, discredit the bastard by introducing the cell phone records, and then use Fitz's testimony to prove that Babbage hadn't checked in to dispatch before pulling Erin over."

And hope, Sean thought.

The four met in the courthouse cafeteria at 7:30 a.m. and went over everything one last time before heading into court. Erin was nervous. Beth said little during the discussion of the hearing details, just sipped her coffee and listened. This was going to be Sean's show. Beth expected that the case would be called early in the morning, so they went upstairs to the courtroom and walked in as soon as the doors opened at 8:30.

They sat in the crowded, noisy courtroom for an hour and a half, waiting for the calendar call. Fitz pretended to be cheerful, but he could only make small talk. Erin was quiet. She sat still, hands folded in her lap. Beth was busy with her other clients, but she checked back periodically to see how they were doing and to confer with Sean. Sean was concerned about the delay. Where was Judge Hart?

Beth had seen the judge early in the morning, in the employees' elevator, so Hart was at the courthouse. Sean wanted to ask Louise, the courtroom clerk, about the delay, but Beth warned him not to. Louise was very busy, and she didn't like being interrupted.

By 10:30, Sean was convinced something was wrong. He looked at Beth. "The judge is two hours late. I'm going to ask Louise."

"Suit yourself," Beth said. "But don't say I didn't warn you."

Sean went to Louise. "What's going on, Louise? Why hasn't the judge taken the bench?"

Louise had a stack of case folders and appeared to be arranging them according to the court's calendar. She looked up. "Judge Hart is going to be out for the rest of the day. Judge Finch is going to call Judge Hart's calendar at 1:30 p.m."

Sean was stunned. "But why? Beth saw Judge Hart earlier this morning. Is he sick?"

"All I know is Judge Hart won't be in for the rest of the day." Louise turned back to her case folders. Sean knew that meant the conversation was over. But he was not going to be put off so easily.

"Does this mean the probation violation hearing is going to be delayed?"

Louise opened each case folder and rubber-stamped something inside each folder, without turning to face Sean. "That'll be up to Judge Finch. Judge Hart has recused himself from the case. And just so you know, the witness, Sergeant Babbage, was remanded by Judge Hart this morning."

"Remanded?" Sean couldn't believe what he heard. "Did you say remanded? Why?"

"I don't know the details. And if I did, I certainly wouldn't be discussing them with you. I'm sure you'll find out soon this afternoon. I've got to get back to work." Louise got up and walked into the file room.

Sean returned to Beth and the others. "Babbage was remanded, and Hart has recused himself from the case. Finch is handling the calendar."

Beth stared at Sean. She opened her mouth to speak, than closed it. "Holy crap," she said. "In my seven years in practice, I thought I'd just about heard it all. But I've never heard anything like this. Finch is bad news. He's all image and no substance. A real asshole."

After lunch, at 1:30, two buzzes sounded in the courtroom, the signal that the judge was about to take the bench. A tall, distinguished-looking man entered. He had gray hair and rimless glasses over blue eyes—the very essence of what a judge should look like, Sean thought. Was Beth wrong about him?

Judge Finch sat down at the bench and immediately started calling the calendar. It was 2:30 p.m. when the court finally got to the Erin Collins matter. Judge Finch called the case. Sean, Beth, and Erin went to the counsel table. Fitz remained in the spectator section sitting in the first row.

"The defendant, Erin Collins, is present with Counsel, Deputy Public Defender Sean Collins, Your Honor." Sean's voice broke in the middle of his sentence.

The prosecutor stood up. "Doris Reynolds for the People, Judge."

Another lawyer, whom Sean did not recognize, came to the counsel table and stood next to Doris. "Are the People ready to proceed with the probation violation matter, Ms. Reynolds?" Judge Finch asked.

"No. I mean, yes, Judge," Doris said.

"Make up your mind, Ms. Reynolds. Which is it?" Judge Finch was frowning.

Doris took a deep breath. "My case was sorely compromised this morning by Judge Hart. He remanded my witness, Sergeant Babbage. I'll represent to the court that I've worked with Sergeant Babbage numerous times in the past and find him a credit to his uniform. There's no doubt whatsoever that Judge Hart deliberately remanded Sergeant Babbage to sabotage the People's case against Erin Collins and to bolster his election prospects."

"I'm not concerned with your election politics, Ms. Reynolds," Judge Finch said. "But I can solve this little problem easily. I'll let Judge Hart have his remand hearing whenever he wants. In the meantime, I'll release Sergeant Babbage on his own recognizance, pending Judge Hart's hearing."

Louise stood. "You can't do that, Your Honor. Judge Hart found Sergeant Babbage guilty of contempt and sentenced him to five days. He's a sentenced prisoner."

Judge Finch's face turned red. "Sit down, Louise. I won't have a clerk interrupt court proceedings. *I'll* be the one who decides what I can do and what I cannot do. If you don't understand that, I'll get another clerk who does."

Louise sat at her desk and looked down. Judge Finch turned to the bailiff. "I'm ordering Sergeant Babbage released OR, forthwith. Please release him and bring him here."

The bailiff got up, and went into the lockup. Within minutes, Sergeant Babbage was brought out. The lawyer who had been standing next to Doris walked over to him. The two conversed in hushed tones.

"Are you ready to proceed with the probation violation now, Ms. Reynolds?" Judge Finch asked.

"We are, Judge," Doris replied.

"Just a moment." It was the lawyer Sean didn't know. "Anthony Giovanni representing the witness, Sergeant Jake Babbage. Your Honor, my client cannot testify today in light of what happened this morning. I need time to talk to him and to decide if there are any constitutional rights involved."

Judge Finch's face had a pained expression. "Can't you take a moment to find out now?"

"I'm sorry, Your Honor," Giovanni said. "But I cannot allow my client to testify today. If the court will continue this matter briefly, I'm sure there'll be no problem."

"Very well," Finch said, petulantly. "The matter is continued to next month, November twenty-two. That should be sufficient time to work out all the problems. This matter is in recess until then."

Finch called the next case. Babbage shook Giovanni's hand, and the two of them left the courtroom immediately.

Sean, Beth, and Erin were still standing there as the lawyers for the next case came forward. They turned and walked out, meeting Fitz in the aisle. "What just happened?" Erin asked.

Erin looked at Beth. "What's an OR release?"

"OR stands for Own Recognizance," Beth replied. "It means that Babbage is released until his hearing without having to put up bail. Instead, he just has to sign a written promise to appear on the hearing date. Of course, if he docsn't show up, he violates that promise and the judge would issue a warrant for his arrest, setting a very high bail amount. The warrant is called a bench warrant."

"But why was he arrested in the first place, and why would the judge release him OR? What the hell is going on?"

"I wish I knew," Fitz said.

28

Hart

Driving to the law offices of Amanda Jordan, Daniel Hart was in a state of near panic. It was all he could do to drive through traffic. At one intersection, he turned right instead of left and went the wrong direction on a one-way street, nearly colliding with oncoming traffic before awkwardly making a U-turn.

If Snake carried out his threat, he would lose his job and, very likely, his freedom. An expert in criminal law, he knew exactly what would happen if a jury found him to be Snake's accomplice. Snake had forced Sarah Collins to perform oral sex on Hart. Hart was forced, too, but he could still be found guilty of forcible oral copulation in concert, which alone carried a sentence of five, seven, or nine years in prison. Snake's murder of Sarah to cover up the forced oral sex would be felony murder with special circumstances, making Hart eligible for life in prison without possibility of parole. Hart was aware of the defenses he could raise. Most important of these was that at the time he was, after all, only a boy. But objectively, he knew it was unlikely any juror would buy this or any of the other possible defenses. The law was clear.

At Jordan's Century City office building, Hart took the elevator to the twenty-fifth floor and entered Jordan's carpeted suite. The reception room was spacious. Background classical music played quietly. Oil paintings hung on walnut-paneled walls. An attractive dark-haired receptionist sat in a corner alcove adjacent to a closed door, answering the phones.

He waited patiently for her to acknowledge him, but she continued to speak into the phone for several minutes before turning to him. He gave her his name and told her he was going to wait until Ms. Jordan came in. Yes, he understood that Ms. Jordan might not be back for another hour. Hart sat in a chair and picked up a magazine.

He wasn't able to read. Other people were waiting as well. An elegantly dressed woman sat next to a pimply teenaged boy, probably her son. Across from Hart, a heavy-set man with combed-back, dark greasy hair and open-necked shirt leafed through a *Sports Illustrated* magazine. People who, like him, had some sort of problem involving the criminal justice system. *Accused criminals,* he thought. *Accused criminals who have sufficient funds to employ an expensive defense attorney to help get them acquitted. And they look at me and think the same thing.*

Hart had a detached, hollow feeling inside that he couldn't completely recognize. Part of it was nervousness. Part of it was fear. Part of it was just being sick to his stomach. But there was something more.

Then he realized. He was grieving. That was it. He was grieving for what he had lost today, this very morning. His career as a judge was over. And maybe his life, too.

Jordan walked in at 11 a.m., with her eyes widening in surprise at seeing him. "Judge Hart, how nice to see you."

"Do you have a few moments to talk?" Hart asked.

"Of course." Jordan looked over to the receptionist. "Angela, please give my apologies to my 11 a.m. appointment," and then, "Judge Hart, come with me."

She escorted him back to a spacious corner office with large picture windows overlooking the expansive Los Angeles Country Club. The floor was polished dark wood with a square Tabriz Persian carpet covering the center area. Jordan sat behind her oversize dark mahogany desk; he sat in one of the plush fabric chairs. "Would you like some coffee, Judge?" Jordan asked.

A grandfather clock stood in the corner behind Hart and he listened to the steady tick-tock.

Hart shook his head. "No, thank you. But please don't call me 'judge,' Ms. Jordan. Especially not here and not under these circumstances."

Jordan's eyebrows raised and she frowned. "What brings you here?"

Being in this office, talking to Jordan, was almost more than Hart could manage. His mouth was dry. There didn't seem to be enough oxygen in the room. He could hear his own rapid, pounding heartbeat, and he could feel the sweat under his arms and on his chest.

"I think I'm going to need a good lawyer," Hart said. He recounted everything that occurred on that July 4th weekend nineteen years ago. Jordan listened patiently, occasionally interrupting to ask a question for clarification. Just the process of telling everything to another human being gave him some small relief. Jordan's eyes were understanding, and if she was shocked by any of the details, she didn't show it. As for Hart, he felt detached from reality. As if he were viewing the conversation from outside of himself, marveling at how professional Jordan was and worrying about what she really was thinking inside. Would she share the same contempt he had for himself. He finished by describing what occurred this morning, including remanding Babbage for contempt. He sat back, waiting to hear her reaction, but thinking to himself ... *had today really happened?*

Jordan got up from her desk, came around, and sat in the chair next to him. She took his hands in hers. He felt their warmth, their softness. "It wasn't your fault," she said. "You were a fifteen-year-old kid, confronted, threatened, and manipulated by a twenty-year-old adult. I can't imagine any teenaged boy that would have handled the situation better."

He couldn't help it. Tears came to his eyes. He said nothing, afraid he might break down completely.

They sat there, neither saying anything. The grandfather clock chimed three times.

"Besides," Jordan said, "the reality is that Babbage isn't going to say anything about your complicity in the murder, because in doing so, he'll implicate himself."

"It really doesn't matter whether or not he says anything. The fact is, I must tell the authorities something. I've kept silent too long. And it's the only way to keep

Babbage locked up once his five-day contempt sentence is completed."

Jordan pondered. "My advice is that you say nothing about the murder. At least, not until I get a chance to review this matter in more detail."

He looked out the window at two tiny figures walking on the green turf of the golf course, twenty-five floors below. It seemed so tranquil.

"All right," Hart finally said. "I'll postpone my meeting with the District Attorney's Office for two days. Babbage will still be in custody, so he won't pose a threat to anyone. I don't know what you could possibly come up with, but I'll give you until then."

"Two days it is," Jordan said. "Until then, say nothing about this to anyone. In the meantime, if you get put in a position where you feel you have to explain something, call me first."

Jordan rose and held out her hand. The interview was over. Hart stood and shook Jordan's hand. It was warm and comforting. The two walked to the door leading back to the reception area, and Jordan held it open. "I'll call you within two days to discuss our options."

Hart walked through, and the door closed behind him. He stood for a moment in the reception area, trying to orient himself. He noticed that he couldn't stop trembling.

29

Captain Greg Becker

Monday, October 30, 2:15 p.m.

Captain Becker watched as Babbage, dressed in full uniform, crisp with freshly pressed creases, his shoes spit-shined, stood in front of the court reporter taking the oath. Becker didn't know what to make of the man. Babbage was a sergeant, highly regarded by his lieutenant, and supposedly looked up to by the cops he supervised. But he'd been accused of sexual misconduct with an arrestee and was ultimately responsible for Fitz's suspension. That worried Becker. Whatever the result of today's hearing, this matter had to be carefully evaluated.

They were in the library of the District Attorney's Office in Van Nuys. Head Deputy DA Chuck Allen was in charge of the Van Nuys' Branch and authorized the meeting. He was mid-fifties, tall and slender with thick salt-and-pepper hair. He sat on one side of the conference table, with Deputy DA Doris Reynolds at his right. Becker sat to Allen's left. Babbage sat on the other side of the table. To his right was the court reporter; to his left, his lawyer, Anthony Giovanni. A tape recorder with a conference-style microphone was on the table between everyone.

Allen pressed the record button on the tape recorder. "Sergeant Babbage," Allen began, "before I start asking you questions, I want to put on the record some key details of today's meeting. If anything I say contradicts your understanding about this meeting, please tell me. If you say nothing, I will assume that you agree with my characterization." Allen looked at his watch. "It is now two-fifteen p.m. on October thirtieth. In addition to this statement being transcribed by a notary and a certified shorthand reporter, it also is being recorded. Do you understand and agree to that?"

Babbage looked at Giovanni, who nodded. "Yes, sir," Babbage said.

"You are here today giving a statement, under informal conditional immunity. You requested formal immunity, through your attorney, last Friday afternoon, October twenty-seventh, indicating that you had information that identified the perpetrator of the heretofore-unsolved nineteen-year-old murder of Sarah Collins. Further, you indicated that you would, under penalty of perjury, disclose that information and testify in court, provided you received a formal grant of immunity. What that means, sir, is that so long as you tell the truth today, nothing you say in this recorded statement can be used to prosecute you criminally, either directly or indirectly. After the district attorney reviews your statement, the decision will be made whether or not to extend to you a formal grant of immunity. If you receive this formal grant, you can never be prosecuted for the rape, murder, or any other crime based upon the acts committed against Sarah Collins on July 4, 1976."

Allen glanced at Captain Becker who nodded.

Allen continued. "You are advised that if you lie, or intentionally misrepresent any fact during today's statement, you will lose your immunity and be subjected to criminal prosecution. Do you understand that?"

"Yes, I do."

Today's statement had been arranged in haste, and Becker could see that Allen was uncomfortable. The events of Friday and the weekend had been absolutely unexpected. What would normally have been routine had become a matter of the utmost importance. The jailing of Babbage by Judge Daniel Hart was simply extraordinary.

But the late Friday afternoon call to Allen by Anthony Giovanni had taken everyone completely by surprise. Giovanni said that Babbage was a witness to a nineteen-year-old unsolved murder. Further, Giovanni said, Babbage now wanted to give a statement identifying the murderer, but would do so only under a grant of immunity.

Normally that procedure would take some time, which was appropriate in light of all that had to be done. But when Giovanni told Allen who the murderer was, all hell broke loose. Any false allegation had to be disposed of immediately, so they all had worked the entire weekend.

Allen said, "Sergeant Babbage, what is your date of birth?"

"July 30, 1955."

Allen continued. "Your lawyer has told us that you have some knowledge about a murder that occurred nineteen years ago. Is that correct?"

Babbage took a deep breath. "Yes. It happened on the fourth of July. Hart was also there."

"You mean Daniel Hart?"

"Yes, sir. Daniel Hart. At approximately twenty-three-hundred hours, Hart approached me and asked if I wanted to party with him. At first I said no, but ultimately I went with him."

"Did he say what he wanted you to do?" Allen inquired.

"He did."

"And what was that?"

Babbage shifted in his seat, sitting up a little straighter. "He suggested we go to Lake Hollywood and get drunk together."

"What were his exact words?"

"I don't recall the exact words," Babbage said. "Something to the effect of did I want to hang out with him and get loaded."

"What did you say in response?"

"I said that I'd promised to take out Sarah Collins. Hart was her children's baby sitter. He knew I was having a relationship with Ms. Collins at that time."

"Go on," Allen said.

"As I said, I asked Hart about Sarah. He indicated that it would be okay to bring her, and that we could all, as he said, 'get loaded' together."

"What did you say?"

Babbage didn't answer immediately. He looked at Giovanni who nodded.

Still hesitating, Babbage said, "I ... I agreed, sir."

Allen's expression gave no indication what he may have been thinking.

"Then what happened?"

"At zero-one-hundred hours we went in my vehicle to pick her up. We drove to the Hollywood Reservoir, forced open the access road gate, drove to the water's edge, and parked. The three of us exited and walked outward on a short pier. There was a small observation building at the end of the pier. We climbed it and sat on the roof, over-looking the water."

"Then what?"

"Sarah Collins and I started kissing, but she told me she felt awkward around Hart, so we excused ourselves and told Hart that we would return later. Hart got angry, but we left him anyway and went to an area concealed by vegetation."

Babbage paused. He glanced around the conference table. Allen had been taking notes on a yellow legal-size pad of paper. The room had grown silent, except for the sound of Allen's felt-tip pen. Allen stopped, looking up. Becker saw Allen's eyes lock on Babbage's, and for an instant the two stared at each other, unblinking.

"Go on," Allen said.

"This is a little awkward, sir," Babbage said. He looked at the court reporter, then toward Deputy DA Reynolds. She had a half-smile on her face.

Babbage again looked at Allen. "Sarah Collins orally copulated me. The next thing I knew, I was struck with a blunt object, probably a rock, on the back of my head. When I awoke, I was sitting against a tree, bound with duct tape. I struggled, but I could barely move my hands and feet. I was still in the brush area. I had a clear, moonlit view of Hart and Sarah Collins."

"What did you see?"

"Sarah was on her knees. Hart was behind her, holding her by the hair with one hand. He had my knife in his other hand. He put the knife against her neck. He told her that if she didn't do what he said, he would 'cut her.' At first she resisted, but Hart pressed the knife to Sarah's neck. She screamed. It appeared that he drew some blood, but I can't be sure. He told her to shut up, and then he forced her to turn around and orally copulate him.

"Sarah gagged and spit, and Hart slapped her across the face. I attempted to get free from the duct tape, but I was still too weak, and I passed out again. When I awoke, I saw Sarah lying on the ground. Her clothes had been removed. She had multiple stab wounds, and she was clearly deceased. Hart was gone, and so was my vehicle. I finally managed to get loose. I made my way out toward the highway, eventually arriving home. My vehicle was parked in front of my house. Inside were Sarah's clothes."

"Did you call the police?"

"No, sir. I used very poor judgment, but I was afraid. I knew that Hart had used my knife, and that Sarah had been in my vehicle. I was also worried that no one would believe me."

"What did you do with her clothes?"

"I burned them."

"Didn't you realize you were destroying evidence?" Allen asked.

"As I said, in my haste, I used poor judgment. I was only twenty at the time."

"Did you hear from Hart later?"

"Yes, sir. He called me the next day. He warned me that if I told anyone, he'd turn the knife over to the police and claim that I murdered Sarah. I asked why he did it. He indicated that at first he wanted a 'blowjob' like she'd done with me, but she refused, so he had to force her. He said he had to kill her to keep her from going to the police. That was the last time I saw or heard from Hart. Until recently."

"Recently?"

"Yes, sir. After all these years, I thought I would never see or hear from him again. I hoped he was either dead or living in another state. But about three months ago, Hart handled a case involving the death of an LAPD lieutenant's wife. The case was well known to most officers. There was newspaper and television coverage mentioning Hart by name as the sentencing judge. I still didn't believe it was him. It was unthinkable to me that the Daniel Hart I knew could actually have become a judge."

Allen continued to make notes on his legal pad. He looked again to Becker. "Do you have any questions you want to ask the witness?"

"Yes," Becker replied. He wished Detective Fitzgerald were here today. No one else had his in-depth knowledge of the murder, but he was still suspended. When Becker found out about today's meeting and that Babbage would be discussing the murder, he had the Sarah Collins murder book brought to him. He'd read it thoroughly. Now, having listened to the statement, he searched his memory for anything that might be in the crime reports that could verify what Babbage was saying, one way or the other. There *was* something significant. The victim's blood had been analyzed. Consistent with Babbage's statement, it showed the presence of alcohol—but also cannabis. She'd been smoking marijuana. This was confirmed by residue found on the thumb and index finger of the decedent.

"You said that Hart asked you to go to the reservoir and used the words, 'get loaded.' Did you actually smoke marijuana that night?"

Giovanni spoke before Babbage could answer. "My client would rather not go into that, Captain. I don't believe it's relevant or needed for the prosecution to make a decision about immunity."

"I disagree," Allen said. "For one thing, we need to know if there is any reason to believe that Sergeant Babbage's memory is impaired. Besides, if this thing goes to trial, the defense will ask, and Sergeant Babbage likely will be ordered by the judge to respond. In short, my office cannot consider immunity unless we have a completely candid statement from your client."

"May I confer with my client?" Giovanni asked. Babbage and Giovanni talked in whispers.

He doesn't know what evidence we have, Becker thought. *For all he knows, we have a cigarette butt with his DNA on it. If he lies to us, he loses his immunity; if he admits to smoking, he could be fired, because the immunity is for criminal prosecution only and doesn't protect him from being fired.*

Finally, Giovanni spoke to the room again. "My client will answer."

"I did smoke, Captain," Babbage said. "But during all the times I've mentioned, my head was perfectly clear. I was not under the influence."

"Did you ingest any other illegal or controlled substance, Sergeant?"

"No, sir."

"What about alcohol?" Becker asked.

"Earlier that evening I consumed one or two twelve-ounce cans of beer, Captain."

Becker asked, "Why did Hart remand you on Friday? For that matter, why did you go to see him in the first place?"

"As I said, sir, I didn't know for sure that he was the same Daniel Hart. Friday morning, I was scheduled to testify. Upon entering the courtroom, I learned that the judge hearing the case was Hart. I started to feel apprehensive. Was this the same Hart I knew? What would he do when he saw me? I decided that I had to be sure it was him before testifying. I asked to see him, saying it was a personal matter. If I determined that it wasn't the same person, I could excuse myself by indicating that I thought he was someone else. But it was him."

"But why did he remand you?" Becker asked.

"At first he didn't recognize me," Babbage said. "I told him who I was, and he reacted with anger, immediately. He demanded to know why I came to see him. Did I actually think I could intimidate him? I'd learn soon just how powerful he was, he said. Who did I think people would believe? Hart, a superior court judge of impeccable reputation, or, as he said, 'a shit' like me? I realized it was a major mistake going to see him."

"You still haven't told us why he remanded you," Becker said.

"I indicated to him that I couldn't go on any longer with this thing hanging over my head. I told him that I was going to my captain and tell everything I knew. Hart reminded me about my knife. I told him I didn't care. That's when he called for the bailiffs and had me remanded."

"Did he tell you he still had the knife?" Allen asked.

"Not exactly. But I'm sure he has it somewhere. It's his leverage."

"I'm not so sure," Becker said. "He'd be a fool to keep it all these years. Especially with his knowledge of criminal law. It's the one thing that would clearly link him to the murder."

"Murderers often do foolish things," Allen said. "But now isn't the time to discuss that. Sergeant Babbage, do you have anything else you want to tell us?"

"That's all," Babbage said.

"One last question," Becker said. He looked at the coroner's report that he had removed from the murder book. "When you were orally copulated by Sarah Collins, did you ejaculate?"

Babbage looked surprised. "That was more than nineteen years ago," he said.

Another dilemma for Babbage, Becker thought. *If he says no, and we have a semen sample with his DNA, we've got him.*

"We're waiting, Sergeant," Allen said.

Finally Babbage spoke. "I don't recall."

"Are you certain?" Becker asked.

"I can see most of the evening in my mind as if it happened yesterday. But I just don't recall."

"More questions? Anyone?" Allen said. He looked around the room. There was no response. "Very well. This interview is concluded."

Giovanni spoke. "Sergeant Babbage will make himself available for further questioning anytime, Mr. Allen. When will the final decision be made concerning my client's immunity?"

"I'll try to get back to you by tomorrow, Mr. Giovanni. Please bear in mind that the decision will have to be made at the highest levels in the District Attorney's Office." Allen looked at the court reporter. "It is now three-thirty p.m. The court reporter is to transcribe this interview, and I will get an order from the grand jury judge sealing this transcript until a final decision on immunity is made."

30

Becker

Becker, Allen, and Reynolds stayed in the library after Babbage, his lawyer, and the court reporter left. Becker wasn't sure what to think. "I'll need to study Babbage's statement carefully and compare it to the murder book," Becker said. "But I don't trust the man. Good cops don't get into the kind of trouble Babbage continually finds himself in."

"The same could be said of Fitzgerald before his suspension," Reynolds quipped. "Babbage had a spotless record before Fitzgerald started messing with him. Number one in his class at the academy, a no-nonsense sergeant beloved by his men—a cop's cop."

"Fitzgerald is not part of this discussion," Becker said. "We need to question Hart and find out why he remanded Babbage."

"We can't question him," Allen said. "If he's involved, he's not going to waive his rights."

"Not necessarily," Becker said. "I say, let's interview him."

"I don't agree," Reynolds said. "Questioning him would just tip him off, and if he does have the murder weapon or other incriminating evidence, he'll get rid of it. Before our meeting, I did a complete analysis of the police reports, analyzed evidence, and photographs. Everything Sergeant Babbage says is confirmed by the physical evidence. The man is obviously telling the truth."

"I'm not so sure," Becker said. *Truth be told,* he thought, *I'd stake my life on Fitzgerald's integrity. And if Fitz says the man's a crooked cop, I want no part of him. On the other hand, this is a nineteen-year-old cold-case murder, and something was going on between Hart and Babbage. Plus, it's not my call—it's up to the prosecutor. Allen seems a reasonable sort. Going ahead would let a jury decide these issues.*

"This whole thing doesn't make sense," Allen said. "Assuming Hart is the killer, remanding Babbage is the last thing he would do—it draws too much attention to himself."

Reynolds spoke up. "I can think of no reason he'd remand Babbage other than what the sergeant told us. I've always wondered about Hart."

"Meaning?" Becker asked.

"The fact that he gives way too much to defendants. And that he's anti-cop. Do you remember the case against that woman physician? The woman killed the pregnant wife of an LAPD defendant and Hart gave her probation—ridiculous. That's why I'm running against him."

"You're running against Judge Hart?" Becker asked. "Isn't that a conflict of interest?"

"It's not a conflict to prosecute a murderer, Captain," Reynolds replied. "The fact that he's a judge I'm trying to unseat is irrelevant. Besides, it's the grand jury's decision whether or not to indict, and if indicted, it's the jury's call to convict. My job is to present the facts to them and let them decide."

31

Fitzgerald

Tuesday, October 31

Fitz sat in a chair outside the closed door of Captain Becker's office. Under normal circumstances, he felt at home in Parker Center, felt the familiarity that twenty-plus years in the same work location brings. But not today. Today he felt out-of-place and conspicuous. He was conscious that every cop who walked by Becker's office could see him in the waiting area and would notice that he was wearing a visitor's badge.

Captain Becker had called Fitz at home and told him to report immediately. There was an impersonal, urgent tone to his boss's voice that deeply concerned Fitz. He worried that he'd done something seriously wrong by going to Erin's probation violation hearing, that he'd somehow further damaged his position. Wasn't it bad enough that he had tried to prevent Babbage from arresting Erin in the first place? Perhaps Becker was going to tell Fitz that he was fired, and he'd have to look to the union to find a way to challenge it.

"You can go in, Fitz," said Sally, Becker's middle-aged secretary. Her desk was directly in front of Becker's office. She'd been glancing at Fitz throughout the time he was waiting in the hallway. *She knows,* he thought.

"Thanks, Sally," he said, and knocked on the door.

"Come in, and sit down, Fitz." The captain was behind his desk and remained seated as Fitz entered. Sitting in front of Becker's desk was LAPD Commander Harold Karp, the high-ranking officer who was to be in charge of Fitzgerald's Board of Rights hearing.

Fitz sat in the chair next to Karp. "I'm not going to delay this any longer," Becker said. He was not smiling, and neither was Karp.

"Captain," Fitz said. "Let me explain ..."

Karp interrupted. "Detective Fitzgerald, wait for Captain Becker to finish. It's important for you to hear what he has to say."

Fitz nodded. He was perspiring. The air of the office seemed hot and stale.

Becker continued. "Yesterday I attended a meeting in the District Attorney's Office. Head Deputy DA Chuck Allen, Deputy DA Doris Reynolds, and Jake Babbage were all there. Babbage gave a statement to the DA that will be of great interest to you. I need you to listen to the voice recording, and then discuss it with us. Commander Karp and I have talked about your upcoming Board of Rights hearing, and we've decided to take some preliminary action in light of this recent development."

Here it comes, Fitz thought.

"Commander Karp," Becker continued, "has agreed to exercise his power as hearing officer to order that you be provisionally reinstated."

Fitz was stunned. He decided he must have misheard. "Come again?" he said.

"That's right," Karp said. "However, you will still have the Board of Rights hearing, and you still face disciplinary action, up to and including termination. For this reason, Detective Fitzgerald, during this provisional period, you must not say or do anything that will jeopardize your provisional status."

"In other words, Fitz," Becker added, "don't fuck up."

"Captain, I'm grateful for the reinstatement, and I promise I won't let you down," Fitz said. "But what the hell happened?"

"I think your question will be answered when you hear the voice recording," Becker said.

He pushed the play button, and they listened. Fitz heard a brief introduction discussing Babbage's immunity statement. He was puzzled, thinking this had something to do with Erin. Then he heard:

> Sergeant Babbage, your lawyer has told us that you have some knowledge about a murder that occurred nineteen years ago. Is that correct?

Fitz was astounded, but he said nothing as he listened with increasing amazement.

Hart the murderer? Babbage the innocent victim?

As the interview played out, he knew he'd have to listen again. And again. To analyze and study Babbage's words carefully. Because, Jesus Christ, it just didn't add up.

The recording ended, and they all sat in silence.

Then: "Fitz," Becker said, "the decision was made last night to grant Babbage formal immunity—so long as what he says is the truth, he will never be prosecuted for his part in the murder. Frankly, I don't know if that was the right decision or not, and I said so. But I was overruled."

"I agree with you, Captain," Fitz said. "Immunity for Babbage is a colossal mistake."

"It's too late to worry about that," Becker said. "Look, Fitz. Sarah Collins's murder is your case. You know more about it than anyone else in the world. That's the reason for the reinstatement. Here's your badge and ID. Now let's get down to business and decide what to do next."

32

Hart

Wednesday, November 1, 11:00 a.m.

Daniel Hart was in his study, sitting at his mahogany desk, an open book in front of him. He tried to read but couldn't concentrate. Instead, he looked out the window at the trees in his front yard. The air was still. Not a leaf moved.

For the past two days, he'd called in sick. It gave him more time to consider his situation. It also gave him a reason to avoid meeting with the LAPD's liaison officer to discuss Babbage's contempt case. Each night, Hart would sleep, wake, worry, and then remain awake for most of the night. Each day, he planned to go to work, but when his alarm went off, he was unable to get up. Instead, he would sleep until ten o'clock or eleven, finally getting himself into the shower.

Amanda Jordan hadn't called him yet, and Hart had decided that he would call her at the end of today to set up a meeting to discuss his situation again. Hart didn't see a way out. But now that he'd taken the time to think about his plight more fully, he was no longer in a state of panic.

Louise had told him that Judge Finch was going to handle the Erin Collins probation violation hearing. Finch hadn't understood that Hart had sentenced Babbage to five days in jail for contempt. By releasing Babbage OR, Finch was, in effect, illegally canceling Babbage's jail sentence. Rupert Finch could always be counted on to do something stupid, but in this case, his incompetence took the pressure off Hart.

Now that Babbage was out of jail, he'd be a fool to implicate himself in a nineteen-year-old murder. Babbage's threats were ridiculous. No way would Babbage open up this case and make himself liable after all these years. Maybe Hart should follow Jordan's advice and say nothing. Because if he told all, the possibilities of what would happen to him were terrifying and unthinkable.

A knock at his front door interrupted his thoughts.

As he walked to the door, he could see through a front window that two black-and-white police cars had pulled up in front of the house. They must be coming to talk to him about why Babbage had been remanded for contempt.

But there were more police than he would have expected. Two other patrol cars had parked down the street, almost out of his line of sight.

Something was wrong.

Hart opened his door. Two plainclothes detectives stood with several uniformed cops directly behind them.

"Judge Hart? I'm Detective Fitzgerald. May we come inside?"

"Yes, sure," Hart replied.

Six more uniformed officers and two more dressed in plainclothes accompanied Fitzgerald into the house. Hart did not recognize any of the other officers. Soon, they were all standing in the middle of Hart's living room.

"Judge Hart," Fitzgerald said, removing documents from the inside pocket of his suit jacket, "I have a warrant to search your house, garage, and automobile." Fitzgerald showed the paper to Hart. "I also have a warrant for your arrest."

Hart was handcuffed and escorted outside to a police vehicle, and waited uncomfortably while officers went through his house and garage.

33

Hart

Hart called Jordan, using an ancient pay phone in the Parker Center jail. He was in a large cell, capable of holding at least twenty inmates, but was, thank God, currently housing only him. His booking process had been utterly humiliating, complicated by the fact that the press had found out about his arrest. News people, including photographers and TV crews, were waiting at the jail entrance. They shouted questions at him and took pictures as he exited the unmarked police car and was led inside the jail by the detectives. His hands were cuffed behind him. His mind flashed back to the scenes he'd seen on television, when well-known people were being taken to jail. The perp walk, it was called. Mobsters, child molesters, and murderers—trying to hide their faces. Now he was one of them. His face burned with shame.

"Daniel," Jordan's voice said, "I was going to call you later today. I have some ideas to discuss with you."

"It's too late."

"What do you mean? You haven't said anything to any-one, have you?"

"I've been arrested. I'm calling you from the jail."

Hart heard Jordan take a deep breath. "My God. When did that happen?"

"Around eleven. They had an arrest warrant and a search warrant. The press knew all about it. They were here when I arrived."

"I hope you haven't said anything to the detectives."

"Not yet. I was fingerprinted, photographed, and booked. I expect the detectives will be coming soon to interview me."

"For God's sake, don't say anything. We have to leave our options open. Promise me you will say nothing."

Hart thought for a moment. "All right. I won't say anything until you and I have a chance to speak. But I've got a more pressing worry right now. My bail has been set at two million dollars. There's no way I can make that."

"I'll make a motion for OR or a reduction. It's too late to get to court tonight, but I'll get hold of the magistrate who's on after-hours bail duty and see what I can do. You might have to spend a night or two in jail. I hope you'll be okay."

"There is no way in the world I'll be okay."

"Just sit tight. I'm going to do everything possible. Perhaps the detectives will consent to a lower bail. I'll fill you in on what I've been able to accomplish when I see you later on."

"When will that be?"

"One, possibly two hours."

34

Hart

Hart sat down on the steel bench against the concrete wall. The cell smelled of urine and feces. Benches lined three sides of the walls, with bars and a sliding jail door on the fourth side. A stainless-steel toilet without a seat was in one corner of the cell. The wall felt cold against his back. The paint was worn and smudged with grease spots where previous inmates had leaned their heads.

Hart recalled standing outside cells like this one so many times during his career as judge, coming into the courtroom lockup to advise defendants of their constitutional rights. They'd looked so pathetic to him, faceless in the dim light of their cells. How ironic that he would be on this side of the jail bars, faceless to those on the other side who were free to come and go as they pleased.

Fitzgerald and a uniformed captain appeared with the jailer, who handcuffed Hart and left. Fitzgerald and the captain then escorted Hart to a small, windowless interview room. There was a Formica-topped Steelcase table with three matching chairs. Fitzgerald took off Hart's handcuffs.

"Judge Hart," he said, "this is Captain Becker."

The fact that a police captain was sitting in on the interview was not lost on Hart. In his entire career, he'd never seen it before—obviously, this was a case where the top brass wanted to make sure there were no screw-ups. Becker pulled out a chair and sat against the wall. Fitzgerald sat behind the table and motioned for Hart to sit on the other side.

Fitzgerald said, "Judge Hart, although I'm sure you know your rights, it is my obligation at this time to advise you. You have the right to remain silent. If you choose to give up that right, anything you say can and will be used against you in a court of law. You also have the right to an attorney. If you cannot afford an attorney, one will be appointed for you at no expense. Do you understand the rights that I have explained to you?"

"Yes."

"Do you wish to give up those rights and speak to us to tell us your side of the story?"

"No, I do not."

"Are you sure?" Fitzgerald had a surprised look on his face. "After all, this whole thing may just be a misunderstanding. We need to know your version of the facts in order to make an intelligent decision about what will happen next."

How often as a DA, Hart thought to himself, had he heard these same words spoken by detectives when he was present at suspects' interviews? "I'm sorry, Detective

Fitzgerald. I've talked to my lawyer, and at this time, I've been advised not to waive my rights. Perhaps later."

Fitzgerald took a business card from his wallet. "If you change your mind, here's my card. Please feel free to call any time."

Fitzgerald and Becker stood and so did Hart. Fitzgerald put back Hart's handcuffs and the three of them walked down a hall to the jailer's desk. "He's all yours," Fitzgerald said to the jailer, an Asian man with close-cropped hair.

Hart was taken to another, smaller cell. "This'll be your home for the night," the jailer said. "Tomorrow you'll be arraigned and transferred to the county jail. But I guess you know the details."

"I do," Hart said. "I'm expecting to hear from my attorney tonight."

The jailer nodded, but said nothing. He opened the cell door. Hart entered. The cuffs were removed. The jailer closed the cell door, locked it, and left.

This cell was a smaller version of one Hart had been in before, except for a bunk bed instead of a steel bench along one wall. Thankfully, there was no urine smell. He lay down and tried to sleep.

Hart is at a county bar cocktail reception. The room is crowded with people—standing, talking, and drinking. The dozens of conversations blend, making it almost impossible to communicate without shouting. He is trying to have a conversation with someone he barely knows, but it's impossible because he can't quite hear all the words. He nods and tries to comment, hoping it's not obvious that he doesn't fully know what's being said.

He looks up and notices a woman across the room looking at him. No—not looking, but rather, staring. He doesn't
meet her eyes. Instead he looks down, uncomfortable. She's
not looking at him, he says to himself, she's only looking in
his direction.

He returns to his conversation, but discreetly glances
to see if the woman is still looking toward him. She is. She
must be someone he's met before, but she is so striking that
he can't imagine not remembering. There is something
strangely familiar. He sneaks another look. Her eyes meet
his. She smiles. He excuses himself and walks over to where
she's standing.

"Do we know each other?" he asks.

"Yes."

"What's your name?"

"Sarah," she says, "Sarah Collins."

"My God!" he says. "You look exactly the same." He sees
that she's dressed the same as she was that night—jeans and
a loose-fitting pullover blouse. She's barefoot, too, and, he
notices, not wearing a bra.

This can't be, he thinks. I saw Snake stab her to death.
She must have survived, after all. Or maybe it didn't happen.
Maybe he just dreamed about Snake and that July 4 night.
It's all a mistake. She's alive, really alive. He is jubilant.

But then Snake appears, wearing a police uniform. He
has a knife. His hand is raised high in the air. He's about to
stab Sarah from behind.

"No, stop!" Hart shouts. He pulls Sarah away, tries to
grab Snake's arm. He fails. The point of the knife strikes his
chest. He feels it enter. He can't breathe ...

"Hart. Hart, wake up," the jailer said. "You've been bailed out." He opened the cell.

Hart was groggy and disoriented, drenched in sweat. The nightmare was still vivid. He felt confused. For a moment he looked at the jailer, not comprehending. Then he became aware.

"Thank God," he said to himself. Jordan must have finally got him an OR, or at least a greatly reduced bail. He followed the jailer to a small desk just outside the lockup. There he signed a release slip that had the bail amount and his court appearance date. The bail amount was still $2 million. How was that possible? Hart wondered.

The jailer then escorted him to the public reception area. Sitting in the reception area was Amanda Jordan and an attractive woman dressed in casual clothing.

Jordan said, "I wasn't able to get you an OR or a reduced bail, Daniel. We did have another kind of luck. Do you remember Gina Black?"

"Of course," Hart said.

"Gina saw you on the news and called me."

Hart felt very uncomfortable. After all, the last time this woman saw him, he sat on the bench, wearing his robe. Jordan grinned. "I guess you're still puzzled, Daniel. Gina put up the two million dollars to bail you out."

35

Fitzgerald

Monday, November 6

Prosecutor Doris Reynolds told Captain Becker to have Fitzgerald in her office at 7:30 a.m. sharp, so that she could "brief" him. Fitz was not looking forward to the meeting, but he decided to do everything he could to avoid pissing her off. Even before he met her at Erin's probation hearing, word was that she was rude, petty, and abrasive—especially if you were on the opposite side. On the other hand, she'd once been nice to Erin when they met in the restroom after that first probation hearing, so she couldn't be all bad.

Fitz arrived at the courthouse at 7:15, took the elevator to the second floor, and entered the double doors bearing the words "District Attorney's Office" in silver block letters. The waiting area was dark, and there was no one behind the receptionist's counter. People probably come in at 8 a.m., Fitz realized. He didn't know where Reynolds's office was and was worried he might have gotten the time wrong. He sat down to wait in the darkened room, hoping she'd come to get him.

At 7:45, Fitz decided that Reynolds might be expecting him to find her. There were two other doors leading out of the reception area. Fitz walked through the nearest and found himself in a large open area containing a series of desks, file cabinets, and photocopy machines. He found a long hallway with offices on either side, and began exploring the maze of offices and hallways.

He heard a female voice, followed the sound, and found Reynolds sitting and talking on the phone. She was in a small, windowless office. He knocked on her open door. She motioned him to wait outside, and that he should close her office door.

He complied and stood in the hallway, waiting. He could hear her talking through the door but couldn't make out what she was saying. After a while, more lights came on and other deputy DAs arrived and went into their offices. They appeared not to notice him. Eventually, Reynolds stopped talking, opened the door, and beckoned him in. He looked at his watch. It was 8 a.m.

Fitz sat down on a small, hard-back steel chair beside Reynolds's desk. "Where the fuck were you at seven-thirty?" she demanded.

Fitz managed to suppress a flash of rage. "I was in the reception area. I thought you wanted to meet me there at seven-thirty."

Reynolds glared. "If I wanted to meet you in the visitor area, I'd have told you."

She took a case file folder from one of the drawers in her desk. She opened it and read silently. While Fitz waited, he looked around the room. Not only was she rude, she was also a slob. She must share the office with someone, since there was another desk on the other side of the room. Reynolds's desk was littered with case file folders, papers, memos, and handwritten notes. In the two-level in-out basket at the left corner of the desk, the top level was marked "in" and was piled with legal newspapers that had routing slips attached. There was nothing in the "out" portion. On the wall behind her desk was a cork bulletin board covered with tacked-up items: four or five snapshots of different cats, including a shot of Reynolds holding a Siamese up to her face. There was also a cartoon showing a judge pounding a gavel while looking at a defendant and saying, "Probably guilty."

Fitz noticed an announcement of an upcoming retirement dinner for some DA; a series of newspaper clippings, describing cases Reynolds had something to do with; and letters of commendation from the LAPD and the sheriff's department. She finally looked up from the file. She wore no lipstick and her hair was slightly disheveled.

"I want to make one thing clear, Fitzgerald," she said. "I'm in charge of this case. I went along with the decision that your suspension be temporarily lifted so you can assist me. If you're not cooperative, or if you otherwise interfere with the investigation or trial, then you'll go back on suspension until your Board of Rights hearing is concluded. Clear?"

"Yes."

Reynolds continued. "Tell me about the arrest and search."

"Not much to tell," Fitz said. "Hart was arrested and refused to waive his rights. We searched his house, his car, and his office and came up with nothing. I didn't really expect to find the knife, or for that matter anything else that would be useful. After all, it's been nineteen years. Besides, Hart, being a judge, is probably too smart to have incriminating evidence lying around."

"Don't overestimate his intelligence," she said. "I've never observed him to be particularly bright in court."

"My main concern," Fitz said, "is that we're moving too fast."

"What do you base that on?" Reynolds snapped.

"I don't think we have enough corroboration of Babbage's statement."

"Fitzgerald," Reynolds said, "listen to me—"

Fitz interrupted. "What bothers me is that we really don't know if we can believe Babbage. We have nothing to connect Hart to the killing other than Babbage's say-so."

Reynolds didn't respond, just looked at him with a strange half-smile on her face. He spoke quickly, afraid she might interrupt before he could explain fully, hopeful that he was getting through.

"The semen sample from the victim's mouth was badly deteriorated," Fitz continued, "but last year I found a private lab, Biotech Markers, who told me they could analyze the sample and likely obtain a DNA profile."

Fitz was relieved that Reynolds let him speak. Maybe things would be all right, after all. "Here's my suggestion," he said. "Let's compare Babbage's DNA to the crime scene evidence—find out if it corroborates what he says. Then get Hart's profile and compare that. That'll clinch it one way or the other, and we can go from there."

"Meaning what?" Reynolds asked.

"Babbage said he saw the victim spit after she orally copulated Hart. That means there should be a match with Hart, and if so, we have our corroboration."

Reynolds half-smile faded. "Is that it?" she asked.

Fitz nodded. "Right." He felt a heavy silence as Reynolds appeared to consider. Outside of the office he could hear the muffled sounds of more DAs coming into work.

Reynolds slammed her hand on her desk. "Damn it, Fitzgerald! You're not thinking clearly," she snapped. "I've studied Babbage's statement carefully, reviewed *all* the evidence. Corroboration is overwhelming. Babbage knows things that no one would know who wasn't there that night."

"The murderer would know it."

Reynolds eyes were on fire. "Haven't you heard anything I've said?"

"I've lived with this case for nineteen years. Isn't a little more time to clinch it worth it?"

"While you were pondering the case with your thumb up your ass, I've tried one hundred fifty jury trials over that same period of time." She continued to glare at Fitz. "I know a liar when I see one, and Hart is a two-faced liar. I used to wonder why he was consistently soft on defendants—now we have the answer."

"But if he's guilty," Fitz said, "won't the DNA comparison confirm it?"

"Either way, it proves nothing. Worse, it contradicts our chief witness, and we all look like fools. Let Hart's lawyer get it, if she thinks there's any value to it."

She stood, walked over to her filing cabinet, and began rummaging through her files. She pulled one out, removed a glossy eight-by-ten picture, and threw on the desk in front of Fitz. It was particularly graphic and gruesome, and one he'd looked at many times over the years. "Look at what Hart did to Sarah Collins. Keep that image in your mind. And keep your mouth shut and do what I say so that we convict this murderer."

Reynolds sat down behind her desk again, arms folded in front of her. "Hart's lawyer, Jordan, will not want to have her client's DNA compared. She'd be a fool to do it. If the comparison is positive for Hart, Jordan would be convicting her own client, since we'd subpoena the results. I don't think any defense attorney would take that chance."

"I'm still worried about Babbage," Fitz said. "I've had experience with him, and I don't trust a damn thing he says. Even if we don't send in Hart's DNA for comparison, we should have Babbage compared."

Reynolds shook her head. "What are you talking about? You're not suggesting we should ask our own witness for a blood sample?"

"We don't need to. We have an exemplar from the Erin Collins case."

Reynolds exploded. "That case ... that case has *nothing* to do with this prosecution." She was shouting and Fitz felt his face redden. "I've been told about your bias against Sergeant Babbage, and also about your unprofessional relationship with that Erin Collins woman. How you attempted to cover up for her. Smarten up, Fitzgerald. If I were you, I'd stay away from her. As it is, she very nearly cost you your job.

"Try to be objective for a moment," she continued. "Look at the facts. Babbage is a highly respected police sergeant who has no motive to lie about Hart. Forget the DNA comparison—we already know that if it's identified, it probably will be positive for Babbage, so it's not going to prove a thing. The jury won't like the fact that his semen was found in the victim's mouth. It makes him look bad, and we need our chief witness to look as good as possible."

Fitz was trying to remain polite, but he didn't know how much more of this he could take. "There's nothing in Babbage's statement that has been or can be verified. It's just his word against Hart's. Babbage claims to have been knocked unconscious, but that can't be verified after all these years. We have no fingerprints, no clothing of the decedent, no murder weapon. No history of criminal behavior by Hart, but a lot of compromising things about his accuser. Please let me get both men compared and see what comes up."

"Fitzgerald," Reynolds said deliberately, her voice thick with rage, "I'm only going to say this once, so listen carefully. If we're going to be on the same team, you've got to get it. There's plenty of corroboration. Hart murdered Sarah Collins, and it's your job to help me prove it. Don't complain to me about what *you* need to be convinced about. Just do your job and find what I tell you we need to win. Let me worry about corroboration. Under no circumstances are you to get DNA compared. Am I getting through to you?" She glared at him.

Fitz stared back at her, thinking that he was crazy for not telling her to get someone else. Every instinct told him this was a mistake and that her path was going to lead to disaster. He realized he could expect nothing from this woman. He'd have to do it alone. One way or the other, he'd have to find out the truth. If she were right, he'd help her. But if she were wrong, it was up to him to stop her, and damn it, he would.

If she didn't stop him first.

Finally, he broke the stare and looked down. Now was not the time to confront this woman. "Yes, ma'am, I understand," he said. "Tell me what you need."

36

Fitzgerald

Thursday, November 9, 7:30 p.m.

Fitz, Sean, and Erin were at the Wharf, sitting at a dockside table overlooking the water. It was a beautiful, unseasonably warm evening for November. The lights from the restaurant reflected on the water and highlighted the moored sailboats and yachts. The three of them were here for dinner. Erin had worked all day and ended her shift in time to eat.

For the past week, newspaper and television coverage had been occupied almost exclusively with the story about the judge accused of murder and his police officer accomplice. Fitz had struggled over whether or not to have this meeting with Sean and Erin. Since his conversation with Doris Reynolds, he'd been in a quandary. He was convinced that it was premature to move ahead with the case and that Reynolds was making a major mistake by not getting Hart's and Babbage's DNA compared to the semen. Fitz had serious doubts that Hart was a killer, but Reynolds had no interest in hearing Fitz's concerns.

He had nowhere to go to talk about his concerns.

Captain Becker supported him, but kept him at a distance since the day Fitz was suspended. Most of the homicide detectives whom Fitz knew were cool toward him since Babbage's prosecution for what he'd done to Erin.

So Fitz decided to talk to Sean, partly because Sean himself was a lawyer and would understand. Sean might also be able to provide some details that had never been mentioned during their years-ago interview at MacLaren Hall.

Erin had been two years old at the time of the murder, so she would know little or nothing about Hart, but Fitz felt she had a right to be part of any conversation about her mother's murder.

Fitz told them about Babbage's statement and that, without consulting Fitz and before he could object, Babbage had been granted immunity. Fitz told them about the arrest of Hart. As Fitz spoke, Sean's face reddened.

"No matter what Babbage said, here's the reality of the situation," Fitz said. "First, he already has immunity. That means he goes free, even if he's the real killer. Second, his story doesn't contradict what I know about the case, so I'm pretty sure he actually was there that night—"

Erin went white. "Wait," she interrupted. "You're telling us that Babbage *was there* when Mom was killed?"

"Yes," Fitz said, quietly.

She shivered. "That bastard who sexually assaulted me, stalked me, and who's still after me?"

"What about Hart?" Sean asked. "Does Babbage's accusation make any sense?"

"That's what troubles me," Fitz said. "Hart lived in the area and could have known your mother." Fitz looked at Sean. "When you were five and I interviewed you at MacLaren Hall, you told me about someone who babysat you. Hart could be the person you were talking about. So things *could* have happened just the way Babbage described."

"I still don't believe it about Judge Hart," Erin said, shaking her head. "Babbage is a cop—he could have looked up the police report and got all those details."

"Not likely," Fitz said. "It's a nineteen-year-old case, and only I have the murder book.

"Murder book? What's that?" said Erin.

"Every homicide detective keeps a murder book on each case," Fitz said, "where all the investigative reports and photos are stored, as well as the full coroner's report. Until a case is cleared, there's only one copy of the murder book. A case is cleared only when the investigation is over and the case is presented to the DA and filed."

"What happens to the murder book after filing?" Sean asked.

"Copies are made for the DA and defense attorneys. If more investigation occurs after filing, the murder book is always updated.

"Without the murder book, Babbage would have to go to archives to get the report, and he'd have to know the DR number or—"

"What's a DR number?" Erin asked.

"All police case file numbers are preceded by the letters *DR*. It's our shorthand for case file numbers," Fitz said, and then continued. "So, he'd either know the DR number or do a computer search to cross-reference it. That would take time. It would also require him to state his name and reason for the request. This morning I checked. I found no record of any request for the case."

Sean was looking out over the water. Finally, he turned back to Fitz. "Whoever participated in my mom's murder should get the same treatment she did. And if Hart played a part, then the son of a bitch should get what's coming to him. I'll deal with Babbage later."

Sean's intensity alarmed Fitz. "Maybe we should call it a night, Sean," he said. "We can discuss this later, after you've cooled down."

"No, goddammit!" Sean said. "We're going to discuss it now." He glared at Fitz. "Look, you've been on this thing since the beginning. You know more about my mother's murder than anyone. What's your appraisal of the situation? Can they really convict Hart?"

Fitz thought a moment before speaking. "This whole thing has moved too fast. We're being forced to go to trial before we have everything we need for a conviction. The plain fact is, after everything at trial is said and done, it's still Babbage's word against Hart's. That's just not enough."

"Why?" Erin said. "You said yourself that Babbage's story fits what you know about the case. Why not let a jury decide?"

"Because they might not get a chance," Sean said.

"We need corroborating evidence in order to get this case to the jury," Fitz said. "Without it, the judge will have to dismiss at the end of the prosecution's case."

"How can that be?" Erin said. "It's up to the jury, isn't it? To weigh the testimony and decide the facts?"

Sean shook his head. "Under the law, Babbage could be considered an accomplice. If the judge finds that to be the case, his testimony has to be corroborated or it can't be considered by the jury."

"But I thought Fitz said that Babbage's testimony fits the facts," Erin said. "Isn't that corroboration?"

"I didn't exactly say that," Fitz said. "What Babbage knows could have been learned from newspaper stories—there was lots of press at the time. After all, he could have just heard about the murder at the time. Much of what he says can't be verified one way or another. And remember, he was fighting a contempt hearing and had a motive to get Hart. It has to be something more. Like the murder weapon—the knife, for instance."

"What about the knife?" Erin asked.

"Our original search turned up nothing," Fitz said. "At this point, we don't have a clue as to who has the murder weapon or even if it exists. Babbage insists that Hart has the knife somewhere, so I'll keep looking for it. But I'm not going to limit my search to Hart. It's also possible Babbage has the knife."

"What else could corroborate Babbage?" Erin asked.

"Not a whole lot," Fitz said. "We're dealing with a nineteen-year-old murder, so what we might usually have is just not available. We really need some way to confirm Babbage's story. He claims he was knocked out, but that can't be proved one way or another."

"What other physical evidence do you have?" Sean asked.

"I don't think it's necessarily good for you to know these details," Fitz said.

"Bullshit," Sean said. "No one has more of a right to know what happened that night than I do."

"Sean, you're upset —"

"Hell, yes, I'm upset," Sean interrupted. "And if you're my friend, you'll stop patronizing me and let me read the fucking murder book." He paused. "How about it, Fitz? If I know everything, I really think I can help."

Fitz looked at Erin. Her eyes met his. She nodded—"It's got to be up to Sean. I don't want to know any details, and I don't even remember my mom. But I'm not Sean."

"Okay," Fitz said to Sean. "I'll show you the murder book. But I'm not going to discuss any details with you until you've read the whole thing. Maybe you'll change your mind once you begin looking at the photographs."

"How long before the trial starts?" Erin asked.

"I don't know," Fitz said. "It's hard to say. The case gets presented to the Grand Jury tomorrow. Once they return an indictment, Hart will need to be arraigned. Since he's bailed out, he's entitled to a trial within sixty days of his arraignment. Most defense attorneys waive the speedy trial rights of their out-of-custody clients, so that they can thoroughly investigate their case and prepare. I'll need the extra time. We'll still be looking for the knife—the more time we have to search for it, the better."

"I've got some money saved, and I'm thinking of taking a leave of absence from the PD's Office until this is over," Sean said. He seemed to have relaxed a little. "That way, I can help on this case, Fitz. Two brilliant minds are better than one."

———

Sean drove Erin home from the restaurant, and was glad he had a chance to speak to her alone. They'd been exposed to too much information tonight, and he needed to discuss it with her, to think things through a bit. Traffic was light and it took almost no time to get to the freeway.

"It just doesn't make any sense," Erin said. "I just can't accept that Daniel Hart, the judge who'd shown me so much kindness, compassion, and understanding, could be the person who killed Mom."

Sean put aside his anger to concede that he, too, was puzzled. "Everyone at the PD's Office is astounded. Hart was one of the most popular judges in the courthouse. It makes sense that Babbage was involved—especially after what he did to you. It scares the hell out of me to think that someone like that could actually be a cop." And to himself he thought, *I won't tell Erin—I don't want to alarm her— but it's too much of a terrifying coincidence that Babbage targeted her in the first place.*

Erin took a breath, started to say something, then stopped for a moment. Finally, she spoke. "Do you know how old Judge Hart is? He seems pretty young. Mom was killed almost twenty years ago."

Sean pondered. "I hadn't thought about it. He does seem young. But you have to be a lawyer at least ten years to be a superior court judge, so he can't be that young. I'll check his profile at the law library."

"Sean," Erin said, "I really think you should go see Judge Hart. Ask him how old he was at the time of the incident. Ask him point-blank if he did it. You might learn a lot just by his reaction."

Sean shook his head. "There's no way he'd talk to me. You've been through the system enough to know that."

"I'm not so sure," Erin said. "Don't you think he owes it to us to tell us what he knows?"

"But he knows that anything he tells me, I'd have to testify to in court. No lawyer would allow him to speak to me."

"It won't hurt you to ask. All he can say is no."

Sean frowned. "I'll think about it. Tomorrow I'll get copies of the police reports and a copy of Babbage's statement. I've got to go over it, detail by detail. It's also important to go to the scene where the crime occurred."

"To the reservoir?" Erin said. "After all these years? What could you possibly learn by going there?"

"I don't know," Sean said. "But after I finish reading the reports, I'm going. I'll think about trying to talk to Judge Hart. I'm sure he won't see me. But you're right, Erin. It can't hurt to try."

37

Doris Reynolds

Friday, November 10, 4:30 p.m.

Reynolds was finishing up for the day and preparing to go home when her phone rang. *Who the hell is calling me now?* she thought. She was in a hurry, and the last thing she needed was a call that would delay her from getting home and relaxing with her cats. For an instant, she considered not answering, then picked up the phone. The secretary told her it was a Robbery-Homicide Lieutenant. Someone named Hardy. "Put him through," Reynolds said.

"Deputy DA Reynolds?" the voice asked.

"What do you need?" she snapped.

"I'm a team leader in Robbery-Homicide. I work for Captain Becker."

"Lieutenant, I'm in a hurry. Get to the point."

"Yes. Right." Hardy paused and Reynolds heard paper shuffling. "I've got DNA results here. I think they might be related to your case. Fitzgerald ordered them. Do you want them, or should I give them to Fitzgerald?"

Reynolds felt a flash of rage that Fitzgerald had defied her, and then realized the profiles had to have been ordered some time ago. "When were the comparisons made?" she asked.

"A while back. Before June, at least."

Reynolds considered. These DNA profiles must have been analyzed before Hart was charged with murder. It probably didn't make any difference to her case, but she didn't want to risk it. There was no telling what Fitzgerald was capable of, and she would take no chances. "Don't give them to Fitzgerald," she said. "Send them straight to me."

38

Amanda Jordan

Tuesday, November 14, 4:30 p.m.

J ordan was impressed with the way Fitzgerald was handling the case. Detectives were usually passive-aggressive toward defense attorneys and sexist—and made it as difficult as possible for her to do her job. They forced her to get a court order before turning over any reports or information about her case and made it clear how annoyed they were whenever she called to ask for anything. But Fitzgerald was different—easy to talk to and respectful—not in any way dismissive. It wasn't necessary for her to do anything more than ask in order to get a complete copy of the murder book. Why couldn't all cops be like him?

Jordan carefully studied the murder book she'd received from Fitzgerald, with its crime reports, photographs, and autopsy results. It was not easy to go through. In her career, she'd seen photos of brutally murdered victims again and again, but Sarah's photos were particularly gruesome, perhaps, even the worst.

There was no denying that things looked bad for Daniel. There were two people there on the night of the murder—and everything in the murder book pointed to those two being Jake Babbage and Daniel Hart.

But something was very wrong. And she was going to have to dig deeper to find it.

The Judge Daniel Hart that Jordan knew was kind, compassionate, and fair. She smiled to herself thinking about the cases she worked on with Daniel when he was a prosecutor. He'd gladly lose a case than take the chance an innocent person might be convicted. As a judge, she appeared in front of him many, many times, and she could always count on him to do the right thing. She looked up to him, and yes, she had to admit, she loved being in his courtroom.

The person who murdered Sarah Collins was a vicious, sadistic sociopath. Jordan had defended such people. They were cold, calculating, shallow, and totally devoid of empathy or human feelings. The very opposite of Judge Daniel Hart. But precisely the characteristics Jake Babbage displayed.

Jordan had started her career as a public defender. It was difficult to get that first job working for the Los Angeles Public Defender's Office, but it had been worth it. In the six years she worked as a deputy PD, she tried over a hundred cases, ranging from drunk driving to death penalty murders. She left the PD's Office to go out on her own in the late 1980s. That, too, had been difficult at first, and she had survived by being a court-appointed lawyer in cases where the Public Defender's Office declared a conflict. Judges, prosecutors, and other defense attorneys had commented on her dedication to her clients, the thoroughness with which she researched her cases, her willingness to go anywhere, anytime to investigate the minutest factual point or legal issue. She worked hard to do all this with style, respect, and good humor. Judges and juries responded by going her way, giving her a win-loss record (almost always a win) that she could be proud of.

But Jordan remained an unknown until she got an acquittal in the famous Huntington murder case. Patricia Huntington had been charged with the poisoning-murder of her husband, Senator Arthur Huntington. Jordan proved to the jury that her client was an abused spouse who lived in constant fear of her life, and killing Senator Huntington was justified as self-defense. The publicity from that case launched her career. After that win, she never had to worry about finding clients or earning a respectable living.

Her thoughts were interrupted by the receptionist on the intercom line. "Amanda, Judge Hart is here to see you. Shall I bring him in?"

"No, I'll come get him."

Jordan walked to the reception area. Hart was seated in one of the straight-back chairs next to a corner end table. Poor guy, she thought, and her heart went out to him. She had never seen him like this before. He looked like he hadn't slept. He was wearing blue wool slacks with a beige camel hair sport coat. His tie was loose and his shirt wrinkled, but his blue eyes were alert—and sad.

She hugged him. He felt stiff and unresponsive. "Daniel, good to see you," she said.

The two walked down the hall into Jordan's corner office. Once seated at her desk, Jordan asked, "You have a new assignment?"

Hart sighed. "I got reassigned after my arrest, handling traffic infraction matters out of the downtown traffic court on Hill Street."

"I'm glad you weren't suspended," Jordan said.

"They can't. As an elected and sitting judge, I can't be immediately suspended or removed from the bench, even though I'm accused of murder. To remove me requires action by the California Commission on Judicial Performance, and it can't do so without a lengthy investigation and hearing. It's easier for the superior court to put me in a traffic assignment until the trial concludes. If I'm convicted, removal is automatic. If I'm acquitted, the Commission can independently decide if there was misconduct and whether further action is necessary."

Jordan shook her head sympathetically. She walked around her desk, sat in a chair next to Hart, and took both of his hands in hers. Daniel's hands were cold and damp. "I know this is a difficult time for you. But you mustn't be discouraged."

Hart shrugged. "I'm not sure anything really matters. There are times when I've considered pleading guilty. All that stops me is the fact that I can't bear to see that bastard Babbage getting away with it."

"You can be certain he *will* get away with it if you plead guilty," Jordan said. "But we need to take things one step at a time. If we can prove he's a liar, he'll lose his immunity and be prosecuted as the real murderer. It's going to be all over for him."

Hart nodded, but it was clear he was not convinced. She took a deep breath. "I asked you to come in so we could take a bit more time to discuss strategy before tomorrow's arraignment in Van Nuys. The grand jury has delivered its indictment. You and I agreed you wouldn't waive your right to a speedy trial, because the case against you is weak, and we don't want to give the prosecution time to strengthen it. We've also found out the name of the Orange County judge who's hearing the case. Jack Fields."

Because Hart was a superior court judge in Los Angeles County, Jordan knew that all judges within the county were automatically disqualified from hearing his case, according to Judicial Council rules. Hence, Orange County and Judge Jack Fields.

"I know who Fields is, but I haven't actually met him," Hart said. "His reputation's pretty good. He's been teaching felony sentencing to new judges at the Judicial College at Berkeley for years."

Jordan knew about the Judicial College, and the fact that Judge Fields taught there indicated that he must be competent. But it said nothing about Fields's judicial temperament, or whether he would have the guts to dismiss this case if that was warranted.

"The prosecution still has no corroboration of Babbage's testimony," Jordan said.

"I'm not surprised. Babbage is a liar."

She nodded and looked directly into Hart's eyes. "There are two items that worry me. The semen and the knife. So far, no knife has been found, and I believe it's unlikely it will show up—but we need to be prepared for any surprises in that area. With respect to the semen,

Babbage said he got a blowjob from the victim before he was knocked out. He claims he doesn't remember whether or not he ejaculated. If he did, the semen found in the victim's mouth should match his DNA. If it does, it does corroborate his story."

"No, it doesn't," Hart replied. "It just means he ejaculated in Sarah Collins's mouth, and that he was with Sarah that night—all consistent with his being the murderer."

She considered. "According to Babbage's statement, you forced Sarah Collins to have oral sex with you, too."

Hart took a breath. "I want you to arrange a comparison of my DNA to the sample from Sarah Collins's mouth. You'll find—"

Jordan held up her hand. "I'll get your side later. Let me continue."

Hart scowled. "You don't seem to understand. I *am* responsible for the death of Sarah Collins. If it weren't for me, she'd still be alive. I'll never be able to live that down."

Jordan raised an eyebrow, although she was too professional to show any other reaction. Her job was to provide the best defense for her client. She'd learned long ago not to be too curious or surprised at anything a client mentioned or didn't mention.

But she still wondered why the prosecution hadn't asked for a blood sample or DNA swab from Hart to compare. Perhaps the physical evidence from the murder scene hadn't been properly preserved and no DNA profile could be obtained from the semen sample. Such facts would be useful to know, but Jordan could not ask without tipping her hand. Besides, she feared if there were a DNA profile, the sample would compare positive for Hart and provide the corroboration the prosecution so far had lacked. She put her hands on his and looked directly into his eyes. "I think it's best for us not to make the comparison. The risk is too great."

"You still don't understand," Hart said, removing his hands from hers, staring back. "I'm not asking your advice on this issue. I'm directing you, as my lawyer, to arrange for the comparison. Period."

"Of course, whatever you want," Jordan said, without missing a beat, as if it was the most logical thing in the world for Hart to want. "But you must realize that a positive DNA result would destroy you in court? As of now, they have no way other than Babbage's word to prove that you were even at the crime scene."

"I was there. I remember every detail as if it happened yesterday. The semen in her mouth was *not* mine."

"But why not wait for the prosecution to move first? And why should we take such an all-or-nothing risk?"

Hart's eyes softened and became sad, enormously sad. "For the truth," Judge Daniel Hart said. "For Sarah Collins. For Sean and Erin Collins. For my conscience."

"Of course," she said, and thought to herself, *my God, of all the people I've ever defended, this man is extraordinary.* Then to Hart: "So be it, then. Tomorrow at the arraignment, I'll make the request."

They walked back to the reception area without talking.

"Good-bye, Daniel. Be strong," she said.

"Thank you," Hart said.

Jordan watched him leave. Was it her imagination, or did he look more determined—more in charge of himself?

39

Jordan

Wednesday, November 15, 1:30 p.m.

The next day Jordan met Hart in the hallway in front of Department R in Van Nuys. The courtroom was still locked, so they sat quietly on a bench outside. She said nothing, but thought it must be humiliating for Hart, a judge, to wait in the public hallway in a courthouse where only a short time ago he presided.

Jordan heard footsteps and turned. It was Doris Reynolds. She had a scowl on her face, and did not meet Jordan's eyes as she walked casually up to the entrance, found it was locked, and then stood waiting. She looked at Hart and shook her head.

She wears too much makeup, Jordan thought.

Presently, the bailiff opened the courtroom door. They went inside and sat in the spectator section, and waited.

The bailiff announced Judge Fields, who entered from a door marked "private" behind the bench. Fields sat at the bench. He looked fit, fiftyish, with thick, graying brown hair. He wore narrow reading glasses, which he used to look down at an open file on his bench. He called the case.

Jordan whispered into Hart's ear, "Let's go." She and Hart walked up to the counsel table. To the judge, she said, "Amanda Jordan, for my client, Daniel Hart, who is present, Your Honor."

Reynolds stood. "Doris Reynolds for the People, Judge. May I take the plea?" Reynolds spoke in a haughty tone that always irritated Jordan when she opposed her.

"You may," the judge said.

"Daniel Hart, you are charged in count one of the indictment with murder in violation of Penal Code Section one-eighty-seven. It is further alleged that said murder was committed in the commission of forcible oral copulation, in violation of Penal Code Section two-eighty-eight-a, subsection c, a special circumstance, making you eligible for a sentence of life without the possibility of parole. It is further alleged that said murder was intentional and involved the infliction of torture, in violation of Penal Code Section one-ninety-point-two-a, subsection nineteen, also making you eligible for a sentence of life without the possibility of parole. Does Counsel waive further reading of the indictment and statement of rights?"

"So waived," Jordan said.

Reynolds smiled. "How do you plead, guilty or not guilty?"

Hart flushed. "Not guilty."

"Do you admit or deny the special circumstance?"

"Deny," Hart said.

"Mr. Hart," Judge Fields said, "your not guilty plea is entered as is your denial of the special circumstance."

He looked at Jordan. "When can your client be ready for trial?"

"Your Honor," Jordan responded, "my client does not wish to waive his speedy trial rights and asks to have a trial date set as soon as possible."

Reynolds raised her eyebrows, and then shook her head. "The People need more time, Judge. I realize we cannot force the defense to waive time, but Ms. Jordan should know that if she forces us to an early trial, the People will oppose any continuance in the future."

"This will be fine with us," Jordan replied.

Judge Fields glanced at a wall calendar. "Trial will be December thirteen of this year. Anything further?"

"Yes, Your Honor." Jordan took a breath, steeled herself for Reynolds expected response and continued. "I ask that the prosecution be ordered to split the semen sample in their possession, so my client can have it analyzed and compared to himself and to an existing DNA profile of the People's primary witness, Mr. Jake Babbage."

Fields looked to Reynolds and asked, "The People's position on this?"

"There's not enough left for a split, but the People do have a sperm fraction that could be compared to that of a suspect. If the defendant voluntarily submits a blood sample, we would arrange to have it typed and compared, but we don't know if the comparison can be made by trial." Reynolds looked at Jordan, a self-satisfied smile on her face. "Perhaps the defendant wants to waive his speedy trial rights and wait for the comparison."

Jordan shook her head and frowned. "We will not waive time, Your Honor, but we will submit a blood sample for my client. May we have an order for a rush comparison? And what about Witness Babbage—can we get his DNA profile for comparison also?"

"I will ask him if he will submit," Reynolds said.

"All right," Fields said. "An expedited comparison is ordered. If Witness Babbage provides a sample, that will be included. If not, the defense will have to make a motion. Court's in recess."

40

Hart

Thursday evening, November 16

It was dark in his living room, but Daniel Hart was not aware of the darkness. He'd been sitting in his leather reading chair for two hours, brooding about his life and listening to the sounds of traffic outside his window. When he first sat down, it was still light outside. His right hand was resting in his lap, holding a Smith and Wesson chrome, five-shot, .38 caliber snub-nosed revolver.

He'd bought the gun six months ago. Because of his job, he felt he needed to have some means of defending himself if someone he'd sentenced ever confronted him on the street. He went to a firing range and learned how to load and aim the weapon, how to squeeze the trigger slowly and smoothly until it fired. He practiced twice a week for a month. He became familiar with the feel of the gun, taking it apart and cleaning it after each practice. He applied for, and received, a permit to carry a concealed weapon.

At first he felt secure driving home every day. But eventually, he started to worry about what he would do

233

if an incident actually did occur. Could he actually shoot someone? And what would he do if he only imagined a danger and actually hurt another human being?

He began to realize how truly deadly a gun could be.

Just looking at it tonight reminded him that death was so close, so easy. What would it be like to hold the gun up to his head and pull the trigger? There was comfort in that thought. It would be a way for him to atone for what he'd done. All the pain, all the guilt, all the worry about the future could be over in an instant.

He picked up the gun and put it against his temple.

At that moment, the doorbell rang.

Hart froze. He could feel the circle of cold steel pressed against his temple. For an instant he thought that this had to be the police again, and he couldn't bear the thought of another confrontation. Maybe he should just squeeze the trigger—end it all and be found immediately.

The doorbell rang again.

No. It was a coward's way out. He must face this, no matter what the consequences.

He put the gun in the drawer of the end table next to his chair. He got up, turned on the lamp beside his chair, walked to the front door, and opened it.

Sean Collins was at the door. "Can I come in?"

Perhaps Doris Reynolds was behind this. If so, Sean might be wearing a wire. But looking at Sean standing there, Hart flashed back to the five-year-old boy he had babysat nineteen years ago. *It's the same kid,* he thought. *Good-looking. Bright eyes. Why hadn't I noticed the resemblance before?*

"Yes, of course," Hart said.

41

Sean

Sean was surprised to see that the interior of Hart's house was dim, lit only by a single lamp in the living room. The whole place had a gloom about it. Faded floral throw rug over hardwood floor, mahogany coffee and end tables, dark-green ceramic lamps on the end tables. Brown—almost black—leather couch and easy chair. An antique wooden floor lamp with a green shade by the chair. There were no knickknacks, no objects d'art to give the room character. Only the plants—lush and green—softened the otherwise sterile room. Ferns on the end tables and coffee table, a ficus tree in one corner of the room.

Daniel Hart motioned toward the couch. "Please sit down," he said. "Would you like something to drink?"

"No thanks." Sean sat stiffly on the couch, posture erect. He wanted to demonstrate that he was all business.

Hart went to the leather chair.

The light from the lamp next to Hart's chair cast shadows on the walls. A small clock on the coffee table in front of the couch ticked softly

Sean could hear the refrigerator compressor in the kitchen. A car passed outside. *Maybe this wasn't such a great idea,* he thought. He felt more nervous than he thought he would, although it surprised him that he was not afraid. If Hart really was the person who'd stabbed his mother to death, then he was a dangerous psychopath, capable of anything. But looking at this sad, quiet man, Sean couldn't imagine that there was any harm in him.

"You know why I'm here," Sean said at last.

Hart nodded.

The two men continued to sit in silence, until Sean spoke again. "I know I shouldn't be asking you any questions, and frankly, I'm surprised that you're talking to me."

Hart looked down, but did not reply.

"I don't know how to say this," Sean began.

"No," Hart said, "I didn't kill your mother."

Sean exhaled. "But Fitz ... Detective Fitzgerald ... said that based upon what he knows, there's every reason to believe you were involved."

Hart wore a pained expression. "Yes. I was involved."

Sean seemed to sit up even straighter.

"I babysat you and your sister."

Sean leaned forward, looking directly at Hart, trying to recall if this was the face of the babysitter he remembered. He couldn't be sure. This Hart looked tired, old. And sad. Utterly sad.

"She was very beautiful," Hart said, absently. "I'm sorry, Sean. So goddamned sorry."

Hart had tears in his eyes. The tears enraged Sean. *Stop playing games,* he wanted to shout. Instead, he kept his tone even and swallowed his anger. "Were you there? Tell me."

"Yes, I was there ... but when things started happening ... I didn't think he'd really hurt her. I thought he might scare her, might threaten to kill her, but not ... not actually rape or kill her. Please believe me. I didn't know. I didn't know."

Hart stared at the floor, took a deep breath, shook his head slowly, and then looked up at Sean. "This has tormented me all my life," he said. "I've tried to make up for it, tried to show myself that I deserved to go on. I know that being sorry isn't enough. I still dream about that night. Sometimes in my dreams I do the right thing, and Sarah doesn't die. Then I wake up." He paused. "Even at fifteen, a person makes choices, and they have to live with the consequences. You can't undo something that you did, no matter how much you regret it."

"You were fifteen?" Sean asked, his voice shaking.

Hart nodded. "Skinny, weak ... almost no life experience. I had no friends. At the time I thought of him as an adult. He must have been nineteen or twenty. I never knew his real name—just 'Snake.' That's what everyone called him at the pet shop."

"Snake?"

"Yes," Hart said. "Because he had these ... pet snakes. Two giant, red-tailed boa constrictors. In the beginning, he hired me to help him—to come by his house every evening to clean up after them and to feed them. Of course, he never actually paid me. He kept them in a shed on this lot where he lived in a trailer. At first, I thought they were magnificent. Snake told me they weren't dangerous unless they were hungry, and even then, they wouldn't ever attack a man, unless he was bleeding. He said the boas could smell blood with their tongues. Boas don't actively squeeze their prey to death, he told me. Rather, they wrap and constrict themselves around their victim as it exhales, making it impossible to inhale, and it ends up suffocating.

"Snake had a volatile temper. If he thought he was being disrespected, he'd flare out of control. One time, he told me that the snakes needed more substantial food than the mice we had at the pet shop, that he needed me to go find and trap a cat or small dog in my neighborhood. I refused, and he went into a blind rage. 'Snakes have to eat, too,' he yelled. He said if I didn't respect that, then he'd feed me to his snakes. I tried to fight him off, but he was too strong—he had huge hands with a grip like a vise. He cut my arm and pushed me into the shed with the snakes. It was so dark. I was so scared ... I tried to get out, but he'd locked the door shut. I thought I was going to die ... He kept me in there for probably thirty minutes ... It seemed like an eternity. Even though nothing happened, I've been terrified of snakes ever since."

"Why the hell would you associate with Babbage after that?"

"I didn't." Hart said. "For a while at least. But then he called me, apologized. Said I didn't need to help with the boas, that he had more work for me. Said he missed seeing me around. So that's when I started babysitting you and your sister. Of course, he didn't pay me for that, either."

"So you just let yourself be used?" Sean asked.

"Looking back at it now, of course I should have realized that I was being manipulated. But at the time, I guess I just felt ... I don't know ... noticed and needed. Snake treated me like I mattered. No one pushed him around, he told me. He took what he wanted, when he wanted it. He bought us beer and hung out with me—as long as I paid and did what I was told. I felt . . . accepted.

"He always had this enormous knife," Hart continued. "He called it his KA-BAR. You don't want to know the details—"

"Yes, I do."

Hart paused. "It must have been at least eight inches long. He kept it in a leather sheath on his belt. He used to take it out to clean and sharpen it almost every day. Said that just having it visible made people show him more respect."

Hart recounted how Babbage had asked him to go to the reservoir to hang out with Sarah and him and to smoke pot. How they drove there, broke in, and sat on the roof of the roundhouse at the end of the pier.

"I don't understand why you went with them in the first place," Sean said. "You were a fifteen-year-old, and they were both adults. What could you possibly have in common with them?"

"Like I said, for me, going out with them that night for the first time, it seemed a reward for being, what I'd call now, Snake's lackey. As for why Snake brought me along, well ... he had me pay for the beer and pot. Maybe he thought he could show me how he did his stuff. I have no idea what was on his mind, but he must have had his reasons for wanting me to come with them. At first, sitting on the roof of the roundhouse, smoking pot, hanging out ... it was okay. Until Snake and your mom started kissing. When Snake tried to go further, your mom said no. She wanted to leave. And that made him mad. As I said, he had a violent temper. I didn't think he was a murderer, though."

"What about his story that he and my mom went into a secluded area in the brush?" Sean asked. "And the blow to Babbage's head. What about that?"

"It's a complete fabrication. I never hit Snake with anything, although I wish to God I had. But I was just a skinny kid. He was a full-grown adult. A powerful man with a wrestler's body. Plus he had a knife. And once everything started, I was petrified. I was afraid if I didn't do what he said, he'd carve me up and feed me to those snakes of his."

Sean shook his head. He felt revulsion so strong that his throat constricted. "There was oral sex performed on both you and Babbage. If that's so and if Fitz can manage to get a DNA marker, you'll show up," Sean said. "That's the corroboration they need. You'll be convicted for sure."

"There won't be any markers. Not from me."

"Are you sure?"

"I remember every detail as if it happened an hour ago. No. I was too scared, too humiliated."

Sean frowned. "But what about Babbage's statement? That you hit her and made her do it to you?"

"It's a goddamned lie! I never hit your mother. Snake did."

Sean's mind was reeling. "I still don't understand. Why would that sick fuck care if you came or not? For that matter, I still don't get why he took you to the reservoir that night. None of your story adds up."

Hart considered. "I've wondered about those things too. Countless times. I'm not sure I know the answers, but ... I don't think he planned on killing her. My guess is he was showing off when he started kissing her. Demonstrating to me how much he was in control of his woman—what a big man he was. When she said no and walked away, he saw it as disrespect and went into a rage—like he did when I refused to help him feed his snakes—and then it all just escalated. Snake forced your mom to do what she did to me so he could involve me in his crime. That way I wouldn't go to the police because I'd have to implicate myself."

"As a public defender, I've seen that before. But those unfamiliar with the system think it makes no sense."

"Look at me now. He's free and I'm going on trial. His strategy worked."

"In other words, you think he *planned* to blame it on you if he was caught?"

Hart shrugged. "It was his insurance."

"You still haven't explained how my mother was killed," Sean said, "and what part you actually played."

"You can't really want to know the details of how she was killed. I sure as hell don't want to think about it, and I was there."

"Damn it, tell me."

Hart sighed. "After your mother finished doing what she did to me, Snake came at her with that knife, the KA-BAR. They struggled. Somehow, your mom managed to knock the knife from Snake's hand and it fell on the ground. I scooped it up and ran away. I should have thrown it into the reservoir but I didn't." Hart paused.

"Go on," said Sean tightly.

"When I came back to see if your mother was all right, I saw her on the ground, crying and struggling, but Snake was straddling her, holding her wrists above her head. When he saw me, he held her wrists with one hand and held out his other hand. He demanded the KA-BAR. I said no. I told him I was afraid he was going to hurt her. He became infuriated. 'Give me the fucking knife,' he shouted. 'If you don't, I'm going to cut off your fucking balls and feed you to my snakes.'"

"Your mother begged me not to. Pleaded with me to help her ..." Hart's eyes again filled with tears.

"You cowardly son of a bitch," Sean said. "You gave him that knife, didn't you?"

"It all happened so fast," he murmured, nodding. "I moved toward him with my arm out to hand it to him, then hesitated. But before I could change my mind, Snake snatched it. He jabbed her with the point and she screamed ... I couldn't believe what I was seeing, what was happening. More screams ... I squeezed my eyes shut and covered my ears with my hands ... I was backing away, when I tripped and fell and hit my head on something hard. I must have lost consciousness for an instant ... and then I couldn't breathe ... I was choking on my own vomit. I managed to scramble to my feet and I ran ... I ran as fast as my legs would carry me ...

"I'm so sorry, Sean. I know I should have stabbed Snake with the knife instead of handing it back to him. Or I should have thrown the damn thing in the reservoir." Hart paused. "God forgive me that I didn't."

Sean's heart was pounding. "Did you help him with the cover-up?"

Hart shook his head. "Once, I almost went to the police. But at the last minute I backed out. Another regret."

"One last question," Sean said. "Why tell me now?"

"You asked me," Hart said simply.

"Aren't you afraid that I'll tell the prosecutor?"

Hart looked at Sean, as if to say, do what you have to do.

"I've got to go," Sean said.

He hurried out without looking back, got into his car, and floored the accelerator. The Celica hesitated, then lurched forward, heading for the freeway. *That fucking coward. A coward nineteen years ago and a coward now.*

Hart would pay.

He would find Fitz tonight and tell him what Hart had said. Fitz would get it to the prosecution. Sean's testimony would cinch the case against Hart.

Up ahead, Sean could see Ventura Boulevard and a red traffic light. He slowed, stopped, and waited for the light to change. Ten seconds passed, twenty seconds. Still the light was red.

Should Hart get the death penalty? When it came to the rest of the world, Sean had always been opposed to it. Since becoming a public defender, he'd dedicated himself to helping the accused. He wanted someday to defend a murder case.

But this was different.

The light turned green.

42

Sean

Erin lived with a roommate whom she'd met in her Alcoholics Anonymous group. Their place was a furnished, two-bedroom apartment in West Hollywood, off Crescent Heights, near Santa Monica Boulevard. They lived on the second floor of a U-shaped, two-story complex. Her roommate worked nights as a waitress at Norm's Restaurant on La Cienega. When Sean called, Erin insisted that he come over immediately. Now they were sitting at a small Formica table in Erin's tiny kitchen, which was filled with the aroma of freshly brewed coffee.

"I'm going to Fitz and tell him everything," Sean was saying. It felt good to talk to Erin about the episode with Hart. Just getting it out had eased much of his anger.

"I don't understand," Erin said. She was wearing jeans and a dark-gray YMCA sweatshirt. She pushed up the sleeves, then leaned over the table. "You said Hart gave the knife to Babbage out of fear. Isn't that something like self-defense? And wouldn't that mean that Hart *wasn't* guilty?"

Sean shook his head. "Hart wasn't protecting himself."

"But he was, wasn't he?" Erin said. "Babbage might have killed him if he'd said no."

"Murder is different than any other crime." Sean explained. "If I hold a gun to your head and tell you to rob a bank or commit any crime other than murder, you wouldn't be guilty because you were forced. But if I hold a gun to your head and tell you to kill someone, you would be guilty. The law doesn't allow you to take someone else's life to save your own."

"That's not fair," said Erin.

"Sure it is." Sean sipped his coffee. "Try to look at it from Mom's point of view. She was helpless. Hart had a knife in his hand. Babbage demanded that Hart hand it over. She knew as soon as Babbage got the knife, he was going to kill her." Sean felt his face reddening.

Erin reached over the table and touched his arm. "It's okay."

Sean nodded.

"In a way, I was lucky being a baby at the time," Erin said. I never really knew her. All the same, I've always wondered what it would have been like." She swallowed the rest of her coffee, got up with her cup and went to the counter, where she picked up the coffee carafe. "Do you want any more?"

Sean shook his head.

She poured coffee and returned to the table. "I don't know about you, but when I was fifteen, I didn't know shit. I got into drugs and wound up on the street. And why? Because I went along with the crowd. I wanted to be liked. Now I'm finally learning to take care of myself."

Sean frowned. He was thinking about the PD's Office. About his clients. Most of them were guilty of just being dumb. Others were a product of where they lived and who they lived with. If your mom and dad are addicts and you get the shit beat out of you daily, are you really to blame when you go out and do the same thing as your parents?

Then he thought of his mom again—begging Hart *not* to give Babbage the knife.

He got up and walked into the living room. He opened the sliding glass door that led out to a small balcony that overlooked the pool. Erin followed him out.

He gazed down at the pool, lit by underwater lights. "I just can't get that scene out of my mind," he said. "Looking at the pictures, reading the police reports ..."

Erin put her arm around his waist. "I know," she said. "I couldn't do it."

The two of them were quiet for a time. The night air was cool and damp. A crescent moon illuminated dark clouds. Sean thought it looked like rain. It felt good to have Erin's arm around him, and he put his arm around her. "Why didn't he just refuse to hand over the knife?"

Erin shrugged. "It's between him and God."

Sean sighed. "What he told me was enough to get him convicted."

A baby in one of the apartments started crying. In another, a man and a woman argued loudly. "Let's go back inside," Erin said. "It's chilly out here."

Sean closed the sliding door. They sat on a grayish-white couch that was not very comfortable. Erin said, "What are you going to do about what he told you?"

"I don't know."

"If you tell Fitz, Hart will go down for sure."

"Isn't that what *should* happen?" Sean said.

"I don't know," Erin said. "It just seems like this stuff is all backwards. *Babbage* is the one who should be on trial, and Hart should be the guy with immunity."

Sean said, "But if I don't say anything, Hart may go free."

"But Hart *should* go free, Sean. He was just a kid. He didn't know any better."

"You wouldn't say that if you were in the same situation our mom was."

"Maybe not. But I've had enough people telling me what I should have done or how I could have 'used better judgment.' What a crock."

She went into the kitchen, and started opening and closing cabinet doors. "I know I have a pack of cigarettes somewhere in here."

"I thought you gave up smoking," Sean said.

"I did."

She returned a minute later with a cigarette in her mouth and a book of matches in her hand. She lit her cigarette. She took a long draw, inhaled, and then she turned and blew the smoke away from Sean. "God, that tastes good," she said. She took another drag. "Sean? Don't say anything to anyone about Hart. Not yet."

"Why not?" he asked.

"You can always spill it later. But until you open your mouth, we're still in control for once."

43

Sean

Friday, November 17, 8:45 a.m.

Sean had some trouble finding Babbage's place. He drove to Chatsworth, but the map showed dotted lines for the streets that led to the address. When he got to the vicinity, apparently the dotted lines signified unpaved and dusty gravel roads. There were few address markings. Eventually, he found what must be Babbage's. The property looked unimproved, covered with dry brush, with a dirt road between two Joshua trees that led to a locked, chain-link gate. He parked on the dirt shoulder across the road and waited. He knew that Babbage worked the graveyard shift and should be coming home soon.

After twenty minutes, a red Toyota pickup truck pulled up to the gate at the front of the property. With the engine still running, Babbage got out of the truck and unlocked the huge padlock that secured the gate. Turning around, Babbage looked in Sean's direction and frowned.

Sean got out of his car and approached. "We've seen each other in court," he said. "I'm not sure that you know this, but I'm Sarah Collins's son."

Babbage looked at Sean for a moment. Sean couldn't tell if there was any recognition in Babbage's eyes, but the look wasn't friendly. "How'd you get my address?"

"It was in the file," Sean said.

"Bullshit. It's confidential information."

"I don't mean the Sarah Collins file," Sean said. "I'm talking about the Erin Collins matter. I was one of her attorneys on the probation violation case."

Without replying, Babbage pushed open the gate, then got back into his truck, drove onto the property, and parked on the other side of the fence. Sean followed and stood at the gate as Babbage stepped out of his Toyota. The road on the other side of the fence continued. Brush and pine trees obscured Sean's view of what lay beyond the road.

"I have a question for you," Sean said.

Babbage pushed the gate closed, locked it, and began to walk away.

"Snake," he called out to Babbage. "That's what they called you, isn't it?"

Babbage stopped, turned. The morning sun was behind Babbage, making it difficult to see his expression. The two men stood in silence, then Babbage came back, unlocked the gate, and held it open.

For an instant, Sean froze. Babbage would be a fool to risk his immunity by harming him. But he realized he was in the presence of a man who was there the night his mother was murdered. It was an eerie feeling, and he hesitated. But he'd come this far and he had to play this thing out, no matter what. He swallowed hard and walked through the gate.

Babbage locked the gate after him and briskly moved up a steep, winding driveway. Sean hurried to keep up, listening to the crunching of gravel beneath Babbage's boots.

It was a clear day. Pine, eucalyptus, and magnolia trees dotted a landscape of weeds and rocks. Dense brush grew in front of chain-link fences on either side of the property and on the steep upward slope, abutting the rear of Babbage's lot. There was an unpleasant cloying smell in the wind that Sean couldn't identify.

At the top of the driveway, an old Airstream trailer glinted silver in the morning sun. Babbage stomped through knee-high bent grass at the side of the trailer with Sean behind him.

A brown shed about the size of a children's playhouse stood at the rear, shaded by a massive oak tree. Next to it sat a pine rabbit hutch. Families of white rabbits were inside.

Babbage took out a gray plastic container from underneath the hutch, unscrewed the lid and scooped out rabbit food. He opened the wire mesh front. The rabbits cowered and crowded to the rear as Babbage poured feed into wooden troughs at the side of the hutch.

Using a hose, Babbage added water to a tank over the rabbit enclosure.

He looked up at Sean. "Who told you I was called Snake?"

"I talked to Hart."

Babbage frowned. He reached into the hutch and pulled out a pink-eyed, trembling rabbit by the scruff of its neck. The creature struggled, but Babbage put it in the crook of his arm, held it tightly with his hand. With his other hand, he reached into his pocket and took out a tiny box cutter and made a sharp movement across the back of the rabbit's neck. A bloody smear stained the rabbit's snowy-white fur. "What did he tell you?"

Sean stared at the rabbit. "Why did you do that?"

Babbage walked over to the large shed, opened the door, gently put the rabbit inside, and closed the door. Sean could hear movement inside, but it was dark, and he could see nothing. "I asked you what Hart said to you."

Sean could feel the morning sun beating down on him. Beads of sweat formed on his forehead. "He told me his version of what happened. Now I want to hear yours."

Babbage reached into the hutch again, took out another rabbit and repeated the procedure. "You're a public defender, right?" He put the second rabbit into the shed, and grabbed another from the hutch.

Sean nodded.

The rabbit squirmed and almost freed itself, but Babbage held on. "Then you must know," he said, as he again made a slit at the back of the rabbit's neck, "that you leave investigation to the pros." He opened the shed door. The frantic rabbit jumped inside. There was more movement inside the structure. "Amateurs muddle up the facts."

Sean's mouth went dry. "What's in that shed?" he asked, knowing the answer.

Babbage walked back to the hutch, reached under, retrieved a towel, and wiped his hands.

Sean had the urge to get the hell away from this man, but he pushed on. "You said in your statement that Hart wanted you to hang out with him. Why would you, a twenty-year-old, want to hang out with a fifteen-year-old?"

Babbage stepped closer to Sean, his face inches away. His foul breath made Sean sick to his stomach. "Do you want to see what's in the shed? I'll show you," Babbage said, grabbing Sean's arm with a vise-like grip. Babbage's eyes were cold.

Sean jerked his arm away. "This is a waste of time," he said, hoping his voice was strong enough to cover his fear. "I'm out of here." Sean turned and headed quickly back down the gravel driveway.

The gate was locked.

Babbage caught up with him, unlocked and opened the gate, but blocked his path with an arm. "You're playing with fire, Chief. If you're not careful, it will consume you. Remember that."

44

Sean

Monday, November 20, 8:30 a.m.

The headquarters of the Los Angeles Public Defender's Office occupied the penthouse floor of the ten-story courthouse in Van Nuys. By PD standards, the office was plush. Meetings were held in a large central conference room that had a view of the entire San Fernando Valley. A long hall stretched from one side of the building to the other with the conference room at the center. On either side of the conference room were offices shared by up to four deputy public defenders. The public reception area was directly across from the central conference room. Sean Collins shared the first office next to the conference room with three other deputy PDs.

Sitting at his desk this morning, Sean thought of how he loved his work and surroundings. More importantly, he enjoyed his interaction with other PDs. They were people he could go to for advice, people who understood the everyday difficulties of defending persons accused of crimes. Most people looked at criminal defense lawyers as one level above their clients. He was sick of people asking him how he could defend guilty people. How he could work to defend murderers and child molesters. People who asked those questions were never satisfied with statements that everyone deserved a defense, no matter how unpopular they were, that innocent people would have no chance if the mere fact that they were accused of a heinous crime prevented them from being defended. But working in the public defender's office he was surrounded with people like himself, who knew that guilt was not a black and white situation.

But now, he was contemplating a move that would require that he give up, at least temporarily, working here.

His phone rang. It was Beth Daniels. "Great news," she said. "I just got a call from Chuck Allen about your sister Erin's probation violation hearing set for Wednesday. They decided to stipulate that Erin's probation be reinstated without a hearing."

"I heard last night they might do that," Sean said. There was relief in his voice.

"It's a smart move," Beth said. "The prosecutor wants a murder conviction and their chief witness, Babbage, would have to testify in your sister's case. So why risk fucking up a murder case just to get a small-fry probation violation?"

After hanging up, Sean picked up his phone and called Erin. He got her answering machine and left a message with the good news.

Sean put on his suit jacket. He walked down the hall to Beth's office. She was sitting at her desk, studying a stack of police reports. She looked up when he came in. "Erin's hearing was the only thing stopping me from taking my leave of absence," Sean told her. "Now that she's squared away, I'm going to HR to arrange for the leave. Also, I've got a critical errand to run, but I'll be back to the office before eleven."

"Any cases that need coverage this morning?" Beth asked. "I'd be glad to handle them for you."

Sean was halfway out the door. "I'm okay. All of my cases were transferred last week, except for Erin's."

"Let me know if there's anything I can do."

Sean nodded. "Thanks. Actually, this morning I made up my mind about this Hart case. Since then, I've felt a lot better. See you when I get back."

45

Sean

True to his word, Sean returned to the PD's Office by eleven. For the last half an hour, he had been research-ing the law of accomplice liability, using Westlaw's online automated case search system terminal. It used to be that in order to find controlling appellate cases, lawyers had to search volume by volume through the books of pub-lished cases. Now, everything was in the West Publishing Company's computerized database, and any subject could be researched in a fraction of the time, without having to open a book. Many older lawyers couldn't adapt to the system, however, giving newer, computer-literate lawyers like Sean a distinct advantage. His intercom line buzzed.

Judy, the receptionist, announced, "Doris Reynolds is in the lobby. She'd like to see you."

"I'll be right out." *Here it comes,* he thought.

He put down the phone, logged out of Westlaw, and walked across the hall to the reception area. Reynolds was standing in the center of the room, hands on hips. She was dressed as if she'd just come from court, maroon skirt with beige blazer. She held a document in her right hand. Fitz was with her. His face was flushed and he appeared ill at ease. *Poor Fitz—caught in the middle—I hope he'll forgive me.*

Fitz spoke first, "Sean, sorry to drop in on you without warning, but—"

Doris Reynolds cut him off. "I'll do the talking." Her expression was dead serious. She handed Sean the document. "This is for you," she said. "It's a subpoena. But perhaps it won't be necessary for you to actually testify, if you tell me what we need to know now. She looked toward the door facing the inner offices. "Is there a place where we can talk? If what you say doesn't add to the case, we'll tear up the subpoena and you can go on your way. Otherwise—"

Sean interrupted. "Follow me, please."

He led them into the central conference room. This was where Sean had interviewed so many clients and witnesses—his turf. It had huge windows, and as usual at this time of day, the afternoon sun bore into the room, making it hot and stuffy. Sean took a seat with his back to the window, forcing Reynolds to look into the sun when she looked at him. As he expected, she took the seat across from him on the other side of the large oak conference table. Fitz sat at the head.

Reynolds took a pen and spiral notebook out of her purse. She looked at Sean, squinting. "I understand you met with Daniel Hart last week. Is that correct?"

Sean nodded.

Reynolds smiled without humor. "What did he tell you?"

"I'm sorry," Sean said, "but I'm not at liberty to discuss that."

Reynolds frowned, looked at Fitz. "Tell him," she said.

Fitz looked uncomfortable. "You'd better answer her, Sean. It's either here or in court."

Reynolds held up her hand to shield her eyes from the bright light. "Let's not play games, Mr. Collins. I know you met with Hart, and I know he described the events of the murder. As a lawyer, you must know that if you don't tell me everything you know now, I'll be able to point out to the jury that you weren't cooperative. Although I can't imagine why you would want to shield the man who murdered your mother."

"I told you," Sean said, smiling. "I'm not going to discuss anything Judge Hart said."

Reynolds reddened. "You'll either tell me now or tell me in court. It's up to you."

"I don't think you understand," Sean said.

"I understand, all right. For some idiotic reason, you want to protect a murderer."

"He's not a murderer," Sean said.

"Is that what he told you?"

"Ms. Reynolds, please understand me. I'm not going to tell you what Judge Hart said to me. Not here and not in court. And there's no way you can compel me to do so."

"Oh?" she snapped. "And just what legal basis are you relying on to avoid being held in contempt?"

"Because," Sean said, "this morning I met with Amanda Jordan."

"And?" Reynolds sneered. "What could she possibly have said that makes you think you can avoid my subpoena?"

Sean smiled, looking first at Reynolds, then at Fitz. "I've just agreed to join Judge Hart's defense team. Anything he may have told me is protected by attorney-client privilege."

BOOK FOUR

46

Judge Jack Fields

Wednesday, December 13

Judge Jack Fields felt uncomfortable sitting in another judge's chambers. The whole room reflected another person and another person's habits, and it made Fields feel out of sorts. Nevertheless, this was going to be his home-away-from-home for the next six to nine weeks while he presided over the People versus Daniel Hart trial. He would have preferred to stay in Orange County and handle that court's business, but he'd been asked by the Chief Justice of the California Supreme Court to handle this case. A Los Angeles County judge had been accused of murder, and the law presumed that any L.A. County judge would be biased toward the defendant.

Two buzzes from the clerk interrupted his thoughts. Fields got up and went to the coat rack to put on his robe. His regular robe was back in his Orange County chambers. He'd brought a spare, but it had a zipper rather than snaps and took longer to put on. That done, he opened the chamber door and went across the back hallway to the courtroom.

The bailiff, Deputy Sheriff Rick Powell, stood up as Fields entered the courtroom. "All rise and face the flag of our country, recognizing the principles for which it stands," he announced. "Court's now in session. The Honorable Jack Fields, Judge, presiding."

Fields did not usually require his bailiffs to recite the formal entry speech when he sat in his home court, but this was different. A superior court judge was being tried for murder, and Judge Fields had to do everything he could to preserve the dignity of the justice system that he loved.

A judge accused of murder was something extraordinary, a matter of great shame. Fields hoped the facts would show that this accused judge was not guilty, that it had all been some colossal mistake. Regardless of the result, this was clearly a disgraceful new low point in the system of law and order that he himself represented. For all these reasons, he'd required his bailiff to use the formal speech each morning when he entered the courtroom. He did this to have people show respect not for him, but for the office he occupied: Judge of the Superior Court of California.

Fields walked up the two steps leading to the bench and sat down.

"Be seated and put all reading materials away," the bailiff said after Fields had taken his place. Everyone sat down, except for the people at the prosecution and defense counsel tables.

As was his habit, Fields studied the courtroom before speaking. Bright fluorescent lights illuminated the room, and the judge's bench gave him a unique view of everything and everyone. It also gave every person an unobstructed view of him, and he felt the weight of all eyes in the room watching, waiting for him to announce that the proceedings were to begin.

It never failed to elate him when he sat down in *his* courtroom. Even when he was having a bad day, he still experienced a sense of euphoria. He felt this way because he was being trusted with the incredible responsibility of deciding other people's lives. Pretty good for an ordinary guy like him.

His gaze took in the podium and the counsel tables on either side of it, the prosecution to the left, the defense to the right. By tradition, the prosecutor sat closest to the jury, because the prosecutor had the burden of proving the case. Since the bailiff was responsible for the security of the courtroom, the defendant, Daniel Hart, occupied the chair closest to the bailiff, to Fields's right. The bailiff sat at a small desk to the right of the defense table and in front of the court's lockup door. Judge Fields looked at Daniel Hart, sitting at the counsel table, directly in front of him. Hart was writing on a yellow legal pad, then must have sensed that Fields was looking at him, because he looked up and for an instant their eyes met. Hart's eyes were deadly serious and profoundly sad. Here was a man that last year would have been a colleague, someone he could have joked with and talked with about the challenges of being a judge. Fields couldn't help wondering whether he was looking into the eyes of a murderer.

"The court calls the People versus Daniel Hart case," Fields said. He made a point of always referring to a defendant by name rather than the label "defendant." Fields felt that trials were, as a rule, dehumanizing, and it was his obligation to remind everyone that they were dealing with human beings. "May I have each of your appearances for the record, Counsel?"

"Mr. Hart is present with Counsel, Amanda Jordan." She motioned to a young man, standing to her left. "Sean Collins will be assisting me throughout the trial, but will do no examination of witnesses, Your Honor."

"Deputy DA Doris Reynolds for the People of the State of California." She'd been looking at Jordan as she spoke, and frowned when the lawyer referred to Sean Collins.

"Are both sides ready for trial?" Judge Fields asked.

"The defense is ready, but we have a request, Your Honor," Jordan said. "We need to know the results of the DNA comparison that Ms. Reynolds has been coordinating."

Reynolds buttoned the jacket on her forest-green pants suit and glared at Jordan. "The DNA profiles of the defendant and of Witness Jake Babbage have been submitted to Biotech Markers, but we do not have the results as yet. We will inform the court as soon as they are available. It's not too late to delay the trial, if the defendant needs the results before proceeding."

Jordan said, "We will not waive time. Will the court order Ms. Reynolds to produce the results the instant she gets the information?"

"No court order is necessary," Reynolds snapped, before Fields could respond.

Reynolds's rudeness surprised Fields, but he said nothing. He needed to get a better feel for this woman, before taking corrective action. His patience was always rewarded one way or another.

"However, a more important issue must be decided before we begin, Judge." She paused, and then looked at Jordan. "The People intend to call Sean Collins as a witness in this case. But, as you can see, Mr. Collins is here in the courtroom at the defense table." She motioned toward the young man Jordan had introduced, who was standing between Jordan and defendant Hart.

"I object," Jordan said sharply. "Sean Collins is co-counsel. The prosecution cannot violate my client's attorney-client privilege. Besides—"

Reynolds interrupted. "There's no privilege involved! Sean Collins is the son of the murder victim in this case. Ms. Jordan can't hide a material witness in the case by making him co-counsel."

Fields thought for a moment. In all his years on the bench, he occasionally had seen members of the victim's family rally around the person accused of the murder. But a victim's son on the defense team? Truly extraordinary. There had to be more to this.

Fields looked at Reynolds. "What's your offer of proof? Exactly what will Sean Collins testify to?"

"Two areas, Judge," Reynolds said, crisply. "First, Mr. Collins was interviewed by Detective William Fitzgerald shortly after the murder took place nineteen years ago. Mr. Collins will describe persons who were friends of his mother and will identify the defendant as being one of the friends."

"That does appear to be appropriate testimony," Fields said. "Ms. Jordan, shouldn't the People be allowed to present that testimony to the jury?"

Jordan shook her head. "No, Your Honor. Ms. Reynolds has not been accurate in her offer of proof. For one thing, Sean Collins was five years old at the time of the murder. He did not identify Judge Hart. In fact, he was unable to describe anyone."

Reynolds's reddened and pointed at Jordan. "Judge, whether *she* likes it or not, the People have a right to call Sean Collins as a witness. It's—"

"For what purpose?" Jordan interrupted. "Even the victim's son believes my client is innocent. Why else would he agree to serve as a member of the defense team?" She pointed back at Reynolds. "It's *she* who's trying to confuse the jury. If Mr. Collins remembers nothing, what possible purpose can *she* have to put him on the witness stand— other than to intimidate and embarrass Mr. Collins?"

Reynolds glared at Jordan. "I resent that. I'm seeking the truth. It's the defense that's trying to conceal and hide evidence. Judge, you've got to see through this. It's for the jury to decide whether or not what Collins has to say is significant. Sarah Collins, the victim in this case, was stabbed fifty times and sexually assaulted."

"Objection!" Jordan shouted.

"Sustained. Ms. Reynolds, stick to the law. Both of you sit down."

Judge Fields considered. The situation presented a real problem. At stake were issues involving fundamental rights. It was well settled that an attorney should not be both a witness and an advocate. But it did appear that the

People had a right to call Sean Collins, if he were actually a witness to important events that occurred long ago. The fact that he now represented the defendant couldn't change that. Fields looked at Reynolds. "What was the other reason you wanted to call Mr. Collins as a witness?"

Reynolds stood. "Mr. Collins recently had a conversation with Daniel Hart. I'm certain that the defendant confessed the murder to him."

Jordan jumped up. "Objection! Outrageous. Totally false!"

"That's why he must testify, Judge!" Reynolds shouted. "In the interests of justice. To find out the truth."

Jordan flushed. "Mr. Collins's conversation with Judge Hart occurred a month ago, at the approximate time that Mr. Collins became co-counsel. Any conversation would be protected by the attorney-client privilege."

"That's nonsense, Judge, and Ms. Jordan knows it. Notice that she said the conversation occurred at the *approximate* time that Mr. Collins became co-counsel. I suggest that it happened *before* he became co-counsel. I'm prepared to prove that the statement is not privileged, and I ask the court to order Mr. Collins to testify, and to disqualify himself from being an attorney on this case."

Fields took a breath and considered. Perhaps Ms. Reynolds was correct. She was clearly an articulate and intelligent lawyer. On the other hand, this issue involved fundamental and constitutional rights—there was no room for error—his ruling had to be correct. "In order to rule on these two important issues," he said slowly, "I'll need to make an under-oath inquiry of Mr. Collins."

"Your Honor," Jordan said. "I object. I don't believe it's appropriate to question Mr. Collins."

"Your objection is overruled. These issues must be determined before a jury is impaneled. If you believe any question violates the attorney-client privilege, you may object and argue your point." Fields looked to his clerk. "Swear the witness."

Reynolds smiled.

Collins stood and raised his right hand. He had a look of cold determination. The clerk also stood, "Mr. Collins, in the cause now pending, do you swear to tell the truth, the whole truth, and nothing but the truth?"

"I do."

Collins walked to the witness box and sat down. "Ms. Reynolds," Fields said, "I'd like you to ask first about events nineteen years ago. Once the court has ruled on that evidence, we can go to the attorney-client privilege issues."

Reynolds remained standing and looked at the witness. "Mr. Collins, how well do you remember your mother's murder?"

"I'll never forget that night."

"Do you remember a subsequent interview with Detective Fitzgerald?" Reynolds indicated Fitzgerald, who was sitting next to her at the counsel table. The detective was looking intently at Collins.

"I remember the day he came to interview me," Collins said.

"You told Detective Fitzgerald about two people you knew, correct?"

"Actually, I have no memory of what I told Detective Fitzgerald."

Reynolds held up a document. "Would it refresh your memory if you saw the police report?"

"I've read it. It doesn't help. I don't remember what I said. It was a long time ago."

Reynolds pointed to Hart. "Do you recall ever seeing Daniel Hart prior to your assignment in the Van Nuys Courthouse?"

"No."

"Think back," Reynolds said. "Back to when you were a child. Surely you remember seeing Mr. Hart?"

Collins shook his head. "I've gone over this again and again in my memory. I just don't remember ever seeing Judge Hart before."

"What about Sergeant Babbage?" Judge Fields inquired. "Do you recall ever seeing him prior to your assignment here as a PD?"

Again Collins shook his head. "I'm sorry, Your Honor. I don't recall ever having seen either of them before. I wish I did."

"Can you honestly say that you *haven't* seen them before?" Fields asked.

"Your Honor," Collins said. "I was too young. I can't remember one way or the other."

Fields looked at Reynolds. "Ms. Reynolds, it doesn't appear that there is anything that Mr. Collins can testify about."

She shook her head. "I don't agree, Judge. I'll need him in order to establish the past recollection recorded exception to the hearsay rule, so that the police report can be read to the jury. Plus, I'll need him to establish the time of the murder."

Jordan stood. "Your Honor, as I said before, we would be willing to stipulate and agree that the police report can be read to the jury. We also would be willing to stipulate and agree to anything that Mr. Collins could testify to regarding that evening."

Reynolds frowned. "The People will *not* stipulate, will not agree, Judge. Under the law, you can't force us."

"We'll discuss that in a moment, Ms. Reynolds," Fields said, then looked at Jordan. "Do you need to cross-examine Mr. Collins on anything said so far, or can we go to the issue of attorney-client privilege?"

"I have no questions, Your Honor. We can go to the next issue."

"Very well," Fields said. "Ms. Reynolds, move on to the attorney-client issue."

"Judge," Reynolds said, "I haven't finished on the first issue yet. I have another argument I want to present."

"I'll hear your argument later. Move on."

Reynolds looked down for a moment, and then looked up again. "Mr. Collins, I would like you to remember back to last month, on November seventeenth, when you attempted to interview Sergeant Babbage at his residence. Do you recall that?"

"Yes," Collins said.

"You told Sergeant Babbage that you'd interviewed Mr. Hart, did you not?"

"I did say that to Mr. Babbage, yes."

"Were you telling the truth?"

"Yes."

"Then as of November seventeenth, you had interviewed Mr. Hart, correct?"

Jordan stood. "Objection, attorney-client privilege."

"Overruled," said Judge Fields. "I'll permit it, subject to a motion to strike."

Fields looked at Collins. "You may answer the question," Fields said.

Collins shifted position in his seat. "Yes."

"What did he tell you?"

"Objection," said Amanda Jordan.

"Sustained," said Judge Fields.

"But, Judge," Reynolds said, "Sean Collins did not become counsel until *after* his visit to Sergeant Babbage."

"You haven't established that yet, Ms. Reynolds," Fields said. "Objection sustained."

"When were you retained as counsel, Mr. Collins?" Reynolds asked.

"Objection," Jordan said.

"Overruled," said Fields.

"The same day that I saw Mr. Babbage," said Collins.

"Before or after?"

Collins hesitated. He looked to Jordan, who did not object. Collins said, "After."

Reynolds smiled. "So at the time you interviewed Mr. Hart, you had not been retained as his counsel."

"Correct."

"All right," Reynolds said. "Tell the court what Mr. Hart said to you."

"Objection. Attorney-client privilege," Ms. Jordan said.

"Sustained," said Fields.

Reynolds stood, hands on hips. "Judge, that ruling is just plain wrong. I've clearly established that the defendant was not represented by Mr. Collins."

"Ms. Reynolds," Fields said, ignoring her rudeness, "I believe if you review the evidence code, you'll see that the privilege extends to times before representation. If it were otherwise, persons accused of crimes would lose the privilege whenever they went to a lawyer, asking for advice."

Reynolds looked down at her notes, a puzzled look on her face. "Wait a minute," she said, then looked to Collins. "Who arranged your meeting with Hart?"

"What do you mean?"

"Did Mr. Hart request that you meet with him before the visit?"

Collins frowned. "No, I dropped in on him, unannounced."

Reynolds smiled. "So he didn't call you for the purpose of getting legal advice, did he?"

"No, he did not."

"I thought so," Reynolds said. "What did he tell you?"

"Objection," Jordan said.

"Sustained," Fields said.

"But, Your Honor," Reynolds said, anger in her voice, "the defendant wasn't asking for advice. There's no possible way that privilege could apply."

Fields was impressed with Reynolds's tenacity. And her point. If Hart didn't go to Collins for advice, maybe the privilege didn't apply. He decided no. It was a difference without a distinction. "Objection sustained," he ruled.

Reynolds exploded. "That makes no sense—you must reconsider," she demanded. "The defendant obviously confessed to Mr. Collins, and then had second thoughts. That's why he hired him as a lawyer. This is a transparent attempt to suppress testimony by hiding behind this so-called privilege."

Jordan stood. "Your Honor, I resent this accusation."

"Careful—both of you," Fields said. "I won't tolerate bickering. Ms. Reynolds, I'm sustaining the objection. Mr. Collins was retained as counsel within two days of the interview. I find that the privilege applies. As to the issue of Mr. Collins's testimony, I will preclude you from calling him. The parties will agree to stipulate to the reading of the report regarding Mr. Collins's interview when he was five years old."

"Judge, I already said we will not stipulate."

"That's your choice, Ms. Reynolds," Fields said. "But regardless of what you decide, Mr. Collins will not testify."

Reynolds fumed. "In that case, the People ask for a stay so that we can take a writ to appeal your ludicrous ruling."

Fields was outraged by her insolence, but he controlled himself, maintaining a calm demeanor. "Your request for a stay is denied." He looked at the clock.

"Court's in recess."

47

Fitzgerald

Monday, December 18, 8:30 a.m.

As the newly selected jury filed into the courtroom, Fitz thought about last week. After two and a half days of jury questioning, a jury of six women and six men was sworn. Reynolds told Fitz she was satisfied with the result. Fitz saw no pattern to Jordan's peremptory challenges, but Sean assured Fitz that the lawyer knew what she was doing. Fitz was still very troubled about the case. He was certain that Babbage was lying, and was frustrated that all his efforts to delay charging Hart until the case was sufficiently investigated had failed.

For the first time in his career, Fitz felt uncomfortable sitting on the prosecution side of the counsel table. Logically, he told himself, he must work with facts, not emotions. Fitz cared deeply about Sean, and if Sean had determined that Daniel Hart was innocent, then damn it, that meant something.

Reynolds's opening statement was first. She wore a just-above-the-knee linen skirt and matching jacket, with a silk blouse open at the neck, revealing the top of her lace bra. Smiling at the male jurors in the front row, she began, introducing herself as the representative of the People of the State of California. Then she became serious, looking intently at the jurors.

"On the fourth of July, nineteen years ago," she began, "that man"—she pointed at Hart, who looked up at her, unblinking—"killed Sarah Collins, a twenty-two-year-old mother of two."

Most of the jurors leaned forward, and the room was so quiet that Fitz could almost hear the jurors breathing. "You will hear the testimony of Jake Babbage, an eyewitness who saw the defendant put the point of a knife against Sarah Collins's neck and draw blood. Who saw Sarah Collins forced to perform degrading sexual acts on the defendant. And who saw the terrible result of the defendant's rage.

"You'll hear from Deputy Medical Examiner Doctor Ethan Crowlich that Sarah Collins was stabbed more than fifty times. Stabbed all over her body. But the most chilling detail is that forty-seven of the stab wounds were not fatal ... were less than an inch deep ... occurred before Sarah's death ... and therefore caused her *excruciating* pain." Reynolds looked at Hart and shook her head in disgust. Fitz looked at Sean. The color had drained from his face, and his hands grasped the edge of the table in front of him—he was visibly shaken.

"All this occurred while Jake Babbage was bound to a tree with duct tape, unable to move, unable to free himself, no matter how much he struggled. He will tell you that the defendant crept up behind him, knocked him out, and then bound him with duct tape. When he regained consciousness, he was forced to watch as his girlfriend was humiliated ... forced to hear her screams. He passed out again. When he came to, the defendant was gone, but the horrible result was there for him to see. Sarah Collins dead. Mutilated by the defendant, Daniel Hart."

Reynolds eyes filled. "This is a horrible case, and I'm sorry that you'll have to endure seeing it and hearing about it." Her eyes narrowed and she shook her head slowly. "The defendant tortured and killed Sarah Collins. He *must* be held accountable—justice demands it."

In the dead silence of the courtroom, Reynolds walked back to the counsel table, sat down, and wiped a tear from her eye.

Fitz was impressed. He'd watched the jury as she spoke. Looking at their faces, he could see they were horrified. It was as if they had endured the torture, the outrage. Reynolds might be a bitch, he thought, but she had just demonstrated that she was a brilliant trial attorney.

Amanda Jordan rose slowly. She walked to a point directly in front of the jury and looked at them, solemnly. Several jurors looked back, arms folded. Two men in the back row avoided eye contact. "The evidence will show," she said, "not only that Judge Daniel Hart is innocent of these charges but that the true murderer"—she paused, cast a scornful look at Reynolds, and then turned back to the jury—"is the very man who accuses him: Jake Babbage."

Reynolds was on her feet in an instant. "Objection. Counsel knows she cannot argue during her opening statement!"

"Overruled," Judge Fields said.

"Jake Babbage is a liar. A liar who waited nineteen years to accuse my client of the horrible crime he himself committed. The evidence will show that not one single shred of Jake Babbage's *story*"—Jordan said the word as if it were a lethal poison—"nor any part of Babbage's *claim*, can be verified or corroborated.

"The obvious question, the question that cries out for an answer is: why? And why now? The testimony at this trial will reveal the answer with clarity. You will find out, why Babbage—a rogue cop—accused my client, a respected and honored judge, of this vicious crime. I'm confident that you will agree, after hearing all the evidence, that the only possible conclusion is that Judge Daniel Hart is innocent of these charges."

Jordan walked back to the counsel table and sat.

Fitz now understood why Sean had joined the defense team. Jordan was one hell of a lawyer and had done a masterful opening statement.

48

Fitzgerald

Fitzgerald was to be the prosecution's first witness. During her trial preparation, Reynolds had asked him detailed questions about his friendship with Sean. Now that Sean had switched to the defense, Reynolds wanted to use Fitz to pressure Sean. She said that she wanted Fitz's testimony to flow smoothly and to show the defense that he believed in his case—very important because of Fitz's relationship with Sean.

Fitz walked to the front of the witness stand and was sworn by the clerk. He sat in the witness box, then stated and spelled his name for the record. How many times had he testified during his career? One hundred? Five hundred? More? It was a blur. He was surprised to realize that he was actually nervous. He glanced down from the witness box at Sean, sitting next to Daniel Hart and Amanda Jordan. Sean looked back at him and nodded, as if to say, "Do what you must." Hart was staring straight ahead, but Fitz could see that his eyes were moist and his shoulders rounded. He looked as if he would rather be any place other than here.

"Detective Fitzgerald," Reynolds began, "what is your occupation and current assignment?"

"I'm a detective, employed by the Los Angeles Police Department and temporarily assigned to the Internal Affairs Division."

"Was that also your occupation and assignment in July 1976?"

"No. At that time, I was a detective in the Robbery-Homicide Division."

"Were you, at that time, assigned to investigate the death of Sarah Collins?"

"Yes, the case was assigned to me."

"And going back to that period, on July fifth, were you called to a crime scene investigation at the Lake Hollywood Reservoir?"

"I was."

"Would you describe for the jury what you observed when you arrived?"

He took a deep breath. So many times over the years he'd obsessed over this case. Now, instead of being happy something was being done, Fitz was caught between an ambitious prosecutor and the one person who mattered most to him.

Fitz looked at Reynolds. "The victim's body was found early Monday morning, July fifth, by some hikers. It was roughly twenty feet from the water. The victim was naked, spread-eagled, and had numerous wounds resembling those created by stabbing. The wounds were in her chest and lower abdominal area. Judging by the volume of blood in the area of the body, it appeared that the body had not been moved from where injuries and death had occurred." Fitz paused and glanced at Sean, who was scribbling notes on a yellow pad. Sean had assured Fitz that he could handle the details of his mother's murder, but could he really?

In contrast, Hart's eyes were on Fitz. Color drained from Hart's face as Fitz described how Sarah's body looked when detectives arrived. At one point, Hart dabbed his eyes with a handkerchief.

As Fitz continued his testimony, he wondered whether it was his imagination or if the courtroom was as unbearably hot and muggy for others. He began to perspire.

Reynolds took an eight-by-ten photograph from a manila envelope and showed it to Jordan, who studied the photograph carefully as if she had never seen it before. She passed the photo to Sean, who looked at it. Hart did not.

Anyone else probably would not have noticed, but Fitz did. Sean glanced at the photo, paled, and then quickly returned it to Jordan. Fitz marveled that Sean could look at all. *No matter how stoic he tries to be*, Fitz thought, *nobody could listen to a description or see the things that Sean was forced to see involving his mom and not be deeply affected.* Before Reynolds could say anything else, Jordan spoke. "Your Honor, may we approach at sidebar?"

"You may," Fields responded.

Jordan, Sean, and Reynolds approached, along with the court reporter. Fitz watched as they gathered at the far side of the bench.

Judge Fields accepted the photo from Amanda Jordan without looking at it.

"Your Honor," Jordan said, "counsel is attempting to introduce the crime scene photo of the decedent. This photo is highly prejudicial and will inflame the jury."

"That's nonsense," Reynolds replied. "The photo is clearly relevant. We have a special allegation of torture-murder, and the jury needs to see these photos to see just how much the victim suffered and the extent of the injuries. It will serve to back up the coroner's testimony."

"But, Your Honor," Jordan countered, "this picture is unduly gruesome. Counsel can get the coroner to describe the wounds and their effect. Showing this picture serves no purpose other than to bias and inflame the jury."

Fields studied the color picture carefully. It was indeed gruesome. It showed a young woman's naked body as it lay on its back on blood-soaked ground. Her head was at an unnatural angle, the lids half closed, but still showing clouded, lifeless pupils. Her mouth was opened as if she had died screaming in agony. Stab wounds were all over her torso. Her breasts, her abdomen, her genitals. Her legs were spread open unnaturally, looking as if the killer had positioned them after death. Blood was everywhere. Fields made up his mind. "I will sustain Ms. Jordan's objection. I do find this picture unduly gruesome, and that its probative value is far outweighed by its prejudicial effect. The jury will not see the photo."

"But, Judge," Reynolds said, "this picture is important for the jury to see—"

Fields cut her off. "I've ruled, Ms. Reynolds. Please don't argue further."

Fields noticed that Reynolds continually referred to him as "Judge" rather than the more respectful "Your Honor." This was consistent with what Fields had heard about her, that she did all she could to control the courtroom and the proceedings. Some lawyers couldn't pull it off, would come across to the jury as wanting to win regardless of whether justice was served. But Reynolds knew how to walk the line, how to pressure the court to go her way. Fields would have to be vigilant and would have to make sure she never crossed the line. But he was already exhausted with her, and the case had only just begun.

He turned away, making it clear that argument was over and that it was time to continue the testimony. The three lawyers went back to their positions at the counsel table.

———

Although he couldn't hear the sidebar, Fitz could see that the pictures were being discussed, and based upon Reynolds's facial expressions, she was not happy with the court's ruling. But that was her problem, not his.

Fitz continued his testimony. He was present when the coroner's investigator arrived on the scene, and he had observed the investigator taking measurements and gathering fluid samples from the victim's body. Fitz described his follow-up investigation the day after the homicide: the autopsy, the interview of Sean Collins at MacLaren Hall, and his interview of Sarah Collins's neighbors.

"Were you able to get any descriptions that would help you in determining possible suspects, Detective?" Reynolds asked.

"None of the neighbors had any useful information. I interviewed the victim's five-year-old son, but he was not able to provide me with any descriptions."

"Exactly what did he tell you?" Reynolds said the words in an even tone, but her eyes bore down on him, seeming to say, *don't fuck this up or else.*

"He said that his mother had two friends he could remember. One was a babysitter he said was named 'Chief' and the other he described as the 'snake man' who lived at the zoo. He was unable to provide any other details."

He checked the Griffith Park area. He found no homeless man living in the park, or in the area of the zoo. There were many who lived in the bed of the Los Angeles River and Fitz questioned them, but no one had any information. He did a search of field investigation cards prepared at or around the murder, looked for any possible suspects who might have a snake tattoo. He interviewed an elderly aunt who lived in Ohio. The father of the two children had been killed in Viet Nam. There were no other living relatives.

"In short," Fitz said, "I hit a brick wall."

"Did anything occur within the last six months that alerted you to suspects in this case, Detective?" Reynolds asked.

"Yes."

"Please tell the jury what occurred."

Fitz shifted in his chair. He'd rehearsed what he was about to say with Reynolds. She'd made it clear to him that he must be very careful in responding to questions, not to show any negative bias to Babbage. "If you destroy this case," she had said, "I'll destroy you."

Fitz finally answered, "I became aware that a witness had given a statement that implicated Daniel Hart."

"What were you told?" Reynolds asked.

"Objection," Jordan said. "Hearsay."

"Sustained," said Judge Fields.

Reynolds asked Fitz, "Without telling us what occurred, did you do anything in response to the statement given?"

"I arrested Daniel Hart."

"Do you see Daniel Hart in the courtroom?"

"We will stipulate to identity, Your Honor," Jordan said.

"We will not," Reynolds said flatly. "Please answer the question, Detective."

"Yes, I can identify him." Fitz knew that Reynolds was doing this for effect. Technically, a defendant had to be identified in open court. In cases involving lineups or eyewitnesses, the identification of the accused was critical. In cases such as this, defense attorneys usually stipulated. But Reynolds had told Fitz that Hart needed to be treated like any common criminal.

"Please indicate the defendant and describe what he is wearing," Reynolds instructed.

Fitz pointed to Hart, who looked back. "That's him, sitting at the counsel table, wearing a brown suit and tie."

Reynolds stood. "May the record reflect that the witness has identified Daniel Hart as the defendant in this case?"

"The record will so reflect," Judge Fields said.

Reynolds looked at Hart, then at the jury. "I have no further questions at this time of this witness." She sat down.

"You may cross-examine, Ms. Jordan," Fields said.

Jordan stood at the counsel table. "Detective Fitzgerald," she asked, "did you search the area surrounding the crime scene for the victim's clothing?"

"Yes, we looked for articles of clothing, or for that matter, anything that would help us identify the victim or the perpetrator."

"How thorough was the search?"

Fitz took a breath and considered. "Our team consisted of eight patrol officers, two detectives, and a criminologist. I personally conducted the search. It included dragging the bottom of the reservoir, combing a radius of perhaps one hundred yards from the crime scene."

"Was this made more difficult because of the surrounding vegetation?"

"It was, but we searched all paths through the brush and all nearby clearings, and examined the base of trees, bushes, and weeds."

"What were you looking for?"

"Anything. Sometimes articles are thrown into a brush area; sometimes a victim is moved from an initial location."

"So blood or blood on rocks or objects would be important?"

"Of course."

"Other than the immediate area where the body was located, did you find any blood on the ground?"

"No."

"On any rocks or trees?"

"No."

Jordan paused and looked down at her notes, then looked up. "Detective, think back carefully. Did you find any duct tape?"

Fitzgerald hesitated, frowned. He looked through his case file. Finally he spoke. "No. None whatsoever."

"One last area of inquiry," Jordan said. "I note in your police report that you determined my client's date of birth to be June 20, 1961, correct?"

Fitz reviewed his investigation folder, then nodded. "That's correct."

"So," Jordan said, "with the murder having occurred on July 4, 1976, by my calculation, my client had turned fifteen just two weeks before, correct?"

"Apparently so, yes." Fitz said.

"And your so-called chief witness, Jack Babbage, his date of birth was July 30, 1955, making him just sixteen days shy of being twenty-one years old at the time of the murder, correct?"

"Correct as well."

"Detective Fitzgerald, doesn't it seem odd to you that a twenty-one-year-old man would have been hanging out and socializing with a boy barely fifteen years old?"

"Objection, irrelevant," Reynolds said.

"Overruled," the judge said. "You may answer, Detective Fitzgerald."

Fitz glanced at Reynolds before replying. She glared at him. She wasn't going to much like his answer, he thought. Too bad. He took a deep breath. "Now that you mention it, yes. It does seem quite odd."

"I have no further questions of this witness," Amanda said.

49

Sean

5:30 p.m.

Sean met Fitz at a public defender hangout, Casa José, a Mexican restaurant one block from the courthouse on Van Nuys Boulevard. The two of them sat at a table, eating chips and salsa. Sean filled their chilled mugs from a frosty pitcher of Budweiser.

"Reynolds would be pissed off if she knew we were meeting," Fitz said.

"Screw her," Sean replied.

"My feelings exactly," Fitz said, smiling. "After I finished my testimony today, she told me to get lost. She wanted to spend the evening coaching Babbage, and she thought I'd cramp her style. There's something weird between them. For her, Babbage can do no wrong. When I tried to reason with her, she came unglued."

"The word among the PDs is that she has a thing for cops," Sean said. "There's a rumor, she's slept with every detective in Van Nuys."

"I can believe it," Fitz said. "Makes me glad I'm assigned downtown." Fitz grinned, then turned serious. "What did you think of my testimony?"

"Very professional," Sean said. "I was looking at the jury, but I really couldn't tell what they were thinking. Reynolds, though, is another story. She's out of control."

"She's a pistol, all right. But it doesn't look like Fields is going to take much shit from her."

"That's one advantage of having an Orange County judge," Sean said. "Her threats mean nothing to him. When this trial is over, he's out of here. He won't care whether the LA deputy district attorneys like him or hate him."

The waiter, a tall, skinny kid Sean recognized as Mike, the owner's son, placed dishes heaped with steaming chicken fajitas, rice, beans, and tortillas on the table between them. "Careful, they're hot," he said.

Sean put a tortilla on his plate, piled on chicken, rice, and beans, and then folded the tortilla gingerly, before taking a bite. Fitz did the same.

Sean looked at Fitz. "I'm sorry I didn't tell you about my switching sides and joining the defense team."

"It's okay," Fitz said. His eyes were bright. "How are you doing on viewing the evidence? I was a little worried about the photo today."

"I can handle it." Sean replied. "It was difficult at first, but ...," Sean's voice broke and he didn't finish. He took a long gulp of beer.

Fitz nodded and looked at him sympathetically, and Sean felt guilty. All of his life, Fitz had been there for him, believing in him and being available whenever Sean needed him. And now when it had mattered most, he'd let Fitz down by not talking to him before making the decision.

The two men ate in silence for a time. "What exactly does Jordan have you doing?" Fitz asked.

"Not much, mostly going over testimony and running errands." Jordan had given Sean strict orders to say nothing about Hart's case. Sean was to meet with Fitz to determine exactly where Fitz stood. And if possible, to find out if there were any upcoming prosecution surprises—all without giving Reynolds any information about the defense.

Fitz drained what was left in his mug. "Tomorrow," he said, "the pathologist, Crowlich, is going to testify."

Sean blinked. It was as if Fitz had read his mind. "Is he any good?"

"The best," Fitz said. He turned and looked around the restaurant, then lowered his voice and said, "Reynolds has something planned."

"With Crowlich?" Sean asked.

"No. A clincher witness. Or as she says, the deadbolt lock to Hart's lifelong cell."

Sean thought he misheard. "What?"

"She won't tell me who it is. Says she doesn't trust me not to tip you off." Fitz grinned knowingly. "She's no fool, and neither am I. But I think I know who it is. She's—" Fitz looked up.

Mike had come up to their table. "You guys want anything else?"

Fitz shook his head. Mike put the check in front them and walked away.

Fitz said, "She's been talking to the Biotech Markers people—crime lab guys. Says they've got some kind of match, but it's preliminary and they need to explain."

Sean's spirits sank. *If Hart's DNA comparison is positive, then I'm the fool.*

50

Sean

8:00 p.m.

Amanda Jordan was sitting at her desk in her office—jacket off, surrounded by law books and police reports—when Sean arrived. "Where's our client?" Sean asked.

"I told him to go home and get some sleep. He's meeting us tomorrow morning in the courthouse cafeteria. What did Fitzgerald have to say?" Before Sean could answer, Jordan asked, "Who's our next witness?"

"The coroner. But—"

"Thought so," Jordan interrupted. "It's going to be an important day." Jordan picked up a document that Sean recognized as the coroner's report. "Something in here caught my attention. It might be the key to a dismissal by the court."

Sean reached for the report and began to scan it. "What is it?" As distasteful as it was for him, he'd read it again and again, and had not uncovered anything inconsistent with Babbage's testimony.

"Let's see how the testimony plays out. It could be nothing, so I'd rather not tell you just yet. If things go the way I think they will, I'll need your reaction, and I'd like it not to be tempered with previous knowledge."

Sean nodded, wondering what Jordan could have discovered. Maybe it was related to Reynolds's secret witness. "Does it have anything to do with Biotech Markers?"

"Not at all."

"Because," Sean said, "Fitz said Reynolds has a surprise witness."

"What?"

"Fitz thinks it has to do with the comparison of Babbage's and Hart's DNA."

Jordan stood, walked over to the floor-to-ceiling window at the side of her desk and stared out into the night sky. "It could be one of Reynolds's ploys. She knows how close you and Fitz are."

"Fitz overheard her talking to Biotech Markers lab people. Something about a match. Something they need to talk to her about."

"Reynolds can't withhold favorable evidence from us—that's clear Brady error and automatic reversal on appeal," Jordan said.

"I think she's going to wait until the last minute to spring incriminating results on us. Maybe we can get Fields to suppress it," Sean said.

Jordan walked back to her desk and sat, considering.

Sean became aware of the tick of Jordan's grandfather clock. *God*, he thought, *Reynolds is ruthless—willing to do anything to get a conviction.* "Doesn't she have to give us the results as soon as she learns of them?"

"That's what she's been ordered to do."

"Why don't we just subpoena the lab results?"

"That's what she wants us to 'do. If they're positive for Hart, she'll nail us."

"But don't we have to assume that Reynolds knows the results, and if they're positive for Hart, she'll use them?"

Jordan shook her head. "I've been opposing her for years. And I'm convinced of one thing: When it comes to Reynolds, we can't assume anything, except she'll do whatever she needs to win her case, ethical or not. We've got to make this decision independent of her. The stakes are too great to gamble."

"I say we should subpoena the results. If they're negative for our client, it proves once and for all that Babbage lied."

"I don't agree," Jordan said.

"But Babbage also said that he saw Hart getting a blowjob, and my mom spitting afterwards."

"That doesn't necessarily mean Hart ejaculated," Jordan commented.

"But doesn't that suggest he did?" Sean said. "That's significant, isn't it?"

Jordan shook her head. "There could be any number of reasons why she would spit—she could have gagged and regurgitated. All it means is that it will be a question of fact for the jury to determine—did she spit, and if so, why? If not, did Babbage lie?"

Sean grimaced and shook his head. "Okay, I get it. Without DNA results, we are still left with Babbage's claims being just that—unconfirmed accusations. But if DNA tests show the ejaculate in my mom's mouth came from Hart, Babbage is corroborated and the court can and will probably use Babbage's testimony to convict Hart."

"Exactly," Amanda said.

"But Hart swore to me that he did not ejaculate, and I believe him. So, if the DNA results are positive for Babbage and negative for Hart, Babbage looks like the murderer, doesn't he?" Sean asked.

"Two problems with that analysis," Jordan said. "First, it proves nothing, because Babbage admitted to having oral sex."

"Maybe," Sean said. "But it sure makes Babbage look guilty, and doubly reduces his credibility. What's the second problem?" Sean asked.

"As you know, Reynolds, as the prosecution, has the burden to prove her entire case beyond a reasonable doubt before she can rest, and before we have any obligation to present our defense. And once she rests, Penal Code Section eleven-eighteen-point-one allows us to ask the judge to dismiss the entire case on the grounds that the prosecution failed to meet their burden. If we were to win that motion, the case would be dismissed and never go to the jury."

"Right," Sean said.

"But if Reynolds rests without offering the DNA test results, we won't be able to mention the DNA results when we make our motion asking the court to dismiss the entire case. So, at a time when we need the results the most, the time when we make our motion to dismiss, we can't use them."

"Unless," Sean said, thinking out loud, "Reynolds stipulates that we can call the expert during her case. Or stipulates that our results are valid." He took a breath. "But Reynolds won't stipulate to anything,"

"Exactly. That's our second and greatest problem," Jordan said.

51

Sean

Tuesday, December 19, 8:30 a.m.

Despite his outward bravado to Fitz, Sean was anxious about the pathologist's testimony. Sean had night-mares after seeing the murder book photos and read-ing the crime report, and now he worried that the awful things he was about to see and hear would further destroy the memories he had of his mother.

He watched as Dr. Ethan Crowlich, MD, deputy medi-cal examiner and pathologist, a white-haired, professo-rial-looking man, was sworn. The physician wore a wool gabardine three-piece suit that was somewhat out of style. In his hand he held a manila file as he stood facing the courtroom clerk and took the oath.

"Doctor Crowlich," Doris Reynolds began, "I'd like you to remember back to an autopsy that you performed nineteen years ago."

Having taken his seat, Crowlich removed his rimless glasses and looked through a file folder he'd brought to the witness box. He put on his glasses and looked at Reynolds.

"Actually, I have no present recollection of that autopsy. I did bring the report, however. If you'll allow me, I can refresh my recollection by looking it over."

"Please do."

Sean took a breath and held it.

Crowlich removed his glasses and studied the report—then he looked up and put on his glasses again. "According to the report, our investigator, Paul Krause, was the first person from the Medical Examiner's Office to arrive on the scene. It was about eleven. He was led to the site where the body had been found. He made preliminary measurements on the body and gathered forensic evidence.

"The body had not been moved or touched but had been photographed by the police. As was his routine, after visual inspection and note taking, Krause put a thermometer into the decedent's liver and determined from its temperature that she had been dead for more than eight hours.

"Using cotton swabs, he took fluid samples from her mouth and vagina, as well as a series of blood samples from surfaces on the body. He observed what looked to him to be a semen-like substance in the victim's mouth. There appeared to be no such semen-like substance on or in the vicinity of the victim's vagina. I performed an autopsy on the decedent the following morning."

"Who was present during the autopsy?" Reynolds asked.

"Just Detective Fitzgerald and myself. And a photographer, of course."

"Please describe your observations, Doctor."

"The body appeared to be that of a healthy, well-nourished female Caucasian, approximately twenty-two years of age, sixty-seven inches in height, approximately one-twenty-five pounds. In the facial region, I observed contusions on the decedent's left cheek."

"Could you tell what caused this?"

"It appeared to be some sort of blunt force trauma, consistent with the use of a hard object. Probably a fist."

"Could you estimate the age of the trauma?"

"From its color, I would estimate that it occurred very close to the time of death."

"What do you mean 'close to'? Within minutes? Hours?"

"I can't be exact," Crowlich said. "The best I can say is that it occurred sometime within two hours of death."

Sean could feel his face burning and hoped it didn't show. To distract himself, he looked over to Hart. It was obvious that the descriptions were having a profound effect on him, also. Pale, he looked not at Crowlich, but at a spot somewhere above the pathologist's head. As a deputy DA, Sean thought, Hart must have heard this type of testimony many times. But now, Crowlich was describing not just some case, but the event Hart had told Sean he'd agonized over for almost twenty years. Was he re-experiencing the ordeal of that night?

Jordan had cautioned Hart not to show emotion during this testimony. "Do anything to distract yourself," Jordan had said. "Stare at Crowlich and think about law school. If all else fails, take copious notes on your legal pad. Whatever you do, *don't* look at the jury. But then, from your trial attorney and judge experience, you know that jurors don't like people staring at them. Even though lawyers do it all the time as they present their case, to get the jurors' reactions to a question, or to communicate with them using body language."

Reynolds continued to ask questions. "What else did you observe, Doctor?"

"The rest of the face appeared unharmed, indicating a single blow. I observed a series of small one-half- to one-inch cuts, starting slightly below the neck and covering the decedent's shoulders and breasts."

"Could you tell what caused these cuts?"

"Some sort of sharp instrument. Probably a knife."

"Did you measure the depth of these wounds?"

"Yes. Most were less than one inch deep and were not life threatening. Three of the wounds were quite deep, three to eight inches."

Reynolds picked up a large cardboard chart. On it was a front-view, generic diagram—an outline of a person, showing the head, torso, legs, and feet.

After it was accepted as People's Exhibit 1, Fitzgerald helped Reynolds mount the large chart on a board close to the witness box. Reynolds walked over to the mounted chart. Within the body outline were various markings. "Doctor Crowlich, referring to this chart, People's One, have you seen this before?"

"Yes, I have."

"Could you tell the court and jury what it is?"

"Yes. This chart is a blowup of a diagram I prepared when I performed the autopsy."

"Will you explain it please?"

Crowlich took a pointer from the side of the witness box. "This is the approximate location of the blunt force trauma to the victim's cheek." Crowlich pointed to an X on the diagram. "Here are the one-half- to one-inch cuts consistent with the use of a knife." He pointed to a series of marks over the shoulder and neck area of the diagram.

"Doctor, do you have an opinion as to the type of knife used?"

Crowlich considered. "Judging from the largest and deepest wound, I would say the instrument was some sort of very large knife with a hand guard. The blade width estimated to be approximately one inch at its hilt, possibly seven or eight inches in length."

"How are you able to determine the presence of a hand guard?"

"The guard prevents the perpetrator's hand slipping from the handle to the blade of the knife. When the instrument was at its full depth, the hand guard made an impression on the victim's body. This also explains the lack of any foreign blood at the wound."

"Returning to your diagram, were the shallow wounds life threatening, Doctor?"

"I would not say so, no," the doctor said.

"Would they be painful?" asked Reynolds.

"Yes." Crowlich replied.

Sean felt his stomach turn and for a moment, he thought he might vomit. He was afraid he might have to get up and leave.

"What about these four wounds, Doctor?" Reynolds pointed to four Xs in the left breast area.

"Those are quite serious." He motioned with the pointer to the second from the right. "Particularly this one."

"That particular one is an injury directly on the nipple, is it not, Doctor?"

Crowlich nodded. "It appears to be."

"What about these wounds, Doctor?" Reynolds pointed to a cluster of Xs at the lower abdomen.

"Those appeared to be postmortem," Crowlich replied.

"How could you tell?"

"Investigator Krause's report indicated no blood surrounding the wounds in that area, meaning the heart was not beating to pump blood to the injury."

"Anything else that you observed that was significant, Doctor?"

"The rest of the body was unremarkable, except for bruises on the wrists and abrasions at the waist, outer thighs, ankles, and feet."

"Any other observations?"

"Only that I noted the presence of semen in the victim's mouth."

"Anywhere else?"

"No."

"Doctor, based upon your observations, do you have an opinion as to the cause of death?"

"Yes. The victim died as a result of this wound." Crowlich pointed to the X that was over the left nipple. "Here the instrument was plunged full depth, piercing the heart. Altogether, there were a total of four fatal stab wounds."

"In your opinion, was this a painful death, Doctor?"

"Excruciating. The series of shallow wounds inflicted a great deal of pain prior to the delivery of the fatal wounds."

Sean felt rage overwhelm his nausea. *What kind of man could do these things to my mom? he thought.* He looked at Hart, who appeared to be struggling to retain composure, his face drained of color. No, Sean thought, *Hart could never do such a thing.* He looked at the jury. They were grim. One of the women was ashen; another was on the verge of tears.

"Do you have an opinion as to whether there had been a sexual assault prior to death?" Reynolds asked Crowlich.

"I cannot say for sure. However, the presence of the contusions on the cheek, coupled with the presence of semen in the decedent's mouth are consistent with forced sexual activity."

"Thank you, Doctor. I have no further questions at this time, Judge."

"Ms. Jordan, you may cross-examine," said Judge Fields.

As Jordan stood, Sean wondered what it was in the coroner's report that Jordan thought could lead to dismissal.

"Were there any cuts or injuries to the palms of the decedent's hands, Doctor?" Jordan asked.

"No, there were not."

"Is that significant?"

"It was ... interesting in light of the other wounds."

"Why is that?"

"Normally one would expect wounds to the palms of the hands. Such wounds are common with stabbing victims. They indicate that the victim was alert and aware during the attack."

"How so?"

"Stab victims typically try to protect themselves with their hands. The absence of stab wounds on the palms of the hands suggests that the victim was either unconscious or that her hands were restrained. The contusions on the wrists suggest there may have been an accomplice holding her wrists while the stab wounds were inflicted."

"Yes," Jordan said, nodding. "Thank you, Doctor. I have no further questions at this time, Your Honor," Jordan said.

The judge looked at Reynolds, who shook her head. "I have nothing further to ask," she said.

"Very well," Fields said. "Doctor Crowlich, you are excused. We'll take our luncheon break at this time. Court's in recess."

Well done, Amanda, Sean thought. He now understood what Jordan had noticed in the autopsy report.

52

Fitzgerald

As he'd done countless times before, Fitz sat at the counsel table, with a prosecutor on one side and a defense attorney at the other. Like before, he waited for a prosecution witness to give testimony to support the State's case. Except this time, he believed that the star prosecution witness was a liar. And Sean, the murder victim's son, the boy he'd watched grow into a man, was on the other side of the table. Was part of the defense team.

Fitz felt out of place, surreal, as he squinted in the harsh fluorescent light.

"The People call Jake Babbage as a witness," Reynolds announced.

Babbage moved with deliberate strides to the witness box, turned to face the clerk, raised his thick hand to be sworn. Babbage wore gray slacks and an ill-fitting blue blazer that didn't accommodate his muscular bulk. He sat, leaned back, splayed his fingers on the counter in front of him, and surveyed the courtroom. His hawk eyes were expressionless, but lingered an instant when he made eye contact with Fitz.

Once again, this son of a bitch is back in court, Fitz thought.

Reynolds walked to the podium, a determined look on her face. "Sergeant Babbage, what is your occupation?"

"I'm a police officer." Babbage replied.

Just like Reynolds to ask this question, Fitz thought. Obviously she was doing this to give Babbage more credibility. Fitz was certain Jordan would object and the judge would sustain, but she'd have made her point to the jury.

But Jordan didn't object.

"How long have you been a police officer?"

"Sixteen years."

Again Jordan just sat passively.

Reynolds continued to push the point, asking Babbage a series of questions about his last assignment, going over his background—including the fact that he was a patrol sergeant who supervised a dozen patrol cops. Babbage's answers were smooth, calm, deliberate, pausing for just the right amount of time, establishing a harmony between questioner and professional police officer.

Reynolds is playing this exactly right, Fitz thought.

The jurors had to be thinking they were in the presence of a prosecution team in control, a team that would guide them through the deliberative process and convince them beyond a reasonable doubt that Daniel Hart was guilty of murder.

And Jordan is letting her get away with it?

Finally, Reynolds got to the facts. Shown the snapshot of Sarah Collins with five-year-old Sean and two-year-old

Erin, Babbage nodded somberly. Yes, that was Sarah and her two kids. Yes, he had a clear recollection of the events nineteen years ago—a time before he became a police officer. He recounted word-for-word the same story that he'd given in his immunity statement. How he and Sarah had gone off to a secluded area because Sarah was uncomfortable kissing in front of the defendant. How the defendant came up from behind and knocked out Babbage. And when Babbage awoke, finding himself bound with duct tape, he saw the defendant use a knife to force Sarah to perform oral sex. And finally, after struggling and losing consciousness, seeing Sarah's mutilated body. Throughout his testimony, Babbage looked at the jury, punctuated his answers with facial expressions of sincerity and concern.

Fitz took a quick look at the jurors. All eyes were riveted on Babbage. Several jurors were scribbling in their notepads. One or two were crying.

"Sergeant Babbage," Reynolds said in an angry voice, her eyes moist, "can you identify the man you saw that night who forced Sarah Collins to orally copulate him, the man who admitted to you that he murdered her?"

"Yes."

"And is this person in the courtroom?"

"He is."

"Could you point him out and describe what he is wearing?"

Babbage pointed at Hart. "That's him. Daniel Hart. Sitting at the counsel table, wearing a dark suit and sitting in the second seat to my left."

"May the record reflect," Reynolds said, "that the witness has identified the defendant?"

"It will so reflect," Judge Fields said.

With a look of utter contempt, Reynolds glanced over at Hart and announced that the People had no further questions.

Hart, still pale, ignored Reynolds's gaze. Instead Hart stared unblinking at Babbage. Fitz stole another glance at the jury. Several were shaking their heads. An older woman in the first row glared at Hart.

Reynolds had buried the defendant, Fitz thought.

Why had Jordan allowed it?

53

Hart

Hart arrived early for the 7 a.m. meeting at Amanda's office. The office was open and Amanda greeted him with a cup of hot coffee and a wonderful smile. He always felt a lift when he saw her. She was wearing a perfectly fitted, charcoal-gray skirt and jacket that accentuated her slim figure with a powder-blue silk blouse that made her eyes look a lighter shade of blue. He knew it was natural for a man to be attracted to his female lawyer, especially someone as beautiful as Amanda, so he guarded himself against that. But he'd always admired and respected her, and never failed to enjoy being in her presence when they worked together professionally. Maybe in another world, things might have been different.

Sean arrived, and Hart's mood shifted downward as they got to work discussing strategy.

Last night, Amanda told him to get a good night's sleep and to be ready to discuss his reaction to what Babbage had testified to so far. *Right*, he'd thought. As if he could get any sleep. Most of the night he lay awake, reliving the night of the murder, agitated and outraged—*there was no limit to Babbage's capacity to perjure himself.* When Hart did fall asleep, the dreams were unbearable flashbacks where, again and again, he failed to save Sarah.

"The critical issue today is also central to the trial—Babbage's recorded immunity statement," Amanda told them. "No detail can be overlooked—nothing left ambiguous and nothing left to chance." She'd hired a court reporter to transcribe and index every word, and she went over the transcript again and again, comparing it to the police reports and pictures in the murder book.

Amanda played the audio recording of Babbage's immunity statement.

As it played, Hart felt his face burn. He fidgeted in his chair, rubbed his temples, and his eyes teared. When Babbage claimed that Hart struck Sarah across her face, Hart couldn't bear to remain sitting. He stood and paced back and forth to the corner window as the recording ran on. *Could anyone really take what Babbage said seriously?* Hart wondered. He tried to be objective, to put himself in the mind of the jurors listening to Babbage. After all, as a judge he'd had to weigh credibility time and again, and Babbage's story was full of holes. But the murder was so violent and so brutal, that the jury might want desperately to attach blame to someone and overlook inconsistencies. After all, Babbage was a police officer and juries wanted to believe the police. When the audio playback got to the part of his driving Babbage's car, Hart couldn't help himself and blurted, "That's absurd. Snake drove a stick-shift

Pontiac GTO. I'd just turned fifteen—I didn't even know how to drive an automatic transmission."

"I don't have to remind you, Daniel," Amanda said gently. "The jury's going to be watching you if any part of the audio recording is played for them. Just scribble notes as you hear it played. Don't say anything or show anything. I know this is going to be hard for you."

"I'll somehow do it," Hart said, wondering if he really could.

Sean spoke up. "Listening to this audio recording and thinking about what Babbage said yesterday during his direct testimony, I get so enraged. Obviously, Reynolds had rehearsed and coached that phony bastard to appear to the jury as a sincere police officer trying to do his job. What a crock. But it looks like it's working for Reynolds. Did you see the jury? They were eating it up."

"Maybe," Amanda said.

Sean continued. "And I thought about that night I visited Judge Hart, and we talked about what happened." He turned to Hart. "You were filled with guilt and recrimination, could barely speak of my mom's death without breaking down. That was honesty—what Babbage is selling at the trial and on his immunity statement is total bullshit. And what galls and irks me is that the jury is swallowing it."

"Actually, that's a good thing," Amanda said. "Because the more they believe now, the more they like him and trust him, the more they will despise him when we reveal what a liar and mendacious bastard he is."

Tall order, thought Hart. But then, if anyone could do that, it would be Amanda—he'd seen her do it countless times before.

Amanda continued. "Sean, tell Erin to be here tomorrow. But have her wait downstairs in the cafeteria—I don't want to tip off Doris."

"Okay," Sean replied. "She keeps asking when she'll be able to come to court and show support for us. As you instructed me, I told her she was going to be a surprise witness, and as a potential witness, she would not be allowed in the courtroom until it was her turn to testify, but nothing more."

"Good," Amanda said. "I don't want to chance Doris seeing her. You realize, of course, that you mustn't talk about the case with Erin?"

"I do now," Sean said. "But that night after I saw Judge Hart, I did talk to her. If we call her as a witness, what if she's asked what was said that night, after I'd interviewed Judge Hart? She'd have to testify to what I told her, wouldn't she? Have I blown everything?"

"It's okay," Amanda said. "If Doris tries that, I'll object—whatever you told Erin is hearsay and can't come in as evidence."

"I hope you're right," Sean said.

"I agree with Amanda," Hart said. "If I were the judge, I'd sustain the hearsay objection and not allow Erin to answer." *But then*, Hart thought, *Judge Fields may not see things the way I do.*

54

Sean

At 8:30 a.m., they were back in court, with the jury seated. As Judge Fields took the bench, Sean noticed he looked tired. No doubt Reynolds was getting to him. But the jurors, once seated, were alert, leaning forward in their chairs. Scanning their faces, he couldn't discern anything about what they might be thinking. As for Reynolds, she had an infuriatingly smug look that Sean wished he could slap from her face.

Judge Fields looked at Jordan and said, "You may begin your cross-examination." And then, "Mr. Babbage, you are still under oath."

Jordan stood. There was absolute silence in the courtroom, and Sean could feel the tension, an electricity in the air. Jordan walked to the podium, took a document from her case folder, examined it, and spoke. "In exchange for your testimony in this trial, you were given a grant of immunity, weren't you?"

"Yes, I was," Babbage answered without hesitation.

"And except for that grant of immunity, you would not be here testifying against my client, would you?"

Babbage sat straight in his chair, his face indignant. He looked toward Reynolds, then back to Jordan. "It was my lawyer's decision to require immunity. As far as I'm concerned, *I don't need it.* I did nothing wrong."

"Really?" Jordan said, tilting her head back, eyes wide with mock surprise. "According to what you told the jury, you contacted the prosecution, asking for immunity on October twenty-seven. You were in jail on that day, were you not?"

Babbage stiffened. "I had been released."

"Objection, non-responsive, Your Honor. I ask the court to strike the response and instruct the witness to answer," Jordan said. "It's a yes or no answer."

"Sustained," Fields said. "Mr. Babbage, were you or were you not in jail that day?"

"I had been in jail on that day," Babbage said.

"And charges were pending against you, when you asked for immunity, were they not?" Jordan asked.

Babbage shifted in his chair, and his face hardened, but he didn't reply.

Jordan turned to Judge Fields. "I ask the court to order the witness to answer."

"The witness is ordered to answer," Fields said.

"Yes. Charges were pending," Babbage said.

Jordan continued. "Let's see if I understand you. You waited for nineteen years to come forward with your ..."—Jordan paused as if searching for the right word—"... story? Correct?"

Babbage glared at Jordan. "With my testimony," he said. "Yes, that's right."

"And during this time, you never bothered to contact the authorities and tell them what you knew?"

"No, because I was afraid," Babbage said, putting his massive hands on the edge of the witness box.

"In fact, Mr. Babbage, you didn't tell anyone until you were jailed by Judge Hart, who had you charged with trying to extort a bench officer, correct?"

"After my confrontation with the defendant," Babbage said, his voice edged with contempt, "I decided that I couldn't go on any longer with this thing hanging over my head. I wanted to put an end to it."

"A conclusion you reached while you were facing charges and still in jail, right?"

Babbage narrowed his eyes. They flashed with hostility. "I came to that conclusion when I confronted the defendant."

"But for nineteen years it didn't bother you, did it?" Jordan demanded.

"It bothered me. But as I said, I was afraid to go to the police."

"Afraid they'd find out you raped and murdered Sarah Collins, correct?"

Babbage shifted in his seat, then sat ramrod straight. "I'm not the one on trial here. Your client is the murderer."

"Objection, non-responsive," Jordan said. "I ask the court to strike the answer."

Reynolds stood. "Judge, it's a perfectly good answer."

"Sustained," Judge Fields said. "The answer is struck. The jury is to disregard it. Mr. Babbage, listen to the question and answer it."

Reynolds face reddened. "May I be heard, Judge?"

"No," Fields said.

Babbage turned to look at the jury. "Of course I was afraid. I was young, in a bad situation beyond my control."

"So afraid that you burned and destroyed the evidence that could place you at the scene of the murder and aid the police in finding out who committed the murder, and then you ran away?"

Reynolds stood. "Objection. Assumes facts not in evidence. And argumentative."

"Overruled."

"As I said, I used poor judgment."

"You admit that your knife was the murder weapon, do you not?" Jordan asked, her voice edged with contempt.

Babbage stared at Jordan for a moment, then said, "That's the knife I saw in the defendant's hands."

He's choosing his words carefully, Sean thought. *The bastard is wary.*

"So you say," Jordan said. Reynolds started to object, but Jordan added, "Can you describe it?"

Babbage said it was an ordinary Bowie hunting knife. Jordan pushed for details. Did the weapon have a hand guard? It wasn't a weapon, Babbage said, but yes, it had a hand guard. How long was the blade? Babbage replied he wasn't sure, then admitted it was longer than seven inches but less than ten. How did he carry it? In a leather sheath on his belt. Did he wear it every day? Not every day, but most days, he admitted.

Asked where he got it, Babbage said he wasn't sure, but probably it was mail order, most likely from an army surplus catalogue.

"Army surplus? So this was a ... combat fighting knife?" Jordan asked.

Babbage reddened. "As I've already said, it was an ordinary hunting knife. Got that?"

"Why would you carry a combat fighting knife on your date with Sarah Collins?"

The long cords on Babbage's neck pulsed, and he said in a loud voice, "I always had it with me. It was a tool I used."

"Did you ever stab anyone else with this 'tool'?"

"Objection!" Reynolds shouted.

"Withdrawn," Jordan said, before Judge Fields could rule, "Did you ever use this 'tool' for protection?"

For a moment Sean thought Babbage was going to leap up from the witness box and attack Jordan. But then Babbage must have realized he was looking bad, so he sat back, gave a thin smile, and said, "It was strictly a utility knife. Period."

Jordan made a disgusted sound.

And then asked, "You say that you had a date with Sarah Collins that night?"

Babbage, adopting once more what Sean regarded as the phony calm and thoughtful look, replied, "Yes."

"You were nearly twenty-one and she was twenty-two at the time?"

"That's correct."

"And you're telling this jury that you took my client, barely fifteen years old, along on your date?"

"Yes," Babbage answered.

Jordan frowned. "Sarah had two children, a five-year-old and a two-year-old. Who was going to babysit those kids?"

"No one. They'd be asleep. I thought it would be okay to leave them alone for a couple of hours."

Fury. Sean remembered the night. The last time he saw his mother. July the fourth. Sparklers. Making circles of light in the air. Mom laughing. Erin dozing. In her high chair. Then, despite all the excitement—Sean in bed. Being tucked in. Kissed. Smelling Mom's flowery scent as he drifted off to sleep.

Sean had an urge to attack Babbage, to shake him, to make him suffer, but steeled himself. He noticed that Fitz was looking at him, concern in his eyes. Good old Fitz.

Jordan continued. "You're telling this jury that Sarah went along with all this?"

"Right." Babbage's cold eyes met Sean's for an instant, then he looked straight ahead.

Jordan glanced toward Sean, paused, and then stared at Babbage. "You're saying," she said, her voice thick with sarcasm, "that your twenty-two-year-old girlfriend did not mind her fifteen-year-old babysitter accompanying you on your date and leaving her little children all by themselves?"

Unruffled, Babbage replied, "Like I said, they were asleep. And I thought Sarah might enjoy having Hart along."

Sean heard a groan from one of the female jurors.

"What about after the murder? Weren't you concerned that they'd wake up alone, terrified?"

"I guess I didn't think about it."

Sean fumed. He remembered how terrified he'd been when he woke the next morning. *At the time Babbage stabbed Mom to death, he knew I was home alone with Erin.*

Jordan, as if echoing Sean's own thoughts remarked, "You were more concerned with your own skin, weren't you?"

Babbage tensed. He leaned forward, glaring, radiating hostility toward Jordan. Reynolds looked up from her notes. "Objection! Argumentative," she shouted.

"Sustained," said the judge. "We'll recess for lunch."

55

Babbage

Reynolds and Babbage met over the lunch hour.
"Fields needs to learn who's really in charge," Reynolds said. They were alone in her office, going over the testimony so far and planning for the afternoon. She'd told Fitzgerald to disappear—said if she needed him, she'd call.

Most of the other DAs were out.

Reynolds continued complaining about Fields. Babbage listened but said nothing. If she wanted him to comment, she could ask. For his part, Babbage was furious. Were it not for his immunity, and based upon what she'd let in, he'd be fired from the department. How could Reynolds have fucked up so badly? Her job was to convict and destroy Hart, but it looked more like Babbage was on trial! She couldn't control Jordan, and Babbage didn't understand why Reynolds deliberately pissed off the judge. It just didn't make sense.

"Your testimony today was acceptable, Jake. But you showed a little too much anger." She got up, walked around her desk, and sat in a chair next to him. She smiled, and her eyes glittered. She patted his leg just above his knee. "Stay calm," she said softly. "Jordan was purposely trying to get you upset today. Just let me do my job."

She crossed her legs, and her short skirt hiked to the middle of her thighs. He could smell her perfume mixed with perspiration. She was old, but her tits weren't bad, and he could see her nipples pressing against her silk blouse. She was acting like one of his projects.

He put the thought out of his mind—he needed her to win the case. Too bad. He'd enjoy making her suffer.

Almost as an afterthought, Reynolds said, "I don't have the DNA results yet. They're due today. If they're positive for Hart, that'll remove any doubt about the case and provide the corroboration we need. Without them—"

"What are you talking about?" Babbage almost grabbed her. The jury had to see through Jordan, he thought. She was a typical defense lawyer, trying to make a big shit deal out of meaningless details.

"I've been pushing to get the results," Reynolds said. "They say they'll have them any minute. I've told them to pull out all stops and to be in court today with the results, or else. They'd better be positive for Hart."

"Or what?" He leaned forward, his voice filled with contempt.

"In some cases," Reynolds replied evenly "and I'm certain it doesn't apply here—in some cases, you can't convict on eyewitness testimony unless there's corroboration. It's the accomplice rule."

Babbage noticed a foul taste in his mouth and suppressed the urge to spit in her face. Had he been wrong to trust his fate to this prosecution bitch? "Are you saying,"

he spoke slowly, clearly—he wanted to get this straight—
"that my testimony means nothing unless there's outside
proof?"

"Not as far as I'm concerned, but Fields is the wild
card. He was wrong not to force Sean Collins to testify
about Hart's statements. There must be a way to get
Fields to reconsider. I'd bet my life Hart said something
to Collins we could use as corroboration—something that
would clinch the case."

That's a bet he'd take. He sprang to his feet. "I'll take
care of that problem." The shit-lawyer had wanted to talk
to him—the time had come to have that meeting.

Reynolds grabbed his arm. "Where are you going?"

"I said I'd take care of the Sean Collins problem."

"Hold on," Reynolds said, not letting go of Babbage's
arm. "I don't want you trying to talk to him."

Babbage removed her hand from his elbow. "Make
up your mind. I've put my career on the line for you, and
I'm not about to see it go into the crapper over some legal
detail."

"Jake, I don't think you understand." She looked
him in the eye. "It would be a disaster for you to speak
to Collins. Especially while you're being cross-examined
and subject to Jordan questioning you about it. It would
give her the chance to claim you're arm-twisting Collins,
and to tell the jury he's the victim's son and part of the
defense team—all the things we've fought to keep out."

Babbage glared. So far her opinion hadn't been worth
shit. "I'll wait for now on Collins, but if he's standing in
the way, don't expect me to sit back and do nothing."

Reynolds considered. "I think we need to ratchet up the pressure on Fields. Let's show him who he's up against. Can you get some cops in the courtroom?"

"I'll call my lieutenant."

"Good. When we finish our case, Jordan will undoubtedly make a motion to dismiss—that's when we'll need the show of support. Fields is weak ..."—she took Babbage's arm again and added—"but he's not stupid. In order for the corroboration rule to apply, the defense must prove you're an accomplice, and I don't think they can."

She returned to her desk and opened the case file folder. "Now, let's go over this afternoon's testimony."

56

Sean

1:30 p.m.

When Sean entered the courtroom, he noticed a balding Asian man, immaculately dressed in a dark blue suit, sitting in the front row of the spectator section. He pointed him out to Amanda, and the two of them walked over to Reynolds, who was sitting at the counsel table with Babbage. She was reading her file and appeared not to notice them standing next to her.

"Is that your witness, Doris?" Amanda asked.

"Don't you know?" Her smug smile triggered a deep rage with Sean. *Can't she show some fucking respect?*

"Stop playing games, Doris," Amanda said.

Reynolds smiled. "He's Arthur Woo, from Biotech Markers, Inc."

"Have you forgotten your obligation to disclose the results to me, Doris?"

"No. You'll find out soon enough." She looked down again at her file.

Before Amanda could respond, the jurors entered the jury box. Fields entered and Powell, the bailiff, called the courtroom to order.

"Request to approach at sidebar, Your Honor," Jordan said.

When the three lawyers were at sidebar, Jordan spoke. "Ms. Reynolds told me that she has a criminalist, Arthur Woo, here in the courtroom, to testify about the DNA results."

"That's correct," Reynolds said.

"But she won't disclose the results," Jordan said.

"That's also correct."

Judge Fields took a breath and sighed. "And why not, Ms. Reynolds?"

"Because, Judge, the results aren't in yet. They're being messengered over, and when they get here, I'll share them with the defense."

"Surely you know at least preliminarily what they are, don't you?" Judge Fields asked.

"I know there's a match, but so far I'm not sure for whom."

"Your Honor, this is nonsense," Jordan said. "I want permission to interrupt Babbage's testimony and question Mr. Woo about the results."

"I object," Reynolds said. "I haven't even decided whether I'm going to call this witness. If and when I decide, Counsel can question him then. Otherwise, the defense can wait and call him as their witness after the prosecution rests."

Fields considered, then looked at Jordan. "At this time, I'm denying your request to question this witness. I must take Ms. Reynolds's representations as true. After all, she is a prosecutor and officer of the court. The side-bar is over."

They returned and Sean took his seat while Jordan went to the podium. *This DNA issue was very unsettling,* Sean thought. The morning had gone well, but Sean worried what this afternoon might bring. Yet, all told, he was satisfied—Jordan was a master at cross-examination, and Sean had learned a lot. But Babbage's testimony was taking a toll on Sean, opening wounds he thought were long scarred over.

No matter how much Sean tried telling himself it was just evidence, he couldn't escape the images—the suffering, the humiliation, the brutality. Try as he might, he couldn't entirely dismiss the fact that Hart could have saved his mom that night.

Jordan looked down at her notes, then looked at Babbage.

"Let's go back to your story—the time between when you left my client alone and when you claim you were struck on the head with a rock. You say you left my client so you could go off to a secluded place and have sex? Correct?"

Babbage agreed, saying that Sarah and he took a path through trees, overgrown weeds, and shrubbery, far away from the shore of the reservoir.

"This is the location where you claim you were hit on your head with a rock, where you say you awoke, bound to a tree?"

Babbage replied that he didn't know what kind of object he was hit with, but agreed it could have been a rock, and yes, when he awoke he was bound with duct tape, but was able to clearly observe Hart and the victim.

A dark-haired woman who Sean estimated to be in her early twenties entered the courtroom and handed two large manila envelopes to Arthur Woo.

"May I have a moment, Your Honor?" Jordan said.

"You may."

Jordan walked back to Woo, and the two conferred in low whispers that Sean could not hear. Jordan took both envelopes and returned to the counsel table, passing one envelope to Reynolds. Both lawyers opened them and examined the contents, a single document.

One or two of the jurors whispered quietly.

Sean looked at Jordan's face but it was impossible to read. He could feel his stomach flip-flop. Jordan held the one-page report in her hands, continuing to study it. Sean could hear the jurors stirring, feel the energy in the room.

Holding the report in front of her, Jordan said, "There's no doubt you saw Sarah Collins perform oral sex on my client."

Reynolds eyed Jordan and looked like a cat ready to pounce.

Babbage leaned forward, his eyes glued to the document in Jordan's hands. "That's right," he said slowly.

"And no doubt that you saw Sarah Collins gag after performing the act, and then spit. Correct?"

"That's what I saw." Babbage frowned—something was about to happen, and he was powerless to stop it.

"You're certain?"

"Yes," Babbage said, squirming.

"Beyond any doubt?"

"Right."

Sean realized the courtroom had become so quiet he thought he could hear his heart beating. He could certainly feel it.

Jordan looked down at the document, then at Babbage. "Perhaps," she said, "you can explain this. Explain why the semen sample taken from Sarah Collins's mouth"—Jordan threw the Biotech Markers report down on the podium—"was positive for you and *negative* for Daniel Hart?"

Doris Reynolds was on her feet, shouting. "Objection! Request to approach the bench!"

Judge Fields assented, and the lawyers assembled at sidebar.

———

Judge Fields let out an exasperated sigh. "All right, Ms. Reynolds, you may argue your objection."

"Judge, in all my years as a prosecutor, I have never seen such appalling misconduct. The People move for a mistrial. In addition, I ask that the court hold Ms. Jordan in contempt."

Fields looked at Jordan. "Explain yourself, please."

Jordan handed the report to Fields. "Your Honor, I'm handing to the court the report from Biotech Markers, Inc. and ask that it be marked as Defense Exhibit A. Ms. Reynolds already has her copy. It contains the results of the DNA comparison of the semen to my client's blood sample and to Mr. Babbage's. As you will see, the sample is indeed positive for Mr. Babbage and negative for Mr. Hart."

"That's beside the point," Reynolds blurted. "There's been no foundation established, so there's no way Counsel can mention this to a jury, and she knows it. It's clearly misconduct."

Jordan responded. "I agree with the prosecution that I should not have mentioned it, Your Honor, but it simply came out in cross-examination. If the court wishes, we can interrupt Mr. Babbage's testimony, and I can put on the expert, Doctor Woo, who's in the courtroom, to establish a foundation."

"I object to that, Judge," Reynolds insisted. "This can only be remedied by a mistrial. The court must do something to correct Ms. Jordan's contemptible conduct."

For once, Fields worried Reynolds might be right. Jordan should have known better than to mention the results before getting court permission.

"I might add," Jordan said, "that Doctor Woo is not my expert, but the People's. He's a director from Biotech Markers, the lab that the prosecution used to analyze the results and make the comparison."

Judge Fields faced a dilemma. The jury had heard the results, which was not proper. But it also appeared that Jordan would have no problem establishing the foundation during the defense part of the case. On the other hand, if Fields granted the prosecution's request for a mistrial, then an appellate court would probably rule that double jeopardy precluded retrial, because once a jury had been impaneled, jeopardy attached. Only the defense could request a mistrial without invoking double jeopardy.

Finally Fields spoke. "Ms. Jordan, there's no excuse for what you did. I expect more from a lawyer of your reputation." Fields then looked at Reynolds. "Your motion for a mistrial is denied."

"But Judge —"

"Hold on," Fields said. "Ms. Jordan, based upon your representation that you will have no problem establishing a foundation for this evidence, I will allow it, and admonish the jury that the results are being offered conditionally, subject to a proper basis being established during the defense case—"

"No!" Reynolds interrupted. "You can't—"

"Ms. Reynolds, I'm not finished."

Reynolds rolled her eyes.

Fields continued. "I will exercise my discretion under Penal Code Section ten-ninety-four and interrupt Mr. Babbage's testimony to allow Ms. Jordan to call Doctor Woo to establish a proper foundation. If he can't, I will reconsider the prosecution's motion for a mistrial. I will not allow you to benefit from any misconduct, Ms. Jordan. As for the contempt issue, I will overlook it for now. Be warned. Any more misconduct of this type will not be tolerated."

Reynolds said, "Judge, your ruling is clear error!"

"That's enough, Ms. Reynolds," Fields ordered. "Your objection is overruled. Your demeanor in this courtroom is utterly unacceptable. I'm sorry you are disappointed with the court's rulings—"

"You're right about that, Judge," Reynolds said.

"Don't interrupt. As I was saying, the fact that you are disappointed with the court's rulings can't be helped. I have to rule according to what I feel the law to be, and I take that obligation seriously. If you disagree, I still expect you to be respectful in your opposition. If you have an appellate case citation that you'd like me to read to support your position, I'll be glad to read it. If I believe it shows that I've made an error, I'll change my ruling. Otherwise, I expect you not to make confrontational or rude remarks to the court."

"Judge, I'm sorry, but that's my style. You'll just have to live with it. Otherwise, I'll have to notify my office that you're prejudiced against the rights of the People of the State of California, and we'll move to disqualify you from this case."

Fields took a deep, determined breath and waited several seconds before speaking. When he did, he spoke deliberately, working to keep any trace of anger out of his voice.

"Ms. Reynolds, I'm only going to say this once, so please listen carefully. Whether you approve of my rulings or not, I'm going to order you to refrain from your confrontational behavior, which clearly constitutes contempt. If you feel you have grounds to disqualify this court, that's your prerogative. But I will not allow you to engage in intimidation tactics. The next time you display confrontational or rude behavior with the court, you will be sanctioned. If your conduct continues, you can expect to spend the night in the county jail. I have no desire to fine you or to jail you, but if that's what it takes to get your attention, so be it."

Reynolds glared. Fields looked back, his eyes meeting hers. For a moment, it seemed that she was going to say something. Then, apparently changing her mind, she looked away. "Very well, Judge," she said. "But rather than have Doctor Woo testify, since he's our expert, the People will stipulate to the foundation."

After all that, Fields thought, *the woman is stipulating. Incredible.*

"The court accepts your stipulation," Fields said, and then turned to the jury. "We will take our afternoon recess."

57

Hart

Thursday, December 21, 7:30 a.m.

Hart felt sick to his stomach. While talking to Amanda and Sean over a light breakfast, he had to excuse himself. He vomited in a stall in the men's restroom and returned to find the two lawyers deep in discussion about the status of the case.

"I can't imagine who Reynolds might call as the next witness," Sean said. He took a bite out of the egg sandwich he had ordered.

"This could be the end," Amanda replied. "Reynolds could call Erin, but I don't think she will. The last thing Reynolds wants is for the jury to see Sarah Collins's daughter tell how Babbage abused her." Amanda was eating a fresh fruit salad and drinking herbal tea.

"I agree," Hart said, sitting down. He took a drink from his water glass, leaving his oatmeal untouched. "Then it's time to talk about whether or not I should testify."

Amanda sipped her tea. "I'm hoping it won't come to that. If you try to tell what really occurred, you'd be supplying Babbage's corroboration, and it would come down to your word against his. The case is going well, but it's always a gamble if it goes to the jury for decision. Babbage is a cop, after all, and we're in Van Nuys. Out here, juries believe police officers."

"But you're a judge," Sean said to Hart. "Doesn't that count for something?"

Hart shook his head. "Accused of murder. A disgrace to the whole community. If anything, they'll be harder on me *because* I'm a judge." And he thought, *if the jury believes everything Babbage says, it would mean a conviction for rape and first degree murder with a special allegation for using a knife, and for torture—that's life in prison without the possibility of parole. It's not likely I could survive very long in prison, at any rate.* Then he said out loud, lying, "Whatever the outcome, I'm prepared to accept it."

"Don't give up yet," Amanda said. "For now, let's concentrate our energy on our motion to dismiss."

"I don't think Fields will dismiss," Hart said. "I wouldn't, if I were him."

Amanda looked surprised. "Why do you say that?"

"If there's any evidence at all of guilt, I'd send the case to the jury. After all, it's their call. No conscientious judge wants to second-guess a jury, especially in a murder case. Sure, Babbage is a liar. I, of all people, know that. After all, I was there. But the jury wasn't, and most judges would leave it to the jurors to assess Babbage's credibility."

Amanda looked at her watch. It was 8:15. "Any other thoughts before we go to court? Sean?"

"I don't agree with Judge Hart," Sean said. "It seems to me that nothing Babbage says makes any sense. He sounds like a murderer trying to cover up and blame someone else."

"I can't be objective," Hart commented. "I've been through more cases than I can count. But this one is completely different for me. I just don't think Fields will grant a motion to dismiss."

"I hope you're wrong," Jordan said.

58

Hart

When court reconvened, Hart studied Amanda as the jurors came into the courtroom. This was a woman he admired and trusted, the lawyer who had impressed him the first day he saw her work in court, and who continued to impress him. Hart had watched Babbage twist the truth inside out and calmly fabricate facts when it served his purpose. It was up to Amanda, using cross-examination—"the greatest legal engine ever invented for the discovery of truth," according to jurist John Wigmore—to strip away the mendacity and reveal Babbage for the lying maggot he was. This morning she'd made some progress. But even with all her skill, it wasn't enough. Hart had watched jurors throughout the testimony, and he could tell that they were clearly sympathetic to Babbage.

"You may continue your cross-examination," Judge Fields said.

Jordan stood, notes in hand, and walked over to the podium. One eyebrow raised, she gave Babbage a long, appraising look. At once, the atmosphere became charged, even though she hadn't spoken a word. *What courtroom presence she has*, Hart thought. *Always perfectly dressed, always calm, always assertive in her manner and tone of voice.* In the jury box, there was considerable stirring as each juror moved to face her.

She read over her notes for a minute, then looked up. "You're a police officer and a patrol sergeant?"

Babbage folded his muscular arms in front of him and leaned back. "Yes," he replied.

"Sworn to protect and serve the people of the City of Los Angeles?"

"That's right."

Babbage sat up straight. He had a slight condescending smile that bordered on a sneer.

Jordan continued. "As a sergeant, your job is not only to supervise but also to maintain high standards of conduct for your patrol officers?"

"Yes." Babbage's eyes narrowed.

"Do you apply those same standards to yourself?"

"Of course."

Jordan paused, an angry look on her face, and stared silently at Babbage. Babbage stared back. Time seemed to stand still in the quiet of the courtroom. Then Jordan spoke, her voice loud and accusatory. "You've testified today, *Sergeant Babbage*, that nineteen years ago, you went to the Hollywood Hills Reservoir with Sarah Collins, a woman and a mother of two children. You smoked pot.

You engaged in oral sex with her. That doesn't set much of an example, does it?"

Babbage didn't answer right away, just stared at Amanda, with eyes radiating hostility. Finally, Babbage took a breath and said, "As *you know*, I wasn't a police officer then—I was just twenty years old at the time."

"Indeed, sir, you've admitted that *you* had Sarah Collins orally copulate you, haven't you?"

"The murderer *forced* the victim into oral sex. What Sarah did to me was what she wanted to do."

"That's what you would have this jury believe," Amanda retorted. "In fact, didn't you use that same argument when you were suspended for misconduct earlier this year?"

"Objection!" Reynolds said, shouting. "I demand a sidebar on this, Judge. Request that Counsel be held in contempt!"

"Your request is denied, and your objection is overruled," Judge Fields said calmly. The witness will answer the question.

"I don't know what you're talking about," Babbage answered.

Jordan glared at Babbage. "It was June thirteen of this year, wasn't it? You were a police officer and a sergeant then, correct?"

"Yes." Babbage tensed, leaned forward, face reddened with anger.

"You were on duty and in uniform in the early morning hours were you not?"

Babbage didn't respond at first. He glanced over to Reynolds. Then nodded.

"Please answer out loud, Sergeant Babbage," Jordan demanded.

"I believe I was on duty then, but I'd have to check to be sure."

Jordan picked up a document. "If you don't remember, Sergeant, I can show you your own report from that night to refresh your memory." Then without waiting for a response from Babbage, Jordan waved the back of her hand at Babbage, voice raised, "You were on duty, a sergeant in full uniform when you stopped a female motorist using your red lights and siren at two-thirty a.m.?"

Reynolds exploded. "Objection. she knows this is improper. I ask the court to admonish the defense lawyer."

"Your Honor," Amanda responded, "the prosecutor opened the door to this line of questioning when she brought up the witness's police officer status. I'm entitled to show that Babbage is a disgrace to his LAPD uniform."

"Your objection is overruled, Ms. Reynolds," Judge Fields said. Then, turning to Babbage, "Please answer the question."

Babbage's eyes narrowed, and he spoke slowly, pronouncing each word. "Yes, I was on duty."

"And after you stopped the woman motorist, still in full uniform, you had her perform oral sex on you, did you not?"

Babbage's face reddened. "A jury has acquitted me of any misconduct in that matter."

"Are you denying that after you used your authority as a police officer to pull over a woman motorist, you had her orally copulate you until you climaxed?"

Reynolds looked like she would burst. "Judge, I object. You cannot allow this line of irrelevant questioning. The People request a sidebar."

"Overruled. Sergeant Babbage will answer the question."

At first Babbage said nothing, just glared at Amanda. His massive hands gripped the top of the witness box, knuckles white. Finally, he said, "I was acquitted of misconduct in that case."

"*Answer the question*," Amanda demanded. "Did you or did you not intimidate and force the female motorist you stopped to orally copulate you to climax?"

"I said I was *acquitted*." Babbage continued to glare.

"Do you deny that you engaged in oral sex with a woman you pulled over for a DUI investigation?"

Babbage exhaled, shifted in his chair as he appeared to consider his response. "You're forcing me to answer yes or no to a question that can't be answered with a yes or no."

"Objection, nonresponsive," Amanda said, then added, "I ask the court to order the witness to answer."

"Mr. Babbage," Judge Fields said. "You are ordered to answer the question."

Babbage considered. Finally he said, "I don't deny it, but there is much more to be said. May I explain?"

"I think you've done enough damage with your explaining, *Sergeant Babbage*." Amanda threw the report down on the table.

"We'll take our noon recess at this time, members of the jury," Fields said. "Please return promptly at 1:30 p.m.

As the jurors filed out, Hart stole a glance. The women were expressionless, but a man from the first row stared at Babbage and shook his head in disgust as he walked.

59

Sean

After the afternoon recess, Jordan returned to the podium. "Mr. Babbage, before the break, you wanted to explain why you intimidated a woman motorist that you pulled over with your police patrol car to perform oral sex. To be fair, I've decided to give you the opportunity to explain yourself to the jury. Please do. What is your explanation for your conduct?"

Sean was puzzled. Amanda had scored a major point earlier when she put Babbage on the spot about his misconduct with Erin. Why would she give Babbage a chance to wiggle out of the box she'd put him in? After all, Sean had been taught, it's a fundamental principle of cross-examination never to give a witness a chance to explain.

"Objection, irrelevant," Reynolds said, standing. "And prejudicial. The defense lawyer is putting up a smoke screen to confuse the jury with this irrelevant event."

"It's highly relevant," Jordan countered, before Fields could answer.

"Overruled." Fields said.

Babbage paused, took a breath. "I was seduced by the woman motorist I pulled over."

"But, Mr. Babbage, you deliberately singled out and pulled over that woman with the intent of intimidating her into giving you oral sex, didn't you?"

"I did not," Babbage said, shaking his head.

"In fact, you knew who the woman motorist was well before you stopped her, didn't you?"

Babbage glared at Amanda. "I deny that."

Suddenly, Sean understood.

Jordan pointed her finger at Babbage.

"Do you deny that the woman you stopped was Erin Collins, the daughter of Sarah Collins, the victim in this case—the woman who was raped and murdered?"

Reynolds jumped up. "Objection! Judge, I insist on a sidebar conference."

"Approach the bench," Judge Fields said.

———

What a day, Fields thought. Then to Ms. Reynolds: "What is your objection?"

"Judge, this is preposterous," Reynolds said, red-faced. "Ms. Jordan is testifying to facts that she has never proven. Everything that Counsel says may or may not have happened is irrelevant to this case. I demand the court admonish the jury to disregard this hearsay."

Fields looked at Jordan. "Ms. Reynolds has a point, does she not?"

Jordan shook her head. "Not at all, Your Honor. My question is for impeachment, to show that the witness is biased, untruthful, and, in fact, the true killer. As an offer of proof, Ms. Erin Collins would testify that she is the daughter of Sarah Collins, and that she was stopped by Babbage and forced into giving him oral sex."

"Officer Babbage was acquitted of all charges in that case, "Reynolds said. "Obviously, the jury in that case didn't believe her story. And where is she? I saw no witnesses in the hall."

"Do you have this woman under subpoena?" Fields asked.

"I do, Your Honor. In fact, she's waiting downstairs in the cafeteria, and I can have her in the courtroom in minutes."

"Good," Fields said. Then to Reynolds: "Do you want to take this witness on voir dire—to question her and verify she's the daughter of Sarah Collins and was stopped by Mr. Babbage?"

Reynolds hesitated, then said, "Yes. But my questioning must be outside the presence of the jury—otherwise it's too prejudicial."

"I object to that," Jordan said. "I've made my offer of proof. Ms. Reynolds knows it's accurate. If she wants to elicit details from Ms. Collins, then let her do it in open court."

Fields considered. *On one hand, Jordan had already overstepped with the expert testimony. Should I allow her to do it again? On the other hand, Jordan has done nothing improper. She's right that her question impeaches Babbage and shows bias. But more importantly, her client is facing life without the possibility of parole, and she's entitled to some leeway.* "All right," Fields said. "I'll allow you to question Ms. Collins, if you wish, Ms. Reynolds. But it must be in front of the jury."

Reynolds took a breath. "Judge, it's wrong to force me to question in front of the jury, and I won't do it. Either you let me examine without a jury present, or I move for a mistrial. I will not examine Ms. Collins in front of the jury."

"Very well. Ms. Reynolds, your motion for a mistrial is denied," Fields said. "Ms. Jordan, you may continue your examination."

The lawyers returned to the counsel table, and Fields spoke. "The objection is overruled. Mr. Babbage, you are ordered to answer the question. Ms. Jordan, please ask the question again.

Jordan rose, pointed her index finger at Babbage and asked, "Do you deny that the woman you stopped was Erin Collins, the daughter of Sarah Collins, the victim in this case—the woman who was raped and murdered?"

Sean was elated. *Let's see Babbage get out of this*, he thought.

Babbage raised his eyebrows, paused. He looked at Reynolds, then back to Jordan. "I do not deny it." He shook his head. "But, she seduced me. She was driving under the influence, afraid of being arrested ..."

"Are you saying you did not know who she was before you stopped her? Do I need to remind you, Mr. Babbage, you are under oath, and that if you lie, you will lose your immunity from prosecution?"

Reynolds, still standing, spoke. "I demand a sidebar conference, Judge."

"Request denied," Fields said. "The witness will answer the question."

All twelve jurors looked at Babbage, waiting for his answer.

Brilliant, Sean thought. Sean noticed that even Hart, who had been writing, put down his pen and glared at Babbage, eyes filled with contempt.

Babbage took a deep breath, sat up straight and responded. "I knew she was under the influence of alcohol and should not have been driving. I didn't know who she was before I stopped her."

"I have no further questions of this witness," Amanda said.

"We are in recess until this afternoon at 3:30 p.m.," Judge Fields said.

Sean watched with interest as the jurors filed out of the courtroom. They looked down, moving slowly. *They know Babbage is the murderer*, Sean thought.

60

Fitzgerald

Thursday, December 21, 3:30 p.m.

It had been a long day, but as the jury entered the court-room, Fitzgerald could see, that despite the day's length, they were still vitally interested in the case. Fitz felt that way too. No one who witnessed today's testimony could fail to see that Jordan had made major progress in attacking the prosecution's case. All of this underscored that Fitz had been right when he urged Reynolds to wait, so that he could do more investigation to establish corroboration. There was so much that needed to be learned before Hart was arrested — before Hart was tipped off that he was a murder suspect.

"Ms. Reynolds, do you wish to further examine your witness?" Judge Fields asked after the jurors were seated.

Doris Reynolds stood, looked at the jury and then at Judge Fields. "I have no further questions of Sergeant Babbage," she said, and then declared, "Subject to the court admitting People's One, the Autopsy Report, People's Two, the Coroner's Diagram, and People's Three, Mr. Babbage's Audio Statement and Transcript, the People rest."

Judge Fields looked at Jordan. "Do you object to the admission into evidence of the exhibits?"

Jordan stood. "Not at all, Your Honor. However, I request the court admit Defense A, the DNA Report."

"I object to Defense A being admitted," Reynolds said.

"Overruled," the judge said. "Exhibits One, Two, Three, and A are admitted into evidence. Anything further before we begin the defense case?"

Jordan stood. "Your Honor, at this time, the defense wishes to make a motion to dismiss under Penal Code Section eleven-eighteen-point-one."

Fitzgerald could feel the tension in the courtroom. The jurors didn't know what the Penal Code section meant, but they understood dismissal. There was no reaction from Reynolds—she knew, as he did, that it was routine for defense lawyers to make this motion in every case. Fitz didn't think much of the case that Reynolds put on, but he knew it was highly unlikely that the judge would grant Jordan's motion.

Judge Fields turned to the jury. "Ladies and gentleman, we must now hold a hearing outside of your presence. Since this may be a lengthy hearing, I'm going to excuse you until tomorrow morning at eight-thirty a.m."

One by one, the men and women of the jury gathered their personal items, put their spiral notebooks on their chairs, and filed out of the room.

Judge Fields said, "We are outside the presence of the jury. Ms. Jordan, you may now argue your motion to dismiss."

"Your Honor," Jordan began, "at the outset, I want to make it clear that I believe the evidence shows that Mr. Babbage is a liar, that his entire testimony is preposterous, and that he sought immunity to escape prosecution for the murder of Sarah Collins. The clear inference is that he picked a story that can't be verified, because otherwise he would be caught by his own lies."

Reynolds interrupted. "That's for the jury to decide, Counsel, not you. I object, Judge."

"Overruled," said Fields. "Sit down, Ms. Reynolds. You'll get your chance to argue. Please don't interrupt." Reynolds glared at Fields and remained standing. Fields looked back at Jordan. "Continue with your argument."

Jordan nodded. "Your Honor, the prosecution has presented no direct evidence that establishes a case against Daniel Hart, or even establishes that Mr. Hart was present the night of the murder. In fact, aside from Mr. Babbage's testimony, there is not a scintilla of evidence, direct or circumstantial that links my client to the murder. Even with the preposterous Babbage testimony, the evidence is so weak that no reasonable jury could convict. But, beyond that, Mr. Babbage is an accomplice, by his own testimony, and as such, must be corroborated in order for this case to go to the jury. There has been no corroboration. Your Honor, the court must grant my motion to dismiss. There is simply no logical alternative."

Jordan continued. "It is uncontroverted that Mr. Babbage destroyed evidence. He says he did it because he was afraid. But of what? If everything occurred the way he claims it did, the logical thing would have been to go to the police immediately, not to burn Sarah Collins's clothing. Going to the police would have allowed investigators to dust Babbage's car for fingerprints and get other forensic evidence. The clear inference is that Mr. Babbage was afraid he would be held accountable for the murder of Sarah Collins."

Reynolds still had not sat down. "I object to this unsubstantiated speculation. There's absolutely no evidence of car fingerprints or blood on the clothing." She pointed at Jordan. "*She* is making this up."

"Overruled," said Judge Fields.

Jordan said, "If Mr. Babbage had come forward on that July fifth, it would have been possible to examine his supposed head injury for lumps and bruises. After all, if he was hit on the head with such force that he lost consciousness for the entire time the murder took place, surely he would have sustained observable damage."

"Let her argue that to the jury, Judge," Reynolds said.

"Please continue, Ms. Jordan," Fields said.

"It's clear that Mr. Babbage is a liar. He's already admitted lying about this incident. When he applied to become a police officer, he lied in response to a direct, material question. He said he had never used drugs, when in fact he had smoked marijuana on the night of the murder.

"But there's a far more serious and dangerous area of testimony where Babbage lied directly to the court and to the jury. This afternoon, Mr. Babbage admitted that while on duty, and in full uniform, using red lights and siren, he stopped motorist Erin Collins, and using his badge, coerced her into orally copulating him. That, by itself, is a reason for not believing anything Babbage says. But in response to my question, Babbage denied that he was aware that Erin Collins is Sarah Collins's daughter. That was either a lie or the world's most bizarre coincidence. Can the court give any credibility to such a man?

"Oh my God," Reynolds said.

"If that's an objection, it's overruled," Fields said. "Continue, Ms. Jordan."

"As I've said, Your Honor, I believe the evidence is clear that Mr. Babbage's story is a total fabrication. He claims he didn't see who hit him, didn't see who stabbed Sarah Collins. He maintains that when he awoke the first time, he was bound to a tree by duct tape. But where did this duct tape come from? He says it wasn't his, but by his own statement we know that he drove to the Lake Hollywood Reservoir in his car. Where would anyone possibly find duct tape at the Lake Hollywood Reservoir after midnight?

"Next, he professes he saw Sarah Collins on her knees in front of my client. But again by his own testimony, he was still in the brush area that *he* had selected because it couldn't be seen from the water's edge. How could he peer through such shrubbery and see what was happening at the same water's edge? And why would he be facing in that direction in the first place? Nevertheless, he wants us to believe that at night, without lighting, he saw through these obstacles and witnessed Sarah Collins orally copulate my client, gag, and spit semen."

Jordan picked up a document, looked at it, and placed it on the podium in front of her. "Your Honor," she said, "by stipulation, the DNA results from the swabs taken from Sarah Collins's mouth are positive for Jake Babbage and negative for Daniel Hart."

Reynolds made a face.

Jordan went on. "After claiming to see what he clearly could not, he conveniently faints again and awakes to find Sarah Collins dead. He removes the duct tape and walks home. How is it that he was able to get free from the duct tape after he awoke a second time, but for some unexplained reason was unable to do the same when he first revived?

"And now we come to the most preposterous part of this obviously manufactured story. He claims that a slight, barely fifteen-year-old boy managed to subdue him, a one-hundred-ninety pound, nearly twenty-one-year-old man. And he would have us believe this same fifteen-year-old boy inflicted numerous, agonizing stab wounds on a one-hundred-twenty-five-pound adult woman, all the while preventing her from using her hands to defend herself."

Jordan turned to where Reynolds was sitting, looking directly at her. "Your Honor, this case has disturbed me ever since I first read Mr. Babbage's statement." She turned back to the judge. "It's filled with inconsistencies and contradictions. It defies common sense. It doesn't make sense that Jake Babbage would bring the fifteen-year-old along on a date.

"It doesn't make sense that a skinny fifteen-year-old boy would knock out a husky twenty-year-old man. And with what object? No bloody rock or duct tape was found by police at the scene. It doesn't make sense that duct tape would somehow magically appear at the Lake Hollywood Reservoir at night and disappear afterwards.

"It doesn't make sense that Jake Babbage could see the water's edge at night without artificial light, after having deliberately picked a spot hidden from the water's edge to have sex with Sarah Collins. It doesn't make sense that Jake Babbage could observe Sarah Collins orally copulate Daniel Hart, watch Sarah spit out the semen, and have the DNA swab show negative for Daniel Hart."

Jordan continued. "It simply doesn't make sense that a skinny boy could subdue a one-hundred-and-twenty-five-pound woman by himself and render her helpless to defend herself. It doesn't make sense that Jake Babbage would burn Sarah Collins's clothing. It doesn't make sense that Jake Babbage would not go to the police immediately. I could go on and on."

Jordan took a breath. "But instead I will make an observation. I have listed a dozen things that make no sense *if* we assume that things happened as Mr. Babbage said in his immunity statement.

"But all of these things make *perfect* sense if Jake Babbage is the real murderer."

"Don't go there, Counsel," Reynolds warned. "Judge, how many times do I have to object to improper argument? This court has demonstrated so much bias against the prosecution that I believe a mistrial should be declared. The People need an impartial judge."

"Ms. Reynolds," Fields said. "I've said that we will deal with your issues during your argument. The next outburst and you will be held in contempt." Fields looked at Jordan. "Please finish your argument, Counsel."

"Your Honor, the DNA results are completely consistent with Jake Babbage having killed Sarah Collins after forcing her to orally copulate him.

"My final point, Your Honor, is that there is not one shred of evidence to corroborate anything that Mr. Babbage has testified to. For these reasons, and in the interests of justice, this case must be dismissed. Thank you."

Jordan sat down.

"Now, you may argue, Ms. Reynolds," Fields said.

Doris Reynolds stood. "Judge, I hope you're not seriously considering granting her motion. Because if you are, I have two things to say to you. First, try to remember that if you grant this motion, the People cannot appeal and the defendant will go free, having escaped accountability for the murder of Sarah Collins.

"The court must let the jury decide the issues in this case. The defense argues that there wasn't enough evidence to send this case to the jury. I vehemently disagree. Officer Jake Babbage testified clearly, candidly, and succinctly. It's true that he did not actually witness the defendant stabbing the victim. But he did testify that he was with the defendant and the victim before the murder.

"He was knocked out. He awoke the first time to see the forced oral copulation by Sarah Collins and the second time to find the victim's body. By then the defendant was missing and so was Officer Babbage's vehicle. That vehicle was driven to Officer Babbage's residence. It doesn't take a rocket scientist to realize that the defendant was the person who knocked out Jake Babbage. The defendant was the person who drove the car to the house and also was the person who forced oral sex, stabbed, and murdered Sarah Collins.

"On the corroboration issue, the answer is very simple. Jake Babbage's testimony does not have to be corroborated because he's not an accomplice. He was unconscious during the murder and did nothing to aid in the crime. If the defendant's lawyer thinks that merely being there makes Jake Babbage an accomplice, then she should go back to law school."

Fields looked thoughtful. "We'll put aside the corroboration issue for a moment. Ms. Reynolds, what are your comments with respect to Ms. Jordan's argument about the internal inconsistencies of Mr. Babbage's testimony?"

"There are no inconsistencies. Defense Counsel's entire argument is speculation, without any foundation in fact. It's up to the jury to evaluate the credibility of the witnesses. If the defendant's lawyer doesn't believe Officer Babbage, so what? The test for a motion to dismiss isn't in the strength of the evidence. The test is whether or not there is any basis for the jury to convict. If they believe Officer Babbage, then they will. If they don't, they'll acquit. I don't see how the court can use the defendant's lawyer's belief that Jake Babbage lied to prevent a jury from rendering its verdict. Let the jury decide who's telling the truth and who's not."

"All right," Fields said. "Let's look for the moment at the corroboration issue. Ms. Reynolds, do you see any corroboration here?"

"That's not an issue that needs to be decided, Judge. As I said, the only time that there's a requirement of corroboration is when the complaining witness is an accomplice.

Officer Jake Babbage was *not* an accomplice. There's not a shred of evidence upon which a trier of fact could conclude otherwise."

Fields looked to Jordan. "Ms. Jordan, the prosecution is right about the credibility issue. I can't substitute your or even my judgment for that of the jury. On the corroboration issue, I tend to agree with you that there is no corroboration of Mr. Babbage's testimony. And Ms. Reynolds has not been able to point to any such corroboration. But she appears again to be correct on the issue of whether or not Mr. Babbage was an accomplice. Has there been any evidence presented that would allow the court to conclude that Mr. Babbage was indeed an accomplice?"

Jordan stood. "Yes, Your Honor."

"All right," Fields said. "Point it out to me, if you can."

Jordan took a deep breath. "Your Honor, the one question that is the key to this entire case is: *Who held Sarah Collins's wrists while she was being stabbed?* The deputy medical examiner, Doctor Crowlich, testified that unless a victim is subdued or unconscious, he would expect stab wounds to the palms of the hands, indicating that the victim tried to protect herself from the stabbing. We know that Ms. Collins was not comatose. There were no drugs in her system that would cause her to lose awareness. There were no blows to the head that could have rendered her unconscious. The only possible explanation is that she was restrained. But how? Not by duct tape. The marks on her wrists were not consistent with having been bound by tape. There was no adhesive residue. Doctor Crowlich's opinion is clear: *These marks were consistent with Sarah Collins's wrists being restrained by someone's hands.* So, while she was being stabbed, another person was holding her wrists so that she could not resist. This is the neutral pathologist's opinion and it cannot be ignored."

Jordan took out the DNA report again. "The DNA from the semen sample taken from Sarah Collins's mouth was positive for Mr. Babbage, indicating that he ejaculated into the victim's mouth. He testified that he was struck while he was being orally copulated. That would imply that the ejaculation had not been completed. This fact then is consistent, at the very least, with his being an accomplice. I would also point out that the acts of burning the clothing and not going to the police are also consistent with his being an accomplice. But I repeat, the one question that is the key to this entire case is: *Who held Sarah Collins's wrists while she was being stabbed?*"

Jordan walked back to her seat at the counsel table. "Perhaps," she said, "the prosecutor has the answer. If not, there can be no case against Daniel Hart, and the court must grant my motion to dismiss." Jordan sat down.

Fitz glanced at Sean and Hart. Sean was smiling. Hart didn't smile, but he appeared to be sitting up straighter.

Fields looked at Reynolds and said, "Any response, Ms. Reynolds?"

She swallowed. "Once again, we're hearing Counsel's interpretation of the evidence. It's up to the jury to determine Officer Babbage's credibility. And I, for one, am not persuaded by the so-called positive semen results. They mean nothing. There could very well have been ejaculation before Officer Babbage was knocked out. So what? As for the coroner's testimony, I see it differently. Doctor Crowlich acknowledged the possibility from a medical point-of-view. The court cannot take this away from the jury based upon a mere possibility. Officer Babbage was not an accomplice."

She sat down.

Fields spoke. "I'll take this matter under submission and rule tomorrow morning before the jury is impaneled. Court is in recess until tomorrow morning at eight-thirty."

61

Babbage

Friday, December 22, 8:30 a.m.

For the first time in two days, Babbage was confident again. Wearing the same sport coat and slacks he'd testified in, he sat at the counsel table between Reynolds and Fitzgerald. She told him to sit next to her so that the judge could see there was no doubt that the prosecution was behind him. As was law enforcement—shown by the visible and clear support of LAPD. Two days ago he'd visited at roll call and made the arrangements. Everyone was willing to do anything to help, but it was damn awkward for Babbage, and it pissed him off to have to beg. But they came, so maybe it was worth it. The first two rows of the audience were filled with uniformed cops. Even Commander Karp showed up in uniform.

The rest of the seats were filled as well. Spectators, reporters, sketch artists, and a bunch that Babbage decided must be DAs and PDs. An overflow crowd waited in the outside hall. Word must travel fast around the courthouse.

Listening to the buzz of conversation in the court-room, Babbage had to admit that, for once, Reynolds might be right. No way, with this much brass, this much support, and this much public, could that gutless judge do anything other than let this case go to the jury.

The bailiff, Powell, announced the judge, cutting through the din. Fields entered and squinted in the bright light of the courtroom. "Good morning," he said. "This matter is here this morning for the court's ruling on the defense motion to dismiss pursuant to Penal Code Section eleven-eighteen-point-one. The parties are present, and we are outside the presence of the jury. The court has considered all argument presented yesterday afternoon and is ready to rule."

Reynolds stood. "Just a moment, Judge," she interrupted. "Before you rule, may the People be heard one last time?"

Fields frowned. "All right, Ms. Reynolds. You have two minutes."

"Judge," she began, turning and motioning with her hand, "look who's here in the courtroom to show how strongly law enforcement and the public feel about this case. They know that ruling against the People would be just plain wrong. You'd be unleashing a murderer onto the public. And since jeopardy attached the moment the jury panel was sworn, the People cannot appeal, and there'd be no way to correct your miscarriage of justice. That's why I'm imploring you to deny the motion and let the jury decide this case."

Fields looked at her, his expression unreadable. "As I said," he continued, "the court has examined your arguments in depth." The judge looked down at a note pad in front of him, then looked up.

The courtroom became still, as if everyone was holding their breath. Babbage glanced over at Hart. *The fucker looks to be frozen, staring straight ahead.*

Fields continued. "Based upon the testimony of Deputy Medical Examiner Crowlich and based upon Witness Babbage's own testimony, I find that he is an accomplice, as a matter of law." Then Fields made eye contact with Babbage. "I specifically find that the Babbage testimony lacks credibility, and that no reasonable jury could convict based upon the People's evidence. Accordingly, the defense motion to dismiss ... is granted."

At first there was a stunned silence in the courtroom, then commotion.

Babbage thought he'd misheard. This wasn't possible. Not after all he'd done. Not with all his supporters in the room. Not in front of the patrol cops he'd supervised, who'd looked up to him and depended upon him. His face burned with humiliation, stung as if he'd been slapped.

The bailiff shouted to the audience. "Quiet! Court's still in session."

Fields looked at Powell, "Bailiff, please inform the jury that the case has been resolved, that the court thanks them for their time and effort, and that they are excused."

"Wait!" Reynolds said. "Take a look around this courtroom. At the supporters of justice. Can you really let a murderer go free?"

"Ms. Reynolds, sit down. I've already warned you. Be advised that if you say anything further, I will hold you in contempt."

"I'll bet you would," she retorted under her breath.

Fitzgerald reached behind Babbage and grabbed at Reynolds's elbow. She turned and looked toward him, her face contorted in anger. "Don't you try to hush me, Fitzgerald. This is your fault, too." She turned back. "Just remember this, Judge. The Los Angeles District Attorney's Office and the LAPD will never accept what you are doing today. Whatever goes around comes around."

Babbage noticed that the bailiff had approached behind Reynolds. *The crazy bitch had stepped over the line.*

"Ms. Reynolds," said Judge Fields, "I find that your remarks constitute direct contempt, and that your conduct occurred after you have been suitably warned. Accordingly, you are remanded and sentenced to spend the rest of today and tonight in the county jail. The sheriff is ordered to keep you in custody and release you no earlier than five-thirty a.m. tomorrow morning."

Fields looked at Hart.

"Mr. Hart, you are ordered discharged. Your bail is exonerated. Good luck to you, sir. Court is adjourned."

62

Sean

Sean had never seen anything like it. Not only had they won, but Doris Reynolds was getting jugged. He grinned at Jordan, who shook her head, indicating now was not the time to gloat. Sean then looked at Fitz. Was that a smile? He couldn't be sure. Sean walked over to Hart and shook his hand. "Congratulations, Judge Hart. Justice was done my faith in the system is restored."

Hart didn't smile. "Thank you. Your support has meant a lot ... to me." There were tears in his eyes.

The bailiff was behind Reynolds. "Please put your hands behind your back, Doris," he said. "I'll need to handcuff you."

"Do you have to do that?" she asked. "I'm not a risk."

"It's policy. Please put your hands behind your back."

"This is nonsense," Reynolds said, starting to move away.

The bailiff put one hand on her shoulder. With his other hand he pressed the talk button on the microphone at his lapel. "I need a female deputy here for backup," he said. Then he said to Reynolds, "Don't make me restrain you."

"Okay, okay. I'll cooperate." She put her hands behind her, and the bailiff snapped on the handcuffs.

The lockup door opened, and a dark-haired female deputy sheriff entered the courtroom. She walked over to Reynolds, grasped her by the arm, and started to lead her away. "Can't you at least wait for my boss, Chuck Allen?" Reynolds pleaded. "I'm sure he'll be able to straighten this out without my having to go to jail."

The bailiff shook her head. "I've got a lot of paperwork to do now to get you out to the jail. But don't worry. I'll put you in a cell by yourself. You'll be kept apart from the other prisoners."

Fitz had started to accompany her into the lockup, but Reynolds shook her head. She looked past him to Babbage, who was still seated at the counsel table. "Jake, I'm sure they'll take me to Sybil Brand and release me from there. Can you find out when I'm going to be released and pick me up?"

Babbage didn't reply.

"Come see me before I get on the jail bus," she said.

The female deputy escorted Reynolds through the door to the lockup. Sean, Hart, and Jordan remained standing while she was being taken away. After the door closed, Amanda, smiling, turned to Hart and hugged him. "Congratulations, Daniel."

Hart did not smile back. He allowed himself to be hugged, but his face was grim.

63

Fitzgerald

Fitz wasn't sure how he felt about the outcome of the case. Fields was correct, of course, because if anything, Babbage was at least an accomplice. And Fitz didn't believe a word that Babbage had said on the witness stand. But Fitz was still left with an unsolved murder.

He was grateful that Sean had handled himself so well. Sean was a great kid. He'd agonized about joining with Hart's defense team, and now he was vindicated.

Doris Reynolds was another matter. She'd created her situation, and now she had to live with it. But Fitz was troubled about her trust in Babbage. He decided he had to warn her.

With the bailiff's help, Fitz made his way into the lockup. Doris was sitting on one of the stainless-steel benches that was in the cell. She had her back against the wall. Her eyes were closed.

"Doris?" Fitz said.

She opened her eyes.

"I don't think it's a good idea for you to have Babbage pick you up. I worry about your safety, especially if you're going to be alone with him. If you need a ride, I'll be glad to give you one."

She frowned. "If you'd done your job, I wouldn't be here now." She stood and walked over to the bars separating them. "Don't worry about Jake Babbage," she said. "Worry about your own career. As soon as I'm out of here, you can expect a call from your captain. I'm going to do everything I can to make certain you're never allowed to mess up another prosecutor's case again. Get out of my sight."

She turned, returned to the bench, and sat down. She closed her eyes again and leaned her head back against the wall. Fitz shook his head. *Maybe she deserves being locked up.* He left the courthouse.

64

Babbage

Babbage stayed seated at the counsel table and tried to make sense of what happened. While some—probably reporters—left, the bulk of the spectators stood in small groups talking. A bunch of reporters came by and surrounded the defense team. Lieutenant Hardy and two of the guys Babbage supervised walked over to him, but Babbage declined to discuss details, telling them it was all bullshit, and that he had to talk to his lawyer.

The judge's ruling made Babbage look like a goddamned fool. Perhaps the time had come for him to act—to show them that no one gets away with humiliating him. All because of Reynolds. It was no surprise she got jailed. She'd deliberately pissed off the judge for no purpose, and with *nothing* to be gained. Daring him to rule against her. Acting like she had power. Like a cat hissing at one of his boas. Playing a stupid, reckless game. And now she was crying about having to spend a night in jail. Shit. A few hours in lockup, then on to her next case.

He had to get out of here.

He got up to leave, when he heard a familiar voice call his name. "What the hell happened, Babbage?" He turned. Commander Karp, face stern, looked at him.

"Sir, I'm as astounded as everyone else. But I'm going to find out."

"Have your rep call me Monday."

Babbage froze. "This won't affect my chances for reinstatement, will it, sir?"

"I can't comment. Ask your lawyer. Or check with the DA." Karp looked at his watch. "I need to get back to a meeting at Parker Center." He rushed away.

Babbage watched Karp leave. What the fuck did he mean? Babbage had assumed his immunity meant the Board of Rights hearing was a formality and that he'd be reinstated as soon as the trial was over. They'd better! Fuming, he decided that he'd have to see Reynolds in lockup after all, to confirm that he'd get his badge back, and that the grant of immunity meant something.

The bailiff, Powell, had returned to his desk and was filling out a form. Babbage approached him. "Do you mind if I talk to Doris?"

Powell shrugged. "Suit yourself."

Powell opened the lockup door and escorted him to Reynolds's cell. She was pacing back and forth as he approached.

"Can you believe this?" she said when she saw him. "That buffoon Fields dismissing the case and finding me in contempt? I knew from the start he was incompetent. But this is not over. The public is not going to stand for this."

She looked at Babbage. He knew his impassive face masked his fury. "Doris, I need some answers—"

"Jake," she interrupted, "besides picking me up, I have another favor to ask."

He wanted badly to hurt her.

"Can you go see my boss, Chuck Allen, for me? I'm sure he's heard by now what happened. No doubt he'll be here shortly. But just in case, tell him I'd like to see him before I get shipped downtown. I also need him to arrange to move my car to my house. It's not safe to leave it here overnight. Also, that bailiff, Powell, took my briefcase and purse. Could you retrieve them from him and bring them with you tomorrow? We can discuss your case then."

"Answers, Doris. Now. I've got to get my badge back."

"No time to talk now," she said. "Find Chuck. Get my stuff." She reached through the bars, put her hand on his arm, and looked into his eyes. "After you pick me up tomorrow morning, we'll talk, and we can decide what to do next. I have some ideas. Okay?"

"Like what?"

"The feds. Another immunity deal. A civil rights case against Hart. I have some friends at the U.S. Attorney's Office. I'll arrange it all—get them to charge Hart. More tomorrow. Trust me." She kept her hand on his arm, kept looking at him, a ridiculous expression on her face.

Babbage removed her hand. "Tomorrow. Eight. See you then," he said.

He walked out of lockup and found the bailiff, Powell. "Reynolds wants you to give me her briefcase and purse."

"I'll have to check with her, but no problem—it'll save me doing an inventory. Wait here."

Powell went back into lockup and returned ten minutes later with a brown shopping bag, sealed at the top with yellow tape. "Reynolds signed the release," he said, and handed over the bag.

Babbage left the courthouse, ignoring Reynolds's request to find her boss. *Fuck her. A little jail would do her good.*

Twenty minutes later, he was on the 405 freeway, headed for home. It was still early in the day, but traffic was congested. The slow pace gave him time to ponder, to evaluate his situation.

He cursed his luck that his fate was tied to such a stupid fucking woman. Now that he thought about it, he realized that ever since he was a child, whenever something went wrong in his life, there was always a woman behind it. His mother ... Sarah Collins ... Erin Collins. Always some fucking woman.

He decided his first priority when he got home would be to call Giovanni and discuss the status of his reinstatement now that the trial was over. Maybe there was a federal angle like Reynolds had suggested, and they'd still need him. Giovanni had worked a miracle getting him back in the department before, and Babbage hoped the lawyer could do it again. He was looking forward to getting back to his regular routine.

Taking the Devonshire off-ramp, he drove east to Haskell, heading north past Chatsworth Boulevard, to his lot.

In his trailer, Babbage put the shopping bag with Doris's stuff on his breakfast table. He reheated some coffee he'd brewed upon waking that morning, poured himself a cup, and sat at the table. He looked at his watch. Ten-thirty. A good time to call Giovanni.

He dialed Giovanni's number. The secretary answered, and told Babbage to hold on, that Giovanni was on another call but would be available presently. Babbage took a sip of coffee and looked out his rear window at the backyard shed housing his boas.

He thought about the snakes. They were something he could rely on. No emotion, just pure logical behavior based on instinct. When they were hungry, they ate. When they weren't, they could give a shit. And they had true power, which they used only when necessary.

Babbage suddenly realized that he had forgotten to feed them this month. Damn. The trial had occupied so much of his attention that he'd had no time to devote full care to them.

"Hello, Jake," Giovanni's voice said. "Trial in recess?"

"It's over," Babbage replied. He took a sip of coffee. It was bitter, but passable.

"Over? What do you mean?"

Babbage was irritated by the surprise in Giovanni's voice. "Over. Finished. Fields dismissed the goddamned case."

Giovanni inhaled sharply. "That's bad news."

"Yeah," Babbage said.

Giovanni didn't reply. Babbage took another sip of coffee and waited. Finally he said, "What's this going to do to my reinstatement chances?"

"I'll put it this way," Giovanni said. "Had Hart been convicted, it would have been iffy at best."

"*Iffy?*" Babbage was incredulous. He'd proven himself on the streets, time and again. He'd trained more rookies than anyone else in his division. "What the fuck are you talking about? Don't all the years I've put in count for something? Didn't you ever look at my performance evaluations?"

"I know, Jake. And if Hart had been convicted, I'd have been able to argue that you'd sacrificed your career to put a murderer away. But now—"

Babbage interrupted. "Why can't you still do that? Nothing's changed." He drank more coffee, decided it tasted like shit. "Reynolds says there's a civil rights case that could be prosecuted against Hart."

Giovanni laughed out loud. "A Section nineteen-eighty-three violation? Bullshit. I've tried a ton of those cases. Hart wasn't a judge at the time of the murder, so no violation. He's been acquitted and no one, not the feds, not the state, no one is going to file anything against him. And with the case dismissed, all that's left is you smoking pot and lying on your application. Not to mention your possible complicity in a murder."

"Bullshit!' Babbage shouted into the phone. "They can't use my testimony, and you know it! The immunity!"

"Calm down, Jake," Giovanni said.

"Don't tell me to calm down. Just answer my fucking question!"

Giovanni sighed. "Jake, immunity just affects criminal issues. As far as a Board of Rights, there is no immunity. They can force you to testify against yourself."

Babbage could feel his insides churning. He felt like smashing the phone into Giovanni's face. He swallowed, knowing he needed to control himself. Taking a breath, he said, "You fucked up, Giovanni. You should've included the Board of Rights in the deal."

"I tried. They wouldn't go for it," Giovanni said.

Babbage said, "This is the first I've heard about it. Don't fucking lie to me—"

"Hold it!" Giovanni interrupted. "I saved your goddamned ass and don't you forget it."

"Why didn't you tell me the Board of Rights wasn't included? I would've refused to cooperate without it."

"Like hell you would," Giovanni retorted, his voice ice-cold. "Without me and the immunity I got you, your ass would be in jail right now, with capital murder charges hanging over your head."

"Goddammit!" Babbage was shouting again. "You didn't save shit! The immunity was my idea! If that's all I got, I could've done this by myself!"

Giovanni didn't reply.

For a moment, Babbage wondered if the connection had been lost. Then slowly, deliberately, Giovanni spoke into the phone.

"Fine. If that's really the way you feel, then do the rest without me."

Babbage calmed himself down. He tried to keep his voice even, low, "You're not getting out of this so easy. You owe me."

"What are you talking about?"

"You've been paid. And for every damn minute you worked. Now do your job."

"I'll do my job, all right," Giovanni said. "If you keep your temper under control. Disrespect me again, Babbage, and I'm off your case. Period. Because if not, we part company here and now."

Babbage took a deep breath. "I'll uphold my part of the bargain if you do yours. Don't tell me what might have been had Hart been convicted. Just find a way to get me back to work and you'll hear no complaints."

"Going back to work is not a possibility," Giovanni said. "Best case, we save your pension. Maybe get you early retirement."

"I don't want early retirement. I'm a cop, goddammit. I want my job back."

"You don't have a chance in hell of getting your badge back. Trust me on this. And do what I say, or else face losing everything."

"And just what are you telling me to do?"

"You've got to make a deal. Admit you lied on your application, and then resign. Give up your right to a hearing. Do that and I think we might still save your ass. You'll be able to work somewhere else. Another city. Maybe become a deputy sheriff."

"No one is going to hire a cop who lied, you stupid, fat fuck."

Silence. Then slowly Giovanni said, "I think you'd better get yourself another lawyer."

"You'd better watch your fucking back, Giovanni." Babbage slammed down the receiver.

He hurried outside to his truck and got in. He forced himself to calm down, fighting back the urge to drive straight to Giovanni's office and shoot the motherfucker. Forcing himself to be logical. As pissed off as he was, he really couldn't blame Giovanni. The lawyer had tried to do his job, had actually tried to look out for Babbage.

The real problem is Doris Reynolds. That stupid, stupid woman. By showing such blatant disrespect for Fields.

By forcing the judge to retaliate at Babbage's expense. Another woman screwing him over. Another woman thinking she could make everything right for Babbage, just by allowing him to fuck her. And she claimed she could make things right. How in the hell did she think she could do that? He stared out the windshield, watching the wind blow through the naked branches of the trees on the hill in his backyard, then it hit him. He could find out what Reynolds had based her comments on when she told him he could go to the feds.

He got out of the truck, went back into his trailer, ripped open the bag, and went through Reynolds's briefcase. Inside he found yellow pads, scribbled notes, and mostly stuff he couldn't read. Behind a thick case file marked "People v. Hart," he discovered an LAPD evidence envelope sealed with red tape, a typewritten note stapled to it from Lt. Hardy. DNA comparisons ordered by Fitzgerald, telling her that unless she saw relevance to these results, no further action would be taken.

What the fuck?

He tore open the envelope and read the report. It was a comparison of three DNA samples. Babbage studied it carefully, trying to make sense of it. Two of the three comparisons matched, but the third was inconclusive, and the report suggested sending the samples to a private lab. The report didn't mention names, only included DR numbers. He recognized one of the numbers as the Sarah Collins case. According to the report, that was the inconclusive comparison.

But the other two samples did match. One was a Sheriff's case, the other LAPD's.

There was only one possible reason Fitzgerald would send out this comparison. To see if the same perpetrator committed all three crimes.

Babbage knew that if Biotech Markers were sent the samples, they'd uncover that the same perpetrator raped all three victims. Babbage had to make certain that those DNA results never got compared to the DNA found on Erin's blouse—his life depended on it.

That settled it.

He spent the rest of the day preparing. Planning had a calming effect on him. He knew that but for exceptional luck, he was a dead man. Luck had favored him before—but only because of careful planning. He'd need to have another phone call made — one like what he'd arranged to make Erin think she was needed at work. But this time he wasn't going to use a hooker to make the call. He had a better idea — one that was sure to convince.

Just before dusk, Babbage visited his boas one last time. They were hungry and alert, their tongues flicking in and out in anticipation of their next meal.

They'd never survive without him.

Using his .22 caliber Derringer pistol wrapped in a towel, he fired one round into each snake's brain. He owed them that much. Carefully, he dragged them halfway up the hill behind their shed.

He buried them in a shallow grave under the shade of a eucalyptus tree.

65

Babbage

Saturday, December 23, 6:00 a.m.

The Sybil Brand Institute was located on City Terrace Drive in East Los Angeles. Opened in 1963, the institution housed female inmates exclusively. Babbage went to the inmate reception center. Without a badge, he was treated like any other member of the public, and told to wait outside. Doris Reynolds would be released as soon as she had completed her exit processing. Babbage went back to his truck and waited, seething.

Thirty-five minutes later, Reynolds walked out of an unmarked door to the right of the public entrance. Her clothes were badly wrinkled. She looked like she hadn't had much sleep.

"Thanks for picking me up, Jake," Reynolds said as she got in the truck. He noticed that she had a jailhouse smell.

As he drove away, she looked at herself in the visor mirror and shook her head. "I never thought Fields would have the balls to do what he did. He sure as hell would never have done it if he were an L.A. County judge."

Babbage said nothing. He drove out to the I-10, entered westbound, heading for the Hollywood Freeway and the Civic Center. The freeway was jammed at the Civic Center, and he worried it might take over an hour to reach Reynolds's house.

"Sybil Brand was way worse than I expected," she was saying, oblivious to his silence. "Even though I got placed in a separate lockup from the rest of the inmates and treated pretty well by the jailers, it was disgusting in the cell. It stunk of piss and shit and was filthy. I don't ever want to go back there."

Finally they reached the Ventura Freeway. Reynolds continued to babble, interspersing directions to her home. After a while, she stopped talking and they rode in silence.

Doris Reynolds lived with her five cats in a three-bedroom house in the upscale neighborhood of Encino Hills, above Ventura Boulevard. After driving for a time along winding tree-lined streets, Reynolds directed him to her house—a one-story, pale-yellow residence surrounded by a well-manicured lawn and brick walkway punctuated by multicolored blooming poinsettias. Babbage pulled into her driveway. Reynolds got out of the truck. "Come in and have a cup of coffee. I need to take a shower and clean up, if you don't mind waiting for me."

"Fine," Babbage said.

The house's entry was well lit, a skylight directly above the hall entrance. The living room was to his right, a bedroom to his left. Reynolds walked into the bedroom. "Make yourself comfortable, Jake. The kitchen is over there. Fix us some coffee. I'll only be a few minutes."

She closed the bedroom door. Babbage walked into the white-carpeted living room with white French-provincial furniture, and embroidered pillows adorning the couches and chairs. There were ceramic figures—shepherds with sheep and dogs—on the mantle above the fireplace. Babbage walked into the kitchen, found the coffee and coffeemaker. While the coffee was brewing, he went out to his truck and retrieved a black grip that he'd packed before leaving to pick up Reynolds. It contained, among other things, his ten-inch marine Bowie knife. He returned to the living room and sat on a couch, placing the grip on the floor behind it.

Two Siamese cats had been sleeping on a white armchair across from the couch, but sensed him immediately and scampered away. There was a oval, white coffee table with a large book of newspaper clippings. Babbage leafed through the book. The clippings were all articles about Reynolds and her cases. Next to the book of clippings were several photos of cats.

Twenty minutes later, Reynolds walked out of the bedroom. She was wearing a terrycloth robe. Her hair was damp. She sat down on the couch near him. She picked up her waiting cup of coffee. "Good. Black and strong. Just the way I like it."

Babbage did not reply.

"Can you believe that son of a bitch granting the motion to dismiss?" Reynolds said. "That's why I went berserk. What a miscarriage of justice."

Babbage shrugged.

She smiled at him. "A lot of men are intimidated by me, Jake. But I can tell that you're not."

She moved closer, and her robe fell open—revealing, as he suspected, that she wore nothing underneath. He glanced at her body. It wasn't bad.

But as she moved closer to him, Babbage felt suddenly awkward. The fucking bitch was being way too pushy. For an instant, he couldn't breathe. When she put her hand on his leg, he shoved her hand away. He decided it was time to begin.

He slapped her across the face.

The force of the blow knocked her off the couch. Reynolds lay on the floor, robe open, tits and cunt showing. She pressed a hand against the side of her face, stunned. He could read the fear in her eyes. "Why?" she screamed. She was crying.

"Shut up," he said.

She started to get up, to close her robe, but he reached down with his left hand, grabbed her arm, and pulled it up and behind her, forcing her to her feet. He reached around with his right hand, across her neck, holding her shoulder. He pulled her arm up behind her and tightened his own arm across her neck, cutting off her air.

"Jake ... you're hurting me ..."

He increased the pressure. This was more like it. He hoped she could feel how excited her terror was making him.

"Please ... please, don't hurt me ..." Her lip was bleeding from his slap. "I'm ... I'm sorry ..." Her voice was breaking. "I didn't mean anything by it ... Jake ..." She tried to smile. "You don't need to force me. I'll do whatever you want. Then you can leave. I won't say anything to anyone."

"I'm not ready to leave, Doris. I like you. I just don't like being rushed."

"If you'll just let me go, I'll do anything you ask. I won't rush you, I promise."

He smiled. "Okay. I'll let you go. But I do want you to do something for me in return. Something very simple."

"Anything, Jake. Anything."

Another smile. "I want you to make a phone call."

66

Hart

Daniel Hart was sitting at his desk in his study at home, looking through mail that had accumulated during the trial. Since this whole Babbage incident had begun, Hart had felt unable to do anything. Now that the trial was over, he needed to try to return to his life's routine.

It was a struggle. He thought he ought to feel good having survived the ordeal, but he felt no relief. The entire trial had caused him to relive that night of nineteen years ago, and his guilt at not having saved Sarah festered like an open wound. It was one of the cruelties of life—some mistakes from the past are irreversible, and the fact that he was only a teenager at the time was no excuse. Yes, he avoided a lifetime in prison, but without redemption, he was trapped in the prison of his mind. Not to mention that Babbage, the source of his misery, was not held accountable for Sarah's death and the suffering he'd caused her children.

True, the case against him had been dismissed, the jury sent home, and he no longer faced the prospect of life in prison. And also true, it was likely (but not guaranteed) that he would be able to resume his judgeship. He still had to face the election and who knows what effect this case would have on that.

But the whole series of events that began with seeing Babbage that morning two months ago had changed everything. There was much more at stake than whether or not he would go to prison. The question in his mind was whether he could allow Babbage to continue to manipulate him. Somehow he had to make Babbage accountable for his actions.

The phone rang. Reflexively, without thought, Hart answered it.

"Judge Hart? This is Doris Reynolds. I need to see you as soon as possible. It's urgent."

Doris's voice sounded a bit shrill to him, her stress obvious. "Can you tell me what it's about?" he asked.

"Not over the phone. But it's very important. Are you free to meet me now?"

Perhaps she'd been able to confirm that Babbage had lied, and his immunity was being revoked. Hart's curiosity was aroused. "All right, Doris, we can meet. Come by my courtroom after Christmas—we can talk then."

"I'm afraid that what I have to tell you can't wait."

"It will have to," Hart said.

"You don't understand." Doris's voice broke. "Judge Hart ..."

Perhaps it was his imagination, but she sounded like she was crying.

"It's absolutely critical that I see you now. Please," she pleaded.

Hart considered. "Can't you tell me more?"

"I can tell you that it concerns Babbage, and only you can help."

"Okay," he said. "When and where would you like to meet?"

"My house. Right away, if you can. I'll give you the address."

Forty-five minutes later, Hart arrived at Doris's. There was a pickup truck in the driveway that Hart did not recognize. Doris drove a sedan. Was there someone here with her? He knocked on her front door. She was dressed in a terrycloth robe when she opened the door. The side of her face was bruised, and her lip was crusted with dried blood.

He blinked. "What happened to you? Are you all right?"

She hesitated for a moment before saying, "Please come inside."

Hart entered. She closed the door behind him.

"I'm so sorry—" she said.

The next thing Hart knew, he was on the floor, stunned and groggy from a blow to the back of his head. Then came another blow, and everything went black.

67

Fitzgerald

At 5 a.m., Fitz got up and went for his daily jog. As always, running in the crisp morning air cleared his brain and invigorated him. He made up his mind. Worrying was nonsense. If anyone could take care of herself, Doris Reynolds could. Besides, he had enough problems of his own to worry about.

At noon, Fitz was at his desk in Parker Center, going through the motions of work. The trial and his suspension had taken him away from too many regular assignments, and he was getting ready for tomorrow's meeting with Captain Becker to talk about what he could do until his Board of Rights hearing was resolved. It was then that the Parker Center lobby receptionist called to tell him that he had a visitor. A Ms. Erin Collins.

"I'll be right there," Fitz said.

He went down to the reception area at the Los Angeles Street entrance. The lobby's large glass windows created a bright, cheerful atmosphere. A huge Christmas tree was to the right of the reception area with a bin labeled "Toys for Tots" at the foot of the tree. High school kids had decorated the tree two weeks ago. Although cool, it was a sunny day, typical of Los Angeles in December. Erin was standing at the reception counter, wearing a visitor's badge.

As Fitz walked into the lobby, Erin came up, hugged him, and kissed him on the cheek. "I thought I'd surprise you and take you out to lunch. It's my day off." She was wearing jeans and an oversized wool sweater, and Fitz couldn't help feeling proud, looking at her. She had become a confident, self-assured woman.

They walked to the Teriyaki Bowl in Little Tokyo. It was a small, narrow place, wedged between a Japanese bookstore and an office building, holding only a counter with stools to the right and a row of booths to the left. They sat in the last empty booth. Menus were propped between salt and pepper shakers. A waiter brought a teapot and two cups.

"Sean called and filled me in on what happened yesterday," Erin said. "I wish I could have been there, but Sean said that I might have to testify, so I couldn't be in the courtroom during the trial. I'm not surprised about Judge Hart. But Doris Reynolds in jail? Isn't that unusual?"

Fitz nodded. "In all my years, I've never seen a prosecutor remanded."

Erin took a deep breath. "Babbage is the real killer. I'm sure of it. That bastard is capable of anything, as far as I'm concerned."

Fitz said, "The main thing is that you can't give him the opportunity to mess around with you again."

Erin glanced at her menu, put it down. "Well, he certainly hasn't bothered me lately. It's almost as if he's forgotten about me."

It's not like Babbage to forget to get even, Fitz thought.

A waiter came by, brought water, and took their orders. Erin took a sip of her water. "Maybe he's found himself another victim."

Fitz then told her about Reynolds asking Babbage for a ride back from the jail. He described the events, including his conversation with Reynolds. "I talked to Captain Becker about my worries, and Becker told me to stay out of it. That it was none of my business and how Reynolds was an adult and could take care of herself."

"Captain Becker's probably right," Erin said. "But how could Doris be so stupid? There's no way I'd ever let myself be alone with that bastard." She shuddered. "I still wake up nights wondering what would have happened if you hadn't come to my rescue."

The waiter brought their food and more hot tea. Fitz watched Erin eat her sashimi, thinking that he never could understand what prompted people to eat raw fish. His own plate of teriyaki chicken was steaming. As Erin poured a cup of tea for herself and Fitz, she said, "Maybe you should go check on Doris to see if everything is okay."

Fitz took a sip of tea, careful not to scald his tongue. "Have you forgotten this is the woman who wanted to put you in jail?"

Erin considered. "She's not so bad. I remember the talk we had in the courthouse bathroom. She wished me luck and seemed genuinely happy I was given another chance." Erin took a breath and sighed. "I think I understand her. She can't stand to lose—can't bear it. Maybe she needs to be kick-ass abrasive and out-of-control tenacious to make her way in a man's world."

Fitz shook his head and didn't reply. He'd had enough of Reynolds and didn't care what drove her.

They continued to eat in silence. "You don't think that Babbage would do anything if he found himself alone with her, do you?" Erin asked.

"I really can't figure the woman out," Fitz said. "With all she knows about him and what he did with you, how can she possibly trust him?"

Erin stared into space for a minute, a far-off look in her eyes. "Looking at my past, God knows I've made some pretty terrible choices. Disastrous choices." She turned to Fitz. "Answer my question. Is Doris in any danger?"

"I don't trust Babbage any more than you do. But he's too smart to try anything with her."

Erin scowled, then shook her head. "Fitz, you have to drive out there and find out for yourself."

He frowned. "I can't do that. First of all, I've been away from my desk for weeks. I've got a mountain of paper-work. But more importantly, Captain Becker ordered me to stay out of it. There's no way he'll let me go."

"Then I'll go by myself."

"You can't do that, either. Remember? You still have that driving restriction on your license. Babbage is just itching for the chance to get your probation revoked again. Besides, what could you do if something was wrong?"

Erin thought for a moment. "Either you go or I'll go. That's all there is to it."

"Erin, I'm sure she's fine."

"I'm going." She got up to leave.

"Hold it," Fitz said, sighing. "All right. You win. I'll go."

"You shouldn't go alone. Why don't you ask Captain Becker to get someone to go with you?"

"Captain Becker ordered me to mind my own business. If there's a problem, I can always radio for backup. Besides, it's probably nothing. Doris herself will likely chew my ass for bothering her."

"Then, let me go with you. If there's a problem, I can call for help on my cell phone."

Fitz considered. If he told Becker that he was taking Erin home, Becker would probably approve. If he went to Reynolds's house with a civilian with him, it would look less like an official police visit. And if Becker ever found out the truth, Fitz could always say that he was humoring Erin. Erin could wait in the car, out of view of Reynolds's house, and if any problem did occur, she could call Becker immediately.

"Okay," Fitz said. "Let's go."

68

Hart

Hart awoke, sitting in a chair. His hands were tightly handcuffed behind his back, hurting his wrists. The cuffs were also somehow connected to the chair, so that he was unable to move his hands. He was in a bedroom. A sock was shoved into his mouth; he had trouble breathing and thought he was going to choke. He had to use every bit of resolve to keep from panicking.

He surveyed the bedroom. It was clearly a woman's room. White and pink wallpaper, white carpet, pink pillows and lace sheets. Hart's chair was against the wall. A door leading into a hallway was to his left. There was a window above the four-poster bed to his right with closed vertical blinds. The head-board side of the bed was against the wall, below the window. To Hart's left was a white dresser with drawers.

Escape wasn't possible, Hart concluded. He could topple his chair, and perhaps that would be heard at the front door, although he couldn't be sure. But he would then be on the floor and helpless. The best he could do was wait to see if an opportunity of some sort presented itself.

A few feet away, Jake Babbage sat on the edge of the bed. At his feet was an open black grip containing duct tape and several pairs of handcuffs. Babbage was directly across from him, grinning. Doris Reynolds was also sitting on the bed. Babbage wore plastic gloves and held a huge knife in his right hand. He was pressing the point against Doris Reynolds's neck. A gun jutted from his waistband.

"I thought you and I might celebrate the end of your trial, Chief," Babbage said. "After all, what with my immunity and your acquittal, we don't have to worry any more about Sarah Collins, do we?"

Hart squirmed, trying to free himself. He tried to say something, but the sock in his mouth made it impossible. He tried to yell, but it came out as a muffled groan.

"I also thought you and I could have a little fun. Like the old days." Babbage turned to Doris. "Unzip his pants and take out his dick."

"Jake," Doris said, "you promised you wouldn't hurt me if I got him here—"

"Shut up," Babbage snapped. "Just do it."

He pushed the point of the knife into her neck. She gasped. "Okay. Okay, please. Don't hurt me."

Reynolds came over to Hart and got on her knees in front of him. Hart twisted in the chair, doing everything he could to avoid her hands, but it was no use. Doris unzipped his pants and reached into his boxer shorts. He could feel her cold hands touching him. She pulled out his penis.

"Put it in your mouth," Babbage ordered her.

"Why are you making me do this?" Doris asked.

"Just do what I say."

Doris bent down, opened her mouth, and put her lips around Hart's penis. He felt the warmth of her mouth on him, felt the edge of her teeth.

Then Doris gagged and pulled away. She looked back to Babbage. She was crying. "Please, Jake."

"If you don't do what I say *right now*, I'm going to kill you."

Doris bent down again, opened her mouth, and drew in Hart's penis. Hart couldn't believe he was in this nightmare, couldn't believe this all could be happening again. And Doris. Even though she had been thoughtless and cruel toward him, she didn't deserve this. No one did.

Babbage got up, walked over to Hart, and spoke softly into his ear. "Doesn't this bring back fond memories, Chief? Memories of nineteen years ago? At the reservoir? Remember that blowjob? Was it as good as this one?"

There was a knock at the front door.

69

Fitzgerald

1:30 p.m.

When Fitz and Erin arrived at Doris Reynolds's house, they parked four doors down, around a curve and across the street. On the way out, they called Reynolds's home number—no answer. Checking with the watch commander at Sybil Brand, Fitz determined that she'd been released at 6 a.m.

Fitz noticed a red Toyota truck in Reynolds's driveway and another car parked in front of the house. The truck looked to Fitz like Babbage's, but the car wasn't Reynolds's. She drove a Lexus coupe. This was a Volvo.

Fitz ran the plates on the computer terminal in his unmarked car. The truck was, as he suspected, Babbage's. The plate on the Volvo parked in front came up as confidential. Fitz recalled from the search and arrest warrant that Daniel Hart drove a Volvo. And as a judge, the plates would come up as confidential.

Something was seriously wrong.

"I need to find out what's going on," he told Erin. "If I don't come back in fifteen minutes, call Captain Becker."

Fitz wrote down Becker's direct number and gave it to Erin. He got out of the car and walked to Reynolds's front door.

Halfway there, he hesitated. *Maybe this isn't a good idea ... Goddammit. I'm going to get to the bottom of this, whether Doris Reynolds likes it or not.*

He went to the door, pressed an ear against it, and listened. Nothing.

He knocked.

Moments passed, then Reynolds partially opened the door. Through a narrow opening of about six inches, Fitz could see that she was wearing a bathrobe, holding it tightly around her. "What ... what ... do you want?" she asked.

"I'm just checking up on you, Doris. The watch commander at Sybil Brand told me you'd been discharged early this morning, but when I called here, there was no answer. Frankly, I was worried."

"There's ... nothing ... to worry about ..." She looked down, avoiding his eyes. "I'm okay."

"What happened to your face?"

She reddened. "Oh ... Sybil Brand ... It was a rough night ... Inmates don't like prosecutors."

Fitz studied her. A bruise on her face was still red, and if it had happened last night, he would have expected it to darken by this time, to be more of a purple color. There was also dried blood on her lip.

"Where's Babbage?" Fitz asked.

She started. "Babbage?" She looked into Fitz's eyes, but he couldn't read the expression on her face.

"His truck is parked in your driveway," Fitz replied.

"Oh ... yes ... he's ... here." She looked down.

"Where is he?"

"He ... he's ... in the ... bathroom."

"Is Daniel Hart here, too?"

Reynolds looked up. Her eyes widened. "Why would he be here?"

"That's what I was wondering," Fitz said. "His car is here, too. Parked in front of your house." Fitz pointed.

Reynolds said, "You must be mistaken. He's not here. I can't talk to you any more."

Fitz didn't move. "I'm not mistaken. That's Hart's car. What's going on, Doris?"

"Do I have to spell it out for you? What's going on here is none of your goddamned business. Just go away."

"All right," he said finally. "I'll go."

Reynolds closed the door.

70

Babbage

Babbage had been out of sight, behind the door, holding his Glock 9mm semiautomatic pistol on Reynolds while she was talking. After she closed the door, Reynolds said, "I did what you wanted. Now please don't hurt me."

"Shut up."

Babbage positioned himself behind Reynolds and held her around her waist while he pointed his weapon at her head. He took her to a spot five feet from the front window where he could see outside without being seen. He watched Fitzgerald walking toward the street. When Fitzgerald reached the sidewalk, he turned to the right and moved until he was outside of Babbage's view.

He must be parked down the street, Babbage thought. It wasn't a good sign that Fitzgerald was being cautious.

He decided that he needed to wait to see whether Fitzgerald was satisfied with Reynolds's responses. The guy didn't seem enough of a gambler to try and force his way into Reynolds's house. But if that happened, Babbage had only one chance of getting out of this successfully, and it would require skill and an incredible amount of luck. But he had succeeded before, facing worse odds.

———

Babbage returned to the bedroom, gun in hand, walking behind Doris. Hart glared at him. Babbage pushed Doris toward the bed. "Don't turn around," he commanded her. "I want you to look straight ahead."

"But why?" Doris asked. "Can't I get dressed? Please, Jake?"

Using his gun, Babbage struck Doris across the back of her head.

Babbage quickly stripped off her robe and positioned her unconscious body on the bed. Then he took the knife and a length of rope from his black grip. He cut sections of rope and tied Doris, nude and spread-eagled, to the headboard and to the posts at the foot of the bed. He then cut a section of duct tape and sealed Doris's mouth. Babbage placed the knife on the dresser, took off his plastic gloves, and put them into the grip.

He came toward Hart, gun in hand. "I'm going to ungag you and take off your handcuffs. If you shout or do anything other than exactly what I tell you, I'll kill you *and* I'll kill Doris. Understood?"

Hart nodded, thinking that Babbage would kill them both anyway. But he needed Babbage to think that he'd cooperate.

Babbage removed the gag. Holding the gun against Hart's head, Babbage unlocked the handcuffs. He backed away but kept the weapon trained on Hart, who bent down to free his legs.

"Don't stand up yet," Babbage commanded.

Hart remained seated, looking up. The knife on the dresser was ten feet away, between where Hart sat and the corner where Babbage had positioned himself. Hart glanced at the knife.

Babbage smiled. "You are so fucking easy to read," he said. "If you think you can get that knife, go for it." He leveled his gun at Hart.

Hart didn't move.

"I have a proposition for you, Chief," Babbage said. "It may even save your life. And Doris's."

Hart said nothing. He knew he and Doris were as good as dead, and that only he could prevent it. He was not going to repeat his mistakes of nineteen years ago, no matter what.

"If Fitzgerald comes back, he's certain to look in this window." Babbage motioned toward the window over the bed. Hart noticed that Babbage was positioned so he could not be seen from the outside. "If Fitzgerald looks in, I want you to go over to the dresser and pick up the knife."

"What if I refuse?" Hart asked.

"Then I'll kill all of you. Including Fitzgerald," Babbage said.

71

Fitzgerald

Back in the car, Fitz told Erin what had happened when he'd gone to Doris's door. Every instinct he'd developed during his entire career told him that this was a life-or-death situation.

"I don't like it," he told Erin. "I've got to do something."

"But what? You still don't have proof that anything's wrong."

"I'll call Captain Becker. Even though he told me to stay out of this, I don't care. I can't just stand by and do nothing."

He dialed Becker's direct number on his cell phone. Becker answered on the first ring. "Captain Becker? Fitzgerald here. Captain, I know you told me to stay out of the Babbage-Reynolds situation, but something's come up, and I think we need to take some action."

Fitz filled Becker in on what had occurred, ending with Reynolds's denial that Hart was in the house. Becker asked, "Hart's car is there? Are you sure of that?"

"Not positive. Hart drives a Volvo and the plates come up as confidential."

"Jesus. If Hart's in there, he must be holding Babbage and Reynolds. That would explain her demeanor."

"Maybe Babbage is the one who's doing the holding," Fitz said.

"That doesn't make sense. Why in the world would Babbage do such a stupid thing? No. If there's a problem, it must be Hart. After all, the two people who tried to put him in jail are Babbage and Reynolds."

Fitz rubbed a hand across his jaw. Babbage was up to something. He knew it.

Becker continued. "And what if that isn't Hart's car or if Hart isn't inside the house? What if Reynolds and Babbage are just in the sack together? That would also explain the situation. Wouldn't it?"

"Except for her bruises and the bloody lip."

"But she told you that she was injured at the jail."

"I'm not sure I believe that," said Fitz.

"I'll tell you what," Becker said. "I'll call the watch commander at Sybil Brand and ask if Reynolds was injured. He'd surely know about it. If she was attacked in jail, then you and I will butt out."

"And if she wasn't?" Fitz asked.

"One thing at a time. I'll call the watch commander now and get back to you. What's your cell phone number?"

Fitz gave Becker the number and hung up. "What did he say?" Erin asked.

Fitz told her. "And if Doris was hurt at the jail?" Erin said. "What will you do then?"

"I'm not sure. Let's find out and then re-evaluate." Fitz said.

Moments later, the phone rang. "Fitzgerald here."

"Fitz," Captain Becker's voice registered concern. "Doris Reynolds was not injured at the jail."

"Then I'm going in, Captain," Fitz said.

"Hold on. You can't go without backup. They'll be on their way ASAP. After they arrive, you'll go in with them."

"But if something's wrong, we shouldn't wait."

"You *will* wait, Fitz. That's an order."

"Yes, sir."

Erin had been leaning forward during the conversation to eavesdrop.

"How long will it take to get backup?" Erin asked.

"Only a few minutes."

Erin shook her head. "Doris could be dead by then. You can't wait."

"I've been ordered to do just that," Fitz said. "I have no choice."

"We'd never forgive ourselves if something happened," Erin said. "You've got to do something *now*."

"Erin, if I go in there with guns blazing, and everything is okay, or Babbage and Doris are just in the sack, it would be the end of me. Especially after my captain ordered me *not* to take any action without backup."

Erin didn't reply.

Finally, Fitz spoke. "Okay. I'll snoop around and see what else I can find out. But that's all."

"I'm going with you," Erin said.

"No. It's too dangerous. I can't let you do it."

"You can't stop me."

"Erin, I won't go unless you wait here for me. I can't risk it. So wait for backup."

"Okay, you win." Erin kissed him on the cheek. "Be careful."

Fitz cut across Reynolds's neighbor's lawn to approach the side of the house away from the front windows. On the south side of the house was a small, opaque window. A few feet from that window was a larger one with closed vertical blinds. From the positioning and size of the two windows, Fitz reasoned that the larger was to a bedroom, with the smaller being an attached bathroom. Because of the slant of the closed blinds, he was unable to see inside.

He approached the opaque window, careful to stay out of the line of sight of anyone who might be watching from the house. He listened at the window, drew his Beretta 9mm, verified that there was a round in the chamber, and slid the safety off. With his back toward the wall, he moved. If he could get on the other side of the window, his angle of vision might permit him to see the interior of the house. Crouching as low as possible he reached the other side.

He looked at his watch. Where was the damn backup? He tried to position himself so that he could see inside without being detected. He thought he saw someone standing inside, looking back. Fitz withdrew, his back against the wall. The sun was beating down and he could feel sweat dripping from his face and under his arms.

72

Hart

Babbage, standing to the side of the vertical blinds, looked out the window and adjusted the slats so that anyone outside could see in without spotting Babbage.

"He's out there," Babbage said. "Pick up the knife."

Hart didn't move.

"I said, 'Pick .... up ... the ... knife.'"

Hart walked over to the dresser, picked up the knife, and looked at Babbage.

"You son of a bitch," Hart spat. "You're not doing this to me twice."

He lunged at Babbage.

Babbage fired one shot. Hart felt a blow to his chest and fell back, unable to breathe. Before he lost consciousness, he looked down. The front of his shirt was soaked with blood.

73

Fitzgerald

Fitz heard the shot. Jesus, he thought. He had to act quickly, whether or not the backup arrived. The Beretta's handle was slippery in his damp palm. He switched hands and wiped his palm on his pants. Shit.

He took a deep breath, focused his thoughts, and exhaled. Then he moved.

Fitz edged toward the front of the house. Reaching the corner, he turned toward the front door. With all his might, he kicked at the deadbolt. The door jamb splintered, and the door flew open.

Fitz burst into the house, gun in both hands, finger on the trigger. Instantly he saw Babbage, whose semi-automatic was pointed right at him. "Drop it," Fitz commanded.

"Not on your life," Babbage said. "The minute I put down this weapon, you'll shoot."

Fitz kept his Beretta on Babbage. "What was that shot I heard?"

"Hart was about to stab Doris," Babbage said. "I had to shoot him to save her life. If you go into the room"— he motioned toward the bedroom—"you'll see him with the knife still in his hands. Go in and see for yourself."

"I'm not moving until you put down your weapon," Fitz said. "If everything you say is true, you have nothing to worry about."

A muffled groan came from the other room. "What's that?" Fitz asked.

"Doris," Babbage said. "Hart tied her up on the bed."

"When did you get here?"

Babbage cleared his throat. "A few minutes ago."

Fitz asked, "Didn't you bring Doris out from Sybil Brand?"

Babbage nodded. "Yeah, but I left. I was halfway home when I realized I forgot my sunglasses, so I came back. Doris let me in. Hart must have been behind the door, because as soon as I came inside, he knocked me out. When I awoke, I was tied up and Hart was out here with Doris, talking to you."

"If you were tied up, how were you able to shoot Hart?"

"I managed to get loose while Doris was talking to you. When Hart came back with Doris, I pretended to still be tied up."

"How convenient," Fitz said. "You've got this all figured out, don't you? Only I don't believe your bullshit story, and no one else will either. Especially when you refused to disarm. And as a suspended cop, you have no right to possess a firearm, let alone point it at another cop who's only doing his job."

"All right," Babbage said. "I'll do what you say."

Babbage began to lower his gun, then raised it again quickly. He fired three times.

By reflex, Fitz fired back.

74

Erin

Erin heard the shots. *Oh no. Please, God, no.*

She pushed open the car door, not knowing exactly what she was going to do. She ran toward the house. She knew she shouldn't go inside, knew that she was risking her life. But she had to find out if Fitz was okay.

The door was wide open, but she couldn't see the entire room—her view was blocked by Fitz, who was slumped against the side of the doorway, not moving. She ran to him, saw his face with his staring, unfocused eyes, and feared the worst. Thank God, he was still breathing, but how badly was he injured? His gun was on the floor, a few inches from his hand. She reached for it.

"Freeze!"

Erin looked up. She saw Babbage standing in the doorway of what looked to be a bedroom directly in front of her. Both arms extended, holding a gun pointed directly at her.

She closed her eyes, waiting for the shot.

Only there was none. Erin opened her eyes just as someone jumped Babbage from behind.

It was Hart. His shirt was soaked with blood. He had a knife in his hand.

As Babbage and Hart struggled with each other on the floor, Erin glanced at Fitz. He was clearly in bad shape. The side of his shirt was soaked in blood, and his arm hung unnaturally. But he was still breathing.

Meanwhile, Babbage had turned around, blocked Hart's arm, and tripped Hart, who fell to the floor. Babbage was on him, grabbing and twisting Hart's wrist, forcing him to drop the knife. Seizing it, Babbage stabbed the blade toward Hart, who managed to block the move with his other arm.

Erin scooped up Fitz's gun.

She had never shot anyone before, and she wasn't sure she could. But she stepped closer to where Babbage and Hart were grappling, trying to aim the gun at Babbage.

The knife skittered away from them and stopped at Erin's feet. Babbage dove for it.

Erin kicked the knife to the side, but lost her balance and fell on her back, though managing to hold on to the gun.

Babbage lunged, but before he could get to her, she raised the gun in both hands and pointed it directly at his chest.

Babbage froze. As the two of them stood up, Babbage's eyes locked on the gun barrel. Erin wanted to pull the trigger, but couldn't.

Babbage smiled.

At once an image of another time flashed in her head— a time when she saw that same smile on Babbage's face. At two-thirty in the morning with the sounds of freeway traffic overhead. Amid the decay of Mission Street and the smell of garbage. Going to her knees, forced to use her mouth, enduring Babbage's pungent stench. She was overcome with rage. Burning, consuming rage. She pointed the gun downward, at Babbage's groin. And fired. And fired again. The sound was ear-shattering, and each time the weapon violently recoiled.

For an instant, Erin thought she missed. But she hadn't.

Babbage lay on the floor, on his back, writhing. "You fucking bitch!" he screamed, his bloody hands between his legs. "You fucking—" She shot again.

Suddenly the room was quiet.

Erin dropped the gun.

She looked at Fitz. He opened his mouth as if to speak, but no sound emerged. Frantically, Erin searched for a phone. She found one on a small table in the adjacent hallway, but before she could dial 9-1-1, four uniformed police officers stormed through the door. One pointed a gun directly at her and shouted, "Freeze. Get down on your knees with your hands over your head."

Erin complied. Her hands were cuffed behind her and she was made to lay face-down on the floor.

One cop, a female, called for paramedics, while another bent over Fitzgerald. "This one's still alive," the cop said. "What's up with the other two?"

A third officer went over and looked at Babbage. "This one's dead—or close to it." He went over to Hart and knelt. "But this one's still breathing."

75

Sean

S ean was frantic. This had been one of the worst days of his life. He had been at home, intending to go out to dinner with Erin to celebrate the end of Daniel Hart's trial, and the end of all the years of not knowing who killed their mother or how she wound up dead at the reservoir. Sean had turned on the TV to watch the six o'clock news, and had seen the story of the shoot-out involving two police officers, a judge, and a kidnapped DA. He'd dialed Erin's cell, but gotten no answer. He had tried Amanda's cell, but only gotten her voice mail, and had left an urgent message to call him back.

Finally, Jordan's secretary returned the call, telling him that Hart and Fitzgerald were at the Tarzana Hospital trauma center, and that Amanda and Erin were on their way there and would meet Sean in the critical care waiting room. Sean raced to the hospital, rushed to the waiting room, and, thank God, found Erin. She was alone, and immediately hugged him.

"It was awful," she said. "There was blood every-where, and I thought Fitz must be dead or dying. At first, the cops thought I'd shot Fitz, but Fitz revived when they were cuffing me. He was obviously in shock, but told them I'd saved his life, then passed out. The paramedics said they thought he'd be okay, but he's still in surgery."

"Are you okay?" Sean asked. Erin looked terrible, with dried blood all over her clothing, her hair a mess.

"Yeah," she said. "I know I look awful, but I can't leave until I know Fitz is okay." She paused, then whispered, "Babbage is dead. I shot him. I've never hurt anyone in my life—I always thought of myself as nonviolent. But so help me God, I'm glad I killed him."

"The bastard deserved it," Sean said. "What about Judge Hart?"

"He saved my life," Erin said. "He attacked when Babbage was about to shoot me. He's alive, but barely. Amanda went to talk to the doctors and to check on him. Apparently Hart was insisting on seeing her."

Just then, Amanda walked in. Her face had almost no color, and she appeared very distraught. "Daniel's in criti-cal condition. He was shot in the chest. Babbage's bullet pierced one lung, causing it to collapse, and damaged the other." She looked at Erin. "It's a miracle he was able to save you. The doctor couldn't believe anyone with a collapsed lung could even move on their own, let alone stand and fight. He's an unbelievable hero, and I don't know what I'll do if he dies."

For the next two hours, they waited, while brows-ing through last year's magazines and ignoring whatever was playing on the wall-mounted television. A doctor appeared and motioned to Amanda, and conferred with her in hushed tones in the hall.

Amanda returned. "Daniel's out of danger, for the time being. Tomorrow morning he's going to be transferred to the Differential Observation Unit. For now, he's sleeping and can't communicate. So I might as well go home and get some sleep myself."

Erin and Sean continued to wait after Amanda left. Erin paced, occasionally going to the nurse's station to ask about Fitz's progress, while Sean managed to doze off on the vinyl couch.

Finally, Fitz was out of surgery. At first they weren't allowed to see him. A nurse explained that only family members were permitted. But one of Erin's Alcoholics Anonymous buddies knew a hospital social worker, and Erin phoned her. Erin explained that Fitz had no next of kin, and that they were the only "family" he had. The social worker understood, and eventually they were permitted to be in the room with Fitz, sitting by the bed.

Erin and Sean were there when Fitz opened his eyes.

He smiled before he went back to sleep.

———

Sean and Erin were at the hospital every day visiting Fitz. Each time, he looked much better. The doctor told them that although Fitz had been hit in each shoulder and in his abdomen, miraculously there had been no vital organ damage, so there was no reason why Fitz shouldn't make a full recovery. As the weekend progressed, Fitz improved. He spent two days in intensive care, then was stable enough to be transferred to the acute medical care unit, where he would stay until he recovered enough to go home.

When Erin and Sean came to visit after his transfer, Fitz was in good spirits, but became concerned when he saw them. "What's wrong?" he asked. "Sean, your face is pale and you look grim, and Erin doesn't look much better."

"I'm okay, but Judge Hart's not doing too well. He lost a great deal of blood and he can't talk," Sean said. "His nurse gave me this envelope from him."

"Can't talk?" Fitz asked, taking the envelope.

"Yeah," Sean said. "The nurse told me that the doctors inserted a chest tube into his pleural cavity. It keeps his lung inflated and drains any blood that accumulates. He's connected to a ventilator via an endotracheal tube. The respirator forces air into his lungs. The problem is, the tube passes between his vocal cords. The nurse said he can hear everything, he's alert, but in pain. He has a steno pad that he writes on."

Sean handed the envelope to Fitz.

Fitz examined it. It was plain white, with the words "For Sean and Erin" scrawled on the front. He turned it over. It was sealed, with the words "Open in the event of my death" written over the flap.

"Let's open it now." He started to tear at it.

"Fitz," Sean said sharply. "Don't."

"It must be a confession," Fitz said. "That's the only thing that makes sense."

Erin scowled. "After all this, after the man saved your life, you still think he's guilty?"

"I don't see how it could be anything else," Fitz replied. "Remember what the coroner said, what Jordan argued to the judge? The marks on your mom's wrists indicated she had been held down. That means Hart must have helped Babbage."

"Not so," Sean said. "There's a simple explanation you would have heard if Judge Hart had testified. He told me that night when I confronted him. He told me everything that happened, and in great detail. And it was way before we knew what the coroner's testimony would be."

"And that is?" Fitzgerald asked, skeptically.

"After Mom was sexually assaulted, Babbage tried to stab her. She and Babbage fought over the knife, and she succeeded in getting Babbage to drop it. Hart scooped up the knife and ran away. Then he made a colossally stupid move, and came back to check on Mom. He saw Babbage straddling Mom, holding her wrists back. She bucked and tried to free her wrists, but Babbage was too strong. That's how she got the marks the coroner observed on her wrists."

"Okay," Fitzgerald said. "Now explain to me how Babbage got the knife?"

"He tricked Hart. Hart initially refused to give the knife back, even thought of throwing it away. Said he was worried that Babbage would hurt Mom. But Babbage said he would not hurt her, just needed the knife to control her. Hart believed him. Remember, Hart was just a fifteen-year-old kid."

"Sean, Sean," Fitzgerald said. "Always the believer." Fitzgerald tore open the envelope, and read the document inside. "I'll be damned," he said.

"What is it?" Sean asked.

"It's his will, leaving everything to you and Erin.

76

The Last Chapter

Saturday, June 8, 1996, 7:00 p.m.

Daniel Hart had been very apprehensive. He'd been anxious about returning to work. Between the trial and his time in the hospital, it had been almost seven months since he'd worked as a judge. All his life, he'd lived under the shadow of Sarah Collins's death. It made him a loner, afraid to get too close to anyone. At first, Hart had wondered whether it would be appropriate for him to return. Would the publicity surrounding him be bad for the court? But then an amazing thing happened. Over the weeks, a steady stream of judges and other colleagues came to visit him—to congratulate and encourage him. At the annual seminar meeting of the judges assigned to the criminal division, Hart received a standing ovation.

And the best news, he'd been overwhelmingly reelected at the June 4 primary. But he couldn't help feeling sorry for Doris after all she'd been through with Babbage. Poor woman.

Things had gone well for Fitzgerald. After he recovered, he was fully reinstated and even received a commendation. And a promotion. He was now Lieutenant Fitzgerald. As for Sean, he'd decided to leave the Public Defender's Office and join the District Attorney's Office, saying he felt a closer tie to victims than to defendants, especially since his experience with the Hart trial.

Today, Hart was nervous about Amanda. He'd invited her for dinner and had spent the entire day preparing the meal. A linen cloth covered his dining-room table, which he'd set with his grandmother's best china and silver. He'd told her that tonight's dinner was to say thank you for all she'd done for him, and to help him celebrate his reelection. But there was more.

Amanda had visited him every day when he was in the hospital. After he'd been discharged, she regularly came by his house with an armful of groceries, sometimes making dinner. For him, it became an important routine when she'd spend one or two evenings a week after work visiting. She'd chat about herself, her day, or anything else. He was surprised at how much they laughed, despite what they had both been through. For some reason, they never ran out of things to say to each other or to laugh about.

Amanda arrived exactly on time, as always.

"Would you like a glass of wine?" he asked.

She nodded. "I'd love one." He went into the kitchen, where he poured two glasses of the cabernet the grocer had recommended and returned handing her one glass. They sat next to each other on the couch.

"The food smells wonderful," Amanda said. They clinked glasses. After sipping her wine, she said, "Congratulations,

Daniel. I'm so happy you were reelected. No one deserves to be reelected more than you. And you are the best." She leaned forward and kissed him on the cheek. Her lips were soft and her breath sweet. He inhaled, savoring the fresh clean smell of her hair.

He took her hands in his. "Thank you," he said. "You saved my life, you know."

"Nonsense. The trial wasn't even close. I never even considered it possible that we could lose."

He was still holding her hands. "I'm not just talking about the trial," he said, looking into her eyes.

Amanda leaned forward and kissed him on the mouth. *It was the sweetest kiss of his life,* he thought.

Acknowledgments

Grant of Immunity came about as a result of a writing workshop I participated in a few years ago. It was there that I met writer/actor Meg Tilly, who inspired and encouraged me and helped me believe that writing a novel was, indeed, something I could do.

I owe much to three professional novelists and gifted writing teachers: the late Bill Relling; the incomparable Jim Frey; and, most of all, UCLA Writing Program instructor, Lynn Hightower, who taught me how to craft my words into a cohesive tale.

Thank you as well to the talented and extraordinary workshop leader Nancy Bacal, and to instructors Reyna Grande and Leslie Schwartz, also of the UCLA Writing Program.

I am grateful to those who have been in my writing groups: April Bosshard, Don Calame (Meg's spouse), James Fant, and Derek Rogers. Their insights, critiques, and comments assisted and guided me through the process of writing and rewriting this story.

Many thanks to all those writers who read my evolving manuscript and offered advice. Specifically, authors Brett Battles, Cara Black, Margo Blair, Sharon Dahl, Eloise

Freeman, Katherine Forrest, Richard Jordan, Bridget Kinsella, Ken Kuta, David McCune, Tony Mohr, Brian Perry, Michelle Rosenblatt, Sheldon Siegel, Corie Skolnick, and Elizabeth White.

I extend my gratitude to readers of successive drafts: Judy Abrams, Elizabeth Baron, Tamara Beard, Matthew Bennett, Ralph Bennett, Sharon Bennett, Aviva Bobb, Larry Crispo, Angelica Dahl, Babbett Goss, Lori Livicich, Kathy Mader, Suzy Miller, Ellen Musgrave, Judy Pieper, Lori Resnick-Fleishman, Lisa Ruston, Bill Speer, and Lisa Stanislawski.

Finally, my thanks to Kyle Hunter, for his wonderful cover design, and Eleanor Gasparik, who patiently and thoroughly, copyedited the novel you are now reading.

About the Author

Garret Holms is a judge and criminal trial expert with more than fiftcen years of on-the-job experience. He has worked all aspects of the justice system, from superior court judge to defense attorney to criminal prosecutor. Holms has tried every type of criminal case imaginable, including special circumstances homicide, sexual assault, police corruption, and gangland murder. Grant of Immunity is his first novel.

Find out more at:
http://www.garretholms.com
Comments or questions about the book?
Email Garret at:
garret@garretholms.com